AF225966

ASSAULT ON DEVIL'S DEN

ERIC BALCH

Copyright © 2020 Eric Balch
All rights reserved.

SARCASCA
RODARIA
DRAKENGUARD
DRAGO
WASKAN
EOSURWOOD
DANOREOUS
BARBICON CITY
BATBICONIA
RELIG
BATTALLIA
WARLORD CITY
WALLTON
TERLI
BROOKSHIRE
RANWALD
DIABLOS
BRATENRO
INDUSTRIA
GOLEMBANE
HALFVILLE
NALSHILL
EGAEA
NECROTIAN EMPIRE
NECROTIA CITY
BLACK PYRAMID
endless sea

CHAPTER 1

Pelagius sits at a table in the corner of a sparsely decorated tavern. There are only a few weapons on the walls and two hunting trophies: an eagle mounted above the doorway, and a black bear standing in the corner. Roughly fifty years old and appearing rather tired, Pelagius stares solemnly at his mug of ale as though nobody else were in the room, a plate of meat untouched and pushed to the side.

There are a few other people gathered in pairs or small groups at the tables throughout the tavern. Humans, elves, and halflings comprise most of the clientele, but other species intermingle as well, including a dwarf, two orcs, and two neanderthals. Some cecropsans, creatures that appear human from the waist up but have the lower body of a snake, and onocentaurs, a cousin of the centaur that is half donkey instead of half horse, occupy a few other tables.

As Pelagius peers into his beverage, he fails to notice Bojan approach the table. Carrying a plate in one hand and a mug of ale in the other, Bojan grasps a chunk of bread in his large red beak. He sets the plate down and brushes crumbs off the black feathers covering his body and straightens his green robes, which are in sharp contrast to to Pelagius' plain brown clothing. Removing the bread from his beak, he places his own mug of ale roughly on the table and plops down in a chair. He glances at Pelagius and gives him a hearty pat on the back. "You've been rather sullen since we got here. Is something wrong?"

Pelagius winces and rubs the upper portion of his back before slumping back into his chair. "I'm in deep thought, Bojan. That last adventure did not go well."

"It went fine. We vanquished the Brotherhood of the Sanguine Skin, after all."

"We only helped, and I barely even contributed. Besides, the leader may be dead, but the rest of the coven remains at large."

"Straktor and Gurrsund are hunting the remaining members. What do you mean you barely contributed? We both helped hunt those skinwalkers and were both there for the confrontation with the leader."

"My courage failed me, Bojan. I froze up in the final battle, nearly getting us all killed."

"We were all frightened by the leader's transformation. None of us were expecting that."

"I've never frozen up in my entire life. You of all people should know this."

"Exactly what are you getting at?"

"I serve the God of Valor. It is my duty to inspire courage and heroism in others. How can I do that if my own courage fails me? I fear that I may no longer be of worth as a Crusader of Ender."

"Even the most courageous heroes in history have had moments like that. Don't let it get to you."

"I'm afraid it's too late for that. I keep thinking back to that moment. Perhaps it is time to retire. If I can no longer keep my own courage, I will be unable to inspire others."

"Retire?" asks Bojan. "You? All you need is another adventure to lift your spirits."

Pelagius gulps down his ale. "My adventuring days may be over."

Pelagius finishes his dinner as Bojan quietly sits.

"I think I'm going to head up and get some sleep. Tomorrow, I must decide on whether or not I can still properly serve Ender." Pelagius leaves the table and heads up the nearby stairs as Bojan watches.

"He seems rather down on himself," observes a nearby patron.

"His confidence has been shaken," says Bojan. "However, Pelagius is not one to stand by and do nothing. Despite his talk of retirement, the next time he discovers a crisis he'll jump right back into the fray."

"What if he actually does retire?"

Bojan stares into his empty glass. "I suppose we all have to hang up the sword sometime. No skin off my back if he does. The world may be poorer for the loss, but there are plenty of younger heroes who could fill that void."

Bojan motions to a nearby waitress for another mug of ale.

Chapter 2

As the setting sun gives way to darkness, a lone figure stands on the hill overlooking the Hamlet of Inolutet. Dressed completely in black and his face concealed by a dark cloth, his piercing green eyes stare into the night as he adjusts a wickedly serrated longsword at his side. Down the hill behind him are seven humanoid figures dressed in identical suits of black, full-plate armor, their glowing yellow eyes peering out from their helmets. After an hour of observation, the two guards at the front gate leave and are replaced by two others.

The Green-Eyed Man turns to his squad. "Now spread out and close in."

The raiders slowly and stealthily move down the hill, hiding behind trees and bushes, to surround Inolutet. As the Green-Eyed Man watches from behind a tree, a troll, nearly nine feet tall, walks to the guards at the front entrance. Like all trolls, he has brownish-gray skin, brown eyes, and sharp claws. He carries a large axe and a warclub on his back. The guards immediately notice him approaching.

"Halt!" says one of the guards. "State your name and business."

"Vorgax," replies the troll, lying. "I have been traveling for days and I need a place to stay for the night."

The guards speak quietly to each other and turn back to him. "Very well. The inn is right this way. Follow me."

The guard turns to walk away and a small black urn appears in the Green-Eyed Man's hands. He removes the lid. As the guard leaves, the troll begins to follow before he suddenly draws his weapons. He smashes one guard against the side of the head with his warclub, crushing his skull before swiftly decapitating the other. Two blue beams shoot out of the Green-Eyed Man's urn and connect with the guards, whose skin turns pale blue as a hazy blue mist retracts from their bodies and returns to the urn. After a few more moments, the urn launches six more beams, which stretch across the hamlet and capture an equal number of souls from the remaining on-duty guards. The Green-Eyed Man comes out from behind his tree, walks through the main entrance, and approaches the troll. "Excellent, Shudgluv."

Shudgluv surveys the scene and hangs his head in shame. "Thank you, sir."

"The raiders should be in position by now," says the Green-Eyed Man. "I think it's time to commence the assault and let these people know of our presence. Shudgluv, you know what to do."

Shudgluv nods and walks into the center of town, joining a female elf about thirty years of age by human standards, placing her actual age at about three hundred. She wields a crossbow with a cylinder mounted on the front containing multiple bolts.

"Hello again, Eeshlith," says Shudgluv. "Do you want to give the signal this time?"

Eeshlith chuckles. "No, I don't have the vocal capacity."

Shudgluv nods and takes a deep breath. He tries to roar, but only a quiet whisper comes out. Shudgluv sighs. "I hate doing this."

"I know," says Eeshlith.

Shudgluv inhales again, but he once again exhales quietly and sighs.

The Green-Eyed Man approaches with clenched fists and rage in his eyes. He stares at Shudgluv before opening one hand and making a waving motion signaling the massive creature to descend to match his height. Shudgluv crouches down and the Green-Eyed Man slaps him across the face. "What is wrong with you, Shudgluv? Do your job and give the signal."

Shudgluv clenches his fist and gnashes his teeth as he glares at the Green-Eyed Man. He emits a low growl. "Fine."

Suddenly, the reluctant troll emits an incredibly loud roar, waking most of the hamlet with a cottage-shaking omen.

CHAPTER 3

A loud crash and blood-curdling screams startle Pelagius from his fitful sleep. Still groggy, he hastily stumbles to the window and looks down to the streets below. Residents of this small hamlet rush out of their homes to combat an invasion. The citizens defend themselves as best they can, but most are easily cut down. As the bodies of the fallen drop to the ground, a blue beam appears, striking them in the chest before quickly withdrawing in a hazy blue mist.

Now fully awake, Pelagius takes action; with no time to don his armor, he slips on his leather padding and retrieves his longsword and a shield. The sigil on the shield depicts a clenched fist wreathed in green flame. Despite his age and current doubts, Pelagius is a seasoned warrior and still retains the passion of youth. Entering the hallway, he knocks on the door across from his room.

"Bojan!" shouts Pelagius. "There's trouble outside!"

Receiving no answer, he opens the door to find the room empty. Pelagius quickly turns and rushes down the stairs. If Bojan had already gone out to assist, that was no surprise. He may have still been in the tavern and is usually quick to action, always wanting to help when there is trouble.

He throws open the front door, bursts out of the inn, and rushes into the battle, swinging his sword at one of the yellow-eyed, armor-clad warriors, who parries his blow with his own sword. The invader pushes back with incredible strength, knocking Pelagius off balance. The umbra warrior thrusts his blade forward, but Pelagius regains his footing, sidestepping the blow, and swings lower than usual, slicing the raider's hand off, with little reaction from the attacker. He drives the blade of his sword into the raider's chest. As he withdraws his sword, the raider slumps lifelessly to the ground and his body disintegrates into a blue haze, which rapidly vanishes.

"As I feared," says Pelagius. "An umbra warrior. This must be the work of one of Babu's soul hunters."

Suddenly, another raider lunges at Pelagius with an axe, embedding it in the ground as the aging hero nimbly sidesteps the blow. With one swift stroke, he decapitates the raider, whose body slumps to the ground and dissolves.

Pelagius turns to see six more umbra warriors chasing after an unarmed inhabitant. As Pelagius gives chase, three of the invaders break off the attack, seemingly distracted by something else, and disappear around the corner. Coming to a quick decision, Pelagius pursues the trio that split off.

The remaining three warriors bear down on their victim, and Bojan emerges from an alley and comes to his aid. The axe warrior swings his axe sideways and it lodges in the wall of a nearby building as Bojan jumps to the side. While the first attacker attempts to dislodge his weapon, the other two surround Bojan. The second raider swings a pair of flails at Bojan as the third attempts to run him through from behind with a large sword. However, Bojan rapidly ducks, turns to the side, and palms the side of the blade, redirecting it away from himself. The chains of the flails catch on the blade and wrap around it, entangling the weapons.

As the umbra warriors struggle to free their weapons, Bojan puts nearly thirty feet between himself and them as a ball of fire appears in his hand. He throws it into the middle of the three raiders and it explodes, engulfing them in flames. When the smoke clears, they are lying motionless on the ground, their bodies quickly disintegrating. Bojan then spots two more warriors trying to sneak up behind him and a third charging at him from an alleyway. He points at the one in the alley.

"Rock-hard bone, skin of stone!" shouts Bojan.

The alley umbra warrior turns to stone and stops in his tracks. Bojan snaps his fingers and the stone raider cracks and shatters. His hand glows green and he makes a throwing motion toward the other two. The pieces of stone fly through the air, pummeling them to death, leaving only a vanishing blue haze.

Pelagius comes around the corner, fighting the three umbra warriors he was pursuing. He blocks blows from one with his sword and the other two with his shield. "I could use some help here, Bojan."

Bojan mutters an incantation and a semi-transparent bubble appears around Pelagius. The raiders attempt to attack him, but their weapons harmlessly bounce off the bubble. A ball of fire then appears in Bojan's hand. He hurls it at the three raiders, immediately incinerating them in a fiery explosion. As the smoke clears, the bubble and the bodies dissipate.

The Green-Eyed Man emerges from around a corner and immediately freezes in his tracks. His eyes grow wide before he balls up his fists and continues his approach.

"I didn't realize that Pelagius and the mighty sorcerer, Bojan the Dragonbird, two of Waskan's greatest living heroes, were staying here in Inolutet tonight. It would seem that I made a slight error."

Pelagius glares at the Green-Eyed Man before raising his sword and pointing in his direction. "That error will cost you. Your days of spreading death and destruction are over."

Bojan glances at Pelagius and grins.

The Green-Eyed Man laughs. "I think not, old man."

A goblin standing just a little over four feet in height walks around the corner and joins the Green-Eyed Man. He has greenish-brown skin, burning red eyes, pointy ears, and sharp teeth. The goblin carries a flail, a metal ball attached to a wooden handle by a chain, and a meteor hammer, a ten-foot-long chain with a cone-shaped metal head at the end. Eight more umbra warriors follow behind him.

"Obviously you can handle a few umbra warriors at a time. Let's see how you do against eight," says the Green-Eyed Man.

The Green-Eyed Man makes a motion toward the eight remaining umbra warriors, who now advance.

Pelagius looks at Bojan. "Should I handle this batch or would you like to take care of them?"

Bojan grins and takes a step forward. "I'll handle these. I have something new that I would like to try."

Bojan looks at the umbra warriors and places his hand on the ground. "Starving stone and famished earth. Teeth of rock and tongue of dirt. Open your mighty jaws and feast upon this bounty."

Bojan's hand briefly glows and the ground under the umbra warriors begins to rumble. Then, a large jagged crack opens directly underneath, causing all eight of the warriors to tumble into the crevasse. Before the umbra warriors can climb out, the crack slams closed. As the crevice seals, the familiar blue mist drifts upward and dissipates. Bojan smiles. "It worked. That was fun."

Pelagius shakes his head. "Tengus."

Bojan grins. "What?"

"You're enjoying this too much."

Bojan shrugs.

The Green-Eyed Man sighs and turns to the goblin. "Zergon, you handle this."

"Yes, sir," says the goblin, stepping forward.

Pelagius looks over at Zergon and notices his red eyes. "So, you brought a soulborn demonkin with you."

"Very perceptive of you," replies the Green-Eyed Man. "It would appear that your eyes are still quite good, old man."

Zergon throws down his flail and walks forward, swinging his meteor hammer over his head, and when he is ten feet away, he throws it at Pelagius, making sure to hold onto his end of the chain. Pelagius blocks it with his shield and the impact forces him back—the force strong enough to dent the metal.

Zergon swings at him again and hits Pelagius in the shoulder, knocking him into a wall before retrieving and throwing his meteor hammer at the crusader's head. The hammer end imbeds in a wall as Pelagius ducks aside. Bojan grabs the chain and sends a blast of magical electricity through it, electrocuting Zergon. The goblin releases his grip on the chain and flies backward several feet, thudding to the ground. Zergon lies still for a few moments before rising to his feet.

"We all know you can do better than that," says Bojan. "Show us what you got."

"Very well," replies Zergon.

Zergon suddenly transforms into a hideous demon. His size increases, as he grows to nearly ten feet tall, forming large wings, horns, claws, and a wicked maw of razor-sharp teeth. The Green-Eyed Man grins under his mask.

"Be careful what you wish for, sorcerer," says Zergon, in a chilling, low-pitch voice.

Pelagius and Bojan look upon this creature with horror.

"Well," says Bojan, "he's more powerful, but we can actually defeat him in this form."

As Zergon approaches them, Pelagius and Bojan prepare for battle.

"Sword of light, blade gleaming bright," chants Bojan, "come to my hand and lend me your might."

A large, glowing sword appears in Bojan's hands. The two heroes then charge at the creature. They swing their swords, cutting deep gashes across his chest. Zergon emits a loud roar and punches Bojan in the chest, causing him to fly back twenty feet to slam into the ground.

Zergon, using his claws, swipes at Pelagius, but the old hero jumps back, barely avoiding the wicked talons. He swiftly lunges forward, driving his sword deep into Zergon's shoulder. The monster roars in pain as the blade pierces bone. He grabs Pelagius with his other hand and pulls him away, causing Pelagius to withdraw his sword. His hand is big enough to wrap around Pelagius's entire body.

"I will crush you," says Zergon.

He tightens his grasp and begins to squeeze. Pelagius screams in pain and drops his sword. The pressure continues to increase as Zergon's grasp grows tighter, and Pelagius is on the verge of passing out when Bojan rises to his feet.

"Breath of the dragon, wings of the beast," chants Bojan.

Suddenly, Bojan opens his beak and a massive stream of fire shoots out. It strikes Zergon's shoulder and a small explosion blows his arm completely off. The severed limb hits the ground with a loud thud and the flesh shrivels and decays until reduced to bone. Zergon shrieks in pain and drops Pelagius, who immediately grabs his sword and scrambles his way back to his feet.

"Thank you," says Pelagius, struggling for air.

Pelagius lunges forward and drives his sword deep into Zergon's chest. Zergon crumples to his knees as Pelagius withdraws his sword. Zergon's breathing becomes labored, and a pair of shimmering, transparent wings, like those of a dragon, seem to sprout from Bojan's back. Flapping these wings, Bojan lifts off the ground and flies toward the evil soulborn with incredible speed. He swings his magical sword as he zooms by, decapitating his opponent. Zergon's lifeless body plops to the ground and he rapidly decays until nothing but the skeleton of a goblin remains. As Bojan's wings fade away, the Green-Eyed Man places the lid on his urn, which quickly vanishes.

Pelagius glares at him. "Your turn. This ends tonight."

As the Green-Eyed Man silently seethes, a bald, ugly, hunchbacked figure with one squinting eye positioned too low on the face and the other eye disturbingly bulged joins him. His ears are misshapen and uneven. One arm is longer than the other, one hand has horribly elongated fingers, and his lips curl a bit revealing discolored and crooked teeth. He holds a pair of hookswords. Seeing the aftermath of the preceding battle, the ugly one aggressively advances, but the Green-Eyed Man holds out his arm, stopping him.

"No, Glakchog," says the Green-Eyed Man. "Your dedication and punctuality are admirable traits of the busurin species, but now is not the time. Retrieve the others and fall back."

Glakchog lowers his weapons and steps back. "As you wish, sir."

As Glakchog slips away, the Green-Eyed Man turns back to Pelagius. "I admit that we have lost this battle. We were unprepared for your interference. We shall retreat for now, but next time we will settle the score."

Before Pelagius can respond, the Green-Eyed Man becomes a blur and disappears.

Chapter 4

The next morning, Pelagius and Bojan are sitting at a table in the inn's tavern and a short, slender serving girl with pointed ears approaches them as a red-eyed raven perches in the rafters, staring ominously at the heroes.

"Good morning, gentlemen," she says solemnly. "What can I get you this morning?"

"Coffee with cream to start," replies Pelagius. "Then I would like some sheep's milk, a demastosuchus egg over easy, and a biscuit with honey."

"And you, sir?" asks the waitress, turning to Bojan.

"Coffee, no cream," says Bojan. "Then I'd like milled and boiled corn and some Sarcascan brie."

"It'll be right out," replies the waitress.

She leaves the table and enters a door next to the bar. Several minutes later, she returns with their coffee and meals. The smell of freshly cooked eggs and corn fills the air.

Bojan has some difficulty drinking his coffee, as every time he takes a sip, some of the liquid spills. "Sometimes I hate having a beak. Now is one of those times."

A few people at an adjacent table chuckle, but Pelagius remains silent as he slowly uses an iron knife to burst his egg yolk and then breaks the whites apart with a spoon. Bojan notes his friend's unusual demeanor is different from the previous night.

"What's wrong?" asks Bojan.

Pelagius looks up at him. "Last night is what's wrong. The Green-Eyed Man's attack is unforgivable. Do you know how many people died last night?"

Bojan shrugs as he places a spoonful of steaming corn in his mouth.

Pelagius takes a bite of his biscuit, some honey dripping on the table. "Thirty-two. Eight of them were Inolutet's guards, which is why we didn't have much help last night. That's thirty-two more innocent souls that Babu will either devour or turn into more umbra warriors."

A human patron at the next table drops his mug of coffee, which crashes noisily to the floor, and turns to Pelagius with a horrified expression. "Umbra warriors are stolen souls?"

Pelagius turns to the eavesdropper. "There's a little more to it than that. Rumor has it that an umbra warrior is formed when Babu magically fuses two or three souls to form one being. How they take on a solid form is unknown, but that is what I have heard."

"So, did you free those souls when you defeated them?" asks the patron.

"I don't know," says Pelagius. "It's possible that the Green-Eyed Man may not have recaptured them, but I cannot say for sure."

"That's horrible," says the patron.

Bojan uses a knife to spear a chunk of cheese and pops it in his mouth. "It could have been worse. If we weren't here, he could have slaughtered the whole town."

Pelagius thinks for a moment as the patron excuses himself and moves to another table.

"True," says Pelagius. "But still, we were unable to save thirty-two souls from that monster's clutches. Think about it, Bojan. The Green-Eyed Man has served Babu for the last sixty years. In that time, there is no telling how many victims he has killed. The number of souls that never made it to the underworld must be astronomical. The thought sickens me, and I'm not going to stand for it anymore."

Bojan takes a sip of his coffee. "What are you going to do?"

"We are going to destroy Babu," replies Pelagius.

Bojan's eyes widen, and he spits some of his drink onto the table in shock. "And how are we supposed to do that? You don't seriously believe that the two of us can just walk into Diablos, infiltrate Devil's Den, and kill Babu?"

"Of course not. Just the two of us attempting such a feat would be suicide. However, we don't need an army. We just need to recruit a few brave heroes to assist us with this noble quest."

"Where are we supposed to find these heroes?"

"You're joking, right? Did you forget where we live? Remember, the kingdom of Waskan values heroism above almost any other trait. There are bound to be plenty of people who would be willing to join our cause. The best place to start would probably be Wallton. I know a priestess who lives there that will join us."

Bojan picks up his bowl of corn and pours the remains into his mouth. "Adotiln?"

Pelagius pokes at his rapidly cooling egg with his spoon. "Yes. Her family was killed by the Green-Eyed Man's minions. She would leap at the chance to bring them justice."

"What if she gets attacked?" asks Bojan.

"She can take care of herself. Most healers are skilled in some form of combat."

"Where in Wallton can we find her? I haven't seen her in years."

"She lives at one of the temples in Wallton's Religious District."

"Sounds like a good plan. When do we leave?"

"As soon as we're done with breakfast."

"What do you mean 'we'? I've been done for a while now. You're the one we're waiting on, slowpoke."

Pelagius chuckles and resumes eating his breakfast.

"So, I see you found your courage," says Bojan.

"I don't know about that," says Pelagius. "Perhaps this quest is a test to see if I am still worthy of being a crusader."

A few minutes later, Pelagius finishes; he and Bojan pay the waitress and exit the tavern. Shortly after they are gone, two red-furred monkeys with small horns pop out from behind the bear in the corner and scamper out the door, quickly followed by the unwelcome raven.

CHAPTER 5

The Green-Eyed Man and his three minions are hiding in a forest several miles from Inolutet. Relaxing by a tree, the Green-Eyed Man removes his mask and hood, revealing a face with the appearance of a thirty-year-old man.

"Boss, why do you bother with a mask?" asks Shudgluv. "Nobody outside of Battallia knows who you are and most of them would have died decades ago."

"It adds to my mystique and inspires fear," says the Green-Eyed Man.

As they lounge, they hear a branch snap and Shudgluv jumps up to investigate the sound. He sees the two fiendlings, the red-furred monkeys with horns, noisily jumping from tree to tree.

"Hey, boss," says Shudgluv, "Thakszut and Nyogsutt are back."

The Green-Eyed Man stands and walks over. "Good. Now we'll see if those two are actually useful."

As the Green-Eyed Man reaches Shudgluv, Thakszut and Nyogsutt land on a branch in front of him.

"Report," orders the Green-Eyed Man. "What is that hero up to?"

"First, let me say this," replies Thakszut. "Watching them from the position we were in was quite uncomfortable. In fact, it was unbearable."

"Yes," says Nyogsutt. "It was difficult to bear. And we barely made it out without being seen."

Thakszut and Nyogsutt burst into raucous laughter. The Green-Eyed Man glares at them and then nods in Shudgluv's direction. Shudgluv draws his axe and chops off the branch that the two fiendlings are sitting on. As they fall, the Green-Eyed Man catches them by their necks and shoves them roughly against a tree. "Report, now!"

Thakszut gags as he claws at the Green-Eyed Man's hands. "All right. They are planning to invade Devil's Den and attack Master Babu."

"Yes," says Nyogsutt. "They are traveling to Wallton to recruit a few adventurers to help."

The Green-Eyed Man releases them from his grip and the two fiendlings drop to the ground. "Interesting. Which route will they be taking?"

"I don't know," replies Thakszut. "They didn't discuss that."

"I see," says the Green-Eyed Man. "Well, we can't allow them to achieve their goal, can we?"

"No, sir," replies Nyogsutt.

"Shall we attack them before they reach Wallton?" asks Glakchog.

The Green-Eyed Man nods. "If possible, yes, but first we must discover their intended path in order to set up a proper ambush. Thakszut, continue to watch them. When you learn the route they plan to take, report back. Nyogsutt, return to Diablos and inform Master Babu that some hero is planning an assault."

"Why does Babu need to know?" asks Eeshlith. "We do plan to kill them before they reach him, don't we?"

"Of course," replies the Green-Eyed Man, "but it would be best to let him know in case they do make it to Devil's Den. I doubt they will stand much of a chance against our master if he knows they are coming."

"I see," says Eeshlith. "What about the rest of us? Are we going to do anything?"

"I need you three to scout ahead and recruit a few minions," says the Green-Eyed Man. "I cannot be in more than one place at a time, so I can't do all of this myself. Now be off. There is no time to waste."

Thakszut runs off in the direction of Wallton. The Green-Eyed Man opens a portal and turns to Nyogsutt as a glowing blue orb appears in his hand. "Take this."

Nyogsutt reaches out and the Green-Eyed Man hands him the orb, which absorbs into his hand. Nyogsutt's brow furrows as he looks at his palm. "What did you give me?"

"Babu will be wanting my latest catch," says the Green-Eyed Man. "That will allow you a one-time summoning of my urn once you are in his presence. Now go."

Nyogsutt jumps through the rift, which closes behind him. Glakchog approaches the Green-Eyed Man. "Permission to speak, sir?"

"This isn't the military, Glakchog," says the Green-Eyed Man. "You always have permission to speak."

"Why do you keep them around? They are poor soldiers and take nothing seriously without the threat of pain."

"Maybe if we treated them better, they would be more cooperative," says Shudgluv.

Glakchog glares at the troll. "You weren't given permission to speak."

"I don't need permission to speak," says Shudgluv, angrily. "Like the boss said: this isn't the military."

Glakchog walks up to Shudgluv and glares into the troll's eyes. "We will treat them the way they deserve to be treated. Anybody who messes around like they do, when there is serious work to be done, deserves to be put through some pain."

Glakchog and Shudgluv glare angrily at each other, each one ready to draw their weapons at a moment's notice. Before anything can happen, the Green-Eyed Man inserts himself between them. "Enough of this! Fighting each other won't get anything accomplished, and I am tired of having to play peacekeeper between you two. Straighten up right now. Is that understood?"

The two bickering minions back off.

"Understood, sir," says Glakchog.

"Yes," says Shudgluv, disgusted.

"Good," says the Green-Eyed Man. "Now be off. We all have work to do."

The Green-Eyed Man opens another portal and Shudgluv and Glakchog step through. Eeshlith moves to join them, but the Green-Eyed Man holds up his hand. She stops as the portal closes.

"I'm sending you ahead to Wallton," says the Green-Eyed Man. "Search for potential allies there."

He waves his hands and another portal opens.

"What are you going to do?" asks Eeshlith.

"There is a chamaran village to the south," says the Green-Eyed Man. "I'm going to pay them a visit and set a little trap for Pelagius in case he happens to go there."

Eeshlith begins to speak, but shudders in silence at the Green-Eyed Man's wicked grin. Saying nothing, she steps through the portal, which dissipates behind her. The Green-Eyed Man then stares in the direction of Wallton, deep in thought as he plots the destruction of Pelagius and his team.

CHAPTER 6

Nyogsutt emerges into a large circular chamber about two hundred feet in diameter. The ceiling is so high that it vanishes in the darkness and massive stone pillars stretch upward and out of sight. Numerous torches light the lower portions of the chamber. A few torches have burned out and red-eyed ravens perch on these. A shaggy red carpet stretches from the door to a large throne made of black stone at the other side of the chamber.

Beings of various species crowd the room and a large, twelve-foot-tall demon sits on the throne. He has black hair, black eyes, greenish-red skin, sharp claws and teeth, wickedly curved horns, and spikes protruding from his back. He wears only a brown loincloth, and a large sword of the deepest shade of black leans against the throne. A pudgy, bearded humanoid standing less than three feet in height and flanked by a pair of busurin stands before this imposing figure. "That is my proposal, Marquis Babu. With my talents in both magic and science, I could greatly enhance your mortal troops beyond their natural limits."

Babu rolls up the scroll he was reading and glares at the gnome. "You're mad. These experiments of yours will more than likely kill my men."

The gnome shrugs. "More souls for you if they don't survive."

Babu clenches his fist and leans forward in his throne. "My home is not part of my designated hunting territory."

"Most norodrian demonkin are not as discerning about their victims. Anyone within their range is fair game."

"Most of my species do not share my responsibilities. The people that live here are under my protection. They are not my prey."

The gnome emits a deranged giggle. "Rumor has it that hunting outside your territory is not an issue for your soul hunters."

Babu stands and approaches the gnome, towering over him as he stares down. "Choose your next words carefully. Those who visit are only protected from being prey while they are welcome. Anger me and that hospitality ends."

The two busurin step back nervously, but the gnome stands his ground. "Apologies, my lord. Now, back to the business at hand."

"Your proposition is denied," says Babu. "I will not subject my troops to almost certain death at the hands of your insane experiments. Now begone."

Babu glances to the side and makes a motion to a few of the creatures in attendance. An onocentaur, a cecropsan, and a humanoid with bright green skin and a katana on his belt step forward. Babu turns his attention back to the gnome. "Yaum, Tymraal, and Julbthu will escort you out."

The gnome bows. "As you wish, sir. You know where to find me if you change your mind. Let's go, boys."

The gnome turns to leave as the three minions surround him and walk him to the door. The two busurin follow, opening the door for him when he fails to jump high enough to reach the handle. As they disappear, Babu turns to Nyogsutt. "Where is your commander, Nyogsutt?"

Nyogsutt bows. "He regrets that he is currently unable to attend himself. He sends me with a message and his quarry."

As Nyogsutt extends his hand, his palm glows blue, and the Green-Eyed Man's urn appears on the floor. Babu picks it up and returns to his throne. As he sits, he opens the lid, holds it above his head, and tips it upside down. A stream of blue mist pours from the urn and flows into his open mouth. When the souls stop flowing, he replaces the lid and the urn vanishes. He returns his attention to Nyogsutt. "Now, what did your commander want you to tell me?"

Nyogsutt stands and looks around. "Where's your bodyguard?"

Babu grunts. "Gulvgrum is running an errand. His presence was not needed for that meeting anyway. That mad alchemist posed no threat to me. Now give me your report."

Nyogsutt proceeds to explain the situation as Babu listens intently. Babu leans back in his throne. "I see. I always thought his tactics attracted too much attention."

"Does this worry you?" asks Nyogsutt.

Babu chuckles. "Pelagius doesn't concern me. I doubt that he is much of a threat in his old age. Once Gulvgrum returns, I will have him inform the guards as a precaution. Tell your commander to clean up his mess."

Nyogsutt bows and turns to leave. "As you wish, my lord. I'll find someone to open a portal for me so that I may return quickly."

"Very well. Now begone. I have more business to attend to."

Chapter 7

Pelagius, now clad in half-plate armor with the Fist of Ender on the breastplate, rides his horse northeast toward Wallton, following the well-traveled road between the small hamlet and the large city. Bojan, wearing a thicker version of his green robes, follows suit on his own mount.

Outside the farmlands of Inolutet is a vast grassland, mostly flat with a few trees and shrubs, along with the occasional hill. Several animals wander around the grassland. A small herd of deer graze in the distance. A group of five leptictidium, small mammals with kangaroo-like legs and a thin, two-inch-long nose, hunt insects by a grove of trees. A giant ground sloth noisily munches on some leaves.

Pelagius and Bojan admire the scenery as they continue down the path, redirecting their horses away from a group of three smilodon stalking a lone megalocerus. Once safely away from the large predators, they pause to watch a couple of coelophysis hunt for mice and insects in the grass and let a herd of apatosaurus wander by. Once the massive dinosaurs have moved on, they resume their journey. Pelagius glances at the setting sun. "It'll be dark soon. We should find a place to stop for the night."

"Excellent idea," replies Bojan. "Why not set up camp by the side of the road?"

"No. These grasslands are too dangerous to remain in after dark."

"Where do you suggest that we stop then?"

Pelagius slows his horse to a stop and pulls out a map. "There is a small chamaran village about five miles away. We can stop there."

"You're forgetting something," says Bojan. "The chamaran only speak their own language and banish any of those who speak another. They're not fond of outsiders and will hide from sight."

"That's true in a traditional, orthodox chamaran village. However, those settlements are set up miles away from commonly traveled roads and non-chamaran settlements. This one is right alongside the road, and the chamaran there have had to adapt to travelers passing through. Although most of them speak only their own language, they have implemented interpreters into their daily lives and built an inn."

Bojan thinks for a moment. "Well, that's different. Let's go."

As darkness sets in, lightning flashes in the distance and a blast of thunder pierces the night air. Soon, rain pours from the sky, forcing the two heroes to don their cloaks to keep dry. As they pass a small grove of trees, Bojan notices a pair of burning red eyes glowing in the brush. A flash of lightning reveals nothing there, but when darkness sets in the silhouette of a lion-sized dog returns to view.

"Pelagius, we've got a Black Dog in those trees."

Pelagius tenses and draws his sword. "Stay alert and we should be able to ride by without any problems."

The eyes follow them as they ride past the trees, staring at them the entire time. Bojan and Pelagius observe warily as the beast slowly edges closer to the road, its eyes flashing between the trees as it stalks them, vanishing when the lightning illuminates the sky and reappearing when the darkness returns. As the two heroes clear the trees, the Black Dog emerges into the open, growling and teeth bared. Suddenly, an unusually bright bolt of lightning flashes across the sky and the beast vanishes without a trace.

"This could be a bad omen," says Bojan. "Black Dogs are often harbingers of death."

"Yes, but whose death does this foretell?" asks Pelagius.

After a few more hours, they finally reach the chamaran village. As they enter, the place appears empty, even abandoned, except for the large red-eyed raven perched on a nearby building. Even when lightning lights up the sky, nobody seems to be around.

"Strange," says Pelagius. "Even with the storm they should have sentries keeping watch."

Bojan and Pelagius leave their horses in a small stable and search the village for signs of life. Pelagius goes over to the inn and pushes open the door. Inside, there is only darkness. Pelagius retrieves a torch from his satchel and lights it with some flint and tinder. He enters the inn, which appears abandoned. Several wooden plates and bowls sit on the tables containing, warm food of unidentifiable origin. Pelagius ascends the staircase and searches the four rooms, each of which is empty.

Returning to the ground floor, he goes behind the desk and opens the door to the innkeeper's quarters. As his torch illuminates the room, he is beholden to the sight of ten chamaran lying motionless on the floor. Gaping wounds, most likely from a sword, cover their bodies. Their green scales have taken on a blue tinge and their yellow eyes stare lifelessly into space. A chill runs down Pelagius's spine as his eyes grow wide, and he takes a step back. Once the momentary shock has passed, Pelagius enters the room and turns over one of the bodies. He looks over the corpse, checking it thoroughly as he examines it. Pelagius moves to the next body when a loud crash from outside causes him to jump and nearly drop the torch.

"Pelagius!" shouts Bojan.

Pelagius rushes out the door and glances around the square. He spots Bojan standing outside an alleyway and runs over. Upon arrival, he sees another dead chamaran slumped against a wall.

"I found one," says Bojan, "but he's dead."

Pelagius examines the body and finds that its condition matches the others. "There are ten more over there. They're all dead too, and from the looks of them, I'd say their souls have been taken."

"So that's eleven dead. How many lived here?"

"About fifty, I think."

Suddenly, the horses let out a fear-filled whinny. Bojan and Pelagius rush to the stable, but one of the horse's whinnies cease before they get there. When they enter the stable, they see five chamaran devouring the dismembered horse.

The other horse is in a state of panic as three more chamaran shamble out the other stalls and attack it. The horse kicks one, caving in its chest and knocking it down. Despite this fatal blow, it rises again and rejoins the attack. Overwhelmed, the horse hits the ground as the chamaran begin to tear it apart.

"Zombies!" exclaims Pelagius. "The Green-Eyed Man somehow knew we were going to stop here."

"How?" asks Bojan. "And how did he have time to do this?"

The eight zombie chamaran turn toward the two heroes and approach them. They are slow and sluggish, barely able to walk as they stumble forward.

"I don't know," replies Pelagius, drawing his sword, "but we don't have time to figure that out now."

Pelagius takes a couple of steps toward the zombies and raises his sword, holding it in front of them. Pelagius starts muttering something and the sword glows green. He suddenly looks up at the zombies.

"In the name of Ender, begone!" Pelagius thrusts his sword forward and a flash of green light fills the stable, reducing the zombies to dust.

Suddenly, the sound of moaning fills the courtyard outside the barn. As Pelagius and Bojan walk out the stable door, a flash of lightning brightens the area and reveals the ten corpses from the inn shambling toward them, as the remaining thirty-two villagers pour out of the other buildings.

"I don't suppose you could do that again," says Bojan.

Pelagius shakes his head. "Not against this many zombies in such a large area."

"My turn, then."

Bojan steps forward, makes a few motions with his hands. "Ever fluctuating space, leave for a new place."

The stable blurs, vanishes, and reappears over the zombies. It comes crashing down, crushing about twenty of them, and shattering upon impact.

As several of the remaining zombies scramble through the debris, a small ball of fire appears in Bojan's hand. He lobs it in the center of the rubble and a massive explosion engulfs it and most of the zombies. Despite the heavy rain, the heap of wood becomes an inferno. A few burning zombies stumble out of the flames, walk a few feet toward the two heroes, and collapse. As the remaining seven zombies continue shuffling toward them, Pelagius sheaths his sword and steps in front of Bojan. He closes his eyes and clasps his hands together.

"Wretched undead," says Pelagius, "may the Flames of Courage consume your corrupted forms."

As he finishes his prayer, green flames appear and seem to wrap around his arms. Pelagius opens his eyes and looks at the seven zombies lumbering toward him. He extends his right arm toward them and a blast of green fire shoots from his arm and engulfs four of the zombies, reducing them to ash. Pelagius then extends his left arm and the green flames incinerate the last three zombies.

CHAPTER 8

The Green-Eyed Man stands at the entrance to a cemetery just a few miles southwest of the chamaran village. The rain continues pouring down as flashes of lightning brighten the night sky. The cemetery itself is in poor condition due to years of disuse. The gate has fallen off its hinges and the sign is missing several letters, which lie on the ground. Several large, red-eyed ravens perch on top of the gate and on the tombstones. As he surveys the cemetery, Nyogsutt comes through a portal onto a tree branch and leaps onto his shoulder.

"So, you're back," says the Green-Eyed Man. "What does Master Babu have to say about the situation?"

"He is unconcerned," replies Nyogsutt. "He has full confidence that they will not make it to Devil's Den. However, as a precaution, he will shore up the defenses."

"That's what I thought he would do," says the Green-Eyed Man.

He looks in the direction of the chamaran village and rolls his eyes in annoyance. "Come out, Thakszut. I know you're there."

Thakszut jumps out of the trees and lands on the Green-Eyed Man's other shoulder.

"I was expecting you an hour ago," says the Green-Eyed Man. "What took you so long?"

"I had a run-in with a large Black Dog," replies Thakszut. "It took me half an hour to lose it, and then another half hour to get back here."

The Green-Eyed Man chuckles. "I forgot that the Grim are quite common in this kingdom. What news do you bring of our heroes?"

"They dispatched the zombies easily," replies Thakszut.

"As I thought they would. Did we slow their progress any?"

"The zombies killed their horses, so yes."

"Excellent," replies the Green-Eyed Man.

The Green-Eyed Man returns his attention to the cemetery and steps through the gate. Nyogsutt taps him on the side of the head. "If I may ask, why are we here?"

"I'm recruiting some help," replies the Green-Eyed Man. "There is a powerful necromancer who lives in a crypt here. One who shares some history with our friend Pelagius."

As the Green-Eyed Man continues down the weed-ridden path, flashes of lightning reveal hundreds of tombstones of various sizes spread throughout the cemetery. Several of them have long since fallen into disrepair, with some missing chunks of rock and others that have crumbled completely. Thakszut and Nyogsutt look around nervously.

"Strange place to live, even for a necromancer," says Thakszut.

The Green-Eyed Man grins. "Well, he doesn't live here by choice. Pelagius imprisoned him here over twenty years ago. He is trapped in a crypt that is actually a pocket realm between this realm and Yatbuju, the realm of anti-life."

"You mean the realm that is the source of undeath and necromancy?" inquires Nyogsutt. "Wouldn't that just make him more powerful?"

"It strengthens his necromantic powers, yes," replies the Green-Eyed Man. "However, being trapped so close to Yatbuju for so long leaves its mark on even the most pure and noble of people, and necromancers are even more vulnerable to its power. So, I don't doubt that there will be some sort of side effect or repercussion from the realm's corrupt touch."

At that moment, a flash of lightning reveals a zombie standing by a tombstone that the Green-Eyed Man is passing by. It lunges at the Green-Eyed Man and Thakszut and Nyogsutt emit monkey-like screams and flee. The Green-Eyed Man quickly draws his sword and with three slashes chops off its head and an arm and slices its torso in half. The remains of the zombie slump to the ground.

"Come back here, you cowards," says the Green-Eyed Man. "One zombie is easily dispatched."

Thakszut and Nyogsutt peek out from behind a tombstone, still shaking with fear.

"One, yes," says Nyogsutt, "but how about a hundred?"

Nyogsutt points past the Green-Eyed Man, who turns to look. A flash of lightning reveals over one hundred zombies making their way across the cemetery toward him.

"I count a hundred and fifty," says Thakszut.

The Green-Eyed Man sheaths his sword. "I should have known that the necromantic energies would seep out of the crypt. I'll warn you just this once. If you want to live, I suggest you jump into that tree."

Thakszut and Nyogsutt quickly leap into a large ash tree nearby and hurriedly scramble fifty feet up to the top branches. The Green-Eyed Man places his palms together and begins to chant. "Burning embers, fires of white, gather round in whirling light!"

As the Green-Eyed Man chants, rings of white flames circle around him, growing in size and intensity until he is not visible within them. "Bright flames of white, reaching out with searing might!"

As soon as his chanting is complete, the white flames expand into a large explosion that reaches the farthest corners of the cemetery, completely incinerating everything, living and unliving, in its path within seconds. The trunk of Thakszut and Nyogsutt's ash tree burns out from underneath, causing it to topple over. They leap from the branches onto the Green-Eyed Man's shoulders just before it hits the ground.

"Impressive, boss," says Thakszut.

"Yes," agrees Nyogsutt. "We knew you had some magical talent, but we've never witnessed one of your powerful spells before."

"Powerful?" says the Green-Eyed Man. "That was weak compared to my most powerful abilities."

With the two fiendlings rendered speechless, the Green-Eyed Man continues on along the now scorched path. Within a few minutes, they reach a large crypt. A flash of lightning reveals a stone structure as tall as a two-story building overgrown with charred vines. Two reaper-like statues, towering five feet above the rooftop and wide enough to take up an entire side of the wall, frame the doorway, their scythes crisscrossing the door with a skull face sitting between them on the door.

"So how do we get in?" asks Nyogsutt.

"We break the skull-seal, of course," replies the Green-Eyed Man.

The Green-Eyed Man clutches his fist and begins to concentrate. After a few seconds, he releases a burst of red energy at the skull-seal. The blast hits the seal and immediately dissipates, leaving no visible damage.

The Green-Eyed Man grunts in frustration. "Too weak. I'll need to use more power."

Suddenly, the skull-seal's eye sockets glow red and it speaks. "None may enter the forbidden tomb. Leave now or meet your doom."

The Green-Eyed Man emits an exasperated sigh. "Why do all of these tomb guardians have to speak in verse?"

He sends forth another ball of energy, which hits the seal and explodes in a small blast. The skull-seal lets out an audible grunt as the blast knocks a chunk from its face but is largely unharmed. "You were warned. You failed the test. Now prepare to be put to rest."

The two reaper statues suddenly turn and face the Green-Eyed Man, their eye sockets glowing red. They then step off their stands, filling the air with the sound of stones grinding together whenever they move, and slowly walk toward the Green-Eyed Man. The ground shakes with their every step.

As Thakszut and Nyogsutt flee, shrieking, the Green-Eyed Man's eyes widen, his arms drop to his sides, and he takes a step back. "Stone juggernauts. I must admit the defenses for this prison are impressive. No matter. I have the perfect solution."

Realizing that these constructs are slow-moving, the Green-Eyed Man blurs and vanishes before appearing thirty feet away. He glances at the juggernauts and grins, knowing that he will have just enough time to build up sufficient power to take them out and destroy the seal in one blast.

The Green-Eyed Man concentrates and, touching his fingertips together, moves his hands and arms in circles. "Force of air, the gentle breeze, gather in my hands. Force of air, strong wind blows, gather your strength, let your power grow."

He then positions one hand in front of him with his pointer finger extended in the direction of the crypt. "Prepare for the ultimate shattering. Force of air, most powerful gale, unleash yourself so that none may sail!"

As he chants these last words, a bright light explodes from his hand and a shock wave ripples through the air, destroying every tombstone in its path and obliterating several ravens. The two stone juggernauts immediately crumble into rubble and the crypt collapses as the shock wave rips through it. Thakszut and Nyogsutt slowly approach the Green-Eyed Man as he walks up to the rubble.

"Well, he's dead," says Thakszut. "What now?"

An expression of pure delight appears on Nyogsutt's face and he enthusiastically clasps his hands together. "Lunch?"

"Too early for lunch," says Thakszut. "Maybe breakfast or midnight snack."

The Green-Eyed Man groans. "He's not dead, you fools. The crypt was merely the entrance to the underground prison. Once I find the door, I can make my way down to the inner sanctum and destroy the seals that keep him imprisoned."

The Green-Eyed Man sifts through the rubble and finds a wooden door in the ground. He clears off the rubble and opens the door, revealing a stone staircase leading downward. Thakszut and Nyogsutt peer into the darkness.

"Let's go," says the Green-Eyed Man.

"But won't the energies of Yatbuju be harmful, if not fatal, to us?" asks Thakszut fearfully.

"Since we won't be exposed to them for very long, they will have no time to cause any long-term effects," says the Green-Eyed Man. "Plus, I'm immortal, remember? Now, let's go."

The Green-Eyed Man takes an unlit torch from the wall and magically lights it as he descends. The stairs descend for what seems like an hour until finally they reach a small room at the bottom. On one wall is a large stone door with another skull-seal, which the Green-Eyed Man easily destroys with a burst of magical energy. He opens the door and begins to enter but pauses. Peering through the door reveals a darkness that even the light from his torch does not penetrate.

"This must be it," says the Green-Eyed Man. "Come on."

"We'll just stay out here," says Nyogsutt.

"Yes," says Thakszut. "We'll stay here where it's safe and not crawling with creepy darkness."

The Green-Eyed Man swiftly grabs the two fiendlings by their tails. "You're both coming with me!"

He then tosses both Thakszut and Nyogsutt through the doorway and steps through behind them. They emerge from the darkness in a well-lit, round, stone chamber about thirty feet in diameter with torches every five feet on the walls. Fifteen feet in, there are five stone pillars three feet in diameter and set in a circle at three-foot intervals. A large glowing chain emerges from the center of each pillar and extends into the center where each one wraps around the single cloaked figure hunched over in a chair. The figure looks up, his face shrouded by a hood, as the Green-Eyed Man tosses his torch aside.

"Who are you?" asks the figure weakly.

"My name is not important," replies the Green-Eyed Man. "Are you Kragus?"

"I am. What do you want with me?"

"I am here to free you from this prison, in exchange for a favor or two, of course."

"I'll do anything to be free of this place. Name the deed."

"An old enemy of yours is undertaking a quest. I want you to provide him with obstacles to slow him down and eventually kill him."

"Name the target."

"The very man who imprisoned you: Pelagius."

Kragus's head quickly lifts up and looks directly at the Green-Eyed Man, revealing his face. Kragus is a human male of unknown age, but he appears ancient. He has long white scraggly hair, a white bushy beard, and a severely emaciated face. Rage fills his bloodshot eyes as he spits on the floor, clenches his gnarled fists, and gnashes his chipped, yellowed teeth. "Your terms are accepted. I shall have my revenge against Pelagius. I will delay his journey and make him suffer like he has never suffered before. When the time has come for him to die, I will make sure that his death is slow, agonizing, and painful. Then, I will force him into undead servitude before I hunt down everyone who shared so much as a friendly smile with him. Nobody of amiable relations shall go unpunished."

Thakszut and Nyogsutt hide behind the Green-Eyed Man during Kragus's rant. Even the Green-Eyed Man appears slightly disturbed by his rage, but soon recovers and grins. "Do whatever you want. Just make sure to kill him before he enters Diablos. Thakszut and Nyogsutt here will lead you to his trail; then they will follow him and keep you up to date on his progress."

"Me?" squeaks Thakszut.

"Us?" says Nyogsutt in an even higher pitch.

"I will haunt Pelagius's every step," says Kragus. "He will see me in every mirror and behind every bush. I shall haunt his nightmares and feed off his fear. He will rue the very day that he dared cross paths with me."

"Right," says the Green-Eyed Man. "But first things first. We need to release you. How do I do that?"

"Destroy the five pillars," replies Kragus. "They are the source of the magic that binds me. Once the pillars are destroyed, the chains will vanish, and I will be free."

The Green-Eyed Man concentrates and remains in a sedate state for a few moments. Then he opens his eyes and unleashes small, concentrated shock waves at each pillar. The shock waves rip through each stone, reducing the pillars to dust. The chains collapse to the floor and disintegrate.

As the last chain fades, Kragus rises from his chair. He stands in place for a few moments before walking through the darkness behind the Green-Eyed Man, who, along with the two fiendlings, quickly follows. As they reach the top of the stairs, Kragus stops, breathes deeply, and seems to grow younger. His hair darkens and shortens as his face becomes less emaciated and his physical stature reverts to that of a young man in his prime.

"Where is he?" asks Kragus.

"In a chamaran village a few miles to the northeast," replies the Green-Eyed Man. "Thakszut and Nyogsutt will take you to the village so you can get an idea of where you want to go."

"Very well," says Kragus. "Beware, Pelagius. I have returned and vengeance shall be mine."

Kragus walks in the direction of the chamaran village, pausing briefly to ponder the presence of a red-eyed raven before continuing. As he disappears over the horizon, the Green-Eyed Man begins to open a portal, but pauses when a raven lands on a nearby tombstone and squawks in his face. The bird stares at him for a moment before taking flight and vanishing into the night sky.

Chapter 9

Morning finds Pelagius and Bojan hiking along the trail with all their equipment that was once carried by their horses on their backs. As they walk down the road, Pelagius suddenly stops and stares into the distance.

Bojan stops and looks at him. "What's wrong?"

"Hopefully, nothing," replies Pelagius. "A memory came to me and I had a horrible thought. Do you remember what's over there?"

"An old cemetery."

"Yes. The same cemetery where we imprisoned Kragus."

Bojan's eyes grow wide. "You don't think he has escaped, do you?"

"It's impossible for him to escape on his own," replies Pelagius. "Somebody would have to free him."

Bojan smirks. "If that has happened, we'll just have to put him back. If memory serves correctly, it was easy last time."

"You have a strange definition of easy. Capturing him was quite challenging."

Bojan laughs. "Ease up, Pelagius. I'm only trying to provide some levity."

"Not the right time, Bojan."

Suddenly, the surrounding air pulsates as several short bursts of shrill whistling emanate around them. With their ears ringing and heads throbbing, Pelagius and Bojan drop their bags and wrap their hands around their own skulls, desperately trying to drown out the noise. Then, the sky darkens, all the plant life begins to rapidly wither and die in a sixty-foot radius, and the flesh rots away from any visible animals, their bones dissolving in a gust of foul wind. Recovering from their sound-induced headaches, Pelagius and Bojan stand back-to-back.

"What's going on?" asks Bojan.

Pelagius begins breathing heavily as a cold sweat runs down his face. "I'm not sure."

The darkness spreads from the sky until it touches the ground, blocking their view beyond the dead plant life. Shadowy figures appear in their peripheral vision, quickly zipping away when they turn their heads. Then, ghostly images materialize before them, some simply pale and translucent, other horribly mutilated and disfigured. A few of these fade away almost immediately, but some of the more horrific ones slowly approach the heroes and stare them in the face before vanishing.

Pelagius begins panting as his heart pounds in his chest. "We're not equipped to combat ghosts. We need to get out of here fast."

Bojan closes his eyes and inhales deeply. "Calm down, Pelagius. These are harmless."

A loud cracking sound causes Bojan's eyes to snap back open. Dozens of skeletons rip through the ground and claw their way out of their graves. They stand and slowly shuffle toward the two heroes, their bones clattering horribly as they walk.

Bojan's eyes grow wide and he starts breathing heavily. Then, his hand crackles with electricity and he lobs a lightning bolt at one of the skeletons. The bolt strikes the undead horror in the skull, passing through harmlessly as the image becomes fuzzy. Bojan narrows his eyes. "It's all an illusion."

Pelagius glances back at him. "Are you sure?"

Bojan nods and takes a step forward, his arms waving in circles in front of him. "Eyes obscured, come to light. Clear my vision and give me true sight."

Bojan extends his arms outward and a wave of energy bursts from within him. Then, the skeletons fade, and the darkness recedes, reverting the surrounding countryside to normal. The wildlife rises and flees the area.

Kragus appears at the top of a nearby hill. "Well done. I wasn't sure if you were going to figure it out. I was about to strike, but you spoiled the surprise."

Pelagius and Bojan look at Kragus in horror as he walks down the hill toward them.

"Who in their right mind would have released him?" asks Bojan.

Pelagius wipes the sweat from his brow and unsheathes his sword. "I can only guess, and he wasn't in the right mind. Surrender, Kragus!

There's no point in fighting. You're outnumbered. Just surrender quietly and you won't get hurt."

Kragus bursts into maniacal laughter. "Outnumbered, but not outmatched. I can defeat you easily now. Did you forget that I am a necromancer? My imprisonment between this realm and Yatbuju exposed me to the source of my necromantic powers. Twenty years of such exposure has greatly increased my power."

"We'll see about that," says Pelagius. "Bojan, it looks like we have to take him down permanently this time. I don't want to prolong this fight, so let's make it quick."

"I think I can do that."

A large fireball appears in Bojan's hand. He throws it at Kragus, hits him directly in the chest, and it explodes on impact, engulfing half of the hill in a massive inferno.

Pelagius looks at Bojan. "A little excessive."

"Maybe," says Bojan, "but I wanted to make sure that we got him."

As Pelagius and Bojan begin to pick up their equipment, evil laughter erupts from within the flames.

"Impossible," says Pelagius as he and Bojan turn toward the fire.

Kragus emerges from the inferno just feet in front of them, completely unharmed. He continues laughing as he slowly walks toward them. "I'm disappointed, Bojan. Is that the best you can do? I would have expected more from the great Dragonbird."

Pelagius hesitates for a moment before he lunges forward and swings his sword. Kragus simply reaches out and catches the blade in his hand. Then, he looks at Pelagius with disappointment. "Your attack was rather slow. Do I sense fear, Pelagius? How very unlike you."

Bojan advances to assist his friend, but Kragus raises his hand and sends a blast of magical energy into his chest, sending him tumbling backward.

"I have grown more powerful than ever," says Kragus. "You, on the other hand, have become weak in your old age."

Kragus's hand flashes red for a moment. Then, he tightens his fist and shatters Pelagius's sword. As the shards of metal fall to the ground, Kragus points at Bojan. "Shards of metal, find your sheath!"

Suddenly, about five metal shards glow red, hover in the air, and shoot toward Bojan at incredible speed. The jagged fragments strike Bojan and rip through his body, knocking him to the ground. Kragus looks over at him. "So powerful, and yet so weak. You really are pathetic, Bojan. Perhaps you are not worthy of the title Dragonbird. I laugh at your helplessness."

Taking advantage of Kragus's rant, Pelagius attempts to punch him. However, without even turning to face him, Kragus rapidly lifts his hand and catches Pelagius's fist. Then, he looks at Pelagius. "Too slow, old man."

Kragus grabs onto Pelagius's breastplate and readjusts his own grip on his hand. "Now, Pelagius, you die."

Kragus's hand again glows red for a moment before what looks like red electricity flows out of him and into Pelagius. Pelagius screams in pain as the vicious energy flows throughout his entire body. Bojan attempts to move to help Pelagius; however, his injuries are too severe for him to provide any assistance. Bojan watches helplessly as Kragus slowly torments Pelagius to the brink of death.

Kragus glances over at Bojan. "What's wrong, Dragonbird? Don't you want to save your friend? Are you really so weak that you can't even gather the strength to stop me? Or do you want to watch him die?"

Kragus laughs malevolently as he continues to force Bojan to watch him inflict more pain on Pelagius. Suddenly, Kragus has an expression of intense pain on his own face and releases his enemy. He groans in pain as he holds his stomach and drops to his knees, screaming in agony. Before their very eyes, he appears to age rapidly. His hair turns solid white and his bones seem to warp.

"What's happening?" asks Kragus between groans.

Pelagius emits a weak chuckle as he struggles to get to his feet. "It seems that your increase in power comes at a price. Your powers have grown to the point that they are too much for your body to handle, and you are doomed to destroy yourself."

Kragus looks at Pelagius. "Perhaps, but I'm not finished with you. Mark my words, Pelagius. I will find a way to counter this effect, and then I will return to finish the job."

Before Pelagius can respond, Kragus punches the ground, appears to flicker, and vanishes. Pelagius limps and stumbles to Bojan. "Are you all right?"

Bojan shifts, wincing as he perches on his elbows. "Oh, just fine. I always have broken hunks of metal stored in my torso."

Pelagius rolls his eyes. "This is not the time for sarcasm. Can you stand?"

Bojan attempts to push himself up and collapses. "What do you think? Does it look like I can stand on my own?" Pelagius helps Bojan to his feet and supports him with his own body. They limp down the road as a large, red-eyed raven hovers above them.

"What about our equipment?" asks Bojan.

"We'll have to leave it and buy new equipment in the next town or village," says Pelagius. "Neither one of us is in any condition to carry it."

The two wounded heroes continue down the road. After ten minutes, they hear a noise behind them and turn to see a wooden cart pulled by a pony coming down the road. They then move to the side of the road to let the cart pass, but as it approaches them, it slows to a stop.

"Pelagius, Bojan, is that you?" A female halfling of about forty years stands up. She is wearing robes with the symbol of Ender, and she only reaches up to Pelagius's waist in height.

Pelagius looks at her and smiles. "Adotiln! Well, this is a pleasant surprise."

"What happened?"

"Kragus has escaped," replies Pelagius. "He ambushed us a little ways back."

"I see," says Adotiln. "Where are you going?"

Pelagius tells her the story of the Green-Eyed Man's attack on Inolutet and of his own quest to end Babu's reign of terror. Adotiln has a solemn look on her face as he finishes.

"I'd like to join your quest," says Adotiln. "It's a very noble and worthwhile venture and it looks like you need help. You'll need someone with the power to heal, and I am a priestess of Ender, after all. Plus, it will give me the opportunity to seek justice for my family."

"Of course," says Pelagius. "I was actually planning on seeking you out when we got to Wallton."

Adotiln laughs. "Well, it's a good thing you were delayed. I have been in Rodaria for over a year and was just on my way back. Now, before we continue our journey, you two need some healing."

"Bojan first," says Pelagius, setting his companion on the roadway. "I think he's worse off than me."

"All right," says Adotiln, approaching Bojan. "Lie on the ground."

"Fine by me," says Bojan, lying down.

"First, we need to get whatever caused those wounds out," says Adotiln.

Adotiln kneels next to Bojan and begins to recite something that neither Bojan nor Pelagius can understand. Her hand glows light blue, and she touches Bojan on the shoulder. The wounds where the pieces of Pelagius's sword pierced his flesh begin to glow blue and the shards are mystically lifted from the wounds. Adotiln pushes them to the side before letting them fall to the ground. Then, she begins chanting and her entire body glows bright blue. She places her hand on Bojan's chest and the blue glow transfers from her to him. Bojan glows bright blue for several minutes and when the glow fades away, he is completely healed. Adotiln then calls Pelagius over and heals him in the same way.

"Thank you," says Pelagius as he rises to his feet.

Adotiln smiles. "It's what I do. Besides, what kind of friend and ally would I be if I didn't heal you?"

"A bad one," says Bojan.

All three laugh.

"Could we trouble you for a ride?" asks Pelagius. "Our horses were killed last night."

"Certainly," replies Adotiln. "There's plenty of room in the back."

"First, we need to go back and get our supplies," says Bojan.

"Do you mean these?" asks Adotiln.

Adotiln pulls back a tarp in her cart, revealing the equipment that Pelagius and Bojan left behind.

"I found this lying on the ground a while back," says Adotiln. "I thought that I might find its owners farther up the road. I took it with me so I could return it to them."

Pelagius smiles. "What would we do without you?"

Bojan grins and chuckles. "Apparently, we would collapse in a dead heap on the road."

Pelagius glares at Bojan. "That's not funny."

"Relax, Pelagius. I wasn't serious."

Adotiln giggles at their exchange as Pelagius and Bojan climb into the back of the cart. Once everyone settles in, they resume their journey to Wallton.

Chapter 10

The Green-Eyed Man follows Kragus into a small shack in the woods. When he enters, he finds Kragus, white-haired with badly distorted bones, reading a tattered, untitled, black-covered book.

"What are you doing?" asks the Green-Eyed Man.

"I am searching for a way to counter the effect that my newfound power has on my body," replies Kragus. "If I can find a way to temporarily reverse the effects, I may be able to take my revenge before I am destroyed by my own power."

"I see. How is that book supposed to help?"

"This is from my old collection of tomes of forbidden lore. If any tome has the answer to my problem, it is this one."

"What is that book called?"

Kragus glances at him with fear in his eyes. "I cannot say. Its name must never be spoken aloud, nor shall it be written down. Even for those of us who delve into forbidden lore, the consequences of saying this book's name out loud are too terrible to contemplate. You know of which book I speak."

The Green-Eyed Man takes a step back in shock, his back against the wall. "The Nameless Tome? How did you get that? I thought that all the copies had been destroyed."

"Most of them have," says Kragus, "but it is believed that between three and five copies still exist, including the original. They are extremely difficult to find. In fact, it took me ten years to track down this copy. And before you ask, no, you can't see it."

"I have no interest in forbidden lore," says the Green-Eyed Man.

The Green-Eyed Man glances over and sees a large red-eyed raven sitting in the window. "A friend of yours?"

Looking at the bird, Kragus shakes his head. "It's not mine. It has been sitting there since I started reading."

"I've noticed it, or others like it, recently," says the Green-Eyed Man. "It almost feels like someone is watching."

The Green-Eyed Man draws his sword and takes a swing at the raven, missing completely as the bird leaps into the air. It flies into the rafters and out of sight as Thakszut and Nyogsutt come through the door and climb onto the Green-Eyed Man's shoulders.

"Anything to report?" asks the Green-Eyed Man.

"Yes, sir," replies Thakszut. "Pelagius and Bojan have been joined by a halfling priestess."

"Interesting," says the Green-Eyed Man. "Do you know who she is?"

"It doesn't matter," says Kragus. "Like Pelagius, Bojan, and the rest of Pelagius's friends, she will soon be dead."

"Her name is Adotiln," says Nyogsutt.

"Adotiln?" inquires the Green-Eyed Man. "She has a personal stake in Pelagius's quest. We must be cautious and eliminate her as quickly as possible."

"What should we do, boss?" asks Thakszut. "Clearly, Kragus is out of action. Should we make more recruitments?"

"No need," says the Green-Eyed Man. "Eeshlith, Shudgluv, and Glakchog are already recruiting more help."

"Whatever help you enlist other than me will be of little consequence," says Kragus. "I assure you that my handicap is temporary."

"I'm sure it is," says the Green-Eyed Man, "but we need someone to delay their trip and possibly even kill a few of them while you are searching for the solution to your problem. Besides, I doubt you'll be ready to face them again before they reach Wallton. If you find a solution, you can try again after they leave Wallton, if they ever do."

"What do you mean?" asks Thakszut.

"Eeshlith has hired Dengor, the leader of the Black Scorpion Crime Syndicate, to send some of his best men after Pelagius," replies the Green-Eyed Man. "She has told me that he has already given the order to eight of his elite thugs. Unless Bojan plans on using one of his exploding fireballs in the middle of a large city, I doubt that they will be able to easily fend off eight of the best that the Black Scorpions have to offer. Nine, if Dengor decides to take part in the venture himself."

Kragus laughs. "A few street thugs won't be able to do anything to Pelagius. He may have grown weaker in his old age, but he is still a skilled warrior. It will take more than the Black Scorpions to slow him down."

"Don't you have a cure to find?" asks the Green-Eyed Man, annoyed.

Kragus waves his hand and a small glowing rift appears in the air. He places the book in the opening, which vanishes immediately. "I've found what I was looking for. It seems that I can use the very energies that cause my powers to destroy me to reverse the effect. All I have to do is concentrate while holding onto someone else, and I will drain their life force from their body and rejuvenate my own. The younger the better. A child would work perfectly for my current condition."

"And how do you plan on capturing this child?" asks the Green-Eyed Man. "You're certainly in no condition to chase after them, and I have more important things to do than kidnap children for you."

"Simple," replies Kragus, putting on a tattered, torn, and filthy hooded cloak. "I merely pretend to be a kindly old man with some candy, and the children will flock to me. I don't have far to go. There's a farm just outside of these woods."

Kragus turns and hobbles out the door.

"Do you really think that releasing him was a good idea, boss?" asks Nyogsutt. "That plan disturbs me."

The Green-Eyed Man shrugs. "He may be helpful to us yet. If he gets out of hand or turns on us, I may have to put him down, but until then I consider him a valuable ally."

CHAPTER 11

Later that night after the sun has set, Pelagius, Bojan, and Adotiln stop to set up camp in a clearing by the road. They sit around a fire with their tents at their backs providing them a makeshift barrier. Bojan turns a spit with a large chunk of beef on it, making sure to cook it evenly. Adotiln gazes at the star-filled night sky and Pelagius studies the remains of his sword. He still has the hilt, but the blade only extends about a foot, where it ends abruptly with a jagged edge.

Pelagius sighs. "This sword served me well for a long time. Ironically, it was the sword that I defeated Kragus with in the first place."

"You've had one sword for that long?" asks Adotiln.

"Pelagius has always taken pride in keeping his blades clean and in good condition," says Bojan. "A well-maintained sword will last for decades."

"I see," says Adotiln.

"I wonder if its destruction is an ill omen," says Pelagius.

"An omen of what?" asks Adotiln.

"I don't know," replies Pelagius, "but it may have something to do with our quest. What if we are doomed to fail? Then those that I bring along would have died for nothing. I don't know if this journey is worth it anymore."

Adotiln and Bojan look at each other with concern and then glance at Pelagius.

"What are you saying?" asks Bojan. "You're not giving up, are you?"

"I'm not as young as I used to be," says Pelagius. "I'm not saying that we should give up. I'm saying that with Kragus on the loose again, this particular quest looks bleak. If Kragus has thrown in his lot with Babu and the Green-Eyed Man, then I don't think we can win."

"Why?" asks Adotiln. "You're the one he wants, aren't you?"

Pelagius nods. "I'm his main target, but Kragus is not the type to take revenge on a single person and be satisfied. He will not rest until his vengeance is complete. Now that he has become as powerful as he is, I do not think we can defeat him this time."

"We can defeat him again," says Bojan. "Did you forget? When he uses his powers, his body is ravaged. We just need to wait until he is in intense pain and then we can get him."

Pelagius looks up at Bojan. "There is just one problem with that plan. By the time that happened, he had nearly killed both of us."

"True," says Bojan. "However, there are two factors that you're not looking at. One, he caught us off guard. Two, we're going to recruit more people. More targets means he'll have to make quicker use of his powers. That, in turn, will lead to him ravaging himself faster."

Pelagius thinks for a moment. "A crude plan, but you bring up a good point."

"Do you see?" says Adotiln. "As powerful as he is, it is still possible to defeat him. You just have to wait for the right moment."

"Which will come when he decides to make his move again," says Bojan. "We have no way of knowing where he went."

Everybody nods in agreement.

"As for the omen of the broken sword," says Adotiln. "Don't worry about it. As long as some of us survive the quest, whether a failure or a success, there will be somebody to carry on."

"You're right," says Pelagius. "In fact, you're both right. We shall continue this quest and worry about Kragus when the time comes. Until then, we should be on our guard. I'm sure Kragus won't be the only thing that the Green-Eyed Man sends our way. When we get to Wallton, we will start searching for new recruits."

Bojan points to Pelagius's shattered blade. "First things first, Pelagius. Unless you plan to attempt to join the Knights of the Broken Sword, you should get a new weapon."

Pelagius chuckles and absentmindedly sheathes the sword. "I have no desire to dedicate the rest of my life to strictly hunting werewolves. I've had enough encounters with shapeshifters after our experience with the skinwalkers. So once again, you are correct, my friend."

Suddenly, a bolt of lightning flashes across the sky and strikes the ground, frightening the pony and scaring a red-eyed raven out of a nearby tree. Several more blasts follow, with one landing directly in the center of the campfire, causing a large explosion that sends the three heroes tumbling backward and plunging the area into darkness. Pelagius, Bojan, and Adotiln jump to their feet and look in the pony's direction as it gives off another terrified whinny. In a grove of trees several yards away, a pair of bright red eyes peek through the brush.

"This is bad," says Pelagius. "It's that Black Dog that was following us a few days ago."

"Not again," says Bojan. "I was hoping we lost it."

Adotiln glances at them nervously. "Is this another of the Green-Eyed Man's minions?"

"No," replies Pelagius. "It's just one of the monstrous creatures that live around here. I'm not certain as to why it is following us, but be on your guard. Black Dogs are dangerous supernatural beasts that could rip out a troll's throat with minimal effort. Plus, one's appearance often foretells of death."

The Black Dog charges forward, growling ferociously as it runs. Bojan makes some motions and mutters something, and a small fireball appears in his hand. He throws it at the beast, and it hits the ground directly in front of it. The fireball explodes upon impact, igniting a small inferno in front of the Black Dog and sending a blast of fire onto the left side of its face. The Black Dog emits a pained whine and when the fire clears, the beast vanishes.

"That should deter it for a while," says Bojan. "Hopefully, that's the last we see of him."

Pelagius and Adotiln nod in agreement. Then, Adotiln calms down the pony while Pelagius and Bojan gather more wood and restart the fire.

"I certainly hope you're right," says Adotiln.

"As do I," replies Pelagius. "However, in my experience, the Grim are incredibly persistent. Even if injured or scared away, they tend to resume the hunt as soon as they are able. He'll probably continue to follow us and try again later."

"We should get some sleep," suggests Adotiln. "That way we're rested for the rest of the trip to Wallton."

"I recommend we take turns keeping watch," says Pelagius. "We'll each take a four-hour shift. I'll take the first watch. Bojan can take the second and Adotiln can take the third. Agreed?"

"Why are you taking first watch?" asks Adotiln. "You two just barely survived a grueling battle."

Bojan yawns and stretches his arms in the air. "She's right, Pelagius. Even with the magical healing, I'm exhausted."

Pelagius emits a groaning yawn. "All right, you can take third watch, but I should still take the first."

Adotiln rises to her feet and stares up at Pelagius, hands on her hips. "You need rest too."

Pelagius sits by the fire and looks Adotiln in the eye. "I'll rest after my turn at watch."

Adotiln groans in frustration and throws her hands in the air. "You are a stubborn old man. Pelagius, I will take first watch. You are too tired to be an effective lookout. Get some rest, and that is final."

Bojan chuckles. "You know you're not going to win this argument, Pelagius. Just take second watch and get the sleep you need."

Pelagius sighs before emitting a deep yawn. "Perhaps you're both right. Very well, Adotiln. You can go first."

Adotiln smiles. "Good. Now both of you get some sleep. I'll wake you if there is trouble."

Pelagius and Bojan nod before retiring to their tents as Adotiln begins to scan the horizon.

CHAPTER 12

The Green-Eyed Man walks into a tavern in a small hamlet just a few miles from Wallton. A male leprechaun, standing barely over three feet, with red hair, a red beard, and burning red eyes, accompanies him.

This particular tavern is not very well kept. It looks as though no one has cleaned in months, and several sections have rotten wood. Broken glass and a few bloodstains litter the floor and tables from the uncountable bar fights that have taken place here, and an unidentifiable musty smell permeates the air. The Green-Eyed Man looks around the room, his face scrunched up in disgust. "Charming place."

As the Green-Eyed Man walks across the room, he notices that most of the patrons are ogres, orcs, and trolls. Also scattered around the room are a few goblins, dwarves, elves, harpies, and humans. He finds Eeshlith waiting by the bar.

Noticing his companion, a look of concern crosses Eeshlith's face. "You brought Alasdar with you? Won't the presence of a soulborn cause unnecessary tension?"

"Perhaps, but he insisted on joining us," says the Green-Eyed Man. "However, he assures me that he will not play a part unless necessary. Lead the way."

Eeshlith leads Alasdar and the Green-Eyed Man to a large table in the corner occupied by a minotaur, a troll, and several other individuals.

"So, these are the Black Scorpion elites?" asks the Green-Eyed Man.

"He is," replies the minotaur, pointing to the troll. "I am Dengor, leader of the Black Scorpions. Allow me to introduce Shurgluz, the leader of my elites."

"Are these the elites?" asks the Green-Eyed Man.

"They are," says Shurgluz. "These are the best that the Black Scorpions have to offer. I assure you that they will get the job done."

"Excellent," says the Green-Eyed Man. "But Wallton is a very big city. How do they plan on finding them?"

"Simple," replies Dengor. "I have the rest of the organization in disguise stationed around the city. When they see Pelagius, they will follow him and report his whereabouts to Shurgluz."

The Green-Eyed Man looks around the room before turning back to Dengor. "And what about the authorities? They're certain to notice a large gathering of Black Scorpion thugs."

Dengor chuckles. "I have already paid off a few of them to look the other way. Of course, I can't guarantee that no law enforcement authorities will show up once the deed is done, but my elites can handle them easily. Trust me."

"I trust you to understand what will happen to you if they fail," says the Green-Eyed Man, staring straight into Dengor's eyes.

Dengor stands up. "Are you threatening me?"

"Not at all," says the Green-Eyed Man, rising from his seat. "I simply wish to bring your attention to the fact that there will be consequences if your men fail."

Dengor slams his fists down onto the table, prompting Eeshlith and Shurgluz to quickly stand up. Shurgluz looks like he is ready to attack, but Dengor waves him down.

"They will not fail!" says Dengor sternly. "They have never failed."

"They had better not, or your organization will cease to be," says the Green-Eyed Man.

"This is not a good way to do business," says Dengor.

"Business has already been taken care of," says the Green-Eyed Man. "You have already been paid half of your fee. You will receive the other half if the job is done. Let's hope for your sake that your elites are as good as you claim."

Dengor thinks for a moment. "There will be no attack."

"What was that?" asks the Green-Eyed Man. "If you recall, we have a deal."

Shurgluz steps around the table, looming over the Green-Eyed Man. "That deal was made on the understanding of doing business. We have no desire to work with someone who threatens us."

"Agreed," says Dengor. "The deal is off."

"Think carefully about your decision, Dengor," says the Green-Eyed Man. "There are consequences for cheating me."

"There will be no cheating," says Dengor. "Your money will be returned, and this mess will be forgotten. That is my best offer."

"I see," says the Green-Eyed Man. "It is a pity that you feel that way. I shall leave the details to my associate. Alasdar, they're all yours."

The Green-Eyed Man briskly walks out the door, with a horrified Eeshlith rapidly following. As they emerge from the tavern, Eeshlith opens her mouth to protest, but an unworldly shriek coming from inside interrupts her, followed by horrific screams. One of the other patrons, who was not involved with the meeting, appears in the doorway and makes it halfway out before something inside, hidden behind the door, grabs him. He holds onto the door for dear life as whatever has hold of him jerks and pulls to get him loose. The unfortunate man looks at the Green-Eyed Man with terror in his eyes.

"Not this!" screams the victim. "Anything but this! For the gods' sakes, help me!"

Suddenly, whatever has a hold of him yanks so hard that the door rips its hinges and pulls him back into the tavern.

"Not the face!" shouts the unfortunate patron.

He emits one last scream of terror and then everything falls silent. A few minutes later, Alasdar walks out the door. "It is done."

The Green-Eyed Man peeks in through the doorway and immediately recoils. "I see you didn't spare anyone, even the bartender and the other patrons."

"I leave no witnesses," says Alasdar.

The Green-Eyed Man shudders in horror. "Well done. Now, seek out their main hideout and relieve them of their funds."

"What do you want me to do with all the money?" asks Alasdar.

"The money we paid Dengor was borrowed from Manthysbia's horde," says the Green-Eyed Man. "He, of course, wanted it back with interest. Therefore, the Scorpions' entire fortune will be added to his stash. I believe that should be sufficient to pay our debt."

Alasdar says nothing. He simply opens a portal and steps through. The Green-Eyed Man turns and walks away from the tavern. Eeshlith angrily follows him and grabs him by the shoulder.

"What was that all about?" asks Eeshlith. "Do you have any idea how long it took me to even meet with the Black Scorpions' leader, let alone arrange a deal? What was the point of all the work I did if that is how you handle business affairs?"

The Green-Eyed Man turns to her. "Do not patronize me, Eeshlith. I knew exactly what I was doing. It was Dengor who chose to break the deal, and so he suffered the consequences."

"I'm not patronizing you. I'm just frustrated that I went through all that trouble just for that to happen. Fear is not the only way to do business, and Alasdar is not the answer to every problem."

"Fear may not be the only way, but in our line of business it is the best way. As Babu's top soul hunter, I have a reputation to uphold. Making friends does not come as a priority in that regard."

"What about keeping friends?"

"As I said, I have a reputation to uphold."

Eeshlith sighs. "Please, I appeal to what's left of your kind, former self. At least be nicer to your friends in your private life. You don't have to maintain a front when it's just us and the others."

The Green-Eyed Man briefly flinches, and his expression becomes softer. "Perhaps you're right. Maybe I can let my old self out every once in a while."

Eeshlith smiles, but the Green-Eyed Man's face reverts to its previous callous state. "But not now. Not until Pelagius is dead. Then, I may be able to relax my guard."

Eeshlith sighs as her smile fades. "It's been sixty years since we joined Babu and even with all the horrible things that we have done, I can tell that your old self is still somewhere inside this evil, callous husk of a human. I think you need to let the old you out more often."

"If I were to do that, I might actually regret the things I've done," says the Green-Eyed Man. "That is an emotion that I cannot afford to feel. For my own sake, I cannot allow myself to fully revert to that man at any time. We've been over this before many times these past sixty years."

"I'm just trying to salvage what humanity you have left," says Eeshlith. "We were friends back then, and we still are. I'm trying to do the right thing and save whatever I can of my old friend."

The Green-Eyed Man glares at her. "If I follow your advice, I will grow soft. Shudgluv is already traveling down that path because of you. I cannot afford to end up a conflicted mess like him. My conscience shall remain buried deep inside me and that is my final word."

Eeshlith sighs and lowers her eyes. "Fine. We'll continue this later."

"Feel free to keep wasting your time if you wish," says the Green-Eyed Man.

Eeshlith sighs once more and thinks for a while. "Answer me this. Why bring Alasdar upon them? Nobody truly deserves that fate."

"As I said, Alasdar insisted on accompanying me," says the Green-Eyed Man. "I don't dare say no when he makes such a request."

"So even you fear his methods?" asks Eeshlith.

"What he does is absolutely horrific. It is by far the most disturbing act that I have ever witnessed, and I have no desire to experience it."

"You've seen him do it?"

"I observed him once. After seeing the results a few times, I was curious, so I stayed in the room while he did the deed. I regretted it immediately."

"What does he do?"

"Trust me, you do not want to know."

"Now who's being soft?" asks Eeshlith, teasingly.

The Green-Eyed Man looks at her with a serious expression. "Nobody is hardened and callous enough to witness Alasdar's actions and not be disgusted and disturbed. Not me, not Babu, and not even Commander Charndergh."

"Commander Charndergh finds it disturbing?" asks Eeshlith. "He's one of the most hardened, evil, and callous individuals I've ever met."

"Indeed, he does," says the Green-Eyed Man. "If you truly wish, I will tell you what he does, but I do not believe that you would want to hear it."

"No, thank you."

"That's what I thought," says the Green-Eyed Man. "Now return to Devil's Den and await further instructions. I will see to a few loose ends here."

"Soul collecting?"

The Green-Eyed Man's urn appears in his hands and he opens the lid. "No need to let the opportunity provided go to waste. I've got a quota to fill anyway."

52

Chapter 13

The next morning, Pelagius, Bojan, and Adotiln roll up the tents and pack them and the other supplies into the cart as a large red-eyed raven looks on. Adotiln feeds the pony, then secures it to the cart. They all climb in and Adotiln gets the pony going. A few hours pass by uneventfully.

"So, how much farther is Wallton?" asks Bojan.

"At the rate we're going, we should be there in three days," replies Adotiln.

"Good," says Pelagius. "That will give us time to stock up on a few supplies before we look for people to join our quest."

"So, Bojan," says Adotiln. "How did you get the title of Dragonbird?"

"Well, when a sorcerer finishes training with his mentor, he is sometimes given a title," says Bojan. "This title is derived from that individual's specialty or some unique ability. There are many other ways one could earn a title, and there are far too many to name. In my case, it derived from two things: the first from the fact that I am part bird and the second from the dragon-like powers that I sometimes manifest. I created those powers, so they are unique to me. Those two factors were combined to earn me the title of the Dragonbird."

"I see," says Adotiln. "I have another question. I have noticed in the past that when you cast spells that sometimes you chant and sometimes you don't. Why is that?"

"That's fairly simple," replies Bojan. "If the spell is new, a sorcerer must chant to form the spell correctly. Sometimes the chant changes over time to perfect the spell. Once a spell has been mastered, the sorcerer in question can summon it up by will alone and chanting no longer becomes necessary. If it is a unique ability that is not often used, like my Dragonbird powers, chanting is required."

"What happens if you create a new spell and don't chant?" asks Adotiln.

"The results could be disastrous," says Bojan. "Anything could happen, ranging from the sorcerer exploding, to an outbreak of a magical plague, to a great magical cataclysm. If you're coming up with a new power, not chanting is extremely dangerous."

Pelagius glances at them. "How do you not know this, Adotiln? The basic principle is the same for your powers as well as mine."

"I don't spend as much time with sorcerers as you, Pelagius," says Adotiln. "I'm not an expert on magic beyond that granted to me by Ender."

"Fair enough," says Pelagius.

The three of them engage in idle conversation for several minutes. Suddenly, something lunges out of a grove of trees and rams itself into the pony, knocking it over and pulling the cart over with it. Pelagius, Bojan, and Adotiln tumble out of the cart. Adotiln manages to roll through and ends up on her feet, but Pelagius and Bojan just fall to the ground. Ferocious growls drown out the pony's cries. As Pelagius and Bojan rise to their feet, they see that their attacker is an amarok, a massive wolf the size of a grizzly bear.

"Not another beast," says Bojan. "First, the Black Dog and now an amarok? What's next?"

As the amarok finishes off the pony, the three heroes slip behind a rock. Unprepared for a fight of any kind, they watch in horror as the amarok has breakfast. Suddenly, his ears perk up and he raises his head. He looks around before fleeing into a large grove of trees.

"What scared him off?" asks Adotiln.

Before anyone can answer, thundering footsteps echo from the other side of another grove of trees. A full-grown Tyrannosaurus rex comes around the corner, walks right to the pony, and steps on the cart, crushing it before sniffing and licking the pony's carcass to see if it is edible. As it prepares to devour the pony, a loud roar pierces the air from above. Both the group of heroes and the Tyrannosaur react and look to the sky as a large dragon flies toward the scene.

"We just can't seem to catch a break, can we?" whispers Bojan.

The dragon is as large as the Tyrannosaur. It has four legs with massive claws on its feet, a long tail, bat-like wings on its back, and a long neck with a dinosaur-like head. It also has a pair of horns on top of its head and an enormous set of teeth.

The dragon swoops and lands several yards from the Tyrannosaur. The two creatures stare and roar at each other. When it becomes clear that neither one will back down, they charge each other. The two beasts collide, and the Tyrannosaur bites one of the dragon's wings. The dragon, in turn, bites the back of the Tyrannosaur's neck, prompting it to let go of its wing.

The fight shakes the ground as the two monsters slam into each other and their shrieks echo for miles. The Tyrannosaur lunges for another bite, but the dragon unleashes a stream of fire and severely burns the mighty dinosaur's face. Squealing in pain, the powerful predator backs away. As soon as the dragon turns to the pony, the Tyrannosaur lunges toward its opponent, jaws agape and headed for the creature's throat. However, at the last possible moment, the dragon lowers its head and shoots a large stream of fire.

The blast enters the dinosaur's mouth and goes down its throat. Now in severe pain and unable to breathe, the wounded Tyrannosaur thrashes and falls to the ground. The dragon approaches and bites on the Tyrannosaur's neck, crushing the dinosaur's throat and severing a few vertebrae with a sickening crunch. The lizard king goes limp and the dragon releases its grip. As the fallen Tyrannosaurus rex flops lifelessly to the ground, the dragon quickly consumes the pony. It then turns back to its victim and begins to devour the fallen predator. Pelagius, Bojan, and Adotiln watch in amazement.

"Should we wait until it leaves?" asks Adotiln.

"No," replies Pelagius. "We should slip away while we have a chance. The supplies have been destroyed anyway. Go through the trees and do it quietly."

The three heroes stealthily sneak away from the dragon, making their way through the woods. After about a mile, they return to the side of the road.

"Well, that was unexpected," says Bojan.

"Indeed," says Pelagius. "Yet another setback. I'm starting to worry about this journey. At this rate, it will take us years to reach Diablos."

"There's a small village farther down the road," says Adotiln. "We can get there before nightfall if we hurry."

Pelagius and Bojan nod in agreement and the three begin walking down the road. Several hours later, as the sun sets, the three heroes leave the road as they cross the farmlands on the outskirts of the village of Austracene. Several small animals, including a group of leptictidium, scurry around as they look for a place to settle for the night.

Just as the last light of day begins to fade, they enter the village. Upon their arrival, they notice that the village is well lit by torches, which is unusual considering that night lighting is uncommon except in big cities. As they survey the area, a pair of guards stops them.

"Halt," says one of the guards. "State your name and business here."

Pelagius approaches them. "I am Pelagius. My companions are Bojan and Adotiln. We simply seek a place to sleep for the night."

"Welcome, sir," says the guard. "Your exploits are well known, even here. You may find food and rest at the Crystal Orc Inn in the center of the village."

"Thank you," says Adotiln.

"Our pleasure," says the guard.

"Your streets appear to be well lit," says Pelagius. "Is there a reason for this?"

"Actually, sir, yes," replies the guard. "Tonight, we are having our annual Returning Heroes Festival. There is music, singing, dancing, drinking, and feasting. You should join in, sir."

Pelagius smiles. "Thank you kindly. When does the festival begin?"

"It starts in an hour," replies the guard. "That should give you time to set up lodging. You may pass."

The guards step aside and the three heroes head to the center of the village, where they find the Crystal Orc Inn, a modest wooden building standing two stories tall. Only a few swords and shields decorate the walls of the lobby. As they approach the front desk, they notice a set of stairs leading up to their left and the entrance to the inn's tavern area to the right. Pelagius approaches the desk, which is currently empty.

"Hello?" calls out Pelagius. "Is anybody here?"

"One moment," replies a rather gruff voice from a room behind the desk.

The door opens and the innkeeper, who is clearly an ogre, steps out. He has bluish-green skin, brown eyes, and sharp teeth, a few of which protrude from his mouth.

"Good evening, strangers," says the innkeeper. "I'm Zynax, owner of the Crystal Orc Inn. How may I help you?"

"Good evening, Zynax," replies Pelagius. "I am Pelagius. My companions and I have been on the road for a few days and wish to find lodging for the night."

"Welcome, sir," says Zynax. "You have arrived just in time. I have two rooms left."

"How much do they cost per night?" inquires Pelagius.

"For you, sir, they are free of charge," replies Zynax. "Tonight, we honor the great heroes of this kingdom and you are one of the greatest. Your adventures are legendary, and your presence is an honor. Therefore, you may stay here as long as you need for no charge."

"Thank you, Zynax," says Pelagius. "We appreciate your generosity. We will take both the rooms. Bojan and I will stay in one, and Adotiln will stay in the other."

"Very good, sir," says Zynax, handing them the room keys. "I hope you will be attending the festival tonight. Many great heroes and adventurers will be in attendance and your presence would be a great honor indeed."

"We will most certainly be there," says Pelagius. "Thank you for your kindness."

"Do we really have time for a festival?" asks Adotiln. "I thought we needed to get to Diablos as soon as possible."

Pelagius glances over at her. "The festival is only one night. Besides, we may be able to recruit an ally or two."

Adotiln thinks for a moment before nodding in agreement.

The three heroes turn to the left and go up the stairs. Upon finding her room, Adotiln immediately unlocks the door and enters. Pelagius and Bojan find their room a few doors down.

As Bojan opens the door, the door to the room across the hall opens as well, and an elderly male centaur emerges. His long, flowing hair is solid white and the brown fur on his horse body is turning gray. He has several scars all over his body from past adventures, and the passage of time shows on his tired-looking face. He has a longsword strapped to his back.

"I thought I heard someone coming up the stairs," says the centaur.

"Forgive the interruption, sir," says Pelagius. "We did not mean to disturb you."

The centaur smiles. "There is nothing to forgive, Pelagius. I was just making sure I heard correctly."

Bojan looks at the centaur and an expression of recognition appears on his face. He taps Pelagius on the shoulder and leans in to speak in a whisper. "Pelagius, I know him."

"You do?" inquires Pelagius, quietly.

The centaur watches them converse in hushed tones, his ears perking up as he pretends that he cannot hear them.

"Remember the stories of a great centaur warrior during the Three-Year War?" asks Bojan.

"Yes," replies Pelagius, "but that war took place nearly one hundred years ago."

"It ended one hundred and five years ago, to be precise," says the centaur.

A look of realization appears on Pelagius's face. "It can't be him."

"I think it is," says Bojan.

Pelagius turns to the centaur. "Are you Celemrod?"

The centaur smiles. "I am."

"But how is it that you are still alive?" asks Pelagius. "You were young when that war started. Your adventures are among the most famous tales in Waskan, but most centaurs don't live past eighty-five and you must be at least one hundred and twenty-five years old."

"I am one hundred and thirty-four," says Celemrod. "I'm not certain as to how I've lived so long. However, when I was young, a seer foretold that I would fall heroically in a great battle. If the seer's words were true, then I have one last battle to fight."

Pelagius's eyes rest upon the sword on Celemrod's back. "Is that White Fire?"

Celemrod unsheathes the sword, revealing that the entire object is solid white. Flames extend from the ends of the hilt, inset with several red gems. "It is. I found its resting place on my first adventure. I have fought many battles with it, and it shall remain with me until the end. Only after my final battle will it find a new owner."

Celemrod then puts White Fire back in its sheath.

"Will you be attending the festival as well?" inquires Bojan.

"Of course," replies Celemrod. "I always come here for the festival. It is interesting to see who shows up."

"What have your impressions of the returning heroes been at previous festivals?" asks Pelagius.

"Honestly, not very many of them are very impressive," replies Celemrod. "The vast majority of those who come are simple adventurers, most of whom have done nothing heroic during their travels. There are a few each year, however, that show potential."

"Have you met any yet this time?" asks Pelagius.

"I have spoken to all fifty of the returning heroes," says Celemrod. "This year, only one of them performed any deeds on his journeys that could qualify as heroic: an elf named Kevnan. The others are simply adventuring in order to seek their fortune or become famous."

"I must speak with him," says Pelagius. "I am undertaking a quest and need to recruit a few heroes to help me. I already have Bojan and Adotiln, but I need a few more."

"What kind of quest?" inquires Celemrod.

Pelagius explains the entire situation to him.

"I see," says Celemrod. "That is quite an undertaking. I would offer to join you, but at my age I would only slow you down. However, I do believe that Kevnan may have what it takes to help you accomplish your mission. You should definitely speak with some of the other adventurers during the festival. I'm sure that some may be willing to join you."

"Thank you for your advice," says Pelagius. "It would have been a great honor to have you on the team. However, I understand your reasons for not joining."

"It was my pleasure," says Celemrod. "I'll see you at the festival."

Celemrod then turns and goes back into his room. Pelagius and Bojan enter their room and close the door.

CHAPTER 14

Meanwhile, the Green-Eyed Man is standing outside of a farmhouse just a few miles from Austracene. As he is about to enter the house, Thakszut and Nyogsutt come running up to him.

"What do you have to report?" asks the Green-Eyed Man.

"They're going to attend Austracene's Returning Heroes Festival tonight," replies Thakszut.

"Anything else?" asks the Green-Eyed Man.

"The only other information we have is that they will be staying at the Crystal Orc Inn," says Nyogsutt.

"Also, there is an unusually large number of ravens in this area," says Thakszut.

"I, too, have noticed the ravens," says the Green-Eyed Man. "They are of no consequence now. Focus on our enemies. Tonight, we shall give them a festival they shall never forget."

The Green-Eyed Man turns and kicks in the front door. He steps into the house and finds Kragus, his health and body fully restored, standing in the center of the room, surrounded by at least thirty corpses. Kragus and the Green-Eyed Man look at each other with surprise.

"Don't you ever knock?" asks Kragus, irritated.

"Knock?" asks the Green-Eyed Man. "Why should I knock?"

"Bursting in like that is very rude. Also, I hope you're going to replace that door."

"I wasn't planning to. I was going to kill the family that lived here and use this house as a point to summon a small army of demons to attack Austracene tonight. I didn't expect to find you here."

"Nobody lives here. This house belongs to me."

"How does it belong to you?"

"This is the house that I was born and grew up in," replies Kragus, "Any family I had left seems to have packed up and moved. Therefore, it was my house and still is. And now, you owe me a new door."

The Green-Eyed Man pulls a small bag of coins out of his pocket and tosses it to Kragus. "Fine, I'll pay for a new door."

Kragus catches the bag. "Thank you."

The Green-Eyed Man looks over the corpses. "I suppose you're planning to reanimate those thirty corpses to attack the village?"

"You are partially correct," replies Kragus. "When you burst in, I was in the middle of performing a ritual to fuse all thirty bodies together to form one monstrous being and then reanimate that. After the ritual is complete, I will send my newly created corpse reaver to attack the village. Your abrupt arrival, however, has interrupted the ritual, and I now must start from the beginning."

"We made an agreement upon your release. Pelagius is not to be killed until he completes his recruitment efforts."

"We made no such agreement. You simply said to slow him down and to kill him before he reaches Diablos. Besides, I do not expect my corpse reaver to be able to kill him. I would need more bodies to form one that powerful. I am simply sending it as a distraction that will hopefully lead to the deaths of a few villagers and possibly injure Pelagius. If my intention was to kill him while he was in Austracene, I would do it myself."

The Green-Eyed Man thinks for a moment. "Fair enough. However, tonight is the night of Austracene's Returning Heroes Festival. There will be at least fifty adventurers there. I sincerely doubt that your corpse reaver will be powerful enough to do much damage, if any. Perhaps I could lend a hand to your ritual."

"What do you have in mind?" inquires Kragus, inquisitively.

"I suggest that we each perform a ritual simultaneously," says the Green-Eyed Man. "You resume your ritual to create a corpse reaver and I will perform a ritual to summon a powerful demonkin, using the location of the pile of corpses as a center point. We will time it so that both rituals are completed at the exact same time. If everything goes according to plan, the demon I summon should be fused with the corpse reaver, forming a more powerful being."

"Excellent idea. It is possible to use a living creature in the creation of a corpse reaver. Although the creature will not survive the fusion, it will become the main base of the rest of the monster, which will make the resulting creature more powerful indeed. Of course, it will not be as powerful as the original host, but it should suffice depending on what kind of creature is used."

"How much of the demon's power would be retained?"

"It is difficult to judge. However, I estimate that approximately one-fourth of the host's power will remain. So, whatever you summon, it needs to be incredibly powerful in order for the desired effect to take place."

"I know just the thing: a morag."

Kragus's eyes widen. "A morag? Are you certain you can summon something that powerful?"

"Certainly," replies the Green-Eyed Man. "Babu has several working for him, so I can call one up at any time."

Kragus smiles. "Perfect. That should create something powerful enough to challenge every hero and adventurer in Austracene."

The two then make preparations to begin their dark rituals.

CHAPTER 15

Several hours after the three heroes checked into their rooms, they emerge from the inn to find the town square is jumping as the festival hits its full swing. Food-laden tables dot the square, where the village's partygoers sit and enjoy a bountiful feast. Several dozen cooking stations are scattered about the area, and each one serves something different.

Adotiln glances around, stretching her neck and pushing up onto the tips of her toes to try to see over the crowd. "How are we supposed to find one specific elf amongst all these people?"

Pelagius scans the horizon. "We'll have to split up and search separately. Meet back here in ten minutes."

The heroes walk in separate directions, pushing their way through the crowds. Several woozy, stumbling adventurers jostle Pelagius, and one spills a mug of ale on his shirt. As he makes his way around the town square, he stops briefly to listen to a few of the adventurers telling the tales of their journeys. Continuing his search, he finds a troupe of minstrels set up by the inn, playing their instruments joyfully as several residents dance nearby. Stopping to listen, he notices an elf nearby playing a mandolin and singing about the quests that he and his friends undertook. By human standards, he appears to be twenty-five years old, which would put him at approximately two hundred and fifty.

Pelagius pushes through the crowd to get a closer look and taps one of the closest townsfolk on the shoulder. "Excuse me. Is that Kevnan?"

The villager nods. "That's correct. A local hero if there ever was one."

"I was hoping to speak with him."

The villager begins to walk away. "I guess you'll have to wait until later, sir."

Pelagius heads back to the inn and finds a crowd gathered around Celemrod, who recounts stories from his past to those who are interested. Looking around, he locates Bojan and Adotiln listening intently. As he approaches, Bojan looks over at him. "Any luck?"

"Yes, but he's busy performing."

Bojan grins. "Then I guess we'll just have to enjoy Celemrod's tales for now."

Pelagius and Bojan return their attention to the elderly centaur. When he finishes his story, everyone remains speechless for a few moments.

"Amazing," says Adotiln. "Absolutely incredible."

"Yes," says an adventurer. "You must share more of your stories."

Celemrod smiles. "There will be plenty of time for that, but first, I believe that Pelagius has something he wishes to discuss with you."

The young adventurers in the audience turn toward Pelagius. However, before he can start, an unearthly noise pierces the night air, immediately halting all activities at the festival and scaring several red-eyed ravens out of their roosts. The entire populace looks in the direction of the sound and immediately sees the source, which is gigantic enough that it is visible from a few miles away.

This creature stands nearly thirty feet tall and has several features indicating its demonic origin: enormous horns on its head, sharp teeth, and a huge tail. However, the creature is in an advanced state of decay and has rotting human body parts of several types sprouting from all over its body. An arm here, a leg there, and a few heads as well; all fused together in a vaguely bipedal form.

"What in the gods' names is that?" asks a villager.

Celemrod and Pelagius take a step forward.

"An abomination," says Celemrod.

"I have no doubt that this is the work of my enemies," says Pelagius.

By this point, most of the villagers are in a state of panic as they attempt to flee. Despite the chaos, Celemrod and Pelagius move quickly enough to rally all the adventurers.

"That thing is coming this way!" says Celemrod. "Now is your chance to show everybody just what you can do! Get your weapons and follow me to battle!"

All the adventurers emit a loud cheer and gather their weapons. Pelagius dramatically draws his blade, only then recalling it shattering upon viewing the jagged edge. Irritated, he tosses it aside as he rushes to the inn, and Zynax is kind enough to let Pelagius take one of the swords off of his wall. Then, all the adventurers follow Celemrod to the edge of the village, where they line up to meet the monster. Celemrod walks up and down the line.

"Now, we all know that we are fighting for our homes," says Celemrod. "I cannot guarantee that everyone will survive this encounter. But rest assured that all those who take part in this conflict will be remembered as heroes."

Everyone in the area lets out a cheer. Celemrod and Pelagius take a spot in front of the rest of the adventurers, along with Kevnan. Bojan, Adotiln, and ten of the adventurers stay behind the line of warriors, forming a mage brigade to support the group with magic from afar.

When the monster is one hundred yards away, Celemrod emits a battle cry and rears up, brandishing his front hooves, then charges forward, followed by Pelagius and twenty of the adventurers. They all catch up to Celemrod quickly and run alongside him in the charge. The other twenty stay behind the makeshift infantry and form an archery line.

At the back of the line, Bojan and the other sorcerers begin flinging various spells at the monster. The creature gets hit with bolts of electricity, fireballs, orbs of blue energy that freeze the areas they hit, and various other spells, most of which have little effect on it. One sorcerer begins chanting loudly and moving his arms in a circle. Magical energy begins building up around him and his entire body begins shaking violently. Sparks of electricity burst from his body, forcing some of the other mages to back away. As he pushes both hands forward, he screams in pain. A stream of magical energy envelops him as it flows out of his hands, but it only flies a few feet before he disintegrates in a burst of power, distracting many of the mages and archers.

"What happened?" asks one of the archers.

Bojan begins directing the mages back into position. "Whatever he was trying to cast was too powerful for his body to handle."

As the mages regroup and resume flinging spells, Adotiln begins praying to Ender.

The rest of the adventurers charge forward, and the archers who remain behind fire their longbows, sending a volley of arrows into the monster. The creature responds by picking up a ball of dirt the size of a large boulder and throwing it at the group.

"Incoming!" shouts Celemrod as he ducks to the side.

The archers attempt to scatter, but the dirt ball lands in the center of the crowd, crushing over half of the archers, and several of the mages.

"I call upon the Flames of Courage!" shouts Pelagius. "Begone, you wretched thing!"

As he says this, green flames appear to wrap around his arms. Pelagius then thrusts both arms forward and streams of green fire shoot from his arms. The flames hit the creature directly in the chest and appear to ignite it. However, the flames soon burn out and the corpse reaver is barely fazed.

Several adventurers rush forward to attack the monster's legs when there is suddenly an orange glow coming from the interior of the creature's mouth. After a while, it opens its mouth and an enormous stream of fire shoots out directly at the crowd, incinerating ten adventurers. Pelagius comes to a stop and blocks the flames with his shield, Celemrod barely manages to jump to the side, and Kevnan leaps into the air and flips to safe ground.

Kevnan runs to the creature's base and stabs one of the legs. The monster brings down its fist, attempting to crush him, but he backflips out of the way before running up the creature's arm, stabbing several rotted, smaller hands with his rapier as they attempt to grab him.

With White Fire faintly glowing, Celemrod charges up the creature's arm. He stops on the elbow and slashes downward, setting its arm on fire and nearly severing the forearm. However, before he can go any farther up, the creature reaches over and grabs him, pulling him away so quickly that he drops White Fire, which flies right toward Pelagius. Pelagius desperately parries the blade and the force of the blow shatters his sword, barely missing his head and knocking him to the ground.

Pelagius groans in frustration and tosses the broken sword aside. "Not again." He looks up in time to see the monster slam Celemrod directly into the ground. It picks him back up and starts to throw him, but Kevnan stabs the creature in a head that forms the shoulder joint, causing the composite arm to slightly drop halfway through his throw. Celemrod slams into the ground just a few feet from Pelagius, whose eyes grow wide in horror.

"Celemrod!" shouts Pelagius as he rushes to the centaur's side.

Pelagius kneels and cradles Celemrod's head in his arms. "You have to get up. Help us finish this fight."

Celemrod groans. "After that, I don't think I can."

"No," says Pelagius. "You're the leader. You can't fall yet."

"I already have," says Celemrod weakly. "It is up to you now. You must lead them to victory."

Celemrod points toward White Fire. "Take it. Take White Fire."

"I can't," says Pelagius. "White Fire is your sword."

"Not anymore," says Celemrod. "It belongs to you now. Take it and finish this fight."

"Very well," says Pelagius. "Thank you, Celemrod. Your deeds shall not be forgotten."

Celemrod smiles as Pelagius lowers his head to the ground. "You know what to do."

Celemrod's eyes close as he slips into unconsciousness. Pelagius picks up White Fire and charges at the monster, now surrounded by the remaining adventurers, who are all chopping the monster's legs while the elf leaps around on top of the creature, stabbing it in several locations of its body. Bojan and the other five sorcerers continue bombarding it with various spells.

Pelagius joins the other adventurers at the monster's legs and slashes one leg with White Fire. The leg is set ablaze, but the damage is not enough to bring the creature down. It swings downward with its massive hand, knocking several adventurers aside.

Adotiln finishes praying and begins to glow bright red. She rises into the air until she hovers twenty feet above the ground. She opens her eyes, which are also glowing red.

"Behold the power of Red Lightning!" shouts Adotiln in a deep, booming, and echoey voice.

She raises her arms in the air and two massive bolts of red lightning shoot out of her hands. Kevnan sees this coming and leaps off the creature into a nearby tree. The two bolts hit the creature directly in the chest and nearly blow it in half.

As the corpse reaver falls to the ground, the red glow around Adotiln fades away. She closes her eyes and plummets to the ground. Fortunately, Bojan quickly jumps with a magically enhanced leap and catches her in midair. With one arm left, the monster continues to swing wildly at the remaining adventurers. Pelagius looks at White Fire and a white flame appears around the sword. He charges at the creature and in one swing slices off its arm and cuts it in half down the middle. The flames from the sword then burn it to ash.

"Finally," says Pelagius with a breath of relief. "It's over."

Bojan approaches carrying an unconscious Adotiln. Pelagius glances over as they draw near. "Is she all right?"

"She'll be fine," says Bojan. "The Red Lightning spell is at the highest level of power she can use without harming herself. She just needs some rest, and she'll be fine."

Kevnan jumps out of the tree and lands by Pelagius. "Nice attack yourself. That's quite a sword."

"Thank you," says Pelagius. "And I assume that you're Kevnan."

"You are correct, sir."

A look of realization appears on Bojan's face, and he taps Pelagius on the shoulder. "Celemrod?"

Pelagius rushes to Celemrod. As he squats to check on the fallen hero, he notices that the elderly centaur is still breathing. "He's alive! If he can hold out until Adotiln awakens, we should be able to save him."

Kevnan and Bojan sigh in relief before surveying the battlefield for more survivors. Then, Kevnan looks toward the village.

"Looks like the villagers are coming to congratulate us," says Kevnan.

Pelagius and Bojan look toward the village and see the inhabitants coming to the field, cheering.

Chapter 16

The next day, Pelagius and the others emerge from the inn to find the townsfolk walking through the village. Most have lowered their heads, and many are crying. As the heroes join the procession, several villagers pulling carts covered with sheets or rugs trudge by. When they reach the edge of town, they find themselves at the village cemetery. Some of the villagers are filling in fresh graves while others are digging new ones and lowering bodies in. They erect stones over completed burial plots and carve names into them. Many others are chiseling away at a large rock, inscribing the names of those of whom nothing remains.

As the burials near completion an onocentaur, opulently dressed in a purple coat, steps forward. "Normally this season of the year is a time for celebration, but yesterday, tragedy befell our village. Today, we set aside our celebration to honor those who fell in last night's attack. We thank each and every one of them for their sacrifices and will honor their memories. Their deaths were not in vain, for they helped to protect our village from destruction."

When the memorial service closes, Pelagius and the others return to the inn and begin preparing their cart for departure. As Pelagius turns to retrieve a large sack, Kevnan approaches. "I hear you are on a quest to destroy Babu."

Pelagius looks at Kevnan. "Correct."

"May I join you?" asks Kevnan.

"Of course," says Pelagius. "I was going to ask you to join us anyway. From what I heard about you from Celemrod, and what I saw you do last night, you seemed like the perfect addition to our team. But if I may ask, why are you so eager to join?"

Kevnan thinks for a moment. "Austracene is my home. Many of those who fell were friends of mine. I owe it to them to bring down the ones responsible for what happened."

"So, you wish to avenge their deaths?" inquires Pelagius.

"You could say that," replies Kevnan, "but I also wish to protect my home. If Babu is out of the picture, he can't threaten my village. I can also document the journey and spread the tale in song once we are successful."

"Fair enough," says Pelagius, "but I cannot guarantee that you will survive."

"That's a risk I'm willing to take," says Kevnan. "Besides, all heroes fall eventually."

Kevnan joins them to help finish loading their food and supplies into the cart. As Bojan is helping Adotiln into the cart, Celemrod approaches Pelagius, with the onocentaur following behind.

"I wish you a safe journey, my friend," says Celemrod.

"Thank you," says Pelagius. "I believe that this belongs to you."

Pelagius retrieves White Fire and hands it back to Celemrod. The elderly centaur looks it over, grins, and returns it to Pelagius. "Keep it. It's yours now. I'm retiring."

"What about your final battle?" asks Pelagius.

"I believe that last night was my final battle," says Celemrod. "The seer said I would fall in battle but did not specify whether or not I would die."

"Thank you, Celemrod. Perhaps we will meet again."

"Perhaps. I am planning on attending the Grand Tourney later this year. It's Diablos' turn to host, so if you survive your quest and are still in Diablos at the time, perhaps I will see you there."

Pelagius grins. "Very well. If I have not started my journey home, I will see you at the Grand Tourney."

As Celemrod says farewell to the others, the onocentaur steps up to Pelagius.

"Well, I am sorry to see you go," says the onocentaur. "It has been an honor having you here."

"Thank you, sir," says Pelagius. "I wish I could stay longer, but I don't want to endanger your village any more than I already have."

"There is one more thing," says the onocentaur. "You may want to be cautious while you are crossing the bridge. We have spotted a few vykonra in the river recently. So far, those vicious frogmen have yet to cause any problems, but it is best to stay alert. In addition, our night watch has spotted a single Black Dog lurking around several times in the past two nights. Some have even reported it appearing inside their homes, only to disappear when they lit a lantern."

A look of concern crosses Pelagius's face. "The Grim seem unusually active recently. We've had a few encounters with one ourselves. Thank you for the warning. We'll proceed with caution."

"Well, have a safe journey, my friend," says the onocentaur. "If you're ever back here, come see me if you need anything. I am Wuhshul, lord-mayor of Austracene."

"Much appreciated," says Pelagius.

Wuhshul leaves to return to his duties. As soon as everybody is aboard the cart, the four heroes depart Austracene. They cross the bridge with no problems whatsoever, and a few days later they arrive at Wallton.

CHAPTER 17

The sun is just beginning to set when Pelagius and the others reach Wallton. They are the last to pass through Wallton's enormous iron gateway before it closes for the night. Coming through the front gate, they find themselves in the city's Craft and Market District, where most of the businesses and shops in the city stand. The streets are nearly empty, and the merchants are preparing to close their shops for the night.

Kevnan looks at Pelagius. "We're going to need to find a place to sleep for the night."

"I already know where to go," says Pelagius. "We can find lodgings at the temple of Ender. My old mentor lives there, and he will be happy to give us a place to stay."

"That works," says Kevnan.

They direct the cart down the street and turn left. After about an hour, they pass through the smaller interior gate that separates the Craft and Market District from the Religious District, continuing down the road until they reach the Temple of Ender.

The temple is a large but plain building that stands two stories tall. The heroes take the cart and horse to the temple's livery stable before entering. When they go through the door, they find themselves in a chamber made of white marble. There are several statues situated throughout the room and doors all along the walls. Directly across the chamber from the main entryway is the door leading to the altar room. As they look around, a monk in a brown-hooded robe approaches them.

"How may I help you?" asks the monk.

"We would like to see Master Glahrug, high priest of the temple," says Pelagius.

"Very well, sir," says the monk.

The monk disappears through one of the doors on the left side of the room. Several minutes later, Glahrug, an elderly male orc about eighty years old, comes through the door. Like all orcs, he has bluish-brown skin, yellow eyes, and sharp canine-like teeth. His hair goes down past his neck and is completely gray. Due to his age, he walks slowly and uses a walking stick nearly as tall as he is. As he approaches the group, he recognizes Pelagius, Bojan, and Adotiln immediately.

"Ah, welcome back!" says Glahrug. "It has been too long. To what do I owe the pleasure?"

"Master, we are on a quest and seek a place to stay for the night," says Pelagius.

"Of course," says Glahrug. "You are always welcome here. Follow me."

He leads them through one of the doors and down a hallway to the sleeping quarters. Since Adotiln usually lives here, she goes to her old room. Glahrug directs Pelagius, Bojan, and Kevnan to the guests' quarters. The room is plain, but cozy with several beds spread out along the walls. As Pelagius enters the room, Glahrug notices the sword by his side.

"Is that White Fire?" asks Glahrug, his eyes growing wide.

Pelagius draws White Fire and hands it to Glahrug. "Yes, Master. It is."

Glahrug examines the blade thoroughly, admiring both the craftsmanship and the legendary artifact itself. "How did you get it?"

Pelagius recounts the story of the night of the Festival of Returning Heroes.

"I see," says Glahrug. "Celemrod chose his successor wisely."

"I'm not so sure. I don't even know if I'm worthy of serving Ender anymore."

"Why is that?"

"My courage recently failed me. I hesitated during an encounter and nearly got everyone killed."

"It sounds to me that you have not had any more lapses since then," says Glahrug.

"I froze up again during an encounter with Kragus," says Pelagius. "His illusions had me terrified before Bojan broke them."

"His confidence was shaken by the first ordeal, and the incident with Kragus has only exacerbated the problem," says Bojan. "However, he's still quite capable of rallying and inspiring others despite his doubts."

"Perhaps," says Pelagius. "We had help at Austracene."

Glahrug hands White Fire back to Pelagius. "Enough doubts. You will find your courage, Pelagius. This quest is proof of that. Is there anything else I can help you with?"

"There is one more thing," says Pelagius. "We would like to recruit a few more heroes to join our quest, but I'm not sure where to start looking."

"What types of warriors are you looking for?"

"Someone skilled with the bow and arrow. I, admittedly, am not well practiced in the art. We could also use another brave warrior."

"I recommend the Silver Knight Tavern. You'll find plenty of adventurers and potential heroes there. I also suggest you seek out the archers' guild. They have the best bowmen around."

"Thank you again, Master."

"My pleasure. Good night, everyone."

Glahrug leaves the room, closing the door behind him, and the three heroes get ready for bed.

Chapter 18

The next day, Pelagius, Bojan, Adotiln, and Kevnan arrive at the Silver Knight Tavern, followed by a large, red-eyed raven that perches in the rafters. The tavern is a large two-story building with two suits of full-plate armor embedded in the walls on both sides of the door. When they enter, they find two more suits of armor inside, placed on the walls near the door. In addition, there are suits of armor wielding various kinds of weapons situated all over the tavern.

As they press their way inside, the smell of ale and simmering meat fills the air. People of many different species populate the tavern. The bartender appears to be a male satyr, a creature with the upper body of a human except for a pair of goat horns and the lower body of a goat, but with two legs instead of four.

Bojan looks around. "There are dozens of people here. Where do we start?"

"Just keep looking around until we find a table and make note of anybody you see who appears to be hero material," replies Pelagius.

"Very specific," says Kevnan sarcastically.

The four heroes walk through the tavern, observing everyone they pass, until they find an empty table in the corner of the room. They sit and order mugs of ale.

"Did anybody see any likely contenders?" asks Pelagius.

Adotiln takes a sip from her small mug. "It's difficult to say. There are so many people here."

"I suggest we separate for now," says Pelagius. "Bojan, you and Adotiln go to the archers' guild. Kevnan and I will conduct our search here."

Bojan downs his ale, with a quarter of it spilling out the sides of his beak. "Very well."

Bojan waits for Adotiln to finish her drink, and then they leave the tavern while Pelagius continues to scan the crowd. After several minutes, they spot a potential candidate on the far end of the building. He is a dwarf about fifty years old, just over four feet in height, and sporting a bushy beard. He wears chainmail armor and has a large maul, with the most massive hammerhead Pelagius had ever seen strapped to his back. That burly character is drinking mugs of ale and besting other patrons at arm wrestling.

"He looks like someone who would take up the cause," says Pelagius.

"How can you tell?" asks Kevnan. "He just looks like a tough guy having a good time."

"Well, hopefully we can convince him to join us," says Pelagius. "Stay here and keep an eye out for any other candidates or any trouble."

Pelagius finishes his ale, crosses to the other side of the room, and approaches the dwarf's table. He pulls up a chair and sits.

"I don't recall inviting you to join me," says the dwarf.

"Forgive the intrusion," says Pelagius. "I have a proposition for you. I would like to recruit you for a quest."

The dwarf snorts. "Nothing against your kind, but I'm not too keen on following an old human around. Try another table."

"Could you at least hear me out?" asks Pelagius. "I think you might be interested."

The dwarf grunts and sighs. "All right, I'll hear you out. If you can best me in two out of three contests."

"Very well," says Pelagius. "Name them."

"The first shall be a drinking game of your choice. The second will be an arm-wrestling contest."

"And the third?"

"That will be decided by me, if we get to the third. So, name your game."

Pelagius summons a waitress. "Three mugs of ale for me and a shot of whiskey for the dwarf."

"Right away, sir," says the waitress.

As she disappears behind the bar, the dwarf eyes Pelagius curiously. "I'm not familiar with this game. You'll have to explain it to me."

"Of course," says Pelagius. "I'm wagering that I can finish my three mugs of ale before you can drink your shot."

The dwarf and the surrounding patrons burst into laughter. "Impossible. You've got guts, old man. What are the rules to this ludicrous game?"

"First, in order to avoid cheating, neither of us can touch the other's glasses," says Pelagius.

"Fair enough."

"Second, you cannot touch your shot until I have finished my first mug and placed it upside down on the table."

"So, you get a one-drink head start?" asks the dwarf. "I suppose that's fair, but it's still impossible to finish the other two before I drink the shot. Is there anything else?"

"That's all the rules," says Pelagius.

The dwarf smiles confidently. "This will be the easiest drinking game ever."

The waitress brings the drinks and places them in front of the two contestants. Pelagius picks up his first mug and drinks it remarkably quickly. When he finishes, he turns the mug upside down and places it over the dwarf's shot glass. His opponent watches, stunned, as Pelagius calmly drinks his last two ales. He looks at the dwarf as he places his final glass on the table.

"Very clever," says the dwarf. "Sneaky, but clever. Be careful who you play that game with, though. A less cordial opponent would not take it as well."

"So, to the arm wrestling then?" says Pelagius.

"Of course," says the dwarf. "This is going to be more interesting than I thought."

The two contestants take positions across from one another, staring each other down as they brace their arms. At the signal of another patron, they begin the contest. The two contestants push forward with all their might, each one trying to drive the other's arm down to the table.

For a few moments, they are at a stalemate. Then, Pelagius begins to slowly force the dwarf's arm down toward the table. The dwarf pushes back and forces Pelagius's arm back up before he begins to slowly push down. He nearly has Pelagius's arm touching the wood when the old man surprisingly forces his way back up and over, nearly taking the dwarf's arm down to the table.

The two contestants battle back and forth in this manner for nearly ten minutes. As Pelagius appears to have victory within his grasp, the dwarf seems to have a sudden burst of strength. He rapidly forces Pelagius's arm back up and slams it down onto the table. A cheer breaks out among the other patrons.

"Very impressive," says the dwarf. "I haven't had someone challenge me that way in quite a while."

"Thank you," says Pelagius. "What's the third challenge?"

"All right, follow me," says the dwarf, rising to his feet.

Pelagius momentarily staggers as he follows the dwarf through a door close by the bar and finds himself in a combat training room.

"This is my third contest," says the dwarf, removing his armor. "We go one-on-one in a hand-to-hand fight. The first one to be unable to stand up within ten seconds loses. Are these terms agreeable?"

"I accept your terms," says Pelagius, removing his own armor.

The two contestants step into the sparring ring and wait a few seconds before engaging in their duel. The dwarf comes up and punches Pelagius in the stomach several times. The old hero is vigilant and remains on his feet, but a sudden uppercut to his jaw sends him sprawling onto his back. A third patron begins counting, but Pelagius is up surprisingly quickly.

"I'm impressed," says the dwarf. "That usually does the trick."

"I'm much tougher than I look," says Pelagius.

The dwarf charges forward and drives his fist into Pelagius's stomach with all his might, sending him sprawling to the floor. Once again, he rises within a few seconds.

"You certainly can take a beating, old man," says the dwarf, "but can you fight?"

"I'm just trying to make sure that this doesn't end too quickly," says Pelagius.

"Awfully cocky for someone getting his posterior handed to him," says the dwarf.

The dwarf charges forward and punches Pelagius in the stomach once again, but this time Pelagius ducks to the side and dodges his uppercut. Then, he punches the dwarf across the face, sending him stumbling to the left. Before his opponent can recover, Pelagius lunges forward and slugs him on the bridge of the nose. The dwarf hits the ground with a thud and is unable to stand in time. After about a minute, the dwarf stirs, and Pelagius helps him to his feet.

"All right," says the dwarf. "Now I'll listen to your proposition. Anyone who can fight like that is someone I'd be willing to work with. The name's Iriemorel, by the way."

While they return to the tavern, Pelagius tells his tale. Iriemorel listens intently as the story comes to a close. "I'm in."

"Really?" says Pelagius. "You've decided that quickly?"

"My hometown has had problems with soul hunters too," says Iriemorel. "I'd like to help put a stop to their raids."

Pelagius smiles. "Welcome to the team."

Chapter 19

Bojan and Adotiln enter a building bearing the sign of the archers' guild. Inside, a human male in his mid-forties greets them. "Welcome. How may I help you?"

"We would like to speak to your best archer," says Bojan.

"I see," says the man. "Then it would be Alithyra you want to speak with. You'll find her in the back at the archery range."

"Thank you," says Adotiln.

The two heroes follow the man through the plain building to the back door. Outside, there are several boxed areas lined up side by side, each one with several targets at various distances. Among the members is a female canin of the saluki breed dressed in a green tunic and pants. She stands roughly six feet tall with a slender build, long arms and legs, a long, narrow head with extended snout, and a small, curved tail. Short, light red hair covers her body, with long, feathery hair on her long ears. She appears young, roughly the human equivalent of sixteen years old. She has a longbow in her hands and a quiver of arrows on her back, and appears to be practicing.

"That's her," says the man, returning through the door.

Bojan and Adotiln approach the young canin, who turns to face them.

"Hello," says Alithyra. "Did you need some help?"

"You might say that," says Bojan. "We were hoping you would join us on a quest."

"I've never been on a real quest before," says Alithyra. "What kind of quest are we talking about?"

Bojan explains the situation to her.

"I see," says Alithyra.

"It is a very dangerous task," says Adotiln. "We would understand completely if you do not wish to join."

"Of course I'll join," says Alithyra. "I would love to help rid the world of such an evil."

"Do you have any other fighting skills or just archery?" asks Adotiln.

"That's rude," says Bojan.

"She's no good to us if she can't fight in close quarters," says Adotiln. "My apologies. I didn't mean any offense."

"None taken," says Alithyra, "I have plenty of combat training and am quite skilled with tonfas."

"Then we welcome you," says Bojan. "Please join us this evening at the temple of Ender. We have other things to discuss."

"I'll be there," says Alithyra.

Bojan and Adotiln leave the archers' guild as Alithyra resumes practice.

Chapter 20

That evening, the six have regrouped at the temple of Ender. They gather around a table in the temple's dining hall, a plain but large room with walls and floors made of white marble and several enormous tables large enough to sit thirty people each. There are also a few dozen smaller tables that could sit between four and ten people. They have gathered at one of these smaller tables on which Pelagius has laid out a map of the Sarcascan continent. Several platters of food surround the map, filling the air with the scent of cooked meats and a variety of spices.

"Before we decide on anything else, we must first determine which route we will take to get to Devil's Den," says Pelagius.

"How many choices do we have?" asks Alithyra.

Bojan holds up a bowl of soup and slurps it down, causing a trickle to run down the side of his beak. "There are several ways into Diablos. Ranwald, Industria, and the Necrotian Empire all have open borders with Diablos. Additionally, Battallia shares a border with Diablos, as do Bratenro and Halfhill."

Pelagius picks up an apple and takes a bite. "Most of those routes would be impractical, however. Ranwald, Industria, and the Necrotian Empire are on the opposite side of the continent. As far as Bratenro is concerned, the stretch of the Great Stony Mountains between the two kingdoms is too perilous and too high to cross."

"So that leaves us with Battallia and Halfhill," says Kevnan.

Adotiln looks at the map. "Battallia is closer to us. That could be a shorter trip."

"In theory, yes," says Pelagius. "However, Diablos and Battallia are not on good diplomatic terms. They are not at war, but King Bloodsworth the First closed off the borders and banned any and all trade with the Diablosians. To cross the border, we would have to convince King

Bloodsworth VII to temporarily open the mountain pass for us. For non-Battallians, getting an audience with him may take months."

Kevnan begins munching on a hunk of cheese. "Then it appears that Halfhill is the best option."

"Possibly," says Pelagius. "Of course, we would have to cross through Bratenro to get there, but after stopping at the village of Ithuweston, we could follow the river through a small mountain pass. That would take us very close to our destination."

Iriemorel bites into a large turkey leg and messily tears off a chunk. "Sounds simple enough."

Bojan sets down his soup bowl and grabs a piece of bread. "It's not as easy as it appears. Remember, Bratenro is ruled by giants. In that kingdom, anything shorter than fifteen feet is considered lower class and inferior. If we cause any harm to a giant, even unintentionally, we will have broken a law and will be executed on sight."

Alithyra cuts two slices from a loaf of bread and sticks a slab of meat between them. "So, we can't even fight in self-defense?"

Having finished the apple, Pelagius tosses the core aside and takes a sip from a nearby mug. "For giants and cyclopes, no. However, the dev are considered to be primitive and inferior even by the giants, so if one attacks us we are free to defend ourselves."

Adotiln grabs the entire platter of cheese and begins shoving small pieces into her mouth. "What's a dev?"

"It's basically a seven-headed cyclops," explains Kevnan. "My troupe encountered one about seven months ago, and they are quite vicious."

Pelagius grabs a knife and spears a chunk of meat. "Of course, the titans are the true ruling class of Bratenro. Standing between thirty and forty feet tall, they are the giants among the giants."

"How big are the giants then?" asks Iriemorel.

"Usually between fifteen and twenty feet tall," replies Bojan. "The cyclopes and devs are about the same."

"So which route are we taking then?" asks Alithyra. "Battallia or Halfhill?"

Pelagius thinks for a moment. "It seems that Halfhill is the best option."

Iriemorel points at the map with his turkey leg, with some juices dripping onto the parchment. "I suggest that we go back to the river and follow it all the way to Ithuweston. The area where the river passes through Tybybik Forest is where the forest is at its narrowest."

"That's plausible," says Bojan. "Except if we do that, we will have to pass through Zreziask Swamp as well."

Pelagius cleans off the map and gives Iriemorel an irritated glance. "We can go around the swamp. The detour will add a few days to the journey, but I think that it would be worth not having to try to find a dry spot to camp in a swamp. Once we get around the swamp, we can rejoin the river and follow it to Ithuweston and take the river passage through the Great Stony Mountains and toward our destination, stopping at the Diablosian town of Ethor to rest and resupply."

"Then what?" asks Alithyra. "Do we go through the Kappa Marsh or around it?"

"Going around Kappa Marsh would take too long," says Bojan. "We're going to have to go through. Don't worry, though. The section we'll be passing through is small enough to get across in a few hours."

Iriemorel finishes off his turkey leg and tosses aside the bone. "And then we just walk right into Devil's Den."

"I'm afraid it's not quite that simple," says Pelagius. "Devil's Den is a vast city-sized fortress whose defenses rival Warlord City. We need to infiltrate the citadel and then find Babu before we can destroy him."

"I see," says Iriemorel. "Are you sure we have enough people to do the job?"

Realizing that the plates are all empty, Pelagius pushes them to the far end of the table. "A small group is what is needed. A large force would attract unwanted attention, not just in Diablos, but in Bratenro and Halfhill as well."

"I think we've had plenty of unwanted attention," says Kevnan. "From what I can gather, Babu knows we're coming."

"All right, look," says Pelagius. "If we go marching through a few kingdoms with a small army, it will raise suspicions, and we would be assaulted by that kingdom's military forces. With a small group, we only have to worry about Babu's minions, any of the Green-Eyed Man's hired goons, and Kragus."

"I see what you mean," says Alithyra, "but this is starting to sound like a suicide mission."

Pelagius sighs and thinks for a moment. "I told you all that it was a dangerous quest. I never made any promises that anybody would survive. If any of you want to back out, now is the time to do so."

No one says a word.

"Thank you," says Pelagius. "I'm happy to know that I can count on all of you."

"So, are we done here?" asks Kevnan.

"We are done for tonight," replies Pelagius. "Everybody, get some sleep. In the morning we will gather supplies and provisions for the journey and then we will depart."

The six heroes clear the plates from the table, roll up the map, and exit the dining hall. Adotiln goes to her room and the others go to the guests' quarters. As soon as they leave, Thakszut and Nyogsutt drop down from the rafters and rush out a window.

CHAPTER 21

The Green-Eyed Man sits in a secluded spot in the forest, deep in thought as he rests, when a rustling tree branch breaks his concentration. He emits an irritated sigh and then shoots a bolt of lightning into the tree, causing a small explosion that blows off several branches, sending Thakszut and Nyogsutt tumbling to the ground and stirring several red-eyed ravens to flight. The two fiendlings quickly get back to their feet.

"Why did you do that?" asks Thakszut.

"Yes," says Nyogsutt. "You could have killed us."

"It was a calculated risk," replies the Green-Eyed Man. "I was in no mood for your shenanigans."

"You're no fun," says Thakszut with a childlike whine.

"Noted," says the Green-Eyed Man. "Now what did you find out?"

"Well, they appear to be done recruiting," says Nyogsutt, "and they started making plans."

"Battle plans?" inquires the Green-Eyed Man.

"No," replies Thakszut. "Travel plans."

"Which way are they going?" asks the Green-Eyed Man.

"South," says Nyogsutt. "They plan to enter Diablos through the mountains' river pass at Halfhill."

"That still covers a lot of ground," says the Green-Eyed Man. "How am I supposed to know where to intercept them from that?"

"Easy," says Thakszut. "They're planning to follow the river most of the way."

"Until they reach Zreziask Swamp," adds Nyogsutt. "They plan to go around that place."

The Green-Eyed Man thinks for a moment. "Excellent. That means I can easily set up traps and ambushes along their planned path. I know just who, or in this case what, to send into the forest after them."

The Green-Eyed Man stands and holds out his arms. When his urn appears, he lifts the lid up a tiny crack, and appears to whisper something into it before opening it completely. A ball of blue energy flies out and a humanoid figure forms. Clearly undead, his skin is gray and shows signs of decay. Chunks of flesh are missing in several places. His coarse hair is long and scraggly, and his eyes are milky white.

Perhaps the most disturbing thing about him is that there are at least a dozen rusty chains, some of which have barbed hooks at the ends, weaving in and out of his body. Several chains emerge from his body and hang from him, but others suspend in the air, moving around as though they were tentacles. Worst of all, he seems to have complete control over them. The Green-Eyed Man grins. "Your targets will be traveling through Tybybik Forest within a few days. Ensure that they never leave the woods."

The creature groans, returns to a mist-like state, and shoots off in the direction of the river. The urn vanishes as the Green-Eyed Man replaces the lid. Thakszut and Nyogsutt look on in horror.

"Boss," says Thakszut nervously. "What did you just do?"

"Yes," says Nyogsutt. "Please tell me you didn't…"

"You are correct," interrupts the Green-Eyed Man. "I have just released Morat."

The Green-Eyed Man smiles evilly, but Thakszut and Nyogsutt tremble with fear.

"I hate Morat," says Nyogsutt. "He's really scary."

"Absolutely terrifying," says Thakszut. "Those chains weaving through his body are the most horrifying aspect."

"What are you two so afraid of?" asks the Green-Eyed Man. "Morat is under my complete control. He can't do anything unless I tell him to."

"That's what scares us," says Thakszut.

The Green-Eyed Man rolls his eyes. "You two are hopeless. Now get back there and keep an eye on them. I'll need you to keep me up to date on their activities."

"Right, boss," they both say.

Thakszut and Nyogsutt scamper off and the Green-Eyed Man sits again to continue making plans.

Chapter 22

Pelagius and the others are back on the road, four days of travel behind them. Kevnan is driving the cart and Adotiln is riding in a small space in the back. Pelagius, Bojan, and Alithyra are riding the horses they purchased before departing, and Iriemorel is riding a pony.

As the sun sets, the six heroes park the cart on the side of the road, tie the animals' reins to a tree, and set up camp. Pelagius, Bojan, Adotiln, and Kevnan are setting up the tents. Iriemorel is chopping some firewood, and Alithyra is feeding the animals. Iriemorel picks up a couple of sticks and goes to start the campfire, but Bojan stops him.

"No need," says Bojan. "I've got a quicker way."

A small ball of flame appears in Bojan's hands, and he lobs it at the pile of logs. It lands directly in the center of the pile and explodes, immediately lighting the fire and knocking Iriemorel back.

"Show-off," says Iriemorel.

Bojan just shrugs and sits on a rock close by. Iriemorel goes over to his bags and retrieves a large sack. He then goes to the fire, puts the sack down, and pulls out a large, black iron pot, a huge chunk of meat, some potatoes, and several types of vegetables, including carrots and onions. He chops up the potatoes and the other vegetables and slices the meat, putting it all in the pot. He pulls out a sealed bottle of goat's milk and pours it in before suspending the pot from a large wooden spit above the fire; then he leaves it to cook. Within minutes, the scent of the concoction fills the air.

Pelagius emerges from a tent. "That smells delicious."

"What are you cooking?" says Kevnan.

"Triceratops stew," replies Iriemorel. "The butcher shop had a special on dinosaur meat."

Alithyra leaves the horses and returns to the others, her nose twitching as she takes in the scent. "I've always heard that cooking dinosaur meat is very difficult. Where did you acquire such skills?"

"I learned it from my father when I was just a boy," replies Iriemorel. "I have several dinosaur recipes that have been a part of my family for ages."

"Impressive," says Bojan, sitting down. "What else can you prepare?"

"Anything," replies Iriemorel proudly. "I learned from some of the best. Just name something, and I can cook it."

"How about Black Dog?" asks Adotiln.

The others look at her.

"A bit unorthodox," says Iriemorel, surprised. "Also, difficult to acquire since Black Dogs are hard to kill and their bodies tend to vanish when they are eliminated. Why do you ask?"

Suddenly, a torrent of lightning illuminates the sky. Then, the fire slowly starts dying down, despite Bojan's best efforts to keep it going. After a minute, the fire goes out completely, leaving the campsite in darkness. A pair of burning red eyes appears and the dark form of the same Black Dog that has been hounding them appears. Half his face seems to have been burned off. Adotiln points in the beast's direction. "Burnscar is back."

Bojan chuckles. "You nicknamed it Burnscar? Personally, I would have gone with Old Crispy Face."

"Enough," says Pelagius. "It's coming this way."

Determined as ever, Burnscar bursts out of a grove of trees and charges toward the heroes. Everyone quickly gets to their feet, drawing their weapons.

"I'll take care of this," says Alithyra.

Alithyra walks a few feet toward the charging Black Dog. She nocks an arrow and fires it off. The arrow hits Burnscar directly in the shoulder, but he rapidly turns intangible for a moment and the arrow passes through harmlessly. Then, he pounces and is upon Alithyra before she can loose another arrow.

Pelagius throws himself in front of her, putting his shield between himself and the angry beast. Burnscar rakes the shield, emitting an ear-piercing metallic shriek as his searing hot claws scorch the surface. The impact pushes Pelagius into Alithyra, knocking them both to the ground. The other three heroes surround the rampaging beast, but it suddenly doubles in size, forcing them back. Iriemorel swings his maul at the monster's head, but Burnscar turns into mist and the hammer-head passes through harmlessly. As the Black Dog reforms, Bojan snaps his fingers and emits a bright flash of light, causing Burnscar to vanish. However, the beast quickly reappears a few feet away, then rushes forward, knocking Adotiln and Iriemorel to the ground. He headbutts Pelagius, who drops his sword and shield and is sent flying about ten feet away, before pouncing on Bojan. Using his front two legs, he pins Bojan's arms to the ground and lowers his jaws toward the defenseless sorcerer's head. Alithyra lunges forward, White Fire in hand, and drives it into Burnscar's side. The beast yelps in pain as he steps off his intended victim. Alithyra quickly withdraws the sword and brings it down upon Burnscar, lopping his head clean off. Everyone sighs in relief as Burnscar flops lifelessly to the ground. Bojan hurries to restart the campfire.

"Well done," says Pelagius.

Alithyra hands White Fire back to Pelagius. "Thank you. I'm fairly handy with a sword, as well."

As the others stand there stunned and impressed, Adotiln looks at Iriemorel and smiles. "You said you could cook anything including Black Dog. Now is your chance to prove just how good you are."

Iriemorel emits an irritated grunt. "I can go ahead and clean the carcass and season the meat, but cooking him will have to wait for another day. I have already started on the triceratops stew, and I don't want to cook two meals in one night."

"Fair enough," says Adotiln. "Better start quickly before the corpse vanishes."

Without saying another word, Iriemorel grabs a large knife and drags Burnscar's corpse off behind some trees. About thirty minutes later, he returns with a large lump wrapped in several layers of brown paper. He puts it into the same bag that held the triceratops meat, then turns to the others, saying, "I'll be right back. I need to dispose of the rest of the carcass. We don't want any scavengers to show up in the campsite." He walks off, only to immediately return. "Nevermind. The body disappeared." Returning to the campfire, he pulls a wooden spoon from his bag and stirs the stew.

CHAPTER 23

Meanwhile, the Green-Eyed Man is still in the forest. Shudgluv has joined him, and the two already appear deep in discussion while a red-eyed raven looks on from a nearby tree.

"That's what I want you to do," says the Green-Eyed Man. "Go to Bratenro and give him the order."

"Why do we need him? You already sent out Morat. He should be more than sufficient to destroy the whole team."

The Green-Eyed Man shrugs. "Call it a contingency plan. On the very small chance that Morat is defeated, we will need something else in place."

"How do you know that he'll want to cooperate, especially since it will be at least a month before Pelagius and the others will even be in that area?" says Shudgluv.

"Offer him lots of food. He is, after all, a simple-minded creature."

"Very well. Consider it done."

"Good. Once that task is complete, return to Diablos and await further instructions."

The Green-Eyed Man then opens a portal and Shudgluv steps through. As the portal closes, another one opens behind the Green-Eyed Man and Alasdar appears. The Green-Eyed Man turns to greet him. "I must say, Alasdar, this is quite a surprise."

"Yes," says Alasdar. "It's a pity it couldn't have been under more pleasant circumstances."

Concern fills the Green-Eyed Man's eyes. "What do you mean?"

"Babu sent me. He grows impatient and demands an update. He especially wishes to know if any of them are dead yet."

"Not yet. Not to worry though. I have begun to set my plans in motion. They will be dead before they even reach Halfhill."

"It would be more efficient for you to kill them yourself. Why are you bothering with recruitment tactics?"

"Pelagius is only a minor nuisance. He is not worth my time. I have my soul hunting duties to attend to. Why don't you help out? They wouldn't stand a chance against you."

"I have no interest in helping you out of the hole you are digging for yourself. In fact, it may benefit me greatly if they actually make it."

The Green-Eyed Man glares at him. "What does that mean?"

"Nothing that you should be concerned with. You should focus on your problem."

"The problem is practically solved. With what I have set up, they won't even make it to Ithuweston."

"They better not. The trip from Wallton to Ithuweston takes thirty-nine days. If by that time Pelagius and his entire team are not dead, you will be leading the first line of defense. If they make it to Devil's Den, who knows what horrors await you as punishment for your failures?"

Fear fills the Green-Eyed Man's eyes. "I have served Master Babu loyally since that day so many years ago. In all that time, I have never failed him."

"Yet," says Alasdar. "Do not forget, Babu saved your life that day. In return for your absolute loyalty, he gave you all the powers of a soul hunter, including your immortality, and he can take all of it away on a whim. I assure you that the consequences will not be pleasant if you should fall from Babu's favor."

"And why did he send you to tell me this?" asks the Green-Eyed Man.

Alasdar smiles. "I volunteered. I wanted to see the look on your smug face when you realized just how much is at stake."

The Green-Eyed Man looks at Alasdar. "The soulborn transformation really does change one's personality, doesn't it?"

"It changes everything," says Alasdar. "The Alasdar you knew is dead. All that remains is what the soulborn transformation left. Of course, you've changed quite a bit yourself since those days."

"Indeed," says the Green-Eyed Man. "Now, if you're done tormenting me with my possible future, I have other matters to attend to."

"Of course you do," says Alasdar. "I'll give your report to Babu, but I suggest that you give this matter more personal attention."

During their conversation, several more red-eyed ravens gather in the trees around them. As Alasdar turns away, he looks up and surveys the treetops. "Be very cautious. You are being watched."

Without saying anything else, Alasdar opens a portal and steps through. The Green-Eyed Man wanders into the forest, deep in thought, disturbed by Alasdar's cryptic warning.

CHAPTER 24

At approximately noon the next day, the heroes have been traveling for several hours and now follow the river through Tybybik Forest. Green-leafed trees of all sizes surround them and leaves, sticks, logs, and other debris cover the forest floor. Several small creatures scurry through the underbrush, including a family group of leptictidium hunting insects by a large tree. A few small dinosaurs occasionally emerge from the thicker part of the forest, only to disappear back into the safety of the brush. Several red-eyed ravens perch in the trees, watching the heroes as they pass by.

Adotiln glances around nervously. "So, how long will it take to get through the forest?"

"Not long," replies Pelagius. "We're crossing through the woods at its narrowest point so, we should only have to camp in the forest tonight. We should emerge into Bratenro early tomorrow afternoon."

"That's honestly a little longer than I was hoping for," says Adotiln nervously.

"Do you dislike the woods?" asks Alithyra.

"I'm not fond of spending time in them," replies Adotiln. "There are too many ways for an enemy or a predator to sneak up on you."

Alithyra smiles. "True, but after spending some time in the woods, you learn to listen for the signs of a potential ambush. Rustling bushes don't always indicate that you are being stalked, but if several sets of bushes rustle at the same time, then odds are there is something hunting you."

"You seem to know quite a bit about the subject," says Bojan.

"I practically grew up in the woods," says Alithyra. "I mastered the bow by going on hunts, and I have been stalked by my fair share of woodland predators. Once you know what to look or listen for, you can stave off an attack fairly easily."

Abruptly, Alithyra's smile fades and she comes to a stop. Her ears perk up, her hair stands on end, and she sniffs the air as she draws her bow. She looks around intently with a serious expression, teeth bared while she scans the vegetation.

"What's wrong?" asks Kevnan.

Alithyra doesn't answer. After several minutes, she lowers her bow and turns to the others. Suddenly, a rusty chain whips out of the bushes and hits Alithyra in the stomach, knocking her down. Before the others can react, Morat emerges. Alithyra gets to her feet and all draw their weapons.

"What is that?" asks Iriemorel.

"Something I was hoping we wouldn't have to fight," replies Pelagius. "We must defeat it before it kills us all."

Iriemorel charges at Morat, swinging his maul. A chain blocks his blow and wraps around him. Acting more like an appendage than a chain, it lifts Iriemorel into the air and swings him violently, while also slamming the dwarf onto the ground. Alithyra looses a few arrows at Morat, with little to no effect, even from the ones that strike their target. A hooked chain wrenches her bow from her grasp. From her belt, she draws a pair of metal tonfas, two-foot-long sticks with a handle jutting from one side about a quarter of the way down the top. She grips the handles so that the longer side runs across her forearms and the shorter side juts out past her fists. She quickly finds herself dueling with the hooked chain, nimbly blocking its blows with her unusual weapons.

Kevnan rushes forward, jumps, and rebounds off a tree, attempting to impale Morat with his sword. Unfortunately, one of Morat's chains hits him in the stomach, impaling him and tossing him aside with a whip-like motion.

Adotiln begins praying to call upon her magical powers, but an attacking chain interrupts her chant. She rolls away before it entangles her, and she draws a pair of large daggers. The chain whips toward her, but she uses her blades to deflect it. A second chain joins it, and she nimbly parries both, then leaps back to dodge two more. A third pair snakes in and wraps around her arms, causing her to drop her daggers and allowing the other four to entangle her body and begin squeezing like a constrictor.

Pelagius attempts to fight his way to Morat, dueling with a chain as though he were sword fighting and blocking blows with his shield. Bojan stands back and a small ball of flame appears in his hand.

"Let's see how he handles this," says Bojan.

He hurls it at Morat. However, to his horror, one of Morat's chains swings at it and knocks the fireball back at him.

"Element of liquid, protect me from the flames!" shouts Bojan as his fireball closes in.

Just before the fireball reaches him, a large bubble of water forms around his body, providing him with a water shield, which successfully extinguishes the rogue flame. An explosion of steam creates a force powerful enough to send Bojan flying several yards backward into a tree. Despite the pain, Bojan rises to his feet.

"Wings of the Beast, come to my aid," chants Bojan.

A familiar pair of shimmering, transparent wings appear on Bojan's back. As the wings flap, he rises into the air and flies forward at amazing speed toward his foe. Morat's chains are surprisingly quick and Bojan finds himself suddenly bound as they wrap around his body. The chains whip around and unravel, sending Bojan slamming into the tree. He bounces off the trunk with a loud crunch and crashes to the ground.

At this point, the chains are overwhelming Alithyra and Pelagius. A hooked chain latches onto Pelagius's arm, preventing him from making full use of White Fire. Despair fills his mind. *I can't believe it,* thinks Pelagius. *This is how it ends for us?*

Suddenly, a rock strikes Morat's head, distracting him enough to cause him to temporarily lose control of his chains, releasing several of the heroes. Alithyra and Pelagius are able to move, and Iriemorel and Adotiln come crashing to the ground. Then, goblin in a loin cloth swings out of the nearest tree.

He is somewhat short for a goblin, but has their usual brownish-green skin. He carries a gnarled wooden staff nearly five feet long. He releases his grip on the vine, flips, and comes down right in front of Morat. As he lands, he swings his staff, hitting Morat in the side and sending him flying into a tree. Pelagius ignites White Fire and moves toward Morat, but the goblin stops him.

"Put the fire away, my friend," says the goblin. "The trees do not like it."

Pelagius, confused by this statement, watches as the goblin walks toward Morat.

"I am Ugai of the Order of the Great Oak," says the goblin to Morat. "Your unnatural presence is poisoning the land. Leave now or be destroyed."

A look of recognition crosses Pelagius's face.

"Who is he?" asks Alithyra.

"He's a druid," replies Pelagius. "A protector of nature. He must have sensed this creature's presence and come to protect his forest home."

Morat rises to his feet and emits a roar-like moan, noisily raising all his chains into the air. Before Morat can do anything else, Ugai plants his staff, which has started to glow, into the ground. After a brief flash of light, several vines, grasses, and roots grow around Morat, weaving in and out of his chain links until he is completely tangled. Then the roots and branches of the tree behind him begin to grow, rapidly intertwining with Morat's chains and leaving him immobilized. Morat struggles in vain to free himself as Ugai looks on.

"Now begone, Scourge of the Forest!" shouts Ugai.

Ugai quickly rips his staff from the ground, causing all the plant material that has grown around Morat to retract and pull his chains in all directions. Morat explodes into a ball of light as the foliage rips the chains from his body.

Pelagius approaches the druid. "Thank you, Ugai. We couldn't have done it without you."

Ugai nods in recognition. Suddenly, a look of horror crosses Pelagius's face and he surveys the scene. He quickly realizes that four members of his team are severely injured, perhaps dying.

Pelagius turns to Alithyra. "What are we going to do? I don't have Adotiln's healing powers and she is just as badly injured as the other three. If we can't heal their wounds, they will die."

Ugai approaches. "Perhaps I can be of assistance. Priests of the cities are not the only ones with the power to heal, you know."

Before Pelagius can respond, Ugai's staff glows and he embeds it into the ground. Glowing cocoons of grass and vines wrap around the four injured heroes. After several minutes, the cocoons stop glowing and slough off; the four heroes rise to their feet, completely healed.

"Incredible!" says Pelagius. "I've never seen anything like it."

"That is the true power of nature," says Ugai.

"Thank you, but why did you help us? I would have thought that you might think we were invading your forest."

"You were fighting an enemy of nature. That makes you an ally."

"I see. Thank you again. Perhaps you would care to join us on our quest?"

"No. I appreciate the offer, and I'm sure that it is a noble quest, but my place is here in the forest. I am its protector, and without it I am nothing. If I leave, I break my oath to the Order of the Great Oak, and in doing so lose my powers of protection. Now, if you'll excuse me, I must rest. I used the most powerful of my abilities in this battle and doing so leaves me drained and exhausted. But rest assured, my friend, as long as you remain a friend to nature, you will always have allies in the Order of the Great Oak."

Before any of the others can respond, Ugai disappears into the trees.

Chapter 25

Adotiln finishes healing Pelagius and Alithyra's wounds as the others set up camp in a small clearing in the forest. Suddenly, Iriemorel throws down his maul. "Are we going to just go about our business like nothing went wrong, or are we going to try to figure out what just attacked us?"

"I agree," says Kevnan. "What was that? Some kind of unknown type of undead monstrosity?"

Pelagius stands up and stretches. "That was a spectre, a vengeful ghost using its rage to fully manifest and attack anyone it encounters."

"Well, thank the gods that Ugai destroyed it," says Alithyra.

"You are mistaken about that," says Bojan.

"Indeed," says Pelagius. "Defeating a spectre is one thing. Destroying it is completely different. It will eventually return once it recovers its energy."

"Unless its soul was enslaved by a soul hunter," says Bojan. "In which case, it will return to its master's urn."

"How do we kill a spectre?" inquires Kevnan.

"We don't," replies Pelagius. "The only way to get rid of an enslaved spectre is to destroy the urn that it is stored in. After it has killed everything in sight, or it is defeated, it will fade away into the afterlife."

"There may be another way," says Bojan. "I have heard rumors that powerful necromantic spells can permanently destroy a spectre, whether free or enslaved."

Pelagius briefly glares at Bojan. "It is possible, but as neither of us dabbles in necromancy, we do not have the ability to try that."

"Why?" inquires Kevnan.

"Magic of any kind takes years of careful training and discipline to master," says Bojan. "The longer you train and practice, the more powerful the spells you can use without destroying yourself. I have never used necromancy and would destroy myself along with the spectre if I were to attempt to use a necromantic spell powerful enough to obliterate it."

"Or worse," says Pelagius. "End up like Kragus."

"What do you mean?" inquires Kevnan. "From the stories I've heard, Kragus's condition is due to years of constant exposure to the energies of Yatbuju."

"True," replies Pelagius, "but such an effect could also be the result of attempting to use a powerful necromancy spell without taking the time to master the required sorcery. Kragus could easily have suffered the same effect had he attempted to use necromancy to destroy a soul when he was just starting to learn his craft."

"Those who were at the battle in Austracene remember the effect that the Red Lightning spell had on me," says Adotiln. "My body was not quite ready to channel that kind of power, but I have adapted enough to not be destroyed by it."

The heroes grow silent as they finish setting up camp. Bojan uses a tiny fireball to start the campfire.

Iriemorel starts unpacking his cooking supplies. "Does anybody have any requests? If I don't have it in my bag, I could probably go hunt for it."

Adotiln looks over at him and smiles mischievously. "How about Black Dog? If you recall, we still have my cooking challenge for you."

"Roast Grim it is then," says Iriemorel.

Iriemorel goes to the camp's edge and brings back two large branches with forks at one end. He drives the straight end of each into the ground on opposite sides of the fire. Then, he pulls out a metal roasting spit and unwraps a large chunk of Black Dog meat. He skewers it with the spit and places it over the fire with both ends of the spit resting in the crook of the branches. He then turns the spit as he seasons the meat.

A few hours later, the heroes finish supping Iriemorel's dish. They sit around the campfire, satisfied. Kevnan strums a tune on his mandolin and sings softly while Alithyra sits close by, both listening and making new arrows out of materials she found around camp. Bojan appears to be deep in meditation and Pelagius is off to one side, sitting under a tree. As Iriemorel cleans and packs his cooking supplies, Adotiln approaches him.

"So, how was it?" asks Iriemorel, glancing at her.

"The meat was a little tough, but it was delicious," replies Adotiln. "I guess you win our little bet."

Iriemorel smiles. "I'm glad you enjoyed it. Black Dog meat is known for being tough and a difficult dish to prepare."

As they converse, a large, red-eyed raven lands on the spit. It eyes the surprised heroes for a moment, squawks in Iriemorel's face, and steals a strip of meat from his plate before roosting in a nearby tree.

"What is with these ravens?" asks Kevnan. "They seem to be everywhere."

"I wish I knew," says Bojan. "I've been seeing them since the Green-Eyed Man's raid on Inolutet. It's almost like we're being watched."

Suddenly, a rustling in the trees puts everyone on the alert. Bojan quickly rises to his feet and Pelagius rejoins the rest of the group as everyone draws their weapons. After a moment, Ugai drops out of a tree into the clearing.

"Ugai," says Pelagius, with a sigh of relief. "We were not expecting you."

"It is good to see you, friends," says Ugai. "However, this is not a social visit. I come bearing news of grave importance."

"What's wrong?" inquires Bojan.

"I sense two great evils in the forest," replies Ugai. "One seems to have a demonic yet human aura, and the other reeks of death. One seems to have been following you, and the other appears and disappears randomly."

Pelagius and Bojan look at each other and then at the rest of the group.

"It could only be the Green-Eyed Man and Kragus," says Pelagius. "Which one has been following us?"

"The one that reeks of death," replies Ugai, striding closer to the group. "Additionally," whispers Ugai, "there are two fiendlings watching you from the trees directly behind Adotiln."

Pelagius looks at Alithyra and nods. Without warning, Alithyra turns and looses an arrow over Adotiln's head. It flies into a tree and the heroes detect a screech of pain from within its branches. After a moment, Thakszut falls out of the tree and hits the ground with a thud, an arrow lodged in his left shoulder. The leaves rustle violently as Nyogsutt flees in a blind panic.

Thakszut struggles to his feet as Pelagius and the others approach him. He tries to leap back into the tree, but Alithyra catches hold of her arrow and stops him in midair. Pelagius grabs him around the waist as Alithyra yanks the arrow from his flesh.

Terror fills Thakszut's eyes. "Please don't kill me. I swear I will never bother you again. Please."

"Calm down," says Pelagius. "I'm not going to hurt you. Just tell me how long you have been watching us and what the Green-Eyed Man's plans are."

Thakszut gulps as his eyes dart back and forth between the heroes. "Following you? We weren't following you. My friend and I were only frolicking through the trees."

Pelagius sighs. "You're a lousy liar. Just tell the truth."

"That is the truth," says Thakszut.

Bojan steps forward, rubs his hands together, and gives Pelagius a wink. "I guess you're not lying after all. Let's just shake on it and we'll send you on your way." Bojan extends his hand. Thakszut eyes him hesitantly and reaches out. They clasp hands and Thakszut shrieks in pain as a small jolt of electricity flows into his body.

"What did you do to me?" asks Thakszut.

Bojan smirks. "I just cursed you with a lie detecting spell. If you lie to us, you'll get zapped again. It would be best if you just told us the truth."

Thakszut gulps. "Fine. We've been following you ever since you foiled the raid back in Inolutet. Per our orders, we were to simply watch you and report your progress to the boss whenever he appeared. As far as his plans are concerned, I only know that he intends to make sure that you never enter Diablos. I don't know how he plans to do it. All I know is that he has something in store for you in Bratenro and a defense force set up somewhere in Diablos."

"Is there anything else?" asks Bojan. "What can you tell us about the ravens?"

"Nothing," says Thakszut. "They've been hanging around the Green-Eyed Man and Kragus as well. They're just as confused about them as you are."

Pelagius looks over at Ugai.

"These ravens are not normal," says Ugai. "They seem somehow unnatural. They are not spirits, but I sense an aura of pestilence on them."

"So, they are diseased?" asks Pelagius.

"No," says Ugai. "The ravens are not diseased."

"What does that mean?" asks Kevnan.

"I cannot say," says Ugai. "All I can discern is that they are watching you. Other than that, I have no other information."

"Nothing else?" asks Pelagius, looking at both Ugai and Thakszut.

Ugai shakes his head.

"That's all I know," replies Thakszut. "I swear. Now, I suppose you have no further use for me."

Pelagius releases his grip on Thakszut. "Unless you wish to help us, we do not. You are free to go."

"What?" asks Thakszut. "You're not going to kill me?"

"You cooperated with us and have not tried to harm us," replies Pelagius. "I have no need or desire to harm or kill you."

"But he serves one of the evil ones," says Ugai.

Pelagius looks at Ugai and then looks back at Thakszut. "True. However, I believe that he serves the Green-Eyed Man out of fear rather than loyalty. Am I right?"

"Yes, sir," replies Thakszut. "I am very much afraid of him and of what he could do to me if I disobeyed him. In fact, now that I have told you his plans, I can't even return to him. If he were to discover my treachery, he would kill me without a second thought."

"Then why not join us?" inquires Bojan. "We can protect you from anything the Green-Eyed Man tries."

Thakszut's eyes seem to brighten at Bojan's offer. Ugai, on the other hand, appears shocked. "What? You cannot be serious. Have you forgotten what this thing is? He will betray you the first chance that he gets."

"Not all demon descendants are inherently evil, Ugai," says Pelagius. "In fact, very few of his species are ever evil. They are more mischievous than anything. The worst things they do are pull unpleasant pranks and heckle those they don't like."

Ugai thinks for a moment. "Be that as it may, he is still a servant of the evil one and I will not allow him to remain in my forest. You trust him if you like, but I will not. The edge of the forest is only a few days away. If he is not out of my domain by then, I will destroy him myself whether, he is with you or not. I will protect this land any way I see fit, even if I have to protect it from you."

With that, Ugai leaps into a tree and vanishes.

Pelagius turns back to Thakszut. "Our offer still stands. Do you have an answer?"

"I cannot go back to the Green-Eyed Man, nor do I desire to do so," replies Thakszut. "So, I will join you."

"Excellent," says Bojan. "What is your name, friend?"

"Thakszut."

Bojan points to his shoulder. "Welcome to the team, Thakszut. Hop on."

"Aren't you going to undo your curse?" asks Thakszut. "I have no reason to lie to you."

Bojan grins. "There was no curse. I just gave you a small zap. It's a standard magical prank."

Thakszut glares at Bojan before bursting into raucous laughter. Then he hops onto Bojan's shoulder and they return to their campsite. They divide up watch duties, and everyone but Bojan and Thakszut enter their tents for the night. Thakszut turns to Bojan. "Is there anything I should do to help?"

"Actually, yes. Go into the trees and scout the perimeter."

Thakszut then jumps off Bojan's shoulder, scrambles up a tree, and proceeds to leap from tree to tree as he surveys the area. When he ventures farther from camp, he encounters Nyogsutt as they simultaneously land on the same branch.

"I'm surprised to see you here," says Thakszut. "I thought you fled to an area farther away."

"I came back to see what happened to you," replies Nyogsutt. "Your conversation was an excellent method of deception. Now come on. We have to keep watching them and report to the boss when he gets back."

"No. I'm done working for the Green-Eyed Man."

"You can't be serious. Do you know what he'll do to you when he discovers you betrayed him?"

"He will try to kill me, but my new friends will protect me."

"If you come with me, we can forget about your temporary betrayal. The boss will never know."

"No. I've made up my mind about this. I'm not working for him anymore."

Nyogsutt reaches out and grabs Thakszut's arm, attempting to make him come along, but Thakszut punches him in the face. Nyogsutt jumps back and glares angrily. "After all we've been through together, I can't believe you would betray me."

"I don't have to betray you," says Thakszut. "If you join me with them, we can still work together."

"I'm not stupid enough to double-cross the boss."

"I'm sorry you feel that way. I guess this is goodbye then."

"You know that I can't keep this information from him. The next time I see the boss, I will have to reveal your treachery to him."

"Do whatever you have to."

Nyogsutt's voice breaks as he fights back tears. "So be it. Farewell, traitor."

Before Thakszut can respond, Nyogsutt leaps away into the darkness. Thakszut then resumes his patrol.

Chapter 26

A few days later, Pelagius and the others emerge from Tybybik Forest onto the plains of Bratenro. The landscape seems to stretch endlessly with only scattered groves of trees and a few occasional hills in view. Somewhere far to the south lies the edge of Zreziask Swamp, and nearly as far to the west looms the section of the Great Stony Mountains that separates Bratenro and Diablos.

Cities and towns of gigantic proportions loom in the distance. Even the wildlife here is of enormous size. A herd of Brachiosaurus roams in the distance and a huge roc bird looms overhead. Various other species, nothing smaller than an elephant, wander through the plains. Trees grow to epic proportions and are even larger than most redwoods.

"My word!" exclaims Kevnan. "The stories of this kingdom are true. Everything here is gigantic."

"It makes me nervous," says Adotiln. "I feel small in places where humans are the majority. Here, I'm afraid I'll get stepped on."

"How do you think I feel?" asks Thakszut. "I'm even smaller than a gnome. Most humans seem like giants to me."

"Where are we going now?" asks Iriemorel, ignoring Thakszut. "It will take weeks to cross this kingdom."

"It will take about twenty-seven days if we go through the swamp," says Pelagius. "Since we're planning to go around it, the journey will probably take between thirty-two and thirty-five days, assuming that there are no significant delays."

"Are we going to just start the journey now or what?" inquires Kevnan.

"No," replies Bojan. "Our supplies are running low. We need to stop at a nearby village, town, or city to restock and rest."

Pelagius consults the map. "The closest place is Terli, the capital of Bratenro. That is where we are going."

"How far is Terli?" asks Iriemorel.

"We should be able to reach it by late afternoon," replies Pelagius.

Kevnan looks at Thakszut. "What about him? His service to Babu and the Green-Eyed Man is well known, and most won't take kindly to us traveling with him."

"I can take care of that," replies Bojan.

Bojan grabs Thakszut and puts him on the ground. "Hold still."

"What are you going to do?" asks Thakszut nervously.

"I'm going to magically disguise you as an ordinary monkey," replies Bojan.

Bojan begins to chant and move his arms in a particular pattern; then he stops and points at Thakszut. A blinding flash of light and a puff of smoke envelops Thakszut, and when it clears, he has the appearance of a normal brown monkey.

"There," says Bojan. "Just don't talk and the disguise should work perfectly."

"How long is this going to last?" asks Thakszut.

"A few days," replies Bojan. "I can undo it earlier; however, you need to look like that whenever we enter a settlement of any kind here to avoid suspicion. I do have a better disguise spell, but it requires an extended ritual. We'll have to wait a little while to use it."

"We should start moving," says Pelagius. "We need to get to Terli before nightfall. Once those gates close for the night, we won't be able to get into the city until morning."

Without another word, the group of heroes starts down to the road toward the enormous city in the distance.

CHAPTER 27

As Pelagius and the others discuss the current situation, Nyogsutt watches silently from a tree at the edge of the forest. Suddenly, he hears a noise behind him. Fearful that Ugai has found him, he turns around and sees the Green-Eyed Man. Nyogsutt drops out of the tree in front of him.

"Oh good," says the Green-Eyed Man. "I guessed correctly when I tried to determine your location. Where's Thakszut?"

"I'm afraid that I have grave news regarding him," replies Nyogsutt.

"Dead?"

"No, sir. Why would that be your first guess?"

"You said that you had grave news about him. Knowing you two, I thought that a bad joke or pun would be involved. So, what? No joking this time?"

"Not this time."

The Green-Eyed Man eyes Nyogsutt with suspicion. "No joking or playful evasion whatsoever?"

"No, sir," says Nyogsutt. "I'm deadly serious."

"Serious? You? This must be bad. What happened?"

Nyogsutt's voice breaks as he fights back tears. "Thakszut has betrayed us."

A look of surprise crosses the Green-Eyed Man's face. "Thakszut? That doesn't sound right. Are you sure that craven little coward isn't pulling a prank on you?"

Tears begin flowing down Nyogsutt's cheeks. "I wish that were so."

"What led to this turn of events?"

As Nyogsutt recounts the events in the clearing, rage fills the Green-Eyed Man's eyes.

"And you just let this happen?" asks the Green-Eyed Man.

"No, sir," replies Nyogsutt. "I tried to talk him into reconsidering, but he refused."

"Did you tell him the consequences of his betrayal?"

"I did. He wasn't concerned."

"Thakszut will pay for his betrayal."

"I assume you're going to kill him."

The Green-Eyed Man looks at Nyogsutt and grins. "I'm not going to kill him. You are."

"What? How am I supposed to do that? I've never killed anyone in my life."

The Green-Eyed Man doesn't answer. Instead, he summons his urn and reaches inside. He pulls something out, but his hand obscures it. He looks at it, and then without warning throws something blue at Nyogsutt, hitting him in the chest and causing him to briefly glow blue. Nyogsutt shrieks in pain and clutches his stomach as he slumps to the ground. He slowly rises to his feet, woozily stumbling as he tries to regain his composure. "What just happened?"

"I have unlocked your Demonic Potential," says the Green-Eyed Man.

"Unlocked it? I thought that one's Demonic Potential could only be unlocked through years of training and meditation."

"There are many ways to unleash one's inner power. I opted for a quicker one."

"How do I use it?"

"When the time is right, you'll know what to do. Of course, gaining such power this suddenly has a price. You will only be able to sustain it for a few minutes. After that, the power will be too much for you to handle and you must revert to normal. Otherwise, the power will rip you apart. Do you understand?"

Nyogsutt simply nods. Then, the Green-Eyed Man teleports away and Nyogsutt jumps back into the tree. He continues to observe the heroes as he tries to determine the best way to stealthily follow them.

CHAPTER 28

The setting sun casts long, looming shadows of the massive iron gate as Pelagius and the others approach. The walls surrounding Terli stretch into the sky, dwarfing the two axe-wielding, armor-plated giants that flank the open entrance.

"Halt!" bellows the first guard. "State your name and business here." The giant's thunderous, booming voice reverberates through the heroes' heads, causing them to clasp their ears.

Pelagius shakes his head to rid himself of the ringing in his ears. Then, he looks at the guard and cups his hands around his mouth. "I am Pelagius of Waskan. My companions and I are on a journey and simply seek a place to stay the night."

"Very well. You may proceed."

"Thank you, sir. Do you have any recommendations for lodging?"

The two guards consult each other. "I recommend the Angry Dragon Inn and Tavern. It is designed for smaller travelers such as yourselves."

"How do we get there?"

"Enter the gate and then turn right. Follow the road until you nearly reach the gate separating our entertainment district from the lower-class residents. The Angry Dragon is right next to the wall."

"Thank you for your help."

Without another word, the heroes go through the gate, which closes after they enter. The streets in this city are fifty feet wide. All the buildings close to the front gate house the city's smaller denizens, and the structures get larger as they go farther back. Standing above everything else, probably in the exact center of the city, is a castle of titanic proportions stretching up nearly five hundred feet tall and quite possibly several miles wide.

"Wow!" says Kevnan, awed by the sights. "This whole place is huge."

"Who lives in that castle?" asks Iriemorel.

"If I'm not mistaken, that is the castle of High King Jaygon," replies Pelagius. "The ruler of Bratenro."

"High King?" asks Adotiln. "There are other kings here?"

"Yes," says Pelagius.

A guard steps out of a watchtower by the gate. "Get moving. The curfew for punies takes effect in thirty minutes. If you're caught outside afterward, you will be crushed on the spot."

"We should probably go," says Pelagius. "We don't want to antagonize the guards."

The heroes turn right and head toward the lower-class residential area. After walking for nearly thirty minutes, they come across the Angry Dragon, a two-story wooden building that seems to have fallen into disrepair. The peeling paint of the sign makes it difficult to read, and several window shutters have fallen off.

Pelagius and the others go through the door. The interior of the Angry Dragon is worse than the exterior. There are no decorations and several broken tables and chairs litter the floor. A foul odor of mysterious origin assaults the senses.

Alithyra sniffs and immediately clasps her hand around her nose as the mystery stench overwhelms her. "Charming. We seem to have been directed to a place that is falling apart."

"Perhaps," says Pelagius. "Remember, in this kingdom anyone less than ten feet tall is automatically part of the lower class. Expect to be treated as such."

Behind the bar, a troll is wiping a mug with a dirty rag. Spread out throughout the room are several people drinking ale. Most are humans, but also among the crowd are a few busurins, gnomes, trolls, and surprisingly, a few chamaran.

A patron sitting at a corner table appears to be a dracian, a humanoid cousin species of dragons. They appear mostly human except that they have scales instead of skin and are sleeker, quicker, and stronger than most humans.

Pelagius approaches the bar. "Excuse me. Are you the owner?"

"Yeah," replies the troll. "I'm Krombron, owner of the Angry Dragon. What can I do for you?"

"My companions and I seek lodging for the night," replies Pelagius. "Do you have any rooms available?"

"I've got three left," says Krombron. "I charge a gold piece a night per room."

Pelagius drops three gold coins on the counter, which Krombron promptly picks up. Then he hands Pelagius three rusty keys.

"Rooms three, five, and eight," says Krombron.

"Thank you," says Pelagius.

He then walks to the others and hands out the keys. "We've got three rooms. Bojan and I will take one room. Kevnan and Iriemorel will take another, and Adotiln and Alithyra will take the third."

"Fair enough," says Alithyra. "What about Thakszut?"

"He'll stay with us," replies Bojan.

The heroes ascend the stairs and find their rooms, each with the same layout. There are, conveniently, two beds in each room. However, the cracked wooden frames are creaky and the sheets dirty and worn. Bojan looks at the single broken window with its torn curtain, grimacing in an expression of distaste. "This is not going to be a pleasant stay."

"Fortunately, it's only for one night, and we've slept in worse places," says Pelagius.

Bojan nods in agreement. Then, he pulls out a piece of chalk and draws a circle in the middle of the floor. He sets a few candles around the circle and lights them.

Thakszut approaches curiously. "What are you doing?"

Bojan snaps his fingers and Thakszut returns to his true form. "Setting up that ritual I mentioned earlier. Get in the middle of the circle and hold still."

Thakszut enters the circle, taking care not to knock over any candles. When he finishes his preparations, Bojan begins to quietly chant. As he chants, the circle begins to glow. Bojan claps his hands together and the candles suddenly melt away completely; the circle becomes a ring of fire. He continues chanting for nearly an hour, flames occasionally jumping from various parts of the circle to punctuate certain parts of the chant.

After an hour, Bojan finishes chanting and extends his arms. When he does this, the circle of flame rushes at Thakszut and engulfs him. Then a flash lights up the room and the flames disappear, leaving the floor unmarked.

Thakszut looks down at himself but sees no change. "I don't feel any different. I don't look any different either. I thought you said that that spell was better."

"It is," says Bojan. "It will also last for a few years, and you can now disguise yourself at will. All you have to do is think of the form you want to take, and you will immediately change into that form. For now, I recommend ordinary monkey. We came in with you looking like that, and it would be suspicious if we left with you looking like something else."

Thakszut thinks for a moment and then becomes a tengu. After a few moments, he transforms himself into a cat. Then, he returns to a normal brown monkey. "I like it. Thank you, Bojan."

"You're welcome," says Bojan.

"Now that that's done, it's time to get some sleep," says Pelagius, pulling back the covers on one of the beds. "We have a busy day tomorrow."

Bojan goes to the other bed and gets in. Thakszut climbs up with him and curls up next to his pillow.

Chapter 29

The next morning, Pelagius and the others go downstairs to the tavern for breakfast. Pelagius approaches the bar. "Good morning, Krombron."

Krombron simply grunts in response.

"What do you have for breakfast this morning?" inquires Pelagius.

"The same thing we have here every morning," replies Krombron. "Moldy gruel, week-old bread, and stale water. If you want something better, I suggest you go to the market and purchase it."

As Pelagius turns to the others, the dracian comes downstairs and approaches the bar. His scales are grayish-gold in color and his eyes are distinctly dragon-like. Aside from these details, as well as very sharp teeth, he appears mostly human. He carries a large greatsword strapped to his back. This sword is nearly as long as he is tall and is close to half a foot wide. He slams his fist on the counter. "Come on, Krombron! I know you have some fresh eggs and meat back there. Cook that for breakfast."

Krombron glares at him. "Fine, Koskru. I'll cook up some eggs and apatosaurus bacon."

Krombron grumpily goes through a door behind him. Soon, the smell of bacon and eggs drifts out from the kitchen into the tavern.

Pelagius turns to Koskru. "Thank you, but you didn't have to do that."

"It was my pleasure, Pelagius," says Koskru. "I've heard of you and your exploits, and despite the way things are around here, you deserve more respect than you are given in this place."

"That's quite a sword," says Bojan. "Are you a soldier here?"

Koskru laughs. "No, I'm a dragonslayer."

"A dracian dragonslayer?" inquires Alithyra.

"That's more common than you might think," says Koskru. "Some are in it for profit, but I only hunt destructive, problem dragons. Of course, even that would get me killed where I come from."

"Where are you from?" inquires Kevnan.

"I am originally from Drago," replies Koskru.

"How is it that you came to be a dragonslayer then?" asks Pelagius. "Dragons are considered sacred in that kingdom."

"That is a fact that I know too well," says Koskru. "No matter what a dragon does there, nobody is allowed to kill or even harm one. A dragon could destroy half the villages in the kingdom, and they would still refuse to harm it. I disagreed with that. It is my opinion that hunting down and killing a dragon which is causing massive, destructive problems is just fine. I went into exile and studied the ways of the dragonslayer. Of course, tales of my deeds spread and as a result, I cannot return to Drago."

"Why not?" asks Adotiln.

"Because dragonslayers are killed on sight in Drago," replies Kevnan.

"That's partially true," says Koskru. "Even in Drago, it is well known that it takes tremendous skill in various forms of combat to take down a dragon. Therefore, the average resident will not take on a dragonslayer unless they can get everyone in town to help them catch one off guard. More likely, they will contact their local law enforcement, who will alert the Dragon Protectors, who will hunt down the slayer."

"It sounds like you would be a formidable ally," says Pelagius. "Perhaps you would like to join us on our quest. We are traveling to Devil's Den to defeat Babu."

"Thank you for the offer," says Koskru. "It would be an honor. However, I must decline. I have heard rumors of a problem dragon somewhere in Waskan. If I remember correctly, it is close to the town of Pethalville. As such, I am traveling there to put a stop to its destruction."

"I see," says Pelagius. "I wish you the best of luck."

"Thank you," says Koskru. "Actually, as luck would have it, once I have taken care of business in Pethalville, I will be traveling to Diablos. I am planning on entering and competing in the Grand Tourney. If you're not finished with your quest by then, come find me and I'll gladly help out."

"Hopefully, we'll be done by then, but I shall seek you out if we are still there," says Pelagius.

Several minutes later, Krombron emerges with several plates of food and serves one to each customer present. The heroes enjoy their breakfast in silence. Several hours later, after visiting the market district to restock food and supplies, they depart Terli and continue their journey south.

<h1 style="text-align:center">CHAPTER 30</h1>

Nearly a week later, Pelagius and the others depart from the river to avoid going through the swamp and now follow a seldom used road.

"Why are we using this road?" asks Kevnan. "Wouldn't it make more sense to use one of the better traveled roads?"

"There would be too much traffic," replies Pelagius. "Those roads would cause unnecessary delays, and we would be at risk of being run over by a giant or titan's carriage. Following this path, we avoid those hazards."

"Of course, we run the risk of encountering other hazards," says Bojan.

"Yes," agrees Thakszut. "Like the Green-Eyed Man's enforcer."

Alithyra's ears perk up seconds before something large bursts out of the trees of the nearby swamp. Before anybody can react, it charges forward and kicks Bojan, who sails through the air, tumbling as he goes, and flies over a grove of trees several yards away. The kick also causes Thakszut to soar through the air, but he lands in the trees.

As the dust settles, the identity of their attacker becomes clear. The creature stands at seventeen feet tall and looks as though it weighs close to four thousand pounds. It has seven heads, each of which has one large eye in the center of its face.

"It's a dev!" says Pelagius, drawing his sword.

As the dev approaches them, the others draw their weapons as well. Seeing this, the dev rips a tree out of the ground and breaks it in half, tossing the half with leaves to the side. Suddenly, it charges forward. The heroes scatter as it swings its makeshift club. Iriemorel then charges forward and swings his maul downward, smashing the dev's foot. The dev shrieks in pain and stamps its good foot, creating a shockwave that knocks Iriemorel to the ground; the dev then stomps on him. As it brings up its foot to stomp down again, Alithyra lets loose ten arrows at once. Each arrow hits a different spot of the body, but one manages to pierce the center of one of its large eyes. The dev clutches the wound and stumbles back, and various colors of light illuminate the air from the other side of the trees.

"What's going on over there?" asks Kevnan.

"Bojan must be fighting a battle of his own," replies Pelagius. "Let's hope we can end this one quickly enough to help him."

Iriemorel struggles to his feet, multiple chain links dropping off his damaged armor, leaving large gaps. He picks up his maul and hobbles toward the dev with Kevnan and Pelagius close behind him. He brings his maul down again, completely crushing the dev's big toe on its right foot. The dev roars in pain, clenches its fist, and punches downward, driving Iriemorel back into the ground.

Kevnan leaps onto its hand and drives his rapier into the dev's wrist. Pelagius runs to the dev's injured foot and begins slashing at it. Alithyra continues loosing arrows and Adotiln mutters a prayer. Kevnan withdraws his sword and runs up the dev's arm; however, the dev manages to grab him and throws him at a downward angle right on top of Pelagius.

The dev raises its tree club high and brings it down toward the two heroes. Seeing this coming, Pelagius tosses Kevnan to the side and barely gets his shield in front of himself. Directly impacting on the spot already scorched and weakened by the Black Dog's claws, the shield completely shatters, snapping Pelagius's arm. Pelagius screams in pain and clutches his arm as the dev raises its club up for another attack. Just then, Alithyra sends an arrow into another one of its eyes, causing it to stumble backward a bit.

Kevnan rushes over to Pelagius. "Are you all right?"

Pelagius rises to his feet, his left arm dangling uselessly by his side. "I'll be fine."

More flashes of light emanate from beyond the trees and a few explosions cut through the air.

"Looks like that fight is still going on as well," says Kevnan.

Pelagius nods in agreement. Just as the dev angrily walks up to them, Adotiln finishes her prayer. Two orbs of white light appear in her hands and she lobs them at the dev. Finding their targets across the chest and another eye, the orbs explode on impact, causing the dev to emit an unearthly shriek of pain.

When the light clears, the dev's chest is severely burned, as is one of its faces. The remaining eyes suffer temporary blindness from the flashes, and the dev swings its tree club randomly. One of these swings manages to hit Pelagius and sends him flying through the air for several feet. Kevnan, however, manages to avoid the blow by leaping over and onto it, then running up the tree club. When he reaches the dev's hand, he stabs deeply into the center of it, causing the dev to drop the tree. The weapon lands on top of Iriemorel as he tries to stand. Kevnan runs up the dev's arm as Pelagius struggles to his feet.

Kevnan leaps onto the dev's shoulder and drives his sword into one of its remaining good eyes. The dev shrieks in pain and swats at the source of the stab. Unable to avoid it, Kevnan gets sandwiched between the dev's hand and one of its heads. Stunned, he drops his rapier, which falls to the ground. Before he can recover, the dev manages to grab him and pulls him off its shoulder. With its remaining eyes, it glares at Kevnan and begins to squeeze him.

"Kevnan, catch!" shouts Pelagius.

Kevnan looks over just as Pelagius throws White Fire like a javelin toward him. He catches it by the hilt, and after some concentration, manages to get White Fire to ignite. He swings the sword in an arc and connects with the dev's wrist. Assisted by the magical fire of the sword, he slices the dev's hand off. The severed hand falls to the ground, loosening its grip upon impact. The dev emits another shriek of pain as it clutches the stump.

Alithyra lets loose more arrows and punctures two more of the dev's eyes. Seeing the source of the arrows with its last remaining eye, the dev pulls Iriemorel out from under the tree and hurls him at Alithyra. Before she can react, Iriemorel crashes into her and they both fly back several feet, knocking down Adotiln in the process. Pelagius retrieves White Fire from Kevnan. Two dark shapes rise behind the trees and ascend into the sky at incredible speed. Then a large explosion fills the air and the two shapes come crashing to the ground, once again out of sight.

"What was that?" asks Alithyra.

"I'm not sure," says Pelagius. "One of those may have been the result of Bojan using his Dragonbird powers, but without a clear view, I can't tell."

They refocus their attention on the dev, who is also distracted by the dark blurs flying through the air.

"We can't take much more of this abuse," says Kevnan. "We need to figure out a way to take this thing down, and soon."

"I know," says Pelagius.

As the dev approaches, Thakszut, now looking like a large gorilla with claws, leaps from a nearby tree and lands on top of one of the dev's heads. He drives his claws into the dev's last remaining good eye and nearly rips it out. Blinded, the dev flails around as it tries to get Thakszut off. However, Thakszut continues to jump to different parts of its body as he drives his claws into its flesh. At last, the dev manages to grab onto its attacker and flings Thakszut into the swamp. Pelagius charges forward as White Fire ignites, but the dev hears him coming and swings his good hand in the direction of the sound. The slap connects and sends Pelagius crashing into Kevnan and Iriemorel.

Adotiln draws her daggers and charges forward, nimbly dodging an attempt to swat her away. She leaps onto the dev's knee and drives her daggers into its thigh. She drops to avoid a swat, slicing down the front of its leg. The dev reaches to grab her, but she ducks around behind it. Then she drives her daggers into the back of its heel, and in a horizontal motion, rips them out of opposing sides, leaving a large gash across the back of the beast's foot. The dev stumbles as he loses strength in the injured foot and drops to one knee. Adotiln leaps onto its back and drives her daggers into the base of its spine. Roaring in pain, the dev falls face-first into the ground. It quickly rolls over, trying to throw Adotiln off, but she runs along its body to remain on top. It sits up and reaches for Adotiln, but Alithyra slams her tonfas into one of its heads. She then darts back and forth between several heads, bashing them with her weapons and keeping it distracted from the halfling on its chest. The tonfas connect with the temple of the leftmost head with a crunch, and the head flops limply to the ground. Taking advantage of the distraction, Adotiln drives her daggers into its chest, only to realize that they are not large enough to pierce its heart.

Pelagius approaches and tosses White Fire to Adotiln, who quickly sheathes her daggers and catches it. The weight of the sword, which is larger than she is tall, momentarily throws her off balance, but she recovers and places the tip of the blade onto the dev's chest. She then ignites White Fire, and using all her strength and body weight, drives the sword into the dev's heart. The dev emits a weak shriek before its heads plop lifelessly to the ground.

Adotiln slides down the creature's body, rushes to Pelagius, and returns White Fire. "You need healing badly."

"Go to Iriemorel first," says Pelagius. "He took the worst of it."

Adotiln runs over to Iriemorel and Alithyra. She kneels by Iriemorel and begins to pray. Suddenly, a huge, forty-foot ball of fire appears in the sky. It passes over them and descends as it goes past the trees. After a few seconds of silence, a massive explosion sets the entire grove of trees on fire and incinerates several red-eyed ravens flying nearby.

"What was that?" asks Kevnan.

Pelagius looks over at the inferno with an expression of dread on his face. "The most powerful spell that Bojan can use without destroying himself. We must hurry. If he's using that spell, then he must be quite desperate. Hopefully, that will end the battle, but we must get over there as quickly as possible so that we may assist him."

Adotiln spends several minutes healing Iriemorel and Alithyra before she moves over to Pelagius and Kevnan. Kevnan's injuries are less severe, but Pelagius's broken arm takes a few minutes to heal even with magic. Thakszut, now back in his true form, stands close by. As soon as everyone is on their feet, they head in Bojan's direction, making sure to go around the inferno.

CHAPTER 31

As the battle with the dev begins, Bojan soars through the air over a grove of trees. While he plummets toward the ground, he makes a few hand gestures and abruptly stops in midair just a few feet from the ground. Then he gently floats the rest of the way down, saying, "Well, that was unexpected."

Bojan rises to his feet, wincing in pain as he grabs his side. "That was quite a kick. I'll have to ask Adotiln to heal my ribs when I get back over there."

Kragus steps from behind a nearby tree and quietly approaches Bojan, a wickedly curved, serrated sword appearing in his hands. As he nears his target, he pulls back his blade and lunges forward. Bojan glances back and leaps to the side, the tip of the blade barely missing him. Bojan rushes to the other side of the clearing and turns back to his attacker. Bojan eyes Kragus suspiciously before picking up a nearby rock and hurling it. Reacting quickly, Kragus catches the stone and tosses it aside. Bojan responds by summoning a sword of glowing energy. "No illusions this time, Kragus?"

"You would see through them in an instant. Why should I waste the time and energy? Instead, let's skip to the end where I kill you."

"A sorcerers' battle it is, then."

As the two sorcerers size each other up, multiple large red-eyed ravens gather in the trees to watch. Kragus and Bojan charge each other and their swords collide with a crash and a bright flash of light. They then each jump back a few feet and move in again. Bright flashes of light accompany each clash of swords. At one point, the two of them jump back as Kragus fires red electricity from his fingers. Bojan blocks this with his sword, which glows red as it appears to absorb the energy, and responds with a bolt of lightning, which Kragus deflects with his own sword. Then they each hurl a ball of fire at each other. The fireballs explode with both barely avoiding the combined blast. They clash again.

"Impressive, Bojan," says Kragus. "I forgot how skilled a combatant you are."

"I'm full of surprises, Kragus," says Bojan.

Using his massive beak, Bojan then pecks Kragus in the face, obliterating his nose and causing him to stumble backward. Before Kragus can recover, Bojan hurls a ball of fire at him and unleashes the red energy from his sword. Both strike Kragus simultaneously and the resulting explosion is quite large. However, Kragus emerges from the smoke seemingly unharmed.

"You'll have to do better than that," says Kragus, realigning his nose with a sickening crunch.

The two sorcerers resume their battle. Swords clash with bright flashes of light as they continue to throw various spells at each other. Bojan gets hit directly in the chest by a bolt of electricity and is knocked to the ground. Kragus brings his sword down upon him, but Bojan manages to block the attempt and kicks Kragus off.

The battle continues with balls of fire, bolts of colored electricity, ice beams, energy rays, and all sorts of magical energies flying back and forth all over the field, causing explosions of all kinds. The swords clash as they bear down upon one another.

"Your powers should begin to take their toll on your body soon," says Bojan. "All I have to do is continue to make you use them until you destroy yourself."

"A cunning plan, but barring any serious injuries, I have absorbed enough life force to last a few days," says Kragus. "I doubt that you can hold out for that long."

The two separate and put several yards of distance between each other. The battle continues as each sorcerer throws everything he's got at the other. As the battle continues, Bojan tires, but Kragus continues, seemingly as strong as ever.

"You can't hold out much longer, Bojan," says Kragus. "This battle will end soon enough."

"Indeed, it will," says Bojan.

Bojan realizes despite his best efforts, Kragus does not seem to have weakened at all. After their swords clash one last time, they each leap back and put some distance between each other. Kragus hurls a large ball of fire at Bojan, who puts up a shield made of water just in time.

"Had enough?" asks Kragus.

"Indeed, I have," replies Bojan. "Now you shall witness the true power of the Dragonbird."

Kragus lowers his sword and backs away a few yards. "Go ahead. It won't affect the outcome of this battle."

"Powers of the dragon, heed my call," chants Bojan. "Grant me your strength and power all."

Suddenly, a wreath of fire surrounds Bojan. As the flames grow in intensity, the mighty sorcerer rises into the air. Bojan vanishes from sight as a fiery explosion envelops him. When the flames clear, the burning shape of a creature that seems to be a cross between a dragon and a bird stands in his place.

As the fire dies down, the creature forms. This dragonbird is massive in size and has the basic shape and appearance of a dragon. However, it has a large red beak, and black feathers cover its wings and back.

The creature glares down at Kragus and speaks, its deep, resonating voice piercing the air. "Behold the dragonbird. Now tremble before my power."

"Impressive transformation, Bojan," says Kragus, "but it will make no difference."

Suddenly, the dragonbird swoops toward the evil necromancer, unleashing a massive stream of fire as it strafes the ground. Kragus leaps to the side and rolls away just before the flames reach him, barely avoiding the blast. As it passes, the dragonbird flicks its tail, hitting Kragus's legs and sweeping them from under him. In an instant, the dragonbird is upon him and traps Kragus under one of its massive talons.

"Surrender, Kragus," says the dragonbird. "This battle is over."

"It's not over yet," says Kragus defiantly.

Kragus closes his eyes and concentrates for a few seconds. "Powers of darkness, hear my call. Unleash yourself, break through the wall."

Suddenly, the ground beneath Kragus darkens and several shadow black tendrils emerge. These things wrap themselves around the dragonbird's leg and pull it off Kragus, who slips out from underneath. The tendrils then fade away.

"Dark Magic!" exclaims the dragonbird. "Are you insane, Kragus?"

"Desperate times, my friend," says Kragus. "Now try this. Dragon of darkness, consume the light. Take my form and grant me your might."

Before the dragonbird can react, shadows burst from the ground and envelop Kragus. Within seconds, these shadows form a shadow black copy of the dragonbird.

"You are insane," says the dragonbird. "Dark Magic is among the most dangerous and corrosive forms of sorcery. You will not survive this encounter."

"If I release the power before it consumes me, I may survive," says the shadow dragonbird in an even deeper voice. "But if I die, I will take you down with me."

The two creatures rush forward and collide. They claw and bite as each one tries to overpower the other. Then, they fly into the air, continuing the battle as they do so. The shadow dragonbird unleashes a stream of shadow black fire, barely missing its opponent. The two creatures separate and hover in the air for a few moments. Then they unleash their fire blasts simultaneously. The two beams collide, resulting in an explosion that envelops both combatants. The force of the blast knocks them out of the air and they both come crashing to the ground. When the smoke clears, Kragus and Bojan have resumed their true forms. Both rise to their feet. However, despite his obvious injuries, Kragus is clearly in better shape than Bojan.

"It would seem that there is only one thing left to do," says Bojan.

Bojan then raises one arm into the air and shouts something incomprehensible. The sky darkens as a forty-foot ball of fire comes over the trees headed right for Kragus.

Kragus runs to the center of the clearing, but the ball's trajectory shifts and continues on its course. Kragus's eyes grow wide with horror as he realizes it is locked on to him and closing in rapidly. Kragus slides to a halt and raises a water shield, but the ball of flame breaks through with ease, landing directly on top of the evil necromancer and driving him into the dirt. It explodes on impact, sending Bojan flying back several yards, sets the grove of trees on fire, and incinerates every raven observing the battle.

When the smoke clears, a crater forty feet across and twenty feet deep at the center lies where Kragus stood. Bojan limps to the crater and peers in. Seeing no sign of Kragus, he sighs with relief and turns to leave, but hears grunting behind him. He turns to see Kragus, now horribly burned, pulling himself out of the crater. Several of his limbs are horrifically twisted and malformed and what remains of his hair has turned white.

Bojan grabs the tattered remains of Kragus's shirt and pulls him up. "That's impossible. How did you survive?"

"It took almost all the power I had," replies Kragus.

"Well, it doesn't matter," says Bojan. "It's over."

"Yes, it is," says Kragus.

Bojan grunts as he suddenly feels a sharp pain in his torso. He releases Kragus from his grip and looks down to see Kragus's sword embedded in his chest. Before Bojan can react, Kragus impales him, pushing the sword through him until the hilt is in contact with his chest and the blade is sticking out of his back.

Kragus leans in beside Bojan's head. "Victory is mine, Bojan. You die first."

Kragus twists the sword and withdraws it. Pelagius and the others come around the side of the burning trees in time to see Bojan slump to the ground with a gravely injured Kragus standing over him, holding a bloody sword. They stop in their tracks.

"No," says Pelagius, stunned.

Kragus shifts his gaze and sees them. He briefly smiles and chuckles weakly before groaning, falling backward, and tumbling into the center of the crater. Adotiln runs as quickly as she can to Bojan as the others look on in stunned silence. After a few moments, they realize that Adotiln has not begun the healing ritual and slowly gather around her.

Pelagius approaches first. "What's wrong? Why aren't you healing him?"

Adotiln turns to him with tears flowing down her face. "There's nothing I can do for him. He's gone."

Dropping White Fire to the ground, Pelagius falls to his knees. He looks at his fallen friend as tears roll down his face. Pelagius remains this way as the other three approach. Realizing what has transpired, they tearfully bow their heads in respect.

"It's my fault," says Pelagius. "If I hadn't made him come along on this quest, this never would have happened."

"It is not your fault," says Adotiln. "Bojan wanted to come. You didn't make him come along. You didn't make any of us come along. We chose to join you."

Rage crosses Pelagius's face. "Kragus! I'll destroy him for this!"

The others look up, taken aback by this statement. Before any of them can speak, Pelagius makes his way into the crater, headed for the motionless form of Kragus, lying at the bottom of the hole, sprawled in an awkward position. One arm is behind his back while the other stretches out to the side and one leg lies unnaturally twisted.

Pelagius walks up to him. "Get up!"

When Kragus does not respond, Pelagius kicks him hard enough to make the body jolt.

"I said get up!" shouts Pelagius. "I know you can hear me, Kragus! Get up!"

Kragus still does not respond.

"Very well," says Pelagius. "I'll finish you where you lie."

Pelagius picks up Kragus's sword and raises it over his head. Before he can swing downward, Kevnan and Iriemorel grab him and pull the sword from his hands.

"That's enough," says Kevnan. "Kragus is clearly dead too, or will be very soon. Mutilating his corpse, no matter how much he deserves it, won't bring Bojan back."

"We should still make sure that he never gets up again."

Adotiln stands and approaches the edge of the crater. "No, Pelagius. There is no valor in striking a coup de grâce. Ender would not approve of such dishonorable actions."

Tears continue to stream down Pelagius's face as he drops back to his knees. After a few moments, he rises to his feet and walks out of the crater. He kneels beside Bojan's body and closes Bojan's eyes. "Do we have any shovels in our supplies?"

"Of course," replies Iriemorel. "We knew something like this could happen. Plus, they could be useful in other situations."

"We need to bury Bojan," says Pelagius. "We'll continue a few more miles south until we can find a suitable place to lay him to rest."

"Why not here?" asks Alithyra.

"We don't have time to dig here," replies Pelagius. "You saw the size of that explosion. A few law enforcement officers from the nearest town are bound to come investigate. We don't want to be here when they arrive, or we'll be arrested for certain."

"What about Kragus?" asks Adotiln.

"Leave him to rot," replies Pelagius. "If the giants want to bury him when they get here, they already have a hole for him."

Although shocked by this statement, the others do not question him. Kevnan and Iriemorel build a makeshift stretcher out of the surrounding debris and carry him off. Pelagius and the others follow as they go to retrieve their supplies. Once they have everything, they load Bojan's body into the back of their cart and move down the road. Thakszut rides in the cart, tearfully looking over Bojan's body.

Just minutes after the heroes depart, two giants arrive on the scene. They both stand eighteen feet tall and weigh about three thousand pounds. Both are also heavily armored, but one wields an axe and the other wields a club.

"It doesn't look like anybody is still here," says the first giant.

"Let's look around anyway," says the second giant. "You check in this area, and I'll look around on the other side of those burnt-out trees."

The second giant walks away and goes around the remains of the tree grove. The first giant looks around until he gets to the crater. He descends into the crater and discovers Kragus lying at the bottom.

"Well, what do we have here?" says the giant.

He bends over and scoops Kragus's body up in his hand. Straightening up, he looks Kragus over. "Looks like this one took quite a beating. It's too bad he's dead. If he were still alive, I could get some information out of him."

Suddenly, Kragus opens his eyes and weakly grabs onto the giant's hand. "I'm not dead yet, but you're not getting anything out of me."

Before the giant can respond, Kragus's hands begin to glow purple. A hazy purplish-black smoke surrounds his hands before flowing over the giant's entire body. A look of intense pain crosses the giant's face. He opens his mouth to scream, but all he can manage to emit is a pain-filled grunt.

As the pain continues to flow through his body, his skin begins to shrivel and dry out. At the same time, Kragus's wounds heal and his bones straighten. After several minutes, the giant's eyes roll back into his head as his skin shrinks and tightens around his bones.

Kragus, nearly fully healed and mostly restored, releases his grip as the giant falls over. Kragus leaps out of the giant's hand shortly before the giant hits the ground. What now lies there has the appearance of a desiccated corpse. The giant's skin shrinks and tightens so much that individual bones nearly pierce the flesh. A weak, pained groan escapes the giant's throat.

"Still alive, I see," says Kragus. "We'll have to fix that."

Kragus grabs onto the dying giant and resumes the process. After several more minutes, the giant's skin sloughs off until only a brittle skeleton remains.

"That's better," says Kragus. "At least now my powers won't destroy me instantly, but I'll have to conserve them until I can absorb more life force. Hopefully, that will also counteract the effects of using Dark Magic. I just hope I never have to use it again."

Just then, the second giant comes back around the burnt trees. "Nothing over there except a dead dev."

When he sees the scene, the giant stops in his tracks. "What the...?"

He looks around the area until he sees Kragus. Rage fills his eyes. "What have you done, puny human?"

"Come on over and I'll show you," replies Kragus.

The giant charges Kragus and swings his club downward. Kragus rolls out of the way as the club crashes into the ground. Moving quicker than the giant, he grabs the giant's hand just before the purplish-black haze surrounds his own. Before the giant can react, the hazy substance surrounds him. Immobilized, all he can do is emit quiet groans of pain as Kragus sucks his life force out of his body. After several minutes, the giant collapses, but Kragus continues to absorb his life force until only a skeleton remains and Kragus is restored to full health.

That should do the trick for a while. However, I may need to absorb more life force before I confront Pelagius and the rest of his crew. At least enough to survive an attack of Adotiln's Red Lightning.

Kragus walks to a fallen log and pulls out a dirty, tattered cloak. He brushes it off before putting it on. He pauses as a large, red-eyed raven lands nearby and starts pecking at one of the skeletons. The bird stares at him fearlessly as he curiously approaches it. It squawks at him before taking to the air and flying away. Kragus watches with a disturbed expression before he pulls up the hood and proceeds to walk down the road.

CHAPTER 32

After traveling for nearly an hour, Pelagius motions to the group to pull off to the side of the road. He walks to a grassy area and looks around. "This should be a good spot."

"Shouldn't we keep going?" asks Kevnan. "Aren't you worried that we'll be caught by sentries looking for the source of the explosion back there?"

"That's not likely. There aren't any major settlements close enough to have seen the explosion from here. Additionally, any giants that went to investigate the area would probably just look around the site and return to their posts."

Pelagius picks up two shovels from the back of the cart and hands one to Iriemorel. He then walks to a soft patch of ground and begins digging. Iriemorel starts to dig as well.

Adotiln turns to Kevnan and Alithyra. "Can you place Bojan on the ground for me, please?"

Without responding, the two gently lift Bojan's body off the cart and place him on the ground. Adotiln motions for them to step aside. She approaches the body and kneels beside it. Adotiln begins a prayer that is immediately recognizable as the healing ritual.

"Why are you healing him?" asks Kevnan.

"It is customary of a servant of Ender to heal all wounds on the body to prepare it for burial," replies Adotiln. "It is a traditional part of our funeral process when cremation is not practical."

Adotiln resumes her prayer and glows blue. She then touches Bojan's body and the blue glow surrounds it, healing the wounds made by Kragus's sword. Afterward, she removes Bojan's green robe from his body and briefly says a prayer. When she touches it, the robe doubles in size. She pulls out a dagger and cuts it in half at the lower end.

With Kevnan and Alithyra's help, she replaces the robe on Bojan's body. She then folds his arms so that his hands rest on his chest and straightens him out. She cuts the rest of the robe into long strips, which she uses to wrap the body; starting at the tip of his beak, she wraps the strips of cloth around his head until it is completely covered. She then wraps his hands and arms before moving to the feet and legs. After that, she uses what's left to wrap up his torso, using small pins from her belt pouch to hold everything in place. Having finished digging the grave, Pelagius climbs out before grabbing Iriemorel's hand and helping him out of the hole. They join the others.

"The preparations are complete," says Adotiln as Pelagius approaches.

"Good," says Pelagius.

"Is this the usual method of conducting funerals?" inquires Alithyra.

"Not quite," says Pelagius. "Normally, followers of Ender and their friends who fall valiantly are given an elaborate funeral and burned on a funeral pyre. Unfortunately, we do not have time for such an event and a funeral pyre would attract too much unwanted attention. In such a case, burials are necessary."

"It will be night soon," says Adotiln. "We should proceed before it gets dark."

Pelagius nods in response. Then he and Iriemorel gently pick up Bojan's body and carry him to the grave. They carefully set him down while Pelagius and Alithyra climb down into the grave. Iriemorel hands them Bojan's body, which they carefully place at the bottom before climbing out. Meanwhile, Kevnan has retrieved his mandolin and begins to strum a solemn tune.

Adotiln steps to the edge of the grave. "Here we lay to rest our good friend Bojan, who gave his life to rid the world of a great evil. Let us remember his sacrifice and let it not be in vain."

Pelagius steps forward. "Perhaps none here knew Bojan better than I. Bojan was with me from the beginning, during my days training at the temple under Master Glahrug. He was there for me during the hardest times of my life, including our first battles with Kragus. Bojan was a hero if I ever knew one. Many of my accomplishments would not have been possible without his help and he deserves the credit for many deeds more than me. Farewell, Bojan. Rest in peace, old friend."

During Adotiln and Pelagius' speeches, everyone present tears up. By the end of Pelagius's speech, everyone is crying. Kevnan struggles to keep the tune right as tears flow down his cheeks. Pelagius picks up the shovels and retrieves two more, which he hands to Kevnan, Iriemorel, and Alithyra. They begin to fill in the grave.

Kevnan and Pelagius return the shovels to the cart and Iriemorel and Alithyra place a rock at the head of the grave. Pelagius returns with a hammer and chisel and hands them to Adotiln, who carves the word Bojan into the rock. A single red-eyed raven lands on the tombstone. Adotiln drives it off with her hammer, but it returns as soon as she walks away.

"These ravens are becoming a nuisance," says Adotiln. "Why are they following us?"

"I wish I knew," says Kevnan.

"I think I can get rid of it," says Alithyra.

Alithyra rapidly draws her bow and looses an arrow, striking the raven in the center of its body. The arrow sends it flying several feet away from the tombstone, and it hits the ground with a light thud. As it dies, the red fades from its eyes and it becomes a normal-looking raven.

"That's eerie," says Alithyra. "Let's get out of here."

Pelagius glances at the setting sun. "There's not enough daylight to continue today. We might as well set up camp here."

The remaining heroes go to the cart and unload it as Thakszut sits mournfully by Bojan's grave.

Chapter 33

As night falls, the Green-Eyed Man stands by the edge of Bojan's crater. "Impressive."

Nyogsutt emerges from some bushes and hops onto his shoulder. "I agree. I was watching from afar, and it was a frightening sight. I'm amazed Kragus survived."

"Indeed," says the Green-Eyed Man. "He was lucky to survive at all, especially after using Dark Magic. Even I would never call upon the powers of the Shadow Realm."

The Green-Eyed Man looks at the skeletal remains of the two giants. "This is somewhat disturbing. There is no magical ability that I am aware of that allows one to leech another's life force to restore oneself."

"Is it Dark Magic?"

The Green-Eyed Man shakes his head. "As dangerous as Dark Magic is, this is worse. This must come from beyond the realms, meaning that Kragus is dabbling in Eldritch Xeno-Sorcery."

"Perhaps you should have tried to read his book after all," says Nyogsutt. "I bet there is information in there that both you and Babu would love to know."

"Even demons know not to mess with the forbidden arts," says the Green-Eyed Man. "Kragus is playing a dangerous game. If he isn't careful, he could suffer a fate worse than death or summon something more horrible than any of us can imagine."

Nyogsutt shudders and looks around, seeking something that can change the subject. He glances at the remains of the two giants. "I bet Master Babu would love a couple of giants' souls."

"I thought of that already, but I didn't get here in time. Either the souls have already moved on or whatever Kragus did to their bodies had a similar effect on their souls. I hope to avoid that power of his at all costs."

"But you're immortal. You can't die."

"I know that, but that won't make the experience any less painful and it would likely take me a while to come back from it. There is only one being I know who I have seen do something worse than what Kragus has done here."

"Alasdar?" inquires Nyogsutt.

The Green-Eyed Man shudders and nods. "Even Master Babu agrees that it is a horrible sight to behold and if it disturbs him, it must be horrendous. The sight of that deed haunts my memories still."

"So why didn't Kragus animate these skeletons?" asks Nyogsutt. "Most necromancers wouldn't pass up the chance to create minions."

"He may have felt too weak to do so safely," replies the Green-Eyed Man. "Additionally, these bones look far too brittle to be of any use. Whatever he did to them severely weakened the skeletal structure."

"Well, I suppose I should return to spying on Pelagius and the rest of his friends. Minus Bojan, of course."

"There is no need. We know where they are going. They should reach Halfhill within the next couple of weeks. I don't have any plans for them until then. As such, spying for information is no longer necessary. However, you do still have a job to do. You remember what that is, of course?"

Nyogsutt lowers his head and tries to fight back tears. "Yes."

"Good," says the Green-Eyed Man. "Then follow them and make your move against Thakszut at the first opportunity."

Without saying another word, Nyogsutt scampers down the road. The Green-Eyed Man watches him leave before turning to look at the crater again.

CHAPTER 34

A few hours later, the remaining heroes sit solemnly around a campfire. Kevnan strums a somber tune on his mandolin as Iriemorel stirs a pot over the fire. Alithyra sits off to one side, using tree branches and stones to make new arrows, while Adotiln prays near Bojan's grave. Pelagius simply stares at the fire, and Thakszut sits nearby as well.

"So, now what?" asks Iriemorel.

"We press on, of course," replies Alithyra.

"No," says Pelagius, looking up from the fire. "I press on. The rest of you must return home. I cannot ask you to risk your lives further. I must continue on my own."

"That's suicide," says Kevnan.

"Perhaps," says Pelagius, "but it is better that only I die than all of us. Therefore, I release all of you from your burdens. Go home."

"Absolutely not," says Adotiln, coming over. "We all knew the risks when we joined this quest, and that includes Bojan. You did not force anybody to come along. We all came because we wanted to."

"She's right," says Kevnan. "We chose to come along and nothing you say or do will make us turn back. I believe I speak for all of us when I say that we are in it until the end."

Pelagius looks up. "Are all of you so inclined to continue?"

"Yes," reply the others.

Thakszut steps forward. "That goes double for me."

Pelagius glares at the fiendling. "You? If you had informed us of what was going to occur, this never would have happened."

"I told you everything I knew about the Green-Eyed Man's plan," says Thakszut. "I didn't know when the attack was coming, and I had no idea that Kragus would get involved. I swear."

"How can I trust your word?" asks Pelagius. "You have told us nothing about the Green-Eyed Man himself."

"Fine," says Thakszut. "I'll tell you what I know. I don't know very much about his past as he rarely speaks of it. I do know, however, that he is not from Diablos, but rather he is a Battallian."

"A Battallian?" says Kevnan. "Everyone knows about the situation between Battallia and Diablos. Why would he be working for a demonkin?"

"Clearly he is a traitor," replies Iriemorel.

"It would seem that way," says Thakszut. "When Nyogsutt and I first saw him, he was not in a good condition. His hands and feet had been removed and metal hooks had been shoved into the stumps. Additionally, he had chains wrapped around his body and over the hooks; he had been suspended from the bridge over Malferno's Canyon."

"From what I have heard, that is Battallia's punishment for treason," says Kevnan.

"True," says Thakszut. "He surely would have died had Gulvgrum not happened upon him and decided to take him to Babu. We followed, curious as to what was going to happen. Instead of devouring his soul, Babu gave him an offer: to restore him to health in return for his services as a soul hunter. It was an offer that he immediately accepted."

"Interesting," says Pelagius. "So far, it sounds like he wasn't working for any demons before being sentenced and punished. I wonder what he did to deserve a traitor's fate."

"He has never told the whole story," says Thakszut. "He only claims that he was framed and betrayed. Upon receiving the powers of a soul hunter, his first act was to free his friends from prison and take his revenge. The spectre you encountered was a man named Morat and it is he that the Green-Eyed Man claims was the mastermind behind his undeserved fate."

"Does he have a name?" asks Adotiln.

"I honestly never learned his name, and he has forbidden his old friends from speaking it on pain of death," says Thakszut. "However, there is some other information. He rescued four friends from prison, but only three serve him. The fourth, a canin named Aldtaw, refused to have anything to do with Babu."

"What happened to him?" asks Kevnan.

"Last I heard, he was locked in the dungeon," says Thakszut. "I believe that he is still alive."

"Is there anything else?" asks Pelagius.

"Well, Eeshlith and Shudgluv claim that his personality was completely different before he came to serve Babu," replies Thakszut.

"So why do the other two still serve him?" inquires Iriemorel.

"Partly out of loyalty to an old friend and partly out of fear," replies Thakszut. "They felt they owed him a debt for getting them out of prison and agreed to join him under Babu. I believe that they did not know just what their roles would be. I have heard them talking when the Green-Eyed Man is not around, and I have heard hints at remorse for the horrible acts that they have committed. However, they will not betray him out of fear of both what he will do to them and fear of Babu."

"That is unfortunate," says Pelagius. "Perhaps once Babu and the Green-Eyed Man have been eliminated, there may be hope for those two. If they truly feel remorse for what they have done, then they may be able to redeem themselves."

"What about Glakchog?" asks Alithyra.

"It sounds like he's too stubborn and far gone to seek redemption," says Iriemorel.

"How are Glakchog, Shudgluv, and Aldtaw still alive?" asks Pelagius. "Sixty years is nothing to an elf, but trolls, busurin, and especially canin don't age much slower than humans. They should be quite elderly by now, if not dead of old age."

"I believe that the Green-Eyed Man used his powers to grant them eternal youth," says Thakszut. "I do not know if it is temporary or permanent, but he certainly went out of his way to ensure that they would not age."

Thakszut thinks for a moment. "There is one more thing. There is also a fifth friend who died during the Green-Eyed Man's arrest. This friend, a leprechaun named Alasdar, is now a soulborn working for Babu."

"What is his demonic form?" inquires Pelagius.

"I have not seen it," replies Thakszut. "However, it must be a horrible sight. The Green-Eyed Man has witnessed it once and he is greatly disturbed by it. Also, while in that form, Alasdar commits an act that even Babu finds disturbing."

"It sounds like we may have a greater evil to deal with than Babu," says Kevnan.

"Soulborns can be powerful," says Pelagius, "but they are rarely more powerful than their creator. However, we must be wary of this Alasdar. If his actions disturb one so vile as Babu, he is an adversary to be feared for certain. Hopefully, we can avoid him. Additionally, I believe we should rescue the friend in the dungeon. What breed of canin is Aldtaw?"

"He is of the Great Dane variety," replies Thakszut.

"Can you guide us to him when we get there?" asks Adotiln.

"Of course," replies Thakszut. "I know the layout of Babu's fortress fairly well."

Thakszut pauses and looks around. Seeing nothing nearby that makes him believe Nyogsutt could be hiding, he leans toward the others and whispers, "There is a secret entrance that only Nyogsutt and I know about."

"Excellent," says Pelagius. "With that information we can avoid the defenses at the castle walls and get inside more easily."

"There is just one problem," says Thakszut. "In order to get to this passage, we must pass through Manthysbia's chamber."

"Who is Manthysbia?" inquires Kevnan.

"Manthysbia is a large dragon with whom Babu has formed an alliance," replies Thakszut. "He listens to Babu, Gulvgrum, Commander Charndergh, and the Green-Eyed Man, and is likely the most dangerous entity in that fortress."

The others look at each other with concern.

"How are we supposed to get past that?" asks Iriemorel. "None of us are experienced or trained in fighting dragons of any kind."

"Maybe we should go back for Koskru," says Alithyra.

"No," says Pelagius. "He has probably moved on by now. So, tell us, Thakszut, how do we get past Manthysbia?"

"Fortunately, he's usually asleep if he's not eating or doing Babu's bidding," replies Thakszut.

"And what if he is awake when we arrive?" asks Adotiln.

"Then we're in big trouble," says Thakszut.

"It's a gamble for certain," says Kevnan.

"So is this entire quest," says Pelagius. "Remember, I never promised that we would succeed, nor that any of us would survive. This new information is quite troubling, and I would not blame anyone if they were to decide to back out now."

"That is not going to happen," says Iriemorel.

The others nod in agreement and Pelagius smiles. "I knew I could count on all of you. Is that stew ready yet, Iriemorel?"

Iriemorel hesitates for a moment and begins unpacking the bowls. "Almost. Pelagius, I've been thinking. We should stop at a nearby town and resupply. We all took a beating in that fight with the dev. You need a new shield and I need new armor."

"I agree," says Kevnan. "I went over our supplies after the funeral and we are running low on several key items."

Pelagius reaches into a nearby satchel and pulls out a map. He looks over it for a few minutes. "The city of Cyclo is a little over a hundred miles to the west. That's the closest settlement to us that would have all the merchants we need. There are several villages and hamlets around, but there is no guarantee that they would have what we need. A trip to Cyclo would delay us for at least a week, but from what you have told me, this side trip is necessary."

"Then Cyclo it is," says Adotiln.

"Very well," says Pelagius. "We will depart in the morning."

After several minutes, Iriemorel fills the bowls and hands them out. The heroes consume their meal in silence.

CHAPTER 35

A few hours later, the heroes divide up night watch shifts, and all except for Adotiln and Thakszut have gone to sleep. While Adotiln sits by the fire, Thakszut patrols the perimeter of the camp, venturing out of sight of the campfire. As he approaches a grove of trees, Nyogsutt leaps out and tackles him. The two fiendlings tumble to the ground. Thakszut gets to his feet quickly, with Nyogsutt rising shortly after.

"What was that, Nyogsutt?" asks Thakszut.

"I am sorry, old friend," says Nyogsutt, "but the Green-Eyed Man has given me orders to kill you. If I don't, he will kill both of us."

"I'm not afraid of what he will do to me anymore. Why not come with me? My new friends will protect us. Or have you decided that fear of the Green-Eyed Man is more powerful than our friendship?"

"Have you forgotten about loyalty? We swore our allegiance to the Green-Eyed Man shortly after he made his deal with Babu."

"And what have we gotten from him in return? Nothing but abuse. He doesn't care about us or anybody else, Nyogsutt. He has been using us for his own personal gain ever since we joined him."

"It's better than death."

"I disagree. I'm perfectly willing to risk death to get away from him."

"Then, my friend, I must do what I have to do," says Nyogsutt.

"Very well," says Thakszut, disappointedly, "but I do plan to defend myself, and I have a few new tricks that I have learned."

Thakszut transforms into a large red gorilla with claws and horns. At first, Nyogsutt appears surprised, but then a look of realization appears on his face. "Not bad, Thakszut, but I too have learned some new tricks."

Nyogsutt transforms into a large, red, lizard-like monkey nearly twice the size of Thakszut's gorilla form. He has enormous curved horns on his head, massive claws on his hands, gigantic teeth, and a long tail with a spiked club at the end.

A look of horror appears on Thakszut's face. "What happened to you?"

"The Green-Eyed Man gave me a gift from his urn," replies Nyogsutt, his voice very deep and gravelly. "Whatever he did unlocked the Demonic Potential within me. Now I can take you on with no problem."

Nyogsutt swings his massive clawed hand downward, barely missing Thakszut, who leaps out of the way. Thakszut jumps over Nyogsutt and onto his back, where he begins to punch, bite, and claw. Nyogsutt howls in pain as he tries to get Thakszut off his back. After a while, he rams his back, and Thakszut with it, into a tree. The force of the blow causes Thakszut to fall off. Nyogsutt then brings his tail down upon Thakszut several times before turning around. He lands a few monstrous punches before grabbing Thakszut by the neck, lifting him up, and slamming him into the ground. Nyogsutt lifts a clawed hand into the air and glares down at his former friend.

Unable to maintain magical concentration, Thakszut returns to his true form. Nyogsutt begins to move his claws downward but stops. He stares down at Thakszut as he hesitates. He raises up his arm and begins to start again, but stops once more.

He then dejectedly lowers his arm, sighs, and reverts to his true form. "I can't do it."

As Thakszut groans and looks up, Nyogsutt runs off into the woods. Thakszut struggles to his feet and stumbles back toward the camp.

Chapter 36

The next morning, the heroes are packing up their tents and remaining supplies. As Pelagius loads some equipment onto one of the horses, he looks around. "Where's Thakszut?"

"He's not in one of the tents?" asks Adotiln. "He was patrolling the camp perimeter last night. I thought he came back after our shift ended. Do you think something happened to him?"

"I hope not," says Alithyra.

"Spread out and look for him," says Pelagius. "We'll finish packing up once we know what happened."

As they begin to fan out, the bushes rustle; Thakszut stumbles into the camp and collapses. The heroes rush to him and discover that he is severely battered and bruised, and possibly suffers from internal damage.

"What happened?" asks Kevnan.

Thakszut only groans. Adotiln immediately begins her healing ritual and after a few minutes, Thakszut is back to full health.

"That took longer than usual," says Iriemorel.

"Demonfolk anatomy is different from humanoid anatomy," says Adotiln. "The magic will always work, but it will take longer on creatures that have a different design than what the healer is familiar with."

Pelagius crouches as Thakszut rises to his feet. "What happened?"

"I was patrolling the camp perimeter, perhaps a little too far out, when Nyogsutt attacked me," replies Thakszut. "It appears that the Green-Eyed Man has given him the task of killing me. I tried to talk him down, but he refused. When I used my new power to transform, he transformed into an even larger and more demonic state. I tried to fight him off, but I never had a chance. The only reason that I am alive is that he couldn't bring himself to finish me off."

"Do you know where he went?" asks Alithyra.

"No," replies Thakszut. "He just ran off. I didn't see which direction he went."

"Will he try again?" asks Pelagius.

"Probably," replies Thakszut, sadly. "He fears the Green-Eyed Man's wrath with every fiber of his being. I don't think that he will report back until he can finish the job."

"Then stay close from now on," says Pelagius.

A loud thumping noise startles the heroes as two sixteen-foot-tall giants with huge swords enter the camp. Thakszut quickly takes on the form of a normal monkey. A third giant appears with a large cart and begins loading the heroes' equipment into it. One of the giants approaches the group.

"Is there something I can do for you?" inquires Pelagius.

"You punies will come with us," replies the leader. "We are aware that you have been traveling through our kingdom and some unusual things have happened since you got here. You are wanted for questioning in the disappearance and possible murder of two guards who were investigating a large fire. Surrender your weapons and come with us."

"I assure you, sir, that we had nothing to do with the disappearances of any giants."

"It doesn't matter. You are punies and foreigners. That makes you the most likely suspects. Now surrender immediately or be destroyed."

Pelagius turns to the others. "Do what he says. This is very serious."

Pelagius places White Fire on the ground, and the others drop their weapons as well.

"Those of you who have armor, remove it," says the leader.

The heroes who are wearing armor take it off and place it on the ground. One of the other two giants steps forward and scoops up their weapons and armor and places them in the cart with the rest of their belongings. The leader makes some sort of motion to the other two and they briefly depart. They return with a large cage on wheels and several smaller creatures of varying species carrying chains.

"Step forward," says the leader.

Pelagius steps forward first. Almost immediately, the smaller assistants shackle his arms, legs, and neck, connecting all his limbs by a series of chains before ushering him into the cart. The process repeats with the others. When they get to Thakszut, a man in a flowing red robe steps forward. He points at Thakszut and a small bolt of energy shoots out of his finger. It hits Thakszut in the chest and immediately returns him to his true form. He is then shackled like the others with chains small enough to fit him. The giants corral everyone into the cage, then shut and lock the door.

The leader approaches the cage. "Since Cyclo is the closest city to here, we will take you to our prison facility there and you will remain there until this matter is cleared up. If we determine that you are guilty of causing these disappearances, you will remain there until your punishment is carried out."

"Well, at least he's taking us where we were going to go anyway," says Kevnan.

The leader bangs his fist against the cage. "Silence, puny! While we are on our way there, none of you will say a word. If I hear another peep out of any of you, your stay will be much more unpleasant. Troops, move out."

With that, the two underling giants begin pushing the cage and the equipment cart along as the leader leads the way. The smaller creatures lead the horses.

CHAPTER 37

Meanwhile, Nyogsutt sits at the base of a tree not too far away. Tears run down his face as he stares at his hands. "How could I do that to Thakszut? We've been friends for ages and now I try to kill him? I can't do it, but I must do it, or the Green-Eyed Man will kill me for sure. How am I going to get through this?"

"It sounds like you could use some help," says Kragus, coming out from behind a tree.

Startled, Nyogsutt leaps into the branches. "What do you want, Kragus?"

"I saw your attempt to destroy Thakszut," says Kragus. "Very impressive, but I was very disappointed with the way it ended. Quite anticlimactic, really."

"I couldn't bring myself to do it."

"I know what happened. Your conscience got in the way. Nasty things, consciences. They constantly get in the way and prevent you from achieving great things."

"You mean horrible things."

"Great and horrible are often interchangeable and merely a matter of perspective. The point is this: as long as you listen to your conscience you will not be able to do what needs to be done."

"So, what do I do?"

Kragus smiles. "I can help you with that. I too was once held back by my conscience. It kept me from doing what needed to be done. That is, until I discovered a way to remove that obstacle."

"How?" asks Nyogsutt, intrigued.

"While poring over some ancient texts of forgotten and forbidden lore, I discovered a ritual that removes the conscience and eventually destroys it," says Kragus, "I haven't been held back by petty thoughts of guilt ever since. Here's what I have to offer: I will perform the ritual on you so that you may complete your task. Of course, this service will not be free. I expect something in return."

"What do you want me to do?" asks Nyogsutt.

"All will be revealed in due time. I simply require that you agree to provide me one favor in return for what I am going to do for you. Do we have a deal?"

Nyogsutt thinks for several moments. "I don't know. I need some time to think about it."

"This is a limited time offer, my friend," says Kragus. "Make your choice now. I will not wait until later. Either you agree to the ritual and gain the ability to kill Thakszut, or you remain in your current miserable state, destined to be destroyed by the Green-Eyed Man. The choice is yours, but you must decide now."

"Very well," says Nyogsutt. "Get ready, Kragus. I shall accept your offer."

Kragus smiles. "Excellent. Come with me."

Kragus leads Nyogsutt to a small clearing in the center of the trees where he has already drawn out an intricate circle with several indecipherable symbols. "As you can see, I was already prepared. Now get into the center of the circle and hold still. This magic involved is not of our world, and if I make even a single error, the consequences could be catastrophic."

Nyogsutt timidly enters the circle and sits directly in the center. Producing the Nameless Tome and opening to a marked page, Kragus disrobes and begins to chant in a language that Nyogsutt cannot understand. As the incantation continues, clouds begin to form overhead, and the wind begins to blow. Flashes of lightning illuminate the sky and the circle glows, its color strange and indescribable.

Kragus chants for several more minutes before his right hand glows the same color as the circle. A pinpoint of light beams out of the circle and centers on Nyogsutt's forehead. As the chanting continues, Kragus approaches the circle. After a few moments, he places his glowing finger on the pinpoint of light on Nyogsutt's forehead. Suddenly, he stops chanting and shouts something incomprehensible.

The light from the circle explodes outward and the light from Kragus's hand drains through his finger, resulting in bursts of light coming from Nyogsutt's ears, nose, eyes, and mouth. Nyogsutt screams in pain and falls unconscious.

After several minutes, he wakes to find Kragus standing over him. "How do you feel?"

Nyogsutt rises to his feet and rapidly shakes his head. After a moment, he inhales deeply. "Better than ever. The guilt I felt over attacking my former friend is gone."

Kragus smirks as he observes the little fiendling. "Good. Now this is what you must remember: Thakszut is no longer your friend. He betrayed you by joining your enemies. He is a traitor and must be destroyed."

Nyogsutt tightly clenches his fists and bares his teeth. "Of course. I feel nothing for Thakszut but hatred. He shall meet the fate that he deserves. When the opportunity presents itself, I will destroy him."

"Excellent. Once that deed is done, I will collect on the favor you owe me. Remember this: the ritual is only temporary the first few times. After a little more than a month, the magic will wear off and your conscience will return. We will need to renew it three or four times for it to become permanent."

Kragus disappears into the trees and Nyogsutt scampers off to locate Thakszut and the other heroes.

CHAPTER 38

Pelagius and the others are sitting in jail cells, one in each room. The jail is dark with the light only coming from a few widely spaced torches on the walls. A dank, musty odor permeates the entire room. The room is huge, possibly hundreds of feet across on all sides and several hundred feet high.

Each cramped cell is only about ten square feet for regular-sized creatures. There are larger cells for the occasional giant or titan criminal, but these larger citizens are rarely arrested. Thakszut sits in a small bird cage suspended from the ceiling. Several giants and a few cyclopes stand guard. They all range between fifteen and twenty feet tall. Kevnan steps to the front of his cell; holding the bars, he looks over at Pelagius, who sits on his tiny, stained and lumpy cot deep in thought.

"How long are they going to keep us here?" asks Kevnan. "We've already told them everything we know about what happened in that area."

"They'll keep us here for as long as they want," replies Pelagius. "It may take them a while to be satisfied with our story."

The door at the end of the room opens and the leader of the giants who arrested them walks in. He walks to Pelagius's cell and glares at him. "We have discussed your stories and we find some interesting holes."

"What do you mean?" asks Pelagius.

"You said that this Kragus died of his wounds and that you left his body in the crater," says the leader. "We have surveyed the area and there is no corpse in that hole There isn't even so much as a skeleton except for the two giant-sized skeletons close by. How do you explain that?"

A look of horror crosses Pelagius's face. "I have a simple explanation. Kragus survived somehow. We left him for dead, and he somehow used your two friends to revive himself. I don't know how, but that is what must have happened."

The leader thinks for a moment. "Very well. I will bring this to the attention of my superiors. If we are satisfied with your story, you and your friends will be free to go. If not, then we will have to resort to more drastic ways of obtaining the information we want."

The leader then leaves the room, locking the door behind him. He returns several hours later and approaches Pelagius's cell. "I have news for you. We have no evidence of the existence of this Kragus. Therefore, we have determined that you are responsible for what happened, and we want you out of this kingdom. We will give you one day to stock up on any supplies you need and then everything will be loaded up and you will be shipped via prison cart to the border. Do I make myself clear?"

"Absolutely," replies Pelagius.

The leader motions to the guards, who immediately unlock the cells. "Now, get what you need and report back here. Don't try to leave the city. I have guards stationed at every gate and they have been informed of the situation. If you try to escape you will be killed on the spot."

"Some of our supplies may take longer than a day to obtain," says Pelagius. "The dwarf needs new armor and it may take a few days for a blacksmith to make it."

"You will get only what can be obtained in less than a day. If he needs armor, he can get it when you get to Halfhill. That is the ruling that has been given and there will be no deviation from it. Any of you who are not back here by the end of the day will be hunted down and slain."

"Very well. We will do as you say."

The leader takes them to the gates of the prison and releases them into the city. He leads the heroes down a wide road to a bustling, but dirty and downtrodden marketplace. Cyclo is just as large as Terli, but without High King Jaygon's massive castle in the middle.

"This is the market for punies," says their escort. "Pick up whatever you need and report back to the prison."

The heroes enter the marketplace and spend the rest of the day obtaining necessary supplies. As the sun begins to set, they return to the prison, new supplies in hand. The guards greet them by taking their equipment and dumping it into a cart. The leader motions toward the mobile cages. "Everybody get in. We will be departing immediately."

The heroes comply and the convoy begins its journey south. One of the guards looks at the heroes and grins mockingly. "Get comfortable, everyone. It's a long trip."

A week later, the prison cart approaches the mountains that serve as a border between Bratenro and Halfhill. When the caravan comes to a stop, the lead guard orders the smaller helpers to unload all the equipment and horses, and release Pelagius and the others from their bonds in the prison cart. They step out and gaze at the section of mountain range ahead. As soon as they unload the equipment, several smaller helpers return their weapons and armor to them.

The leader approaches them. "Once you enter the mountains, you will have left Bratenro, but you will not actually enter Halfhill until you reach the other side. All that matters to us is that you get out of our kingdom and do not return. If you need to return to Waskan, you'll have to leave Diablos through Necrotia or Industria. Your presence will not be tolerated in this kingdom. Is that understood?"

"We understand," says Pelagius.

"Good," says the leader. "Now be off with you. I don't want to see you around here again."

The prison caravan turns and begins its journey back to Cyclo.

Pelagius turns to the others. "We will have to lead the horses and travel on foot from here. The mountain passes are too dangerous to ride them through."

The heroes then begin to lead their horses up a path on the closest mountain.

CHAPTER 39

The Green-Eyed Man sits at a corner table of a poorly lit tavern. There are no decorations on the walls and the furnishings are bare. Behind the bar is a gaki, a species of demonfolk with a human-like body but with a huge engorged stomach, the head of a horse with three eyes, twisted horns, sharp talons, and bright red skin. He occasionally picks up and munches on a large chunk of cooked meat as he serves drinks. A river runs right through the building at a corner of the bar and several kappas sit in this area. After several minutes Eeshlith, Glakchog, and Shudgluv enter. Eeshlith sits at the Green-Eyed Man's table while Glakchog and Shudgluv approach the bar.

Glakchog motions to the bartender for a mug of ale. "You wanted to see us, sir?"

"Yes," says the Green-Eyed Man. "I've been thinking about my attack plans, and I have had a change in thought. I do not want any of you to be involved in my defensive line."

Shudgluv grabs a gallon-sized mug of ale and turns toward him. "What? Why not?"

"Because I have a better idea," replies the Green-Eyed Man. "I want you to hide in the mountains near the river pass."

"I see," says Eeshlith. "So, you want us to attack them on their way into Diablos."

"Not exactly," says the Green-Eyed Man.

Shudgluv joins them at the table and takes a large gulp. "I'm not sure I follow."

"If they enter Diablos, they will encounter my defense force," says the Green-Eyed Man. "If they fail to penetrate my defensive line, they will have to retreat. Assuming, of course, that any of them survive."

Glakchog approaches the table and stands nearby, sipping from his ale. "Of course."

"That's where you come in," says the Green-Eyed Man. "Once they emerge from the pass, I want you to follow them. With you cutting off their escape, they will have nowhere to go once they reach me."

Glakchog downs his ale and motions to the waitress for another. "Shall we close in and attack once the battle has begun?"

The Green-Eyed Man shakes his head. "No. You will be there as backup. Only attack if they begin to retreat."

Shudgluv finishes his drink. "What should we do if the battle goes badly for you?"

The Green-Eyed Man chuckles. "Join in if they defeat a few of the others. If the battle somehow appears to be lost, retreat back to your camp, and I will join you later."

Eeshlith stands and goes to the bar, where she orders a glass of wine. "So we are to make sure that none of them leave Diablos alive?"

Realizing his mug is empty, the Green-Eyed Man motions to the bartender for a refill. "Actually, I would like you to let one survivor escape if possible."

"Why?" asks Eeshlith.

"So the survivor can tell the tale of the doomed quest," replies the Green-Eyed Man. "After hearing of such a catastrophic failure, nobody will ever take on such a foolhardy quest again. Just make sure that Pelagius is not among the survivors."

Eeshlith eyes him skeptically. "That sounds like it could backfire and just inspire more adventurers to attempt this quest."

The Green-Eyed Man rolls his eyes. "If that happens, we'll just eliminate those adventurers as soon as possible. My plan stands as is. Is that understood?"

Glakchog quickly finishes his drink. "Understood, sir."

"Good," says the Green-Eyed Man. "Get into positions as soon as possible. They will be arriving in Halfhill within the week."

The three minions get up and walk out the door as the Green-Eyed Man sits back to enjoy his second mug of ale.

CHAPTER 40

Several days later, the heroes set up camp for the fast-approaching night on a flat surface overlooking a cliff. Most sit on some rocks with their backs to the cliff, but Pelagius sits by his tent in the middle of the area. Iriemorel turns a large piece of meat on a spit.

Alithyra's nose begins to twitch and she glances in Iriemorel's direction. "That smells delicious. What are you cooking?"

"Megalocerus venison," replies Iriemorel. "Hopefully, it will be similar to preparing ordinary venison since the megalocerus is a type of deer. Albeit a very large species."

"Did we have to camp so close to a cliff?" asks Kevnan.

"There wasn't much other choice," replies Pelagius. "This is the only section of flat ground at this altitude for miles. The only other option would have been to find a cave, and that would put us at risk of camping in some large animal's home."

"Or disturbing a tribe of barbarians," says Adotiln. "Personally, I don't want to have to deal with either one."

The air around them begins to pulsate and a familiar high-pitch whistle pierces the night, causing them to grab their ears and double over in pain. Then, the sky turns red and the mountains around them erupt in bursts of fire. Spectral forms dance in the flames, rushing the heroes before vanishing and reappearing to repeat the process.

The heroes jump to their feet and draw their weapons, swinging wildly at anything that comes near. Pelagius breathes heavily as fear begins taking over his mind. He closes his eyes and takes a deep breath. "Everybody, relax. Bojan and I encountered something like this before. This is all an illusion. Kragus must be nearby."

"Then let's find him," says Iriemorel.

As the others continue swinging at the ghostly figures and at empty spaces trying to locate their enemy, Alithyra begins sniffing the air. Seemingly catching a scent, she raises her bow and scans the horizon, her nose twitching as she attempts to locate her quarry. Then, she stops moving, aims toward a large flame, and releases her arrow, which flies rapidly toward her intended target. Suddenly, it stops in midair and the illusion drops, returning everything around them to normal. Kragus stands by a large rock, holding the arrow just an inch from his eye. He quickly tosses it aside. "Very clever. I should have known that I couldn't hide from the senses of a canin. Your shot was a little too slow to strike me, though."

Alithyra smiles. "It was enough to break your concentration and cause you to drop the spell."

"We won't fall for that trick again, Kragus," says Pelagius. "Surrender now. You're outnumbered."

"Not for long," says Kragus.

Kragus snaps his fingers and the campfire spreads out into a line between the heroes and Pelagius, forming a semicircular pattern ending at the edge of the cliff. The line briefly erupts into a wall of fire before dying down, leaving only a line of scorched rock.

"If that was an attempt to separate us, you failed miserably, Kragus," says Pelagius.

"I'm not done yet, Pelagius," says Kragus.

Kragus slams his fist into the ground, causing the rock to crack along the scorch mark. The section of cliff that all but Kragus and Pelagius are standing on begins to give way. The others try to run or leap to safety, but none of them are quick enough. Their section of ground topples down the mountainside, taking them with it.

Pelagius glances over in horror as his teammates' rock crashes on another section of cliff about forty feet below and shatters. From his vantage point, most of his teammates land safely on the outcropping, but he clearly sees someone go over the ledge on a large chunk of rock and plummet out of sight. Pelagius looks up at Kragus.

"Now, Pelagius, it is just you and me," says Kragus.

Chapter 41

As they plummet down the mountainside, the heroes desperately cling onto anything they can for dear life. They fall for about forty feet until their section of cliff hits. Their now-fragile boulder shatters on impact, sending them flying in all directions. Alithyra hits the ground right by the cliff wall with a thud and manages to avoid any falling rocks. Thakszut flies through the air and grabs onto a tree root growing out of the mountainside. Iriemorel and Kevnan slam into the ground with a thump and are almost immediately buried in the rocky remains of their ride. Adotiln, who was unfortunately closest to the ledge, flies over the next ridge on the rock she was clutching. She desperately leaps for the side, hoping to grab hold of the cliff. However, she misses and plummets into the unseen depths below.

As the dust clears, Alithyra stands up gingerly, although mostly uninjured, and Thakszut drops down to join her. Alithyra begins sniffing the air around the rock piles as they search for the others. "One of them is right here."

Thakszut takes on his gorilla form and they begin clearing rocks. After several minutes, they find Kevnan first. He groans as they lift the last rock off him.

Alithyra reaches out and helps him up. "Are you all right?"

"I'll live," replies Kevnan, wincing in pain.

After a few more minutes, they find Iriemorel, who stands with no problems.

"You okay?" asks Thakszut.

"I'm fine," replies Iriemorel.

Kevnan looks around concern. "Where's Adotiln?"

"She went over the edge of the cliff," replies Alithyra sadly.

"We've got to go find her," says Kevnan.

"No," says Iriemorel. "It is highly unlikely that she survived. Besides, Pelagius is up there alone with Kragus. If we don't get back up there soon, he'll die as well."

"What if she did survive?" asks Alithyra. "We can't just abandon her."

Iriemorel sighs. "This is just as difficult for me as it is for you, but I've seen more than my fair share of falling accidents and most of them are fatal. Even if she did survive the initial fall, by the time we find her she will likely have passed on, and Pelagius will be dead as well. Right now, we have to help Pelagius. We can save him if we hurry."

"Maybe we can do both," says Thakszut. "I am an excellent climber. I can go search for Adotiln while the rest of you go help Pelagius."

"Very good," says Iriemorel. "Go. The rest of us need to find a place to start climbing."

As the others search for a path to climb up the cliff, Thakszut returns to his real form, goes over the ledge, and climbs down the mountainside using tree roots, grooves in the rocks, or stones jutting out the side as hand- and footholds. He descends for about one hundred feet or so before he finds Adotiln, alive and well, hanging from a tree root jutting out of the side of the mountain. To get a better grip, she draws one of her daggers and wedges it into a crack between the rocks.

"Adotiln, are you all right?" shouts Thakszut as he makes his way down.

"At the moment," replies Adotiln.

"Hang on. I'm on my way."

"I think I can make the climb, but I would welcome your assistance."

Thakszut returns to his gorilla form and picks up his pace, swinging down the mountainside as Adotiln uses her daggers as climbing spikes to scale the cliff. Suddenly, something comes out of a darkened area and hits Thakszut in the chest. The impact sends him flying backward several feet, but he manages to grab onto a rock before he falls. As he recovers, he sees that his attacker is Nyogsutt in his monstrous form.

"Hello, old friend," says Nyogsutt. "I have come to finish what I started."

"I don't have time for this right now," says Thakszut. "Since we both know that you can't bring yourself to kill me, let's just skip the fight. I'm trying to save a friend."

"I have changed since our last encounter. Thanks to Kragus's help, my conscience has been eliminated. I can kill you with no problem at all. Especially since you can't defeat me."

"I see. Well, in that case, I won't hold back."

Thakszut transforms again. This time he changes into a duplicate of Nyogsutt's monstrous form, but with green skin instead of red. The two fiendlings leap at each other simultaneously, collide in midair, and begin to bite and tear at each other as they fall. After a moment, they separate and grab onto the cliff. Nyogsutt leaps at Thakszut and drives his shoulder into Thakszut's stomach. They fly several feet to the left before grabbing onto the mountain and swing-climbing back up. Adotiln continues her ascent, hugging the side of the cliff to avoid falling debris knocked loose from the fight.

Thakszut and Nyogsutt continue their midair battle. They slam into each other, punch, claw, bite, and kick as they swing through the air. Adotiln briefly loses her grip and slips, barely hanging on, but manages to reestablish her footing.

Thakszut glances in Adotiln's direction and Nyogsutt takes advantage, clawing him right across the face and nearly knocking him off the mountainside. However, Thakszut manages to grab onto a large rock jutting out.

Nyogsutt grins malevolently. "Is she distracting you? We can't have that. I want you fully focused on our battle. Let me remedy the situation."

Nyogsutt then begins swinging and leaping in Adotiln's direction. Horrified, Thakszut chases after him. Adotiln continues her ascent as Nyogsutt closes in. He grabs onto a thick tree root close to her and swings toward her, his claws aimed at her hands. She releases her grip on one of her daggers and swings to the side, causing Nyogsutt to miss. She maneuvers herself back to her original position, dislodges one of her daggers, and stabs him in the eye. Nyogsutt cries out in pain, grabbing his eye and leaning as far back from her as possible.

Taking advantage of the distraction, Thakszut swings around and slams his body into Nyogsutt's side, ramming him into the side of the cliff. Stunned from the impact, Nyogsutt nearly falls off the cliff as he barely holds onto his root. Thakszut pushes off the side and flips over Nyogsutt, using the momentum from his flip to kick his former friend in the stomach with both of his feet.

The force of the impact causes Nyogsutt's root to snap and he flies several feet away from the edge of the cliff before plummeting into the unseen depths below, screaming all the way down. Thakszut watches with tears in his eyes as Nyogsutt disappears. He quickly returns to his gorilla form and checks on Adotiln.

"You okay?" asks Thakszut.

"Fine," says Adotiln. "Cutting it a little close, though."

"Climb on my back."

"I think I can make it up myself."

"Perhaps so, but I can scale the cliff much faster than you. We'll be able to help Pelagius much quicker if I give you a ride up."

"Good point."

Adotiln clambers onto Thakszut's back and he climbs up the cliff. At one point, he stops and sadly looks down. "Goodbye, old friend. I'm sorry it had to end this way."

He then resumes his ascent.

CHAPTER 42

Meanwhile, Pelagius stands on the mountain staring down Kragus on his own. Kragus grins with arrogant malevolence. "It's over for you, Pelagius. Your entire group couldn't have defeated me, so you stand no chance at all alone."

"If my entire team would have been less than a match for you, then why did you get rid of them?" asks Pelagius.

"Simple. Killing you in a one-on-one encounter will inspire a greater reaction in your friends, who will be more crushed to know that they have let you down instead of fighting alongside you. I want to watch despair creep into them as they realize that they were too late to save you. That will be a much more gratifying reaction."

"I see. Quite devious of you. Still, I will not back down."

"Of course. I would be disappointed if you did. I'll tell you what. Just to show that I'm not such a bad guy, I will allow you to pray to Ender one last time before you die."

"You're too kind," says Pelagius sarcastically.

"Make it quick, though," says Kragus. "I won't wait all day."

"How do I know you won't attack me while I'm praying?"

"You of all people should know that I am a man of my word. I swear on my own life that I will not attack you for the first minute of your prayer."

"Very well."

Pelagius kneels with his sword in front of him, blade down. He mutters a prayer lasting about a minute. As he finishes, the wind begins to blow and a faint yellowish glow appears to surround him. Pelagius opens his eyes, revealing his new yellow, glowing eyes.

Kragus appears puzzled. "What's going on?"

"Allowing me to pray was a mistake," replies Pelagius. "Ender has granted me the Righteous Fury. Now I am your equal in power level and can call upon any of my powers I want without further prayer."

"I see," says Kragus. "I wasn't aware you had access to that power. An act of desperation will make no difference. I will still destroy you."

Kragus draws his sword, still stained with Bojan's blood. Kragus and Pelagius charge and their swords collide. They pull back and meet again and again. Kragus shoots red energy from his fingers, but Pelagius blocks it with White Fire. Pelagius lunges forward and shouts as he pushes his swordless arm forward. Kragus is hit in the chest with some sort of yellow energy and flies back several feet. He charges back at Pelagius and their swords clash once again.

"Impressive," says Kragus. "You're actually providing a challenge for me. However, you can't hold this up forever. If you truly are my equal in power, then that power will shortly begin to tear your body apart."

"Which is why I intend to make this quick," says Pelagius.

Pelagius ignites White Fire and sweeps it across as the two swords part. The white flame catches Kragus across the face and he stumbles backward. Pelagius grasps White Fire, still ignited, with both hands and begins swirling it around in a circle. As he does this, the green fire of the Flames of Courage encircle his arms.

As he circles White Fire, the green flames swirl along his arms and join the white flames encircling the sword until only a swirling pattern of white and green fire surrounds the blade. He then swings the sword in an overhead arc and points it at Kragus, firing off a tornado of green and white fire that spirals toward Kragus, hitting him directly in the chest and completely enveloping him. Kragus screams in pain as the flames engulf him. When the flames and smoke clear, Kragus is still standing. Aside from some burns on his flesh, he is still in perfect fighting shape.

"Is that the best you've got, Pelagius?" asks Kragus mockingly. "How disappointing. My turn."

Blackish-red energy resembling lightning surges from Kragus's body. After several seconds, an enormous blast of this energy streams forward and hits Pelagius, who screams in agony as the energy envelops him and flows throughout his body. When it stops flowing, Pelagius takes a few steps forward. Despite the smoke coming off his body, he is still standing and ready to continue the fight.

The two warriors charge forward again, White Fire still wreathed in flame and Kragus's sword surging with that blackish-red energy. The swords clash and the two energies collide. The reaction is more violent than either had anticipated, resulting in a huge explosion of energy that is a combination of the two. The blast engulfs both men and they fly back several feet, screaming in agony. As they rise, it becomes clear they are both in severe pain. Both are badly burned and bleeding. Kragus's bones have begun to twist and warp, and Pelagius's left arm hangs limp by his side. They hobble toward one another and the swords scrape again, this time without the energies. Their swords clash repeatedly. Kragus takes Pelagius by surprise and briefly knocks White Fire aside.

As Pelagius recovers his grip, Kragus slashes him across the chest and stabs him in the thigh. Kragus removes his sword from Pelagius' leg, and Pelagius swings downward and cuts deeply into Kragus's right shoulder. They continue fighting in such a manner with each man taking and receiving hits. Suddenly, Pelagius ignites White Fire midswing and hits Kragus's sword with a blow strong enough to make him nearly drop it. While Kragus regains his grip, Pelagius slashes across both his legs. Kragus's knees briefly buckle, causing him to drop. He struggles to stand again, but is unable to do so.

"Surrender," says Pelagius.

"Never," says Kragus.

As he tries to stand, Kragus thrusts his sword forward and stabs Pelagius in the knee, causing him to fall. They drag themselves closer to each other and continue their fight. They swing their swords, but this time the blades do not meet. Instead they slash each other across the chest. Their blades drop to the ground and they sit there panting for a few moments and gather their remaining strength. They then strike at each other with everything they've got left and their swords collide. However, this time White Fire's blow shatters Kragus's sword. Shocked, Kragus stares at the broken blade. Pelagius takes advantage of the opening and uses his own body weight to lunge forward, stabbing Kragus right in the chest.

Kragus grunts in pain as the blade pierces his torso and emerges from his back. The pressure of the blow forces the air from his lungs and he gasps for breath. Glancing down, his eyes grow wide as he realizes what has happened. "Well played, Pelagius."

Pelagius withdraws his blade and Kragus topples over backward.

"This can't be the end," says Kragus, "Curse you, Pelagius. May death torment you for the rest of your days."

With one last choking breath, his life departs. As soon as he dies, his body twists and warps. His flesh desiccates into a state like that of a mummified body. The dry, shriveled skin stretches across his bones, and his eyes dry out into nothingness.

As Kragus dies, the Righteous Fury leaves Pelagius's body and he falls over on his side. Within seconds, he is unconscious.

Chapter 43

Alithyra, Kevnan, and Iriemorel climb up onto the ledge. When they reach the top, they take a moment to catch their breath and survey the scene.

"What happened?" asks Kevnan. "Are we too late?"

They rush to Pelagius and find him wounded and unconscious but still alive. Kragus, on the other hand, is obviously dead. As they hover over Pelagius, wondering what to do, Thakszut appears at the ledge and puts Adotiln down next to Pelagius before reverting to his true form. Seeing her alive fills the others with joy, but expressions of relief must wait. Adotiln immediately heals Pelagius's wounds, but he does not regain consciousness.

"Why isn't he coming around?" asks Kevnan.

"From what I'm sensing, he called upon the Righteous Fury," says Adotiln. "Use of that power is always dangerous and draining."

"Will he be all right?" asks Alithyra.

"He'll be fine," replies Adotiln. "He just needs some rest. Righteous Fury is incredibly powerful. It is only used as a last resort because it feeds off your own life force. It won't kill him this time, but he can't safely use it again for a few weeks."

The heroes are silent for a few moments.

Kevnan points to Kragus's corpse. "What should we do with that?"

"Are we certain it's even real?" asks Iriemorel. "He could be hiding and giving us an illusion of his body."

Adotiln walks up to Kragus and gives the corpse a swift kick, causing it to jolt. "It's real. I think that Pelagius would agree that even Kragus deserves a burial."

Iriemorel points past the tents to an area above a rocky wall. "There's a patch of soft soil just above that rock."

Kevnan picks up a couple of shovels, tosses one to Iriemorel, and slings Kragus's body over his shoulder. "Let's take care of that, then."

Kevnan and Iriemorel proceed to bury Kragus while Alithyra and Adotiln place Pelagius in his tent and wrap him in blankets to keep him warm. When the other two return, Adotiln proceeds to heal everyone's injuries. Thakszut slips away from the group and begins climbing down the cliff.

CHAPTER 44

Thakszut slowly descends the mountainside. When he reaches the section where he and Nyogsutt battled, he searches for the scratch marks left by Adotiln's daggers. After several minutes, he finds the correct spot and continues his descent. Nearly half an hour later, he reaches the bottom of the cliff. This area is a small rocky valley within the mountain range.

Rocks of all sizes, some of which are wickedly jagged, comprise most of the area. Although it is darker down here, Thakszut has excellent night vision and can see very well. He searches the area for a few moments before finding Nyogsutt, now back in his true form, lying motionless and awkwardly sprawled over a large rock. Thakszut slowly approaches, tears running down his face. "I'm sorry it had to end this way, old friend."

As he gets closer, he notices that Nyogsutt is still breathing. The breaths are shallow and labored, but he is still alive. Nyogsutt weakly opens his remaining eye as Thakszut approaches.

"You're alive," says Thakszut. "How is that possible?"

"I don't know," replies Nyogsutt weakly, "but I won't be alive much longer. My body is broken. I will be dead very soon." He briefly chokes and coughs. "I'm glad to see you down here. We can make amends before I die."

"Make amends?" inquires Thakszut.

Nyogsutt's breathing becomes heavily labored. "It would seem that the impact undid Kragus's ritual. I am back to my old self."

Tears begin to pour down Thakszut's face. "I'm sorry for what I did to you. I had no choice."

"I understand. However, I'm the one who should be apologizing. It was only out of fear that I followed the boss's orders. Had I been as brave as you, I would have joined you on Pelagius's side. Can you forgive me?"

Nyogsutt weakly extends his hand and Thakszut takes it, clasping it in both of his. "Forgive me, Thakszut. I am truly remorseful for everything I have done to you. I'm sorry."

"I forgive you, my friend. I feared the Green-Eyed Man just as much as you. I know why you made the choices you did, and I could never hold it against you."

"Our time as enemies was brief, but I wish that we never were enemies at all."

"Take heart, Nyogsutt. We part as friends once more."

Nyogsutt smiles weakly. His grip loosens and his body goes limp. Life leaves his eyes as his hand slides from Thakszut's grasp and flops to the side. Thakszut stands over his fallen friend with tears running down his face. After several minutes, he picks up Nyogsutt's body and places him in a nearby crevice. He then piles rocks over the crevice to serve as a grave.

Thakszut bows his head in respect as he continues to cry. "Goodbye, old friend."

Thakszut turns away and begins to make his way back up the cliff.

CHAPTER 45

A few hours later, Pelagius stirs in his tent. He groans lightly as his eyes flutter open. He slowly sits up, wincing in pain as he does so. Adotiln, who has been sitting close by, steps forward to assist him. "Take it easy. You're still suffering from the aftereffects of Righteous Fury. It will be a few more days before you're strong enough to continue the journey."

"Adotiln?" says Pelagius weakly.

"Yes, it's me," says Adotiln. "Do you remember much of what happened?"

"I remember facing off against Kragus and calling on the Righteous Fury. I also remember an intense battle, but it gets a little fuzzy there. What happened?"

"I did not see the battle, so I can't give you the details. I can tell you that despite suffering horrendous wounds, you managed to somehow kill Kragus."

Pelagius emits a sigh of relief. "Finally, that chapter of my life is over. What did you do with the body?"

"We buried him," says Adotiln. "Even he deserved that much."

Pelagius grunts in agreement. "And his copy of the Nameless Tome?"

"I'm afraid he didn't have it on him."

"No matter. He would likely have hidden it well. Consider it to be lost. How long have I been unconscious?"

"About four hours. We were beginning to worry."

Pelagius looks at her. "You should have continued without me. The success of the quest is more important than I am."

"No," says Adotiln. "Without you, there is no quest."

"Nonsense," says Pelagius. "Even if I am to die before reaching Devil's Den, the quest must continue. Babu must be defeated, even if you have to do it without me."

"Regardless of what you say, we will never leave you behind. You would have done the same for any of us."

Pelagius lies back down. "You're right. How much longer until we can continue?"

"A day or two," says Adotiln.

Iriemorel enters the tent carrying a steaming bowl smelling of cooked meat and vegetables. Adotiln helps Pelagius sit up and Iriemorel hands it to him.

"This smells delicious," says Pelagius. "What is it?"

"Well, Kragus destroyed most of our food supplies, so I had to go hunting," says Iriemorel. "Unfortunately, the only things that seem to inhabit this area are mountain goats and yetis. I couldn't catch any goats."

Pelagius looks up at him. "So, this is yeti stew?"

"Yes. It tastes better than it sounds. One yeti is big enough to supply meals for a week. I hope you enjoy it. That creature almost killed me before I could bring it down."

"Thank you."

Pelagius puts a spoonful of the stew into his mouth. "That is quite good. Your cooking never ceases to amaze me, Iriemorel."

"Thank you, sir," says Iriemorel. "I'll be outside if you need any more."

Iriemorel leaves the tent. Adotiln turns to Pelagius. "I'll be out there as well. Just call if you need anything. For now, just try to regain your strength."

Adotiln leaves the tent and joins the others outside. Iriemorel is back at the campfire cooking more stew. Alithyra is making some new arrows and Kevnan quietly strums his mandolin. Thakszut is not present.

"Where's Thakszut?" asks Adotiln.

"He climbed down the cliff," replies Kevnan. "He said that he wanted to pay his last respects to an old friend."

"Nyogsutt?" says Alithyra. "Didn't this 'friend' try to kill him?"

"Yes," says Adotiln, "but you have to remember that they were friends for their entire lives until Thakszut joined us. Even though Nyogsutt tried to kill him, Thakszut still has respect for his former friend. This loss of friendship, compounded by the fact that he was forced to kill Nyogsutt, has surely affected him deeply. He wants to say goodbye."

Pelagius opens the tent's flap and peers out. "I understand his pain. Before Kragus was corrupted, he and I were good friends. When he turned to evil, it saddened Bojan and me greatly. That's why we imprisoned him instead of killing him when he was defeated. Despite all the horrible things he had done after his betrayal, we couldn't bring ourselves to destroy him."

"I never would have imagined that," says Alithyra. "Especially after your expressions of hatred after Bojan's death."

"I was speaking in grief and anger," says Pelagius. "It was from the pain of losing a friend due to the actions of a former friend. Until he killed Bojan, I held onto some hope that somewhere deep inside Kragus was still the good man he used to be. The death of Bojan proved me wrong."

"How did the three of you meet?" asks Alithyra, "I've heard tales of many of your adventures, but not very much from your early years."

Pelagius grins as he struggles to his feet, exits the tent, and limps to sit on a nearby rock. He sips from his bowl. "That was thirty-five years ago, and it is a unique tale itself. It is a long story though, and I do not currently have the energy to weave the tale. If we survive this quest, I will tell you on the journey home."

"I still can't imagine you being friends with Kragus," says Kevnan.

"Kragus was a good man before he was corrupted," says Pelagius. "He didn't start out as a monster."

"Kragus's situation seems unusual. I've known great people who practiced necromancy on a regular basis, but none of them became corrupted by it."

"Necromancy wasn't the problem. Kragus delved into forbidden lore from beyond the realms. Terrible knowledge and magic of those that should not exist. That is what corrupted his mind."

"What caused him to resort to such dangerous magic?"

"That too is a story for another time. I do not wish to discuss that right now."

Pelagius finishes his meal and places his empty stew bowl on the ground. "That was delicious. I needed that. Now, if you'll excuse me, I'm going to get some rest."

Pelagius gingerly walks back to his tent and disappears behind the flap while the others go back to what they were doing. Unknown to any of the group members, a mysterious ogre is watching them from the shadows. He continues to observe them for several minutes before he quietly slips behind a large boulder. He checks to make sure that nobody is watching before opening a portal and stepping through.

CHAPTER 46

The ogre emerges in a shadowy, foreboding location. It appears to be the hallway of some building. Although it is very dark here, it is clear that stone comprises the entire structure. Water drips from several places on the ceiling and various types of fungi and moss grow on the walls. Dirt and mud cake the floor, and a few bones lie scattered about. The stench of death and decay permeates the air.

The ogre walks down the hallway and opens a rotten wooden door. He steps through into a large dark chamber even filthier than the hallway; several dozen red-eyed ravens perch around the room. At the end of the chamber, a figure sits in what appears to be a moldy, rotten wooden throne. The figure's body is humanoid in shape, but the darkness obscures its features.

"What do you want, Tohirata?" inquires the mysterious figure.

"My lord, I have interesting news," replies Tohirata. "I'm sure you have been hearing the rumors of Pelagius's quest to destroy Babu."

"Of course I have. However, my spies have lost track of Pelagius's group after they were arrested. Did you find them?"

"Yes, master. They are camped in the Great Stony Mountains. Pelagius has managed to kill Kragus."

The mysterious figure falls silent for a few moments. "Did they bury him?"

"Yes, my lord," says Tohirata.

"Have some of your men keep an eye on his grave. My spies tell me that Bojan is also dead. Is that right?"

"Yes, my lord. He was not with them, and I heard them mention that he had been killed by Kragus. I believe he is buried somewhere in Bratenro."

"Excellent. This quest is quite advantageous to my plans. The death of either Pelagius or Babu, or even both, will benefit us."

"What would you like for me to do?"

"One of my spies in Diablos has informed me that the Green-Eyed Man is sending an agent to dispatch Pelagius and his team in Halfhill," replies the mysterious figure. "Of course, the Green-Eyed Man is also commanding a defense force in Diablos in case this agent fails. If the Green-Eyed Man falls from Babu's favor, it could also be of great benefit to us. I want you to make sure that the agent fails his mission, but at the same time try to make sure that at least one member of the team does not survive."

"Which one, my lord?" inquires Tohirata.

"It does not matter. Just try to make sure that one of them dies. The method is up to you. I also want you to send word to one of your men to sabotage the efforts of the Green-Eyed Man's defense force. Report back to me when both tasks have been accomplished."

"Yes, Lord Scirrhus."

Tohirata bows as he exits and closes the door, followed by several of the ravens.

Chapter 47

The Green-Eyed Man sits at a table in an unremarkable tavern, drinking an ale, and suspiciously eying a nearby red-eyed raven. After a few minutes, a dwarf walks in. He has dark brown hair, a bushy beard, and burning red eyes like Alasdar's. Spotting the Green-Eyed Man, this new arrival walks over to join him.

"Sit down, Urbelkru," says the Green-Eyed Man. "What is the status of our defense force?"

Urbelkru summons a waitress to get him a drink. "They are ready and waiting for your order. As soon as you give the word, they'll be ready to mount the defense."

"Excellent," says the Green-Eyed Man. "You have done well."

"Thank you, sir," says Urbelkru. "Will there be anything else?"

"Yes. I have an assignment for you."

Receiving his drink, Urbelkru takes a large gulp. "What do you want me to do?"

"I need one last trap for Pelagius and his team before they enter Diablos. I have chosen you to take that job."

"Where do you want me to go and what should I do?"

"You will station yourself in Halfhill close by Ithuweston. As for your exact actions, that is up to you, but I want them dead. There is something else you should know. A daemon spice merchant named Ralkgek is currently traveling through Halfhill and will be in Ithuweston at about the same time that Pelagius arrives. I need you to keep an eye on him and make sure that he doesn't join Pelagius's team."

Urbelkru finishes his drink and tosses the mug to the bartender. "You can count on me, sir. I won't fail you."

The Green-Eyed Man sits back down and Urbelkru turns to leave. However, the Green-Eyed Man stops him. "One last thing. Do not underestimate Ralkgek."

Urbelkru laughs. "What possible threat can a simple spice merchant pose to me?"

"Such arrogance will cost you. Ralkgek is a retired Diablosian military captain. He is an incredibly skilled warrior and is also a rather formidable sorcerer. Heed my warning, Urbelkru. Do not underestimate him."

Urbelkru rolls his eyes and impatiently inches toward the door. "Are you done? I have work to do."

"Very well," says the Green-Eyed Man. "Ignore my warning at your own peril."

Without any more interruptions, Urbelkru leaves the tavern. He passes Alasdar coming in.

Alasdar approaches the Green-Eyed Man's table. "Is everything in order?"

"Of course," replies the Green-Eyed Man. "Urbelkru will, hopefully, take care of them in Halfhill. If not, then my team will. It would be easier if we had your help."

"How so?"

"You are the most powerful soulborn in history. If you were to attack Pelagius's team, they would all be dead within a minute. I've seen what you can do, and nothing can stand in your way."

Alasdar smiles evilly. "I have no interest in helping you stay in Babu's favor. In fact, it would be more entertaining to see what would happen if you fail. I won't cause either event to happen. Until I decide that I want to help, I shall simply observe."

The Green-Eyed Man looks at Alasdar sadly. "So, the old Alasdar truly is dead. There was a time when you would have given your life to help me."

"I did, and look how we ended up. No, old friend, I will not help you this time. I will be looking out for my own interests."

"And what are your interests?"

"That is not your concern."

The Green-Eyed Man emits an exasperated sigh. "Why are you here?"

"Babu wants an update on the situation, and I volunteered to come get it."

"I've given you the status report," says the Green-Eyed Man.

"Indeed, you have," says Alasdar. "Enjoy your drink."

Alasdar leaves the tavern and the Green-Eyed Man settles back into his chair to enjoy his ale.

CHAPTER 48

Several days later, Pelagius and his team finally emerge on the other side of the mountains and enter the kingdom of Halfhill. Although a few forests loom in the distance, Halfhill is mostly comprised of plains and grasslands stretching as far as the eye can see. Towns and cities are clearly visible in the distance, and farmlands dot the landscape.

In contrast to the enormity of Bratenro, the structures of Halfhill are quite small. Although there are several visible that are large enough to house human-sized creatures or larger, most house smaller creatures like halflings, gnomes, and leprechauns.

Scanning the horizon reveals very few large animals. Unlike Bratenro, there are no herds of massive animals roaming the land. Most of the animals visible are smaller creatures such as the leptictidium and compsognathus, or compy, a small predatory dinosaur about three feet long and weighing around only six pounds. The only large predator visible on the plains is the gastornis, a flightless predatory bird standing nearly six feet tall with a large slightly hooked beak, powerful legs, and taloned feet. As soon as they set foot on the plains, a small group of red-eyed ravens spots them and begins hovering nearby.

Kevnan surveys the area. "Everything here is so small."

"Welcome to Halfhill," says Pelagius. "This kingdom is run by the halflings and they comprise the majority of the population here."

"Where to now?" asks Iriemorel.

Pelagius consults the map. "We'll continue following the river to the village of Ithuweston. Stay on your guard. Most of the wildlife here is too small to threaten us, but the apex predator here is the gastornis and it is very dangerous."

"Ithuweston is only a few miles away," says Adotiln. "We should be able to reach it this afternoon."

The heroes continue to follow the river, which curves to the left after a mile. By mid-afternoon, they reach the village of Ithuweston. Similar to Inolutet, Ithuweston is mostly a farming community. Farmlands surround the village on all sides and go for miles in several directions.

Inside the village, there are a few other businesses as well, including a blacksmith. There is an inn, known as the Moon and Shadow, close to the center of town and a small temple nearby, although it is unclear as to which god this temple belongs.

As the heroes come to the center of the village, several of the villagers come to greet them. Among them is a somewhat portly halfling, and although average height for a halfling, he is slightly heavier. "Greetings. Welcome to Ithuweston. I am Tyso, lord-mayor of Ithuweston. How may I assist you?"

"Hello, Tyso. I am Pelagius of Waskan. We are travelers on a quest that brings us through here. We simply seek a place to stay for a few days while we resupply for our continuing journey."

"Of course," says Tyso. "Guests are always welcome. The Moon and Shadow has rooms available. If there is anything you need, be sure and let me know."

"I am in need of some new armor, and my cooking supplies are running low," says Iriemorel.

"You can visit our blacksmith for the armor," says Tyso, "and our butcher for the food. If you are interested in rare and exotic herbs and spices, there is another guest in town you could speak to: a daemon spice merchant from Diablos named Ralkgek. His selection of spices is exquisite."

"Where can I find him?" asks Iriemorel.

"He is staying at the Moon and Shadow," replies Tyso. "When he's not there, you can find him at his cart next to the butcher's."

"Thank you," says Iriemorel.

The heroes head over to the Moon and Shadow Inn. The inn is a modest building that is clearly not designed with larger patrons in mind. Everyone except Adotiln and Thakszut must squat to get through the door and shuffle along the floor on their knees. Inside, the lobby is sparsely decorated with only a few weapons on the walls. Immediately upon entering, guests find themselves at the front desk. To the left of the desk is a stairway leading to the second floor and to the right is a doorway leading into the inn's tavern. Visible from the doorway is the tavern's bartender cleaning glasses.

Pelagius goes up to the front desk. "Hello?"

A halfling comes out of the back and gets up onto a stool behind the desk. "How may I help you?"

"We need rooms for six," says Pelagius.

"I can give you three rooms," says the innkeeper. "Two in each room. The rooms are two gold pieces a night, paid daily."

Pelagius hands him twelve coins and receives three keys.

"Rooms two, three, and four," says the innkeeper.

The group heads upstairs and goes into their rooms. Pelagius and Thakszut take one room, Kevnan and Iriemorel take another, and Adotiln and Alithyra take the third. As Pelagius is unlocking his door, a door down the hall opens and someone comes out. He looks human except that his skin is blue, and he has a pair of wings on his back. It is apparent that he is in his later years, judging from the aged look on his face. The stranger grins politely. "Good afternoon, sir. I didn't know anyone else was staying here."

"We just got here. My name is Pelagius."

"I'm Ralkgek. It's a pleasure to meet you. Well, I'd love to stay and chat, but I must go attend my spice cart."

"No need to apologize. Business must be taken care of."

Ralkgek smiles as he passes by and goes down the stairs. Pelagius enters his room, which is very clean and well-kept, and proceeds to settle in.

Later that day, the heroes are out exploring the town. Iriemorel has found his way to the blacksmith's shop. The shop is a large brick building with smoke pouring out of a tall chimney, and several red-eyed ravens perch on the roof and on the sign. Instead of a door, the shop is completely open air, lacking a front wall.

Inside, various metal objects hang from the walls and a stone counter separates this area from the workshop, which is plainly visible and consists of a massive firepit filled with flames and hot coal, over which is the chimney. Several anvils sit around the space, as well as hammers, chisels, and other tools of various sizes. There is also a large tub of water. Various types of tools sit in both the firepit and the tub of water.

The blacksmith is at one of the anvils, pounding on a red-hot object with a large hammer. He is a busurin, with the typical hunchback, hairless head, and one squinting eye and one bulging eye. The hump on his back is over twice the size of a typical busurin hump, and his arm and leg muscles are massively bulged, large even by busurin standards.

Iriemorel approaches the counter. "Excuse me, sir."

The blacksmith stops what he is doing and looks over at Iriemorel. "Just a moment."

He pounds on the object a few more times and sticks it into the tub of water. The liquid sizzles as steam rises out of the tub.

The blacksmith approaches the counter. "What do you need?"

"I need some armor," says Iriemorel. "Full-plate, if you can."

"It can be done. Takes one week." The blacksmith grabs a length of rope, some paper, a quill, and some ink. He then steps around the counter. "Hold still. I need to measure you."

Using the rope, the blacksmith begins measuring Iriemorel. As he takes measurements, he dips the quill in the ink and writes notes on the paper. After several minutes, he finishes and steps behind the counter. "Your order will be ready in one week. It'll be two hundred pieces of gold. Half now and half when your order is complete."

Iriemorel reaches into a pouch on his belt and pulls out one hundred gold coins, counting them as he places them on the counter. Gorthax counts them as well and places them into a metal container behind the counter. "Thank you. What is your name?"

"Iriemorel."

The blacksmith writes this down. "Very good. I'll get right on it. If you need anything else, please let me know. If you have any questions, my name is Gorthax."

Gorthax turns and returns to his workshop to begin preparing his new order. Iriemorel leaves to take care of some other tasks. On his way out, he passes Pelagius coming in.

Pelagius approaches the counter. "Hello?"

Gorthax comes up to the counter. "I'm a bit busy."

"I won't keep you long," says Pelagius. "I'm looking for a shield."

"What kind and how big?" asks Gorthax.

"A round shield, about three feet in diameter."

Gorthax walks to the far side of the room and from the wall pulls a shiny metal shield of Pelagius's description. He hands it to Pelagius. "How's that?"

"This is exactly what I'm looking for," says Pelagius. "I don't suppose you can add the symbol of Ender to it?"

Gorthax grunts. "I can't customize a shield that I've already made. If you want a custom-made one, you'll have to place an order with me."

"How long will that take?"

"I'm just starting on some armor for a dwarf. That project will take me about a week. Once that is done, I can work on your customized shield, which will take about another week."

"Never mind. I can't wait for two weeks. How much for it as is?"

"Fifty gold pieces."

Pelagius reaches into a pouch on his belt and counts out fifty gold coins, which he hands to Gorthax. Gorthax counts them as well to double check, smiles, and places them in his metal box.

"Very good," says Gorthax. "It's yours now."

"Thank you," says Pelagius.

Pelagius turns to leave and Gorthax returns to his new project.

CHAPTER 49

Most of the heroes' business is complete and they are getting some much needed rest, despite the eeriness of the ever-growing number of ravens. Most of the group is in the town square conversing with the locals. Iriemorel is at Ralkgek's spice cart.

"What do you have in stock, Ralkgek?" asks Iriemorel.

"I've got the usual spices," replies Ralkgek. "Various chili powders, nutmeg, and cumin among others, as well as some herbs like basil and rosemary. I also have some Diablosian Cayenne."

"Diablosian Cayenne?"

Ralkgek smiles. "A special type of red pepper grown only in Diablos. It's hotter than the cayenne found in the rest of the world. If you like spicy foods, Diablosian Cayenne is definitely for you. With it, you can make the spiciest chili you'll ever taste."

Iriemorel smiles, intrigued by this sales pitch. "That sounds very interesting."

"It seems to me that you are a dwarf who enjoys spicy food," says Ralkgek.

"Love it," says Iriemorel.

"Well then, you'll love Diablosian dishes. Diablos is well known for its hot foods. Although I do not have them all, Diablos has hotter versions of many spices known for their heat. Of course, we also enjoy some sweetness as well. For that, I have Diablosian Cinnamon, which is even sweeter than any other type of cinnamon in Sarcasca. Baked goods made with Diablosian Cinnamon are to die for."

Suddenly, a large battle axe flies right by Iriemorel's shoulder and slams into Ralkgek's cart, splitting it in half. The containers rupture, spilling various spices out of the cart and onto the ground. The sound of the blow causes all of town square to go silent and everybody, Iriemorel and Ralkgek included, looks in the direction it came from. Directly in the center of the square stands Urbelkru. The heroes all draw their weapons, as does Ralkgek, and Thakszut takes on his gorilla form.

"Missed," says Urbelkru. "Sorry."

Ralkgek clenches his fists and grits his teeth as veins pop out on his forehead. "You owe me for all that spice and the cart, soulborn."

"Sorry, Ralkgek, I don't have any money on me," says Urbelkru spitefully. "I'll ask Master Babu to reimburse you. How does that sound?"

"I don't appreciate the sarcasm," says Ralkgek.

Urbelkru smiles. "Just stay out of my way, spice merchant. I'm here for Pelagius and his team."

"I assume that the Green-Eyed Man sent you," says Pelagius.

"You are correct," says Urbelkru. "Now if you'll excuse me a moment, I'm going to change into a more comfortable form."

Urbelrku's skin turns orange and he grows to twelve feet tall. His body widens and becomes more circular until he takes on a blob-like appearance and becomes translucent. One large red eye appears in the center and a varying number of tentacles sprout and retract as his now amorphous body continues changing shape and size.

Ralkgek picks up the axe that destroyed his cart. "Stand back. I want the first shot."

Ralkgek charges at Urbelkru and swings the axe. The blade connects with a seemingly central part of the blob-like body and splits open a deep gash, which closes in seconds. Ralkgek hears a sizzling sound and looks at the axe, which appears to be slowly melting away. Before Ralkgek can react, a tentacle slaps him across the chest and face. He flies backward, screaming in pain, and crashes into his cart, which shatters the rest of the way on impact.

Kevnan leaps into the air and lands on top of Urbelkru, stabbing his rapier into Urbelkru's eye. He withdraws the sword only to discover that the eye has the same properties as the body. The apparent wound closes in seconds and the blade of his sword dissolves until it snaps in half. Kevnan's feet sink slightly into the body and his boots immediately begin to smoke and sizzle. "Get me out of here!"

Thakszut, who has begun his attack, stops in his tracks. He realizes that he can do nothing against Urbelkru and remain unharmed. Iriemorel charges forward and swings his maul at Urbelkru. He connects and smashes out a chunk just below Kevnan's feet. Kevnan hits the ground with a thud, rolls away, and removes his boots as quickly as possible. The wounded area on Urbelkru's body immediately closes as the acid burns the surface of Iriemorel's maul. Pelagius comes in and swings White Fire. However, before he can ignite it, a tentacle wraps around his arm and the sword. Pelagius screams in pain as the acid burns his flesh and he loses his grip. Urbelkru then pulls White Fire from Pelagius's hand, and forming a massive maw below his gelatinous eye, swallows the sword.

Suddenly, Adotiln, who has been quietly praying at the far side of the square, begins glowing light red and rises into the air. "Everybody, stand back!"

The others immediately back away from Urbelkru. Adotiln raises her arms and shoots two massive bolts of lightning out of her hands. They strike Urbelkru right in the center of his gelatinous body, resulting in an explosion that sends globs of orange goo flying through the square. Adotiln slowly sinks down to the ground, and although obviously exhausted, she remains on her feet. White Fire lies on the ground unharmed and Pelagius picks it up.

"Well done," says Pelagius.

Ralkgek stirs as he tries to rise from the wreckage of his cart, groaning and grasping his head and back. As Adotiln goes to heal her friends, one of the villagers emits a frightened shout. Upon looking in the direction he is pointing, everyone sees that the small orange blobs are quickly moving across the square. Before anyone else can react, the small globs come together and Urbelkru reforms. Adotiln drops to her knees in exasperation.

"You'll have to do better than that," says Urbelkru in a liquid voice reminiscent of thick, bubbling mucus.

Alithyra looses an arrow at him, which goes straight through. The arrow, dissolving as it continues, strikes a nearby lantern into a small barrel of oil, causing a fiery explosion. It reaches Urbelkru, who emits a pained shriek when the fire touches his body. As everyone looks on, they see that the parts of Urbelkru the flames touch burn and drop off as ash.

Alithyra's ears perk up and her eyes widen as she realizes the implications. "Fire! He's vulnerable to fire!"

Pelagius ignites White Fire and charges forward. He slashes Urbelkru across the body a few times, burning away several tentacles. However, between shrieks of pain Urbelkru wraps a tentacle around Pelagius's waist and hurls him across the square. Pelagius flies by Ralkgek and crashes into the remains of the spice cart.

Alithyra begins loosing burning arrows; although they help, they cause minimal damage. The others grab lit torches and begin stabbing at Urbelkru with them. Urbelkru's blob-like body gets smaller as more of him burns away. At one point, he extends a massive tentacle and knocks almost everyone away.

Ralkgek limps forward. "I think I can finish this."

Ralkgek concentrates for a moment. Then, he extends one hand, palm up and fingers curled before tightly clenching his fist. "Engulf!"

Urbelkru is suddenly engulfed in flame. He emits an unearthly shriek as the flames reduce him to ash. Everyone breathes a sigh of relief and Pelagius hobbles back over.

Adotiln smiles and begins to make her way over to her wounded friends, but stops with a look of suspicion on her face. She draws her daggers, rapidly turns, and quickly moves one dagger in front of her chest. A metallic clang reverberates through her blade as she blocks something unseen. She quickly pushes the invisible weapon to the side and stabs forward, striking her invisible foe with a clang, followed quickly by a shattering sound. An inhuman figure appears and pieces of a broken gem clatter to the ground.

The thing standing before her is humanoid in shape, with a tall and slender frame composed entirely of metal. Although shocked, the others react quickly and join Adotiln. The thing makes a quick survey of the situation and leaps onto a nearby rooftop. It then flees the scene and disappears on the horizon.

Chapter 50

Later that day, after Adotiln heals everyone's wounds, the heroes gather at a table at the inn's tavern. Ralkgek approaches them, much to the group's surprise.

"What was that thing?" asks Adotiln.

"It could only have been an assassin golem," says Ralkgek.

Everyone at the table develops an expression of horror, except for Thakszut, who looks confused. "What's an assassin golem?"

"You are familiar with golems, right?" asks Kevnan.

"You mean those large humanoid things made out of metal or stone and brought to life with magic?" asks Thakszut.

"Exactly," says Pelagius. "All golems are built to serve a purpose. Regular golems are usually built to guard something or someone. Their intelligence is minimal, and they can only follow basic commands."

"Assassin golems are much worse," says Ralkgek, "They are imbued with much greater intelligence and are able to follow complex commands and even scout targets and learn. They can even turn invisible at will. Frankly, I'm amazed that you were able to detect it."

"I almost didn't," says Adotiln. "I thought I heard a very soft clanking sound, but only briefly. I was about to dismiss it when I heard a quiet footfall behind me followed by the sound of a sword being drawn. After that, I honestly got lucky."

"So why didn't the Green-Eyed Man just send an assassin golem to begin with?" asks Iriemorel.

"Because Babu does not use them," replies Thakszut. "Otherwise I would have known about them."

"He's right," says Pelagius. "Assassin golems are not as durable as regular golems. If exposed, they are easily damaged and are the easiest golems to destroy. As such, they rely on stealth rather than brute force to accomplish their tasks. Babu and his minions prefer to inspire fear and are far less subtle. This assassin golem was not sent by Babu or the Green-Eyed Man. Someone else deployed it."

"Who?" asks Alithyra. "Very few of the kingdoms make use of them."

"True," says Ralkgek. "Of all the Sarcascan nations, only Industria mass produces them."

"But Industria is on the other side of Diablos," says Kevnan. "Why would they send one over here after us?"

"I said they're the only ones who mass produce them," replies Ralkgek. "I never said that nobody else makes them. This one may have been privately owned or it may have been sent by the government of some kingdom you offended; in which case, it could have been stalking you for years."

"So why did it target Adotiln?" asks Thakszut. "Why not all of us?"

"Assassin golems are opportunistic," replies Pelagius. "Adotiln was the farthest one away from the main group at the time. It simply saw the opportunity to take one of us out and took it."

"It's also possible that it only had one target in the group, which may or may not have been Adotiln," says Ralkgek. "If it was supposed to kill all of you, it wouldn't have done it in front of the rest of you. Either Adotiln was specifically targeted, or it was told to kill just one of you and Adotiln happened to be the one who was by herself at the most opportune moment."

"That still doesn't answer who sent it," says Kevnan.

"I'm afraid it will not be easy to answer that," says Pelagius. "Whoever this mysterious third party is, he will remain in the shadows for now. Having an unknown enemy opposing us will make our quest that much harder."

"I think our mystery party had another hand in play today," says Alithyra. "That lit lantern and the barrel of oil were not in that spot when the soulborn first arrived. Sometime between the soulborn's arrival and when I loosed my first arrow, somebody moved those two objects into place."

The others think for a moment.

"Very strange," says Ralkgek.

"Could it have been done by the same person or by another mysterious party?" asks Iriemorel.

"That is another difficult question to answer," replies Pelagius. "I think that someone may have their own agenda that was helped by both the events of today."

"How would causing setbacks to two opposing parties favor one's own agenda?" asks Kevnan.

"And what would that agenda be?" inquires Thakszut.

"That is another part of this mystery," replies Pelagius. "The answers will have to remain shrouded for now. We have no clues or leads to examine for any of this. For now, we must focus on the task at hand."

The group then orders food and drinks and spends the rest of the evening in deep thought over the day's bizarre events.

Chapter 51

Several days later, the blacksmith delivers Iriemorel's new armor to the Moon and Shadow Inn. With some help from Pelagius and Kevnan, Iriemorel dons his protection. The armor is plate mail, or full-plate, which covers his entire body, leaving no flesh exposed. Even the helmet has a face guard that flips up and down.

"How is it?" asks Pelagius.

Iriemorel adjusts the breastplate. "Uncomfortable, as armor typically is, but it fits perfectly."

"That armor should keep you well protected," says Kevnan. "Provided that nobody happens to hit the exact spot of a joint."

"It won't matter much if you face an opponent with a weapon made of war-iron or infernal steel," says Pelagius. "Anything made from either of those two metals can cut through any type of armor as though there were none."

"Speaking of weapons, I need a new one," says Kevnan.

Ralkgek enters the room and leans against the doorway. "I think I can help with that. For a price, of course."

"What price?" asks Pelagius.

"I want to join your quest," replies Ralkgek. "That soulborn destroyed my livelihood, and I hold his master directly responsible."

"You want to join us strictly for revenge and not out of a need to protect the innocent from him?" inquires Pelagius.

"Basically, yes," says Ralkgek.

"Certainly not the most noble intentions," says Adotiln.

"It shouldn't matter how noble my intentions are," says Ralkgek. "Whether to protect the innocent or avenge a personal wrong, my goal is the same as yours."

"He has a point," says Kevnan.

"I agree," says Iriemorel. "We need all the help we can get."

Pelagius thinks for a moment. "What can you contribute to our team?"

"As you saw in the square, I am an experienced sorcerer," replies Ralkgek.

"Do you have a title?" asks Kevnan.

"Of course," replies Ralkgek. "I am Ralkgek the Fiendish Cold-flame."

"How did you earn that title?" asks Alithyra.

"I specialize in elemental magic," replies Ralkgek. "You know, magic that makes use of fire, ice, air, and earth. Plus, I am of demonic descent, hence the fiendish part."

"If you also specialize in air and earth magic, why are they not included in your title?" asks Kevnan.

"That would make it too long," says Ralkgek. "Plus, I tend to use fire and ice more often than air and earth."

"How is it that you can help us procure weapons?" asks Pelagius.

"I have a trunk that contains a few weapons that I used during my time in the military," says Ralkgek. "Come. I'll show you."

Ralkgek exits their room and the heroes follow him down the hall and through the door to his room. Inside, Ralkgek grabs a key off a desk and goes to a large trunk in the corner. He unlocks the trunk and opens it.

The trunk has several weapons inside of varying types. They are mostly swords, axes, and daggers, but there are a few crossbows too. The first weapon Ralkgek pulls out is a large black sword with a blade about four and a half feet in length and a few more inches in width than a longsword. He straps it to his back. "This was my preferred weapon in the day."

"The color of the blade," says Kevnan. "Is that infernal steel?"

"Yes, it is," replies Ralkgek. "Cuts through even plate mail like butter, after a few strikes. Only armor made of infernal steel or war-iron stands a chance to block it, and even then, only about half the time."

Ralkgek reaches into the trunk and pulls out a large battle axe with a black blade which he hands to Iriemorel. "I don't have a maul, but this axe should serve you well."

Iriemorel pushes the blade away. "I appreciate the offer, despite the stereotype it presents. Even with the damage, my maul's head is still structurally sound. I respectfully decline."

Ralkgek grunts in annoyance and returns the axe to his trunk. "As you wish."

Looking at Kevnan, Ralkgek reaches back into the chest and removes a sheathed katana. He unsheathes it, displaying the intimidating sharpness of the curved, slender blade. The hilt guard on it is circular and the hilt itself is long enough to hold with two hands. He hands it to Kevnan. "This is much better than a rapier. I'm sure you've heard stories of warriors skilled with this sword."

"Indeed," says Kevnan. "They are famous for their sharpness, and their cutting abilities are legendary. One could easily slice an opponent or two in half. However, it's useless against armor."

"For the most part, that's true," says Ralkgek, "but look at the blade."

Kevnan pulls the sword out of its sheath, revealing a black blade. His eyes grow wide as he inspects the weapon. "Infernal steel."

"Now, armor that would normally block a katana will not be a problem," says Ralkgek.

"Infernal steel is incredibly rare," says Pelagius. "How do you have this many weapons constructed of it?"

"Perks of being a captain in the Diablosian military," says Ralkgek. "War-iron is just as rare and only given to the elites."

He turns to Adotiln. "I believe I have some daggers that you may like."

"Thank you for the offer, but no," says Adotiln. "I've got extras in case I lose the two I used."

"Well prepared," says Ralkgek. "Excellent."

Ralkgek thinks for a moment. "Bring Alithyra in here. I have something for her too."

Kevnan exits the room and returns a few moments later, followed by Thakszut and Alithyra. They look in awe at the new weapons. As Alithyra approaches, Ralkgek pulls a longbow from the bottom of the trunk.

"Thank you kindly," says Alithyra, "but I already have one."

"This one is special," says Ralkgek. "This is the Seeker Bow."

Alithyra's eyes grow wide as she stares at the bow in awe. "The legendary enchanted bow that never misses its target?"

"The very same," says Ralkgek. "I obtained it from an enemy combatant during a military campaign. I rarely use it and it's just wasteful for it to sit in a chest."

"Thank you," says Alithyra.

Ralkgek squeezes the center of the bow and utters something in an unknown language, causing the Seeker Bow to briefly glow before shrinking. When the glow fades, the Seeker Bow has the appearance of a small wooden dowel. Ralkgek hands it to Alithyra. "That will make storage easier and carrying it more discreet."

"That will definitely be easier than carrying around two bows," says Alithyra.

Ralkgek looks over at Thakszut and frowns. "Unfortunately, I don't have anything for Thakszut."

"That's fine," says Thakszut. "I prefer my own abilities anyway."

Ralkgek turns to Pelagius. "Is there anything you would like from my little collection?"

"No, thank you," says Pelagius. "White Fire is all I need."

Ralkgek closes the trunk and turns his key, locking it. "Very well. One more thing, and this is important. Do not take those infernal steel weapons with you into Battallia. They are illegal there and you will be arrested on the spot."

"We were arrested in Bratenro," says Kevnan. "Surely we can clear up any misunderstandings like we did there."

"Clear them up?" says Iriemorel. "We were banished from Bratenro."

"And we got lucky in that regard," says Pelagius. "Remember, if there is one kingdom where you do not want to get arrested, it's Battallia. The Battallian government is legendarily harsh in its enforcement of the law. The minimum penalty for breaking a law in Battallia is sixteen months in prison. The possession of an infernal steel weapon in Battallia may be as low as sixteen months in prison or it could go as far as the punishment for treason."

"Oh," says Kevnan.

"So then, are we ready to continue our quest?" asks Alithyra.

"Not yet," replies Pelagius. "We need a few more days to finish resupplying, and we need to procure the services of a couple of boats to carry us on the river."

"I was hoping for a brief delay," says Ralkgek. "I need a few days to train Kevnan in the basics of using a katana."

"Very well," says Pelagius. "Oh, and stay on your guard. That assassin golem may still be around somewhere."

Everyone nods in agreement; then they depart to get a few tasks done.

CHAPTER 52

Tohirata nervously approaches his master, and Scirrhus leans forward, partially entering the light. "What is it, Tohirata?"

"My lord, Urbelkru has been destroyed," says Tohirata. "However, the assassin golem failed. None of Pelagius's team perished."

"Intriguing," says Scirrhus. "How did it happen?"

Tohirata tells him of the events as reported to him by one of his spies.

"I see," says Scirrhus. "Recall the golem and cancel its mission."

"You do not wish to try again, sir?" asks Tohirata.

"There is no need. The goal was to give Pelagius an idea of something bigger happening. With our involvement revealed to him, that task has been accomplished. A death would have gotten the point across in a more dramatic fashion, but the desired result was achieved without it."

"What shall I have the men do now, my lord?"

"Aside from our spy in the Green-Eyed Man's group, nothing. For now, we simply observe."

CHAPTER 53

That evening, the heroes, including Ralkgek, sit at a table in the Moon and Shadow's tavern. A young halfling waitress approaches their table. "Good evening. How may I help you this evening?"

The waitress writes down their orders and then goes through a door by the bar. The heroes enjoy their drinks while they wait for dinner.

"While we're all in one place, there is one thing that I think we need to discuss," says Ralkgek.

"What would that be?" asks Pelagius.

"Once we get into Devil's Den, we will be in the middle of enemy territory," says Ralkgek. "There is a strong possibility that something could go horribly wrong, and in that case, we would need to be able to make a quick retreat."

"That will be very difficult if we are in Babu's inner sanctum," says Thakszut. "Next to impossible, actually."

Pelagius thinks for a moment. "How do you propose we do this? Teleport out, use a portal, or run as fast as we can?"

"Despite my considerable magical abilities, I have very little experience with teleportation or portals," says Ralkgek. "Which would make my use of such powers dangerous at best and suicidal at worst. However, I do have a friend in the town of Ethor who has mastered the art of magical transportation: an elderly goblin sorcerer named Shukrat. Also known by the title Shukrat the Ghoststepper."

"Ghoststepper?" asks Adotiln.

"Yes," says Ralkgek. "Apparently, during his time under his sorcery master, he gained so much proficiency with teleportation and portals that he could appear anywhere in an instant. The other students started calling him the Ghoststepper because he would just appear and step up behind or beside someone. After he completed his training, Ghoststepper became his official title."

"How far will he be able to go with us?" asks Alithyra.

"He is too old to accompany us to Devil's Den," replies Ralkgek. "However, he has mastered teleportation, portals, and even dimensional gateways to the point that he can concentrate one use of these powers in a small object. If he is willing to help, he may give us one or two of these objects that we can use to return to his home immediately in an emergency."

"Wouldn't that put him in danger of being targeted by Babu's forces?" asks Kevnan.

"Not in this case," replies Ralkgek. "In his youth, he was a high-ranking government official with considerable influence in the royal court. In fact, he is a personal friend of King Demonicus and even though he is long since retired from government duties, he still retains the title of viscount and the influence of his youth. As such, Babu and his minions wouldn't dare touch him, or they would all have to answer to King Demonicus himself."

"An ally like that would be invaluable," says Iriemorel.

"Do you think he would be willing to help?" asks Pelagius.

"Absolutely," says Ralkgek. "He is a kind old goblin and will even be willing to take you in for a few days."

"This is too good of an opportunity to pass up, Pelagius," says Alithyra. "Shukrat could be of great help to us."

"Ralkgek, if Shukrat is willing to help us when we get there, we will take you up on your offer," says Pelagius.

"You won't regret it," says Ralkgek.

The waitress arrives with their food and they enjoy their dinners in silence.

CHAPTER 54

The Green-Eyed Man walks down a large hallway made of reddish-black stone. Lit torches line the walls, spaced evenly every five feet. Every once in a while, another corridor opens and goes in another direction. As he passes by an open door, he peeks inside and sees the grand hall, where a large oni is stirring a massive pot. He stops and sniffs the air as he takes in the meaty aroma of whatever stew the oni is preparing. Continuing, he comes to a wooden door about twenty feet high and ten feet wide. The door is reinforced with metal bands, and a large metal ring serves as a doorknob. Waiting by the door is an imposing figure standing over twelve feet tall. He has grayish-red skin, red eyes, sharp claws, and massive sharp teeth, and horns on his head.

"What is it, Gulvgrum?" asks the Green-Eyed Man. "Why did you call me here?"

"It was not I who sent for you," replies Gulvgrum. "Master Babu sent for you personally."

The Green-Eyed Man's eyes widen as a cold sweat seeps out of his pores. Gulvgrum opens the door and they enter the throne room. Babu sits on his throne reading, a large piece of parchment; he dips a massive quill in an inkwell and begins writing. He then rolls up the parchment and hands it to a minotaur flanking him. "Tell the baron that if he wishes to have more troops, he needs a better reason than some strange technology on the other side of the border. It's Industria. There's always something strange over there."

"My master is concerned that the Industrians are preparing an invasion on his territory," says the minotaur. "He will send me back to make the request again."

Babu sighs. "Unless he has proof that they are planning to attack, I cannot grant more troops. Industria is our ally and has no reason to invade. Besides, too large a gathering of soldiers, even this far south, will put Battallia on alert and they may declare war. The baron's request is denied. That is my final word."

The minotaur nods and exits the room. After making sure that nobody else is waiting, Gulvgrum approaches the throne and bows. "I have brought him as you asked, master."

Babu swats a raven off his throne. "Well done, Gulvgrum. Take your place."

Gulvgrum rises and stands to the right of Babu's throne. The Green-Eyed Man slowly approaches the throne.

"That's far enough," says Babu.

The Green-Eyed Man stops halfway between the throne and the door and bows. "You wished to see me, master?"

"Silence!" shouts Babu. "You know why you are here. Urbelkru failed his mission. Pelagius and his team are on their way here, and now Ralkgek has joined them."

"There were unforeseen circumstances, my lord," says the Green-Eyed Man. "We all thought Urbelkru to be invincible. Their victory was a fluke."

"Your excuses mean nothing. You gave me your word that they would never live to enter Diablos and yet they will soon be on their way. Your failure is most disappointing. From what I have heard about your defense force, it sounds as though they will fare no better."

"One member of the team had a slight accident, but he has been replaced. I can assure you, master, that we will not fail you."

"You had better not. If you do, your punishment will be more horrible than you can imagine. You are not the only soul hunter under my command, and I can replace you."

Babu snaps his fingers and a large door behind the throne opens. From this door steps a rhinoran. Although their bodies are humanoid in shape, rhinorans have the head, horns, and feet of a rhinoceros, as well as gray skin. Rhinorans are also considered giants and this one is bigger than Babu.

"I believe you know each other," says Babu.

"It's been a long time, Hazgor," says the Green-Eyed Man.

Hazgor smiles.

"If your defense force fails, Hazgor will serve as your replacement," says Babu. "Until then, he will remain hidden."

"You would replace me with him rather than Garu? Hazgor can barely see me from where he stands."

Babu chuckles. "Garu is a coward. He would not make a suitable replacement no matter how far you fall from my favor. He serves his purpose, but Hazgor is still my choice."

Babu makes a motion to Hazgor and he goes back through the door behind the throne.

"I hope you realize the stakes here," says Babu. "Your immortality is not at risk, but if you fail, you will beg for death before I'm through with you. Do you understand?"

A chuckle to one side of the chamber gets the Green-Eyed Man's attention. Quickly glancing over, he sees Alasdar standing by the wall.

"Yes, master," replies the Green-Eyed Man. "I understand perfectly."

"Good," says Babu. "Now get out of my sight and prepare your troops for Pelagius's arrival."

"Yes, master."

As the Green-Eyed Man rises to his feet, Gulvgrum steps down and escorts him to the door. Before he can leave, Gulvgrum grabs him by the arm. "If your methods weren't so aggressive, we wouldn't be in this situation. Past soul hunters were far more subtle. You, on the other hand, attract too much attention."

The Green-Eyed Man pulls away. "The tactics of the old guard were inefficient. Collecting souls is my job and the old method is far too slow."

"Well, now your job is to ensure that this foul-up doesn't affect our master," says Gulvgrum. "Now get out."

The Green-Eyed Man leaves the throne room and walks back down the hallway. Suddenly, he stops and turns down another corridor that eventually ends at an iron door. He unlocks it to reveal a stone staircase leading down. At the bottom of the stairs is another iron door, which the Green-Eyed Man opens.

Behind this door is a dark, dank dungeon filled with cells. Many are empty, but several hold prisoners of various species. The Green-Eyed Man walks through and stops at one close to the back wall. In this cell is a canin of the Great Dane variety, currently shackled to the wall, covered in sandy brown hair. He is nearly eight feet tall but has a scrawny build due to his years in prison.

He looks up as the Green-Eyed Man approaches the bars. "Well, this is a surprise. Come to visit, old friend?"

"Hardly, Aldtaw," replies the Green-Eyed Man. "I was just coming to remind you that you're due for a torture session sometime this month."

"What happened to you? You've changed so much since that day. You used to be a good friend. I still can't believe you betrayed me the way you did."

"You turned your back on me. You refused to take my offer after I broke you out of prison."

"How could I take such an offer? I still can't believe the others agreed to it. What you would have asked me to do would have been more horrible than I can imagine. The fact that the others can still live with themselves is beyond me."

"I broke you out of a Battallian prison. You owed me for that, and the offer I gave you was your means of paying me back for that favor. The others realized that and took it. You refused it, so I did what I had to. What happened to that legendary loyalty the canin are known for?"

"Even we have our limits. You asked me to choose between my own moral code and becoming your servant. That ultimatum was a betrayal."

"Had I known how ungrateful you would be, I would have left you in that cell."

"I wish you had. Nothing the Battallian penal system can do is worse than what I would have had to do if I had taken your offer."

"There is no hope for you, Aldtaw, unless you reconsider," says the Green-Eyed Man.

"What makes you think I will ever be willing to accept that offer?" says Aldtaw.

"It's an opportunity to save yourself," says the Green-Eyed Man, "and our friendship."

"Our friendship died when you locked me in here," says Aldtaw. "I will never join you or Babu. That is my decision and it will stand."

"Very well. Your fate is sealed. You will die down here. When the dungeon master has had his fill, I will allow him to let you die. You will suffer horribly and perish in agony."

"If that is my fate, then so be it. At least my conscience will be clean. Unlike the others, I won't have to die with blood on my hands. When you and the others die, you will all have to answer for what you have done."

"They will. However, if you don't remember, I am immortal. I can't die."

"You can die. It is well known that your urn is the source of your immortality. If it is destroyed, you can die just as easily as the rest of us."

"I keep my urn well protected. It is not possible for anyone to destroy it."

"You've kept it well protected so far, but you can't keep that up forever. Someday someone will catch you off guard and that will be the day you finally die, Ma…."

Rage fills the Green-Eyed Man's eyes. He throws open the door, enters the cell, and clasps his hand over Aldtaw's muzzle. "Do not say that name! The others are forbidden to speak it, and so are you!"

Aldtaw shakes his head until the Green-Eye Man releases his grip and glares into his eyes. "What are you going to do about it?"

The Green-Eyed Man turns and looks toward a door opposite of the one he came in. "Nakhurd, get in here!"

The door opens and a large troll steps through. Screams of agony echo from within.

"What do you want?" asks Nakhurd. "I'm busy over there."

"When you get around to torturing Aldtaw, make sure that this session is exceptionally agonizing," says the Green-Eyed Man. "I want him to suffer like he has never suffered before."

Nakhurd smiles evilly. "Understood, sir."

"That is all," says the Green-Eyed Man. "As you were."

Nakhurd goes back through the door. The Green-Eyed Man turns back to Aldtaw.

"There," says the Green-Eyed Man. "Try to speak my former name again, Aldtaw, and I'll make a deal with Master Babu to grant you true immortality so that you may be tortured to the point of death and beyond without passing away."

"You've practically made me immortal already," says Aldtaw. "Like the others, you have used the power of your urn to keep me from aging. I would have died in here by now if you had not."

"It is true that you cannot die of old age while you are here, but you can still be killed. Keep that in mind before you try to call my bluff."

Locking Aldtaw's cell, the Green-Eyed Man leaves the dungeon and returns to preparing for Pelagius's arrival.

Chapter 55

Meanwhile, Eeshlith, Glakchog, and Shudgluv camp in the mountains near the river pass. They each have a tent set up and are sitting around a fire eating a meager meal and keeping warm. Eeshlith and Shudgluv seem troubled.

"Remind me why we keep doing these things," says Eeshlith.

"We're following orders," says Glakchog, barely paying attention as he eyes a nearby raven. "It's as simple as that."

"I think we originally went along with him because we felt we owed him a debt for getting us out of prison," says Shudgluv.

"If what we have been doing was repaying a debt, then it is long since repaid," says Eeshlith. "Why, then, do we keep doing the horrible things he asks of us?"

"I don't know," says Shudgluv.

Glakchog looks at them. "As I said, we are following orders. We were all in the Battallian military. We were all soldiers, and we still are in a way. A good soldier follows orders without question and that is what we are doing. Disobedience earns disciplinary action."

"Disciplinary action in this case meaning death," says Shudgluv.

Eeshlith looks at Glakchog. "It is true that we were all soldiers at one point, but none of our commanders ever asked us to do anything as remotely horrible as what we have been doing all these years. Do you mean to tell me, Glakchog, that you feel no remorse for your actions?"

Glakchog glances at her. "I am a soldier. That's all there is to it. Personal feelings must be set aside in the line of duty. It does not matter how horrible the act is. If you are given an order, you follow it. That is how I live my life."

Shudgluv sighs. "Sometimes a good soldier has to know when to disobey an order."

"Absolutely not," says Glakchog. "I thought I made myself clear. A good soldier follows orders to the letter no matter what. And that is what we are going to do. Remember, the Green-Eyed Man placed me in charge whenever he is not around. So, when I give an order, you had better follow it. I don't care how you feel personally about it."

"There was a time when you would have agreed with Shudgluv," says Eeshlith.

"That was a mistake," says Glakchog. "I have paid for that error. Now I know that orders must be obeyed no matter what."

Eeshlith stands up. "You know, Glakchog, you were born for this."

"What does that mean?" asks Glakchog.

"Your ability to justify what we have been doing is uncanny," says Eeshlith. "You are a natural. Murder is second nature to you."

Grabbing his hookswords, Glakchog leaps to his feet. "I am not a murderer!"

Glakchog swings a hooksword angrily in Eeshlith's direction. Fortunately, Shudgluv's warclub blocks the attack.

"That doesn't help your case," says Shudgluv. "If you want to kill her, you'll have to get through me. Take me on, if you're not a coward."

Eeshlith steps between them and pushes them apart. "I can handle myself in a fight. However, fighting each other is not going to solve anything or get the job done. I suggest that everybody calm down now."

Glakchog angrily throws his weapons down and stomps off to the other side of the camp.

"Thank you," says Eeshlith. "It's nice to know that at least one of you agrees with me."

"Glakchog has always had a nasty temper," says Shudgluv, "but, then again, so do all busurin."

"You do agree with me, right?"

"Absolutely. In fact, I've been considering leaving for some time. I haven't come to a decision yet, and I don't know how I could get out alive. However, I'm beginning to care less and less about the latter part."

"Even if we made it out alive, there's no telling if the Green-Eyed Man's anti-aging spell would hold or not. Betrayal may break the spell."

Shudgluv chuckles. "That wouldn't be a problem for you. Sixty years is nothing to an elf."

"True," says Eeshlith, "but it is a long time for a troll."

"I'd be willing to risk it," says Shudgluv.

"I don't know how much longer I can continue down this path either. However, I do not feel as though I can leave yet."

Shudgluv gives her a confused look. "Why not?"

"I haven't given up on the Green-Eyed Man yet," says Eeshlith. "I still feel that our old friend is somewhere inside, desperately trying to get out. As his friend, I feel it is my duty to salvage what is left of his humanity and direct him to redemption."

Shudgluv sighs. "You're wasting your time, Eeshlith. The Green-Eyed Man is beyond redemption. He just enjoys his job too much."

"I disagree," says Eeshlith. "He has had several opportunities to kill Pelagius, but he continues to simply delay and toy with him. Why do you think that is?"

"I'm pretty certain he's doing it for a sadistic laugh."

"No. I think that subconsciously, he is remorseful for what he has done. He can't break free from Babu's control himself, but Babu's death may release him. I believe that deep down, he is hoping that Pelagius is successful in his quest."

"I doubt it. Babu's power over his mind is total."

"We don't know that for certain."

Shudgluv sighs again. "Look, I believe you're doing the right thing. I want nothing more than to have our old friend back, but I'm afraid that it is too late. When he disowned his name, he turned down the path of darkness once and for all."

"I still think we can lead him back," says Eeshlith.

"Perhaps," says Shudgluv. "If I may ask, when will you be convinced that he is beyond all hope?"

"When he actually attacks one of us. Although he has threatened to do so many times, he has yet to even hint at making a move. I don't think he can bring himself to harm us."

"That's a dangerous gamble. What if he kills you?"

"Then I'm counting on you to do what's necessary. Please just bear with me a little longer."

"Very well. I'll see this out with you."

A sad expression crosses Shudgluv's face.

"What's wrong?" asks Eeshlith.

"Aldtaw," replies Shudgluv. "I wish there was some way we could get him out of there. I'm certain that they won't keep him alive much longer. Eventually, the Green-Eyed Man will grow bored of punishing him and will have him executed."

"Death would be a relief for poor Aldtaw. He's been tortured almost constantly for sixty years."

"I agree, but I don't think it will be a quick execution, especially if Alasdar is the one who kills him."

Eeshlith shudders. They both then look in Glakchog's direction and see him returning to the tents.

"We'll have to finish this discussion later," says Eeshlith. "Glakchog is coming back."

Eeshlith and Shudgluv sit as Glakchog returns to fireside.

CHAPTER 56

The Green-Eyed Man is close by the river that Pelagius and the others will be traveling down; about one hundred yards away is the edge of Malferno's Canyon. The surrounding landscape is heavily mountainous but is also comprised of plains and a few hills, with several groves of large trees huddled by the river. The Green-Eyed Man stands in front of a line of six individuals. Among them are a centaur, satyr, a gaki, and two banoks.

Banoks are also a species of demonfolk, best described as man-bat creatures. Banoks stand about eight feet tall but only weigh about fifty pounds. Their bodies are humanoid in shape, but they have the head of a bat, complete with a mouth full of razor-sharp teeth and five-inch-long fangs. Their beady eyes glow bright red. Fur covers their heads, torsos, and legs. The hair color varies, but in the case of these two, one has light brown fur and the other has black fur.

Banoks also have wings that consist of a layer of skin that connects to the center of their backs, stretching in between their long fingers and down to their feet. Due to this body design, banoks, much like bats, are clumsy on the ground but very quick and agile in the air. The Green-Eyed Man walks up and down the line as though he were inspecting them.

"Everything seems to be in order," says the Green-Eyed Man. "Except for one thing."

"What's that, boss?" asks the gaki.

"With three eyes, you should have noticed that something is missing, Slythrogg," says the Green-Eyed Man. "Now, has anyone seen Tzauhrag?"

"Who's Tzauhrag?" asks the centaur.

"He's Nataka's replacement, Digrigonkh," replies the Green-Eyed Man.

"What happened to Nataka?" asks the satyr.

The Green-Eyed Man sighs in frustration. "And these were the best I could find."

He turns to the satyr. "He was killed in an accident, Faoghehm. Now I will ask again. Has anyone seen Tzauhrag?"

"I guess we lost him," says Slythrogg.

The Green-Eyed Man emits an exasperated groan and tosses his hands in the air. "How do you lose an oni?"

The others, except for the two banoks, converse, but nobody is able to come up with an answer.

The Green-Eyed Man rubs his forehead with his thumb and forefinger. "This is ridiculous. How did I gather such incompetent henchmen? I should kill you three right now, but I don't have time to find replacements."

"What about them?" asks Slythrogg, pointing to the banoks.

"They're smarter than the three of you," says the Green-Eyed Man angrily. "I can tell you one thing. If Tzauhrag doesn't show up, I'm going to make his death very unpleasant. Now, did you three at least remember to bring your weapons?"

Slythrogg reaches behind a tree and pulls out two bastard swords.

"Very good," says the Green-Eyed Man. "And you two?"

Digrigonkh reaches behind a large rock and pulls out a war hammer, a weapon that resembles a hammer but is about three times the size. Faoghehm, who wears flowing blue robes similar to what Bojan used to wear, pulls a mace from under his robe.

"Good," says the Green-Eyed Man. "At least you're not completely incompetent. Now, if only Tzauhrag would actually show up."

"I'm here, boss," says a deep voice in the trees.

An enormous demon emerges from the grove of trees. This creature is about seventeen feet tall and weighs over three tons. His body is humanoid in shape, but he has two large horns on his head and enormous fang-like teeth. He has wild, disheveled black hair and blue skin. In his hand he carries a kanabo, a club made of heavy oak, covered in metal from the middle to the end, with vicious-looking spikes covering the top third. Wielding this weapon takes great strength as it is very heavy, weighing at least thirty pounds.

The Green-Eyed Man glares angrily at him as he emerges. "Your punctuality is very disappointing, Tzauhrag."

"Sorry, boss," says Tzauhrag. "I got stuck in some mud in the swamp."

"I suppose I should have expected as much from a stupid, lumbering oaf like you," says the Green-Eyed Man.

Tzauhrag emits an angry shout and raises his kanabo in the air.

"I would think twice about that if I were you," says the Green-Eyed Man.

Tzauhrag brings his kanabo down, and it crashes to the ground just inches from the Green-Eyed Man. "Insult me again and I will crush you."

"Crush me and you die," says the Green-Eyed Man. "Remember, I am immortal. You can't kill me."

Tzauhrag emits an angry grunt and picks his kanabo up, revealing a crater in the ground at least two feet deep.

"Now that we're all here, let's discuss our tactics," says the Green-Eyed Man. "We will hide in the trees by the river. Pelagius's group is large enough that they may require two boats. After the first boat passes our spot, Tzauhrag will rush out and smash the second boat. Then, Faoghehm will hit the first boat with a ball of flame. Once that is done, the rest of us will come out of hiding and take on the survivors."

"Who gets who?" asks Slythrogg.

"Pelagius is mine," says the Green-Eyed Man. "Faoghehm should engage Ralkgek. It is best that a sorcerer take on another sorcerer. The rest of you can take on whoever is left. Now, is the plan understood?"

"Yes," they all say in unison.

"Excellent," says the Green-Eyed Man. "Remember, failure is not an option. Some of them may be allowed to retreat. I have a surprise waiting if they do, but they should not be allowed to reach Devil's Den. Pelagius should be here sometime within the next few days. Spend that time training in the tactics we discussed and make sure that you are hidden when any boats come down the river. Start training now."

Slythrogg's stomach gurgles. "Boss, I'm famished."

The other henchmen back away in fear as Green-Eyed Man eyes him nervously. "How long has it been since you have eaten?"

"An hour," says Slythrogg.

"Go gorge yourself then," says the Green-Eyed Man. "We don't need you going feral. The rest of you, start training."

The Green-Eyed Man and his minions disappear into the trees as Slythrogg leaves to hunt.

CHAPTER 57

In the throne room of Devil's Den, Babu writes on a piece of parchment, dipping his massive quill in a jar of ink as he continues. He rolls up the scroll and hands it to a nearby busurin. "Deliver this to your master. Tell him that troops on the Necrotian border are not needed. Those skeletons he is seeing are likely just a crew building something for their master."

"Very well," says the busurin. "He won't be happy."

"That is not my concern," says Babu. "Even if one of those skeletons wanders over the border, they are easily dispatched by the forces he has. Off with you now."

As the busurin leaves the room, Gulvgrum turns to Babu and bows. Babu acknowledges him. "Speak your mind, Gulvgrum."

"Master, if I may be so bold, I think it would be wise to increase defensive preparations in case the Green-Eyed Man's defense force fails," says Gulvgrum.

"He assured me that it will not."

"Of course, master. And they had better not for his sake, but it is always wise to be prepared."

Babu thinks for a moment. "You make a good point."

"Thank you, master," says Gulvgrum.

"Inform Commander Charndergh to mobilize his men along the walls. Once our wall defenses are on alert, this fortress is impregnable."

"Master, they now have Thakszut on their side. With his knowledge of this fortress, he could lead them to secret entryways that we are unaware of. Once inside, they would be able to easily infiltrate the inner sanctum."

"That's what you're here for, Gulvgrum. As my bodyguard, it is your job to protect me if they should penetrate our defenses."

"But there are seven of them and only one of me. I can't hold all of them off. I am well aware that you can easily handle yourself, but I also know that you prefer not to sully your own hands unless you have to. I will need help if they make it here."

Babu listens intently and considers the possibilities. "Very well. Once you have spoken with Commander Charndergh, seek out a few helpers."

"Yes, master," says Gulvgrum. "I will make sure to recruit enough to outnumber them three to one."

"No. Just get six others."

"But that will make the numbers even, not including you."

Babu grins arrogantly. "Exactly. One defender for every attacker. Only if they defeat their opponent will they be able to come after me. If they are able to make it this far, they should at least be given a sporting chance."

"Forgive my questioning, master," says Gulvgrum, "but that sounds risky."

"Those are my standing orders, Gulvgrum. Anyway, if necessary, I can call out Hazgor and Garu. Also remember that I do have other precautions."

"It shall be done, master. Did you have anybody in mind for my team or shall I pick them?"

"I will let you decide who will be on your defense team. However, you will need a powerful sorcerer to counter Ralkgek."

"I know just the man," says Gulvgrum. "Or I guess I should say, cecropsan."

"Tymraal?" inquires Babu.

"The very same, master."

Babu smiles malevolently. "Excellent. Get to it, then."

Gulvgrum turns to leave, but Babu stops him. "I almost forgot. There is one more thing."

"Yes, master?" inquires Gulvgrum.

"Set up the inner sanctum's divider defenses and place one of your defense minions in each area that the dividers lead to. It will be more entertaining if they are separated and forced to duel with an adversary one on one."

"But one of those paths leads directly to the throne room. One of them is certain to make it here."

"The one who uses that path will face you, Gulvgrum. And since the other paths lead to various areas of the fortress, it will take his allies a while to get here even if they defeat their opponents."

Gulvgrum smiles. "It shall be done, master."

"And find a way to get rid of these cursed ravens," says Babu.

Gulvgrum bows and leaves the throne room.

Chapter 58

Pelagius and the others have finally acquired a couple of boats and sail the river through the mountain passage that separates Halfhill from Diablos. Pelagius is in the lead boat with Ralkgek, Kevnan, and Thakszut, while Iriemorel and Alithyra are in the second boat with the horses and most of the supplies. A halfling captains each boat. Pelagius turns to one of the captains. "Thank you for allowing us to use your boat. Getting through the pass would be difficult without it."

The first captain shrugs. "Your offer was more than generous. I would have been a fool to turn down the commission." The captain glances at Ralkgek. "Take the oars for a moment."

Ralkgek takes the oars as the captain looks at a map.

"Steady as she goes," says the first captain. "We should emerge on the other side of the mountains very soon."

"Once we get into Diablos, how far is it to Ethor?" asks Kevnan.

"About a day," replies Ralkgek. "We'll have to find a place to camp once night falls, but we should reach Ethor sometime tomorrow."

After several minutes, the boats exit the mountain pass and enter Diablos. As they clear the pass, Glakchog, Eeshlith, and Shudgluv slowly descend from their campsite and follow the heroes at a distance. The landscape of this kingdom is mostly savannah and mountains, with patches of forest and swampland dotting the landscape. The river curves slightly north, coming precariously close to the edge of Malferno's Canyon, a gigantic, seemingly bottomless fissure nearly a mile across at its widest point. The fissure is so large that it cuts the kingdom of Diablos in half. A single smoking volcano looms in the distance on the far side of the canyon.

A large variety of animals roam the plains, including at least one pride of lions and a herd of thousands of zebras and wildebeest. Dragons and wyverns, a cousin of the dragon with only two legs and wings where the front legs would be, circle in the sky and roost on the mountainsides. Gastornis and phorusrhacos, a large cousin of the gastornis also known as a terror bird, as well as many species of dinosaurs, wander the land.

"Amazing," says Alithyra, surveying the countryside.

"I don't see very many thorps, hamlets, or villages," says Adotiln.

"Diablos is still very much a wild country," says Ralkgek. "Most of the inhabitants live in larger towns or cities. There are a few smaller settlements scattered throughout the kingdom, but nowhere near as many as you'd find elsewhere."

Soon, the boats drift past a grove of trees. Tzauhrag bursts out, swinging his kanabo in an underhanded sweep, smashing it against the underside of the second boat and shattering the vessel completely. The blow catapults the captain into the river, knocks Iriemorel, Adotiln, and Alithyra several feet away onto the bank, and obliterates the horses. The supplies scatter and sink into the river. The other four heroes and their captain barely abandon ship in time as Tzauhrag turns and brings the kanabo down upon their boat, smashing the second vessel to pieces.

As the heroes drag themselves onto shore, the Green-Eyed Man and the rest of his defense force emerge from the trees and attack. The two captains flee the scene, disappearing into the trees. The Green-Eyed Man engages Pelagius, and the two men begin a sword duel, with each strike and step taking them closer and closer to the edge of the canyon. Faoghehm takes on Ralkgek, Digrigonkh engages Kevnan, and the two banoks go after Thakszut and Alithyra. Slythrogg pauses to pick up and munch on a dead horse before engaging Iriemorel.

Adotiln draws her daggers and turns to face Tzauhrag, who does not attack, but simply observes the battle for a while. Weapons clash, magical energies explode, and general chaos is everywhere. Suddenly, Tzauhrag moves toward Pelagius and the Green-Eyed Man, who are dangerously close to Malferno's Canyon. A bewildered Adotiln watches as the oni strides right past her, and is rather insulted that her opponent ignores her.

As their swords clash, Pelagius and the Green-Eyed Man stare each other down. They both notice a shadow overtaking them and glance back to see Tzauhrag approaching. The massive oni is upon them remarkably quickly, swinging his kanabo in a sideways sweep through the air. Pelagius quickly drops to the ground, barely avoiding the strike. The Green-Eyed Man is not so lucky. He receives a direct hit and goes flying through the air, plummeting straight down the canyon.

Before Pelagius can react, Tzauhrag turns and charges another part of the battle. Pelagius rises and watches as Tzauhrag swings his kanabo and hits Slythrogg in the head. Slythrogg falls to the ground and before he can react, Tzauhrag brings the kanabo down upon him, crushing his skull completely. At the exact same time, Alithyra lets loose two arrows and brings down the banoks, but the actions of Tzauhrag immediately bring the rest of the fight to a halt. Without saying a word, Tzauhrag disappears into the trees. Surveying the scene, the remaining two defenders hastily retreat and Eeshlith, Shudgluv, and Glakchog flee back to the mountains. "What just happened?" asks Kevnan.

"I wish I knew," says Pelagius. "It seems that the oni had his own agenda."

"Or he was working for someone else," says Ralkgek.

"It doesn't matter either way," says Pelagius. "Back to the boats. We need to see what we can salvage. Hopefully we still have a day's worth of food and equipment."

The heroes return to the river and begin retrieving their scattered supplies as the captains emerge and survey the damage. Pelagius approaches the two hired halflings. "I'm sorry for your boats."

The first captain sighs. "They're not the first boats I've lost. With the amount you paid me, I should have all the funds I need for the supplies to rebuild."

The second captain nods. "In the meantime, we should be able to use the scraps to build a raft for the trip back."

The two halflings begin pulling some of the larger remaining pieces out of the river. Pelagius rejoins the others and they stack a few intact crates along the riverbank and start checking the items that fell in the water. After an hour, they have salvaged everything they can, including the remains of the two boats. The two captains begin lashing the wood together into a makeshift raft.

"Well, it's not very promising," says Pelagius, "but hopefully it will last until we can get to Ethor."

Iriemorel approaches Pelagius. "I'm afraid it's worse than you think."

"What's wrong?" asks Pelagius.

"While we were able to salvage enough supplies to reach Ethor, we weren't so fortunate with our food," replies Iriemorel. "The little we were able to scrounge was what landed on the shore. The rest was either ruined by the water, washed farther down the river, or stolen by scavenging kappas. We don't even have enough food to make it to Ethor. Unless...."

"Unless what?" asks Alithyra.

"The only other possible source of food we have here are the horses," says Iriemorel.

"Can't we go hunting?" asks Kevnan.

"No," replies Thakszut. "It's too close to nightfall."

"He's right," says Ralkgek. "The sun has already begun to set and hunting here after dark is extremely dangerous."

Pelagius thinks for a moment. "Very well. Get to it, then."

Iriemorel walks off and drags one of the horse corpses out of the river. He then begins the task of preparing it for cooking.

"We had better set up camp," says Ralkgek. "It will be getting dark soon. Tomorrow, we'll have to see if the captains left enough of the scraps to build our own raft."

The heroes then begin unpacking the remaining supplies and setting up camp for the night as the two captains begin navigating their raft back up the river. When he finishes his task, Iriemorel tosses the rest of the carcass into the river and begins packing the meat away. He then pulls another horse out of the water and repeats the process. When he finishes, he brings several chunks of meat into the camp, and after building a fire and a makeshift spit, begins roasting them.

"Unfortunately, we lost all of the herbs and spices in the river," says Iriemorel. "This meal may be somewhat bland because of that."

"I'm sure it will be fine," says Pelagius. "You've never let us down before. Even the Black Dog you prepared was delicious."

As Iriemorel continues to cook dinner, Pelagius helps to set up camp.

"Where are the tents?" asks Pelagius.

"Somewhere in the river," replies Kevnan. "We managed to find a few dry bedrolls, but only five. One fell in the river, but I've got it drying by the fire. And that's it for sleeping arrangements."

"Well then, until that one dries, we'll have to have three people on watch," says Pelagius.

The evening continues as the heroes go about their business. Several red-eyed ravens perch nearby to observe. The heroes enjoy their dinner in silence as the sun sets. Pelagius, Adotiln, and Ralkgek agree to take the first watch.

CHAPTER 59

The next day, the heroes stumble into Ethor, where several red-eyed ravens already perch on the rooftops. The hour is close to sunset, and they are clearly exhausted from an entire day of hauling their remaining supplies all the way to town.

"How much further?" asks Iriemorel, leaning on his maul for support.

"We must travel to the center of town," replies Ralkgek. "That is where Shukrat lives."

Two human guards wielding halberds approach.

"State your name and purpose," says the first guard.

"I am Ralkgek and these are my traveling companions. We wish to see the wise sorcerer known as Shukrat."

"I'm sorry, but that is not possible," says the second guard, "We have received orders that nobody is to see Shukrat without his approval."

"Who gave this order?" inquires Pelagius.

"Our superiors received the order from higher up," replies the first guard. "Without Shukrat's permission, we can't permit anyone asking to see him to enter town. Please leave and find lodging elsewhere."

Pelagius turns to Ralkgek. "Clearly this is the work of one of Babu's men."

Ralkgek nods in agreement and turns back to the guards. "What if we refuse?"

The guards shift into a more threatening stance, brandishing their weapons menacingly as several red-eyed ravens gather. "Then we will be forced to use any means necessary to prevent you from entering town."

"I do not wish to fight you," says Ralkgek. "I'm sure that we can work something out. Shukrat is an old friend of mine. I'm sure he would grant permission for you to admit us if he were here."

"But he is not here," says the second guard. "Now be on your way."

Ralkgek sighs. "Fine. If that's the way you want it."

Ralkgek reaches for his sword, but Pelagius stops him. "Don't. There must be another way."

"There is no other way," says Ralkgek. "Stay out of it if you wish, but I am getting us in no matter what."

Pelagius steps back. "I will have no part in this. Just don't kill them."

Ralkgek draws his sword as the guards advance. One guard swings his halberd downward, but a wooden staff halts his attack. An elderly goblin stands between the guard and Ralkgek. He is short for his species, stooped over due to his age. His skin has taken on a slightly lighter tone than that of a younger goblin, and his face appears ancient. He wears a tattered white sorcerer's robe.

"Viscount Shukrat!" exclaims the guard, surprised.

"Violence will not be necessary," says Shukrat. "If these people seek an audience with me, then they shall have one."

Ralkgek and the first guard back away, but the second guard retains his threatening stance.

"Stand down," says the first guard.

"No," says the second guard. "I have other orders."

"What other orders?" inquires the first guard.

"To ensure that nobody sees Shukrat at all," replies the second guard.

Before anyone can respond, the second guard lunges forward. He swings his halberd down toward Shukrat. To everyone's amazement, the elderly goblin catches it by the blade and stops the attack. "I'm sorry to do this, but you leave me no choice. Goodbye."

A brief flash emanates from Shukrat's hand. The light travels up the halberd and surrounds the guard, who screams as the light engulfs him and flashes brightly. The halberd and the guard's now empty armor clatter to the ground. All that remains of the treacherous guard is a fine ash that blows away in the wind.

"Will there be any more problems?" asks Shukrat.

"No, sir," says the guard. "They may pass."

Shukrat turns to the weary heroes. He looks at Ralkgek disdainfully. "You disappoint me. Picking a fight with a couple of guards because they wouldn't let you through."

"I'm sorry, old friend," says Ralkgek. "I shall use better judgment in the future."

"See that you do," says Shukrat. "Now, let us retire for the evening. Everyone, gather in a circle around me."

The heroes quickly form a circle around Shukrat. The elderly goblin closes his eyes and seems to enter a trance. Before any of them realize it, their surroundings change from the town's gate to that of a cozy living area in front of a lit fireplace.

Shukrat sits in a large cushy chair in front of the fire. "We can talk business tomorrow. For tonight, please rest. You will all need to regain your strength. I have guest rooms down the hall to your right with beds your size. Please sleep comfortably."

The heroes thank him and then turn to the indicated hall. As they enter the guest rooms, Shukrat closes his eyes and drifts off to sleep as well.

CHAPTER 60

Upon awakening, Pelagius and the others emerge from their chambers and return to the living room. There, they find Shukrat and Ralkgek drinking coffee and already engaged in conversation. Shukrat sees them enter.

"Ah, good morning," says Shukrat cheerfully. "Please help yourselves and have a seat."

Pelagius takes a cup and gets some coffee from the top of the wood-burning stove. He sits in a chair by Ralkgek and the others follow.

"Thank you," says Pelagius. "I suppose you probably know why we are here."

Shukrat nods. "Ralkgek has already explained the situation. I believe I may be able to help in some ways."

"Can you teleport us into the fortress?" asks Kevnan.

"No," replies Shukrat. "Nor can I open a portal to the inside. I have never been inside of Devil's Den. Even for someone of my abilities, using transport magic to get to a location that I have not even seen is too dangerous to attempt. The potential consequences of such an action are far too deadly to even attempt it."

"What can you do?" asks Iriemorel.

"I can help you plot a route to the fortress, and I can provide you with a quick means of escape," replies Shukrat.

"Have you seen the outside of the fortress?" inquires Alithyra. "If so, then couldn't you just teleport us to the edge of the wall?"

"I have never gone anywhere near Devil's Den," says Shukrat. "If I were to attempt such a feat, you could re-materialize in the masonry. I have personally witnessed the outcome of such a blunder, and I can promise you that it is not a pleasant way to die."

"We must approach on foot anyway," says Thakszut. "Commander Charndergh has set up permanent magical detection along the outer wall. Any attempt to get near the fortress by means of magic will instantly be noticed, which will result in Babu's entire defense force coming down upon us."

"What was your plan for getting in?" asks Shukrat. "You will not be able to enter through the main gate."

Pelagius chuckles. "Thakszut has suggested that we enter through Manthysbia's lair."

"His lair is unguarded aside from him," says Shukrat. "Of course, that is an extremely dangerous point of entry."

"It's the only option," says Thakszut. "Other than the gate, the only way in is through there."

Shukrat thinks for a moment. "Well, if you must, you must. However, I advise you not to engage Manthysbia. He is an old and powerful dragon that could possibly be more than a match for even Babu."

"Then we should slip in while Manthysbia is sleeping or out," says Iriemorel. "Do you know his routine, Thakszut?"

"Unless Babu has a task for him, he is rarely ever out, except for a brief period at night to hunt," replies Thakszut. "However, he sleeps for the majority of the day."

"How brief of an excursion are we talking about?" asks Ralkgek.

"An hour," says Thakszut. "Maybe less, depending on how long it takes for him to find his prey and bring it back. Unfortunately, the exact time he goes hunting is not consistent. He goes out at a different time every night with no discernible pattern."

"Then a daytime raid appears to be the best option," says Pelagius. "We will just have to make absolutely sure that we do not wake him. Where does the passage in his lair lead?"

"It leads into the dungeon," says Thakszut.

"I suppose we should start planning the raid and get started," says Iriemorel.

"There will be time for that later," says Shukrat. "Right now, you need to rest and resupply. I have something for you that I need to work on before you depart. The project I have in mind requires at least two days' time."

"It is true that we must resupply," says Pelagius, "but we must get started as soon as possible. The longer we delay, the more innocent souls we endanger."

Shukrat sighs. Then he turns and smacks Pelagius in the head with his staff. "Think for a moment. Currently, Babu is more focused on defense. He is not going to waste potential defensive resources by sending out a massive soul hunting party. He won't attack us either. He wouldn't dare risk the wrath of King Demonicus by bringing harm upon me or the citizens of this town. Now, rest and regain your strength, or you will fail."

"As you wish," says Pelagius, rubbing the lump on his head. "There is one other thing. Do you know anything about these ravens that have been following us? A druid told us that they had an aura of pestilence."

"I've noticed them around here even before you arrived," says Shukrat. "I have seen the phenomenon before. If they have an aura of pestilence, then they may be the servants of a powerful carcinomancer."

Kevnan's eyes grow wide. "That's not good. Why would a carcinomancer be interested in us?"

"Unfortunately, I have no answer for that," says Shukrat. "All I can say is, we have no idea if this carcinomancer is an ally or an enemy, so stay alert. Now, I believe you need to go purchase supplies."

"You are correct," says Pelagius.

The heroes depart to find more supplies, but Thakszut remains behind. As he stares into the fireplace, Shukrat comes up behind him. "Why did you not go with the others?"

"Even with the shapeshifting powers that Bojan gave me, the townspeople will not be fooled," replies Thakszut. "And since my service to the Green-Eyed Man is no secret, I'm certain I would not be welcome here."

"I see. Well, although I do have some work to do, I think there is something I must do for you first."

"What is that?"

"In order for you to survive the coming challenges, we must unlock your Demonic Potential. I have enough experience with demonfolk to be able to do that."

"I thought that Bojan already did that when he granted me my shapeshifting powers."

Shukrat shakes his head. "No. All he did was cast a spell that granted you the ability to shapeshift and then performed a ritual to extend the spell's duration. I would like to help you unlock your true Demonic Potential."

"Will I become a monster like Nyogsutt?" inquires Thakszut.

"What happened with him?"

Thakszut tells him everything he knows about Nyogsutt's power and actions.

"From what you have told me, it was likely that Kragus did something else aside from unlocking Nyogsutt's Potential," says Shukrat. "He may have performed a ritual that buried Nyogsutt's goodness deep within him, allowing his dark side to take over for a time. Simply unleashing your true power should not have that effect."

"Will my Demonic Potential manifest the same way his did?" asks Thakszut.

Shukrat thinks for a moment. "It's possible that it may manifest in a similar manner. However, in my experience, every Potential has been unique. No two demons have ever had the exact same powers. Some have been similar, but never identical."

Thakszut ponders the offer for several minutes. "Very well. I accept your offer."

Shukrat approaches Thakszut and places his hand on Thakszut's head. He then closes his eyes and begins to concentrate. "Great power within, hear my call. Awaken and reveal yourself." Suddenly, Thakszut glows and a mysterious wind blows through the house. Then, all is still and silent and the light surrounding Thakszut fades away. Shukrat opens his eyes and removes his hand from Thakszut's head. "Now, concentrate. Find the power within yourself and activate it."

Thakszut closes his eyes and begins to meditate. After several minutes, he grows to twice the size of a large gorilla and his color changes from red to white.

Thakszut opens his eyes in amazement. "Incredible! The power I feel is amazing."

Shukrat smiles. "I know something even more amazing. I have, of course, seen both you and Nyogsutt from afar. With my abilities, I am able to peer inside a demonfolk and view the Demonic Potential within. While Nyogsutt's power was impressive, yours is at least twice as powerful."

"What did you say?" asks Thakszut, shocked.

"You heard me," replies Shukrat. "If you had access to your Demonic Potential when you fought him, you would have defeated Nyogsutt easily within seconds."

Thakszut remains silent, stunned by this revelation. He then reverts to his original form.

"There are some limitations, of course," says Shukrat. "You can't remain in that form for very long. At least not right now. Also, you can't use your shapeshifting powers while your Demonic Potential is active."

"Thank you, Shukrat," says Thakszut. "Thank you for everything."

Shukrat smiles. Then, he turns to leave and enters his workshop to begin the project he mentioned earlier.

CHAPTER 61

Pelagius, Iriemorel, and Kevnan are loading the new supplies into a modified cart that is able to traverse swampland. As the others pitch in, Shukrat approaches Pelagius. "I have something for you. Something for each of you, in fact."

Shukrat produces seven small blue spheres.

"What are these?" asks Kevnan.

"Portal spheres," replies Shukrat. "If you need to escape from Devil's Den quickly, just throw them on the ground and a portal leading back here will open up. I have made one for each of you in case you get separated. Also, the portal created from one of these spheres will only stay open for a short time. If you need to use one, enter quickly. I could have made more if you had been willing to wait a few more days."

"These should do fine," says Pelagius. "Thank you."

Shukrat hands out the spheres. "Before you depart, I have a word of warning. The Kappa Marsh is a dangerous place. Like any other swamp, it is filled with many hazards."

"Is there something specific we should be looking for?" asks Ralkgek.

"Yes," replies Shukrat. "Rumor has it that a large deinosuchus has been spotted in the marshes recently."

The heroes glance at each other nervously.

"Thanks for the warning," says Pelagius. "We will proceed with extreme caution."

"Wait," says Shukrat. "There is more."

"I hope it's good news," says Iriemorel.

"Unfortunately, no," says Shukrat. "There is also a rumor that a group of slavers have been operating nearby. It is quite possible that they have been camping in the marsh."

Pelagius looks at the others. "We'll have to be sure to avoid them."

The others nod in agreement. Later, after some words of farewell, the heroes climb into the cart. Pelagius takes the reins and gets the horse moving. Shukrat watches as they depart from Ethor and travel down the road toward the swamp.

CHAPTER 62

The heroes slowly trudge through the Kappa Marsh. Water covers nearly the entire area, with only patches of soggy land dotting the landscape. Trees grow both on patches of land and in the water. The humidity is nearly overwhelming, and the heroes sweat profusely as they travel. The air is thick with flies and mosquitos, and leeches wriggle in small pools of water. Every once in a while, a meganeura, a massive dragonfly with a wingspan of two and a half feet, flies by.

"What a miserable place," says Ralkgek. "The mosquitoes are eating us alive."

"Enough complaining," says Pelagius. "We have already established that this is the quickest route. If we must suffer a little on the way, then so be it."

"We're not suffering a little," says Ralkgek under his breath.

The heroes continue their journey. After a few more hours, they stumble upon a somewhat dry, recently used clearing, surrounded by red-eyed ravens roosting in the trees. Several large tents encircle a smoldering campfire. Charred bones of some recently eaten meal litter the ground. Scattered about the site are a variety of weapons and other tools, including several sets of manacles and empty cages of all sizes.

Pelagius freezes in alarm. "This could be a problem. I believe that we may have found the slavers' encampment. Back up slowly. It would be best if we slipped around this area."

They all begin to slowly and quietly reverse their steps. As he backs up, Thakszut accidentally slips and sets his foot in the water, making a slight splashing sound. Everyone freezes as though expecting the slavers to charge in and attack at any moment. However, nothing seems to happen.

"Be careful," whispers Kevnan.

"Sorry," whispers Thakszut.

Suddenly, the water behind Thakszut explodes and a massive set of jaws, nearly eight feet long and attached to an enormous crocodile-like head, emerges from the water. The creature extends half of its body, roughly twenty-five feet in length, out of the water. Thakszut attempts to jump out of the way, but he falls dead center into the creature's mouth, and its jaws rapidly snap shut with a loud bang. The creature briefly drags itself out of the water before it slips back in and disappears into the depths. The sight stuns the others into a brief silence.

"What was that?" asks Alithyra.

"I think that was the deinosuchus we were warned about," replies Kevnan.

Pelagius is shaking with grief and rage. "No, not Thakszut! I can't believe we lost him."

"I wouldn't worry about that right now," says a mysterious voice.

Alarmed, the heroes draw their weapons. Suddenly, they find themselves surrounded by twenty individuals. Fifteen of them are human and the other five are dwarves. Each brandishes obviously lethal weaponry and some hold weapons meant for taking captives. Roughly half wear flowing robes indicating that they are mages.

Alithyra's eyes widen, her hair stands on end, and she bares her teeth. "The slavers!"

The others begin to move in to attack, but Pelagius waves them down.

"Don't," says Pelagius. "There are too many of them. If we try to fight, we will all die."

"But if we don't fight, we'll be sold into slavery," says Iriemorel.

Ralkgek looks around, sizing up each slaver. "If we fight, we'll be annihilated. There are ten sorcerers here. We won't stand a chance."

Pelagius nods. "Let's surrender for now. We can figure out how to escape later."

"Your courage is failing you again, Pelagius," says Iriemorel. "We should fight."

Pelagius shakes his head. "There is a great difference between courage and overconfidence. Even the greatest champions of valor should know when not to fight. We surrender. That is my decision."

The others reluctantly agree, and most lower their arms. Iriemorel stands firm, but finally concedes as well. "Fine. I see your point."

The largest of the slavers, obviously the leader, steps forward. "Excellent choice. A fight would not have ended well for any of you. Now you will come with us."

Some of the other slavers come forward and disarm the heroes. They then bind them with manacles and load them into the cages. Ralkgek and Adotiln's manacles glow when locked.

"What are these?" asks Ralkgek.

"Mage restrainers," replies one of the slavers. "We know you are well versed in magic and that she is a priestess. We are not taking any chances."

"All right, men, let's move out!" shouts the leader. "We need to get away from that deinosuchus. Plus, these ravens are giving me the creeps."

Three or four slavers lift each cage and they follow their leader deeper into the marsh. A few minutes later, the water by the abandoned campground explodes again and the deinosuchus slams onto the dry ground. It appears to be struggling to keep its massive jaws shut and thrashes from side to side. Suddenly, something from within forces its jaws open; Thakszut, now in his giant white monkey form, holds the massive maw wide. He steps out, releasing the bottom jaw from the grasp of his feet. However, before the deinosuchus can bite down on his upper body, he releases the grip of one of his hands from the upper jaw and catches it.

He continues to struggle against the mighty jaws of the deino-suchus as he barely manages to hold its jaws open. Suddenly, his muscles bulge and his hair turns light gray. With a sudden burst of strength, he wrenches the jaws back open with a sickening snap. He releases his grip from the lower jaw as he folds the upper jaw backward beyond its natural range of movement. Its jaw practically destroyed, the massive animal collapses. When Thakszut releases its broken jaw, it slips back into the water and sinks into the depths. With a heavy sigh, Thakszut returns to his natural form. "Where did everybody go?"

Thakszut scours the campsite. After a couple of minutes, he finds the indentions where the cages were, and the footprints left by the slavers. He then follows the tracks, staying well clear of the water's edge by jumping through the trees alongside the path.

Chapter 63

Thakszut tracks the slavers deep into the marsh. Finally, after a few hours of traversing the trees and undergrowth, he spots another large, semi-dry clearing. As luck would have it, the slavers have set up camp here. Thakszut climbs into the treetops to avoid the sentries' line of sight while cautiously trying not to stir up the ravens, and stealthily makes his way around the camp.

After observing the campground and avoiding the detection of the eight lookouts, he determines that there are about twelve slavers here in addition to the ones standing guard in the trees. He quietly sneaks up behind the guard closest to him. Once he has gotten close enough, he uses his shapeshifting powers to transform into a massive green snake. Before the guard realizes what is happening, Thakszut wraps himself around the guard's throat and tenses his muscles to constrict. He squeezes and squeezes, tightening his grip as the guard struggles for air until the unlucky slaver slips into unconsciousness and ceases to move. Thakszut wedges him between two large branches, and after changing back, ties him up with several large vines. Thakszut also manages to catch the guard's weapon, a massive spear, before it can hit the ground.

"That's one down," whispers Thakszut. "If I can take out the rest, I shouldn't have a problem getting into the camp."

Thakszut stealthily moves through the trees toward the next closest guard. As he comes up behind him, he accidentally breaks a small twig. The guard reacts to the snapping sound and turns in his direction. Reacting quickly, Thakszut throws the spear and leaps higher into the trees. The guard turns just in time for the spear to hit him in the stomach. The force of Thakszut's throw is powerful enough that the spear head emerges from his back. The guard grunts in pain, but before he can cry out, Thakszut is upon him in the form of a large green serpent. He coils around the wounded guard's throat and chokes him just like the last one. Realizing that this one will likely die from the wound, Thakszut quietly lowers him out of the tree and into the waters of the swamp. The body quickly sinks from view.

"That was too close," whispers Thakszut to himself. "I need to be more careful."

Thakszut returns to the trees and resumes stalking the remaining guards.

CHAPTER 64

Pelagius and the others sit in their cages, shackled and bound. Pelagius is deep in thought.

"So, what is your plan for escaping?" asks Ralkgek. "If it involves my magical abilities, then we've already failed."

"I'm thinking," says Pelagius. "Don't worry, I'll come up with something."

"Hurry," says Alithyra. "If you don't come up with a plan soon, we will all be sold into slavery."

"I think we have a couple of days," says Pelagius. "If they were done hunting for slaves, they'd be taking us to the slave market already. The fact that we are still here means that they're still looking to capture more. My guess is that they are planning a raid on a nearby village."

"How do you know?" asks Iriemorel.

"That's actually fairly standard for slavers," says Kevnan. "My previous group had encountered a few slave traders. They would remain in one area until all of their cages were full and then they would transport their catch to the slave market."

"I've heard about the raids," says Adotiln, "but I didn't know there was a slave market on this continent."

"For the most part, there isn't," says Pelagius. "At least not a legal one in most kingdoms. However, the Necrotian Empire, Barbiconia, and Battallia all have some form of legalized slavery."

One of the slavers walks over to them. "Quiet over here! No unauthorized chatter between slaves! If I have to come over here again, somebody will get a merciless beating."

The slaver walks away. The captured heroes wait a few moments before resuming their conversation.

"So then how do we escape?" asks Adotiln.

"Well," says Pelagius, "if one of us could somehow pick the locks, then that person could free Ralkgek, assuming it wasn't Ralkgek to begin with. If he can catch them off guard, he should be able to eliminate the sorcerers in quick succession."

"Great," says Ralkgek, "so does anybody know how to pick locks?"

The others just stare blankly. At that point, the slaver guarding them comes back over.

"I warned you!" shouts the slaver. "I guess I'll just have to make an example of someone. Perhaps the old man."

The slaver grabs onto Pelagius's cage and begins to drag it toward the trees. When he gets to the tree line, he stops and begins to unlock Pelagius's door. Suddenly, a massive white-haired hand shoots out of the trees, grabs the slaver, and pulls him into the brush. The sounds of a struggle ensue, attracting the attention of the remaining eleven men and causing them to investigate. The noises stop as they arrive.

"What was that?" asks the leader, looking at Pelagius.

Pelagius shrugs. Then the unconscious or lifeless body of the slaver comes flying out of the underbrush. He bounces off Pelagius's cage and continues through the air for a few more yards, landing on top of Ralkgek's cage. The slavers ready their weapons for battle, but none will approach the tree line.

"Come out of there, coward!" shouts the leader.

Suddenly, seven spears come flying out one after the other. Each spear hits a different slaver, killing three instantly and fatally wounding four others. A giant white monkey leaps from the trees and lands between two of the remaining slavers. Towering over them, he grabs them by their heads and slams them into each other, causing a loud crunch to fill the air. The giant white monkey tosses their limp bodies aside and turns to the leader. The leader looks around at the carnage.

"If you want them, you can have them," says the leader.

He pulls a small white ball out of his pocket and throws it to the ground. It explodes in a blinding flash and when everyone's vision clears, the slaver is gone. The giant white monkey returns to his true form. To everybody's amazement, it is Thakszut.

"You're alive?!" says Pelagius. "How? We saw the deinosuchus eat you."

Thakszut searches through the pockets of a few slavers, extracting a set of keys. "I'll explain later."

A few minutes later, the heroes have all been freed. Pelagius looks around nervously as the sun begins to set. "We should move on."

"Move on?" says Iriemorel. "But it will be dark soon. We need to set up camp."

"We will have to find another place to camp," says Pelagius. "If we stay here, we will be captured again for certain."

"Why?" asks Alithyra.

"Twenty is a small group, especially for a raiding party," says Pelagius. "My guess is that there is a much larger force somewhere nearby and the leader left for reinforcements. If we stay here, then we could potentially have over one hundred more experienced slavers bearing down upon us. If we continue, then we are less likely to encounter the main group."

The others think for a moment.

"I agree with Pelagius," says Kevnan. "If we were to encounter the main attack force of a raiding party, there is no possible way that we could win."

"Then we move on," says Ralkgek.

They then gather up all their supplies, equipment, and weapons and leave the clearing. They continue forward toward their destination.

Chapter 65

Back in the mountains, Glakchog is on watch duty. He sits by a well-made campfire, sharpening his hookswords with a smooth stone, warily eyeing a red-eyed raven perched on a nearby rock. He slowly lifts his head up and glances at a rocky outcrop behind him. Glakchog shakes his head and rolls his eyes. "I know you're there, Brelgvu. Come out. The others are asleep."

A small demon steps from behind the rocks. Although humanoid in shape, he is about the size of a spider monkey, complete with long, slender limbs, a slender body, and a long and thin tail with a wickedly curved barb on the end. He has claws on his hands and feet, a set of horns on his head, and bright red skin.

"What do you want, imp?" asks Glakchog.

"Is that any way to treat an old friend?" asks Brelgvu. "I sense that you are troubled. What is on your mind?"

"Why should I tell you?" asks Glakchog. "Whenever I express concern about anything, you just belittle me."

Brelgvu walks up to Glakchog and places his hand reassuringly on his shoulder. "Because I'm the only one you can ever truly confide in. Remember, your so-called friends would think you were weak if you were to ever tell them what you tell me. I am tough on you to make you stronger."

Brelgvu grins wickedly as Glakchog emits a weary sigh.

"I know I'm a good soldier," says Glakchog.

"You're not a good soldier," says Brelgvu. "You're a great soldier. Almost a perfect soldier."

"Then why do I feel this way? The more I think about it, the more I feel that the others may be right. Have I really been doing the right thing all these years? The atrocities I alone have committed under his orders are more horrible than anything I have seen in any war."

"The others are weak. Their constitution is pathetic. Only poor soldiers question the orders of their superiors. You surprise me with these thoughts. Think not of these so-called atrocities. You were following orders without question like a good soldier would. A true soldier would not be fazed by such sights."

"I have never met a soldier yet who was not conflicted about something."

"And you are conflicted about the missions you have done for the Green-Eyed Man?"

Glakchog nods. "I have taken so many lives in order for him to collect the souls. Most of them were civilians. The only military presence has been town guards. I want to be the best soldier I can, but following orders like that goes against any military code, especially since we are not at war."

Brelgvu looks at Glakchog and thinks for a moment. "You disappoint me. I thought you were an excellent soldier, but it seems I was wrong. You are pathetic. To question your commanding officer in such a way is practically treason. Perhaps you no longer wish to rise to the next level."

"You're wrong," says Glakchog. "I want nothing more than to reach the next level."

"Then think hard about the path you wish to take," says Brelgvu. "If you tread any farther down this road that your friends have pointed you to, there will be no turning back. That road will strip away your soldier's pride and you will never become the perfect soldier."

Glakchog sighs. "All right. I will bury my conscience deep within me, and I will no longer question any order."

Brelgvu grins malevolently. "Excellent. Perhaps there is hope for you yet. Before I go, there is one more thing."

"What is that?" asks Glakchog.

"Eeshlith and Shudgluv have been plotting," says Brelgvu. "They plan to betray you and the Green-Eyed Man at some point in the future. You see, your friends are pathetically poor soldiers. A true soldier never turns on their superiors while their commanding officer still lives."

"Should I expose their plot to the Green-Eyed Man?"

"No. You will need proof of their plot, and I do not intend to reveal myself as a witness."

"Then what should I do?"

"Well, poor soldiers always hold back the great ones. You cannot reach the next level while they live. Bide your time and wait for the right moment. When that moment comes, strike them down before they can do the same to you. If done correctly, it will appear as though your enemies did the deed. Once they are dead, there will be nothing to stop you from achieving your goal."

Eeshlith shifts in her tent.

"I had better depart before they wake up," whispers Brelgvu.

The evil imp then disappears into the shadows.

CHAPTER 66

Babu is sitting on his throne, distractedly writing on parchment and agitatedly eyeing the ravens perched around the chamber, when one of his servants enters and bows.

"Forgive the intrusion, master," says the servant.

"What is it?" asks Babu. "Can't you see I'm busy here."

"The mercenary you hired is here. He seeks an audience with you."

Babu rolls up the scroll, sets it aside, and leans forward on his throne. "Only one?"

"Yes, master. He says it's important."

Babu looks at Gulvgrum before addressing the servant again. "Send him in."

The servant departs and Gulvgrum turns to Babu. "Does this trouble you, master?"

"We were told that there is only one mercenary," replies Babu. "We hired more than that. I suppose we shall have to see what news he brings."

The door to the throne room opens and the leader of the slavers steps through. He walks halfway to the throne and bows.

"Where are your men?" asks Babu.

"Forgive me, my lord," says the slaver. "They are dead. We failed to complete the mission."

Gulvgrum advances angrily toward the slaver, but Babu waves him down.

Babu rises from his throne and approaches the slaver. "How disappointing. Tell me, how did you bungle such a simple task? All you had to do was surround them. With your superior numbers, you should have been able to capture them easily, and then bring them to me. How did they defeat you?"

The slaver gulps nervously. "We did manage to capture them after a deinosuchus distracted them by eating the fiendling, but a giant white monkey attacked our camp."

Babu pauses as he takes in this news. "A giant white monkey?"

"Yes," says the slaver. "Despite its size, it somehow stealthily eliminated the guards and then took down the others with ease. I barely escaped myself."

Babu turns to Gulvgrum, a knowing look in his eyes. "So, it seems that Thakszut has unlocked his Demonic Potential."

"That could be problematic for us, master," says Gulvgrum, "You've seen the potential within him. His true power is unheard of among demonfolk."

"We will have to modify our plan. Inform the internal defense squad to prepare for a powerful demon."

Gulvgrum passes the slaver and exits the room. Babu turns back to address his failed minion. "It seems that your failure was not without its upside. Now we have information that could prove vital to our defenses."

The slaver breathes a sigh of relief. "So, shall I get reinforcements? With double the numbers, we can easily complete the mission."

Babu grins and motions to the slaver to stand. The slaver rises as Babu glares at him.

"That won't be necessary," says Babu.

"I promise you, my lord," says the slaver. "We will not fail this time."

Babu's grin turns to a scowl. "Your services are no longer required."

The slaver's eyes grow wide with horror as Babu's massive hand wraps around his throat. The slaver grabs at Babu's paw but is unable to free himself from the evil norodrian's clutches.

Babu's free hand lunges forward and his claws plunge into the slaver's chest. With impressively fast motions, Babu does two things at once. He rapidly flexes his wrist at the slaver's throat and viciously snaps his neck. At the same time, he rips out a blue haze from the slaver's chest. He releases his grip and the slaver drops lifelessly to the floor; Babu devours his soul and returns to his throne. A few minutes later, Gulvgrum returns and surveys the crumpled heap on the floor before bowing to Babu.

"Your orders have been carried out, master," says Gulvgrum. "A demon with powers to match Thakszut's will join our defenses."

"Did you have a specific demon in mind?" asks Babu.

"Yes, master," replies Gulvgrum. "Basmorg."

"Excellent," says Babu. "Now, dispose of that before it stinks up my throne room."

"As you wish, master," says Gulvgrum.

"When you're done with that, send in the next audience seeker."

Gulvgrum drags the lifeless slaver out of the room as Babu returns to his thoughts.

CHAPTER 67

Several days later, Pelagius and the others have left the swamp behind and now hide in a grove of trees close by Devil's Den. The infamous fortress is vast in size and intimidating to behold. The walls surrounding the massive castle are nearly thirty feet high with watchtowers spaced apart every ten feet. The wall itself stretches farther than the eye can see in both directions and a large, black, spiked castle stretches into the sky beyond it. The main gate looks like a massive maw of teeth surrounding the doorway. Two guards constantly patrol each section of the wall and at least one stands on top of each watchtower. The heroes eye the wall nervously.

"So how do we get in?" asks Kevnan.

"I already told you," replies Thakszut. "We need to sneak around to the entrance to Manthysbia's lair."

"There aren't enough trees for us to remain concealed without going deeper into the swamp," says Alithyra. "The only way to do this without being spotted is to go along the wall."

"It's impossible to sneak up to that wall without being seen," says Ralkgek. "There are too many guards."

"They have to change the guards sometime," says Pelagius. "That is when they will be less vigilant."

"The guards should be changing within an hour or so," says Thakszut. "If we time it right, we can make our move without being seen."

Iriemorel glances up and then quickly ducks down in alarm. "Quiet. Look on top of the gate."

The others look in the indicated direction and see a fearful sight. Standing on top of the gate is a green-skinned demon. His appearance is similar to that of a daemon, although larger and more monstrous in appearance. He has a pair of bat-like wings on his back, massive claws, large horns on his head, and a long tail with a nasty-looking stinger on the end.

"That must be Commander Charndergh," says Kevnan. "I didn't expect the commander to be a daemon."

"He's not a daemon," says Ralkgek. "He is a devilspawn."

"So Babu has True Demons under his employ as well?" asks Kevnan.

"That would appear to be the case," says Pelagius.

Iriemorel turns to Thakszut. "Something you forgot to tell us?"

"I swear I didn't know," says Thakszut. "I have never personally seen Commander Charndergh before. I always avoid the barracks, and I've never been allowed on the wall."

"What are we going to do?" asks Adotiln. "True Demons are natives of Malferno. We can't possibly defeat one."

"If we do this right, we won't have to fight him," says Pelagius.

"I'm hoping we don't," says Ralkgek. "Even the weakest devilspawn could be more than a match for us."

"We'll discuss it later," says Pelagius. "Right now, we need to be quiet so he doesn't hear us. We will wait until he leaves before we sneak up to the wall."

The heroes silently watch Commander Charndergh and the guards on the wall. After several hours pass and at least two guard changes occur, the commander remains at his post as night falls. The moon is full, and a sliver of red appears on one side.

"So much for a daytime assault," says Iriemorel.

Pelagius nods. "We'll just have to modify our plan."

Charndergh continues his watch for a few more hours, and the red sliver on the moon continues to grow. Finally, when the moon is half covered in red, Charndergh leaves his post. Shortly after, the guards begin to change again.

"Now," whispers Pelagius. "The eclipse should help mask us in additional shadows."

Without another word, the group quietly rushes up to the wall and presses up against it. They then begin to slowly inch their way along the wall, remaining pressed firmly against it and being as quiet as possible. They occasionally pause and listen nervously as the guards move around above them.

After what feels like uncountable hours, they can see the wall's edge. As they continue to inch their way toward it, a loud booming reverberates from atop the wall. The sound continues and seems to be getting closer until it is right above them. Just as they round the corner, they hear another loud noise. Curiously, they peek around and see that a large oni has jumped off the wall and now patrols the grounds just outside the fortress.

They duck around the corner as the oni turns in their direction and hold fast against the wall, silent and terrified as they hear the beast's booming footsteps coming closer. The sound stops just around the corner and they hear the demon breathing and grunting. Several minutes pass without anyone making a sound. Then, the oni grunts and its booming footsteps resume. However, instead of coming around the corner, they now seem to be getting farther away.

Pelagius nervously peeks around and sees the oni heading in the other direction. He motions to the others to continue and they resume inching their way along the wall until they reach a massive cave opening. An eerie wind blows across the opening and steam rises from the hole. Above, no guards patrol the wall, and the guard towers here are beginning to crumble.

"This area isn't guarded at all," says Kevnan.

"Of course not," says Thakszut. "This is the entrance to Manthysbia's lair. Babu feels no need to have this section patrolled."

"So how are we going to do this?" asks Ralkgek.

"If Manthysbia is out, it will be easy," says Pelagius. "We can just go in and follow Thakszut to the entrance. If he is home, then we'll have to sneak around him while he sleeps."

"Let's hope he is asleep when we enter," says Thakszut. "If we walk in on him when he is awake, we won't stand a chance. If he wakes up while we are there, we can easily hide until he goes back to sleep or leaves. Anyway, if everyone is ready, then follow me."

When nobody objects, Thakszut enters the cave opening. The others follow down a ramp-like slope on the ground. After walking for several minutes, they go through another opening and enter a massive cavern. Mountains of gold and other treasures glistening and glowing brightly fill the entire space.

Curled up on a pile of gold in the center of the cavern is a sleeping dragon of massive proportions. The heroes duck behind mounds of treasure and survey the scene. Thakszut motions for everyone to follow and they begin to quietly make their way around to the other side of the cave. Suddenly, Iriemorel trips on a small statue and he crashes loudly into a pile of gold. The others rapidly duck behind various large treasures as Manthysbia's eyes shoot open. Iriemorel quickly buries himself in gold just as Manthysbia glances in his direction. The dragon surveys the cavern and stands. He takes a couple of steps forward and his massive foot stomps down just inches from Iriemorel's hiding place. The others silently quiver behind their mounds, dreading what may happen next.

"Who goes there?!" asks Manthysbia, his booming voice echoing through the cave.

He pauses as though waiting for an answer. "I know that someone is here. There is no point in hiding. I'll find you eventually."

Manthysbia then begins searching his cave. He turns over large statues and checks behind and under piles of treasure. He nearly steps on Iriemorel again, coming within less than an inch of him. Manthysbia stops and looks down at the pile of gold that the dwarf has concealed himself in. He lowers his head to inspect more closely. He eyes the pile suspiciously and sniffs the area. He moves his massive paw forward and begins to move gold and treasure aside. Suddenly, Thakszut throws a small stone statue into the tunnel, quickly returning to his hiding place. The statue shatters as it hits the ground, causing the sound to echo down the tunnel. Manthysbia quickly snaps his head up and looks down the tunnel.

"You won't escape so easily," says Manthysbia.

The dragon then charges down the tunnel. He spreads his wings and flies out of the cave, quickly vanishing from sight. The terrified heroes emerge from their hiding places.

"That was too close," says Pelagius. "Try to be more careful next time."

"I am very sorry," says Iriemorel.

"We can settle this later," says Thakszut, nervously eying the tunnel. "We must move on before he comes back. It won't be long before he figures out that he was tricked."

The heroes make their way to the back of the cave, following Thakszut. Using his shapeshifting powers, Thakszut takes on his gorilla form. He pushes aside a large boulder to reveal a door, behind which is a passageway leading up. When they glance back to make sure that Manthysbia is still out, they see the moon is now completely red. The heroes enter the passageway and Thakszut closes it up behind him. Manthysbia returns seconds after Thakszut closes the gap.

Chapter 68

Tohirata enters his master's throne room. He approaches the throne and, dropping to one knee, bows. Scirrhus leans forward into the light, revealing his frightful appearance. This sickly-looking creature is barely discernible as human as he is extremely emaciated with pasty skin covered in weeping sores and long, scraggly, greasy, matted black hair. Sunken cheeks accentuate his expressionless face and he shows no emotion as his unblinking, bloodshot yellow eyes stare at his minion.

"Rise," says Scirrhus. "What have you to report, Tohirata?"

Tohirata rises to his feet. "My spies have informed me that Pelagius and his followers have entered Devil's Den. They now fight for their lives."

"Excellent," says Scirrhus. "Everything has gone as expected and events have been set into motion that cannot be stopped."

"Shall we interfere with the battle, Master?"

"No. We must let this play out as fate sees fit. Either outcome will be beneficial to my plans. For now, we must turn our attention elsewhere."

"Yes, Lord Scirrhus."

Tohirata exits the chamber as the mysterious Scirrhus leans back in his dingy throne.

CHAPTER 69

The heroes emerge in a large circular stone chamber. The entire room is bare except for seven doors on one side, guarded by a cloaked figure.

Thakszut looks around, puzzled. "This is new."

"What do you mean?" asks Ralkgek. "How can this be new?"

"I don't know," says Thakszut. "That passage normally leads to the dungeon. I've never seen this room before."

"This is no normal room," says the cloaked figure. "You stand in an area between the realms. Only the doors lead out."

"Let me guess," says Pelagius. "Only one door is the real one, the others are traps, and we have to guess which one is real."

"Wrong," says the cloaked figure. "They are all real. Each door leads to a different location in Devil's Den. However, each door can be used only once, and only one may pass through at a time."

The heroes glance nervously at each other.

"So, I guess we divide and conquer?" asks Iriemorel.

"We're stronger together than apart," says Kevnan. "It would be best if we didn't separate."

Pelagius nods. "Agreed." He returns his attention to the figure. "How do we know you're telling the truth and that six of the doors aren't traps?"

The mysterious entity shrugs. "You don't. You'll just have to take my word and pick your doors. Either that, or you can stand in this room for eternity and starve to death. It's your decision."

Pelagius sighs and glances at the others. "I don't think we have a choice. We have to play Babu's game for now."

They turn back to the figure.

"So how does this work?" asks Ralkgek.

"Simple," replies the cloaked figure. "We will do this in an orderly fashion. I will select one of you, and the chosen individual will pick a door. Once that person has gone through, that door will vanish, and I will select the next person."

"Who is going first?" asks Thakszut.

The cloaked figure scans the room and points at Pelagius. "You shall go first."

Pelagius steps forward and examines the doors. "I choose the third from the right."

"Excellent choice," says the cloaked figure.

Pelagius steps forward as the figure opens the door. He goes through and sure enough the door vanishes, leaving only a wall in its place. Pelagius finds himself standing alone in a reddish-black stone hallway in front of a large wooden door reinforced with metal bands. He reaches out to the door handle and grasps it firmly.

"I guess this is it," says Pelagius to himself.

Pelagius opens the door and finds himself in Babu's throne room. As he walks to the center of the room, he sees Babu sitting on the throne, reading an unfurled scroll, flanked by Gulvgrum.

Seeing Pelagius approach, Babu scowls and rolls up the scroll and sets it aside. "So, Pelagius, you picked the door leading here. I knew that one of you would arrive here immediately, but I must admit that I was not expecting it to be you. It will be a real treat to personally watch you die."

Pelagius draws his sword and readies his shield. "I will not be dying here today. I have come to end your reign of terror, Babu. Step forward and face me; if you're not afraid."

Babu glares at Pelagius as he crushes a nearby raven. "I do not fear you, old man. However, you have to get through Gulvgrum in order to face me."

Gulvgrum turns and grabs two weapons off the wall. A large infernal steel bastard sword and a massive morningstar. Gulvgrum turns to Babu.

"If I must defeat your bodyguard first, then so be it," says Pelagius.

"As you wish," says Babu. "Gulvgrum, finish him slowly."

Gulvgrum steps down from beside the throne and approaches the lone hero. Pelagius stands firm as this large demonkin with two menacing deadly weapons draws near, wondering if he can possibly defeat such a creature.

CHAPTER 70

Alithyra emerges through her chosen doorway to find herself standing in a dark, dank, empty cell. The cell bars are rusty and most of the stone floor has worn away due to water damage. A pile of bones sits next to the wall underneath a set of shackles.

"It would seem that this section has fallen into disuse," says Alithyra to herself. "Hopefully, I can get out."

She pushes on the door and it swings open with an incredibly loud, rusty creak. When it is halfway open, the hinges give way and the door comes crashing to the ground, making a loud banging noise that reverberates down the halls. She steps nervously into the hallway and looks around. Seeing nobody coming and only a wall on her right, she turns left and begins to search for a way out. She draws her bow and nocks an arrow as she goes along.

As she continues, the dungeon becomes less worn down. Some cells even show signs of recent occupation, but she finds no living prisoners. Eventually she comes to a part of the dungeon that seems to be in use. She reaches an end in the hallway, but the dungeon continues both left and right. Hearing muffled screams, she checks the right door and finds it locked. She considers breaking down the door and going in to rescue any of the poor souls inside, but on the left she spots a pitiable sight. In one of the cells she sees a canin of the Great Dane breed chained to the wall, bruised and battered with his head hanging down as his body slumps forward as far as the chains allow. Recognizing him from Thakszut's description, she rushes to his cell, grabbing a set of keys off a nearby hook.

Unlocking and entering the cell, she approaches him. "Aldtaw? Are you still alive?"

Aldtaw's eyes flicker open, and he weakly raises his head to look at her. "Who are you?"

"My name is Alithyra. I'm here with a team led by Pelagius to destroy Babu. I'm going to rescue you while I'm here."

"Were you the one who caused that terrible noise on the other side of the dungeon?" asks Aldtaw.

"Unfortunately yes," says Alithyra. "As luck would have it, nobody has responded. I think nobody else heard it."

"I wouldn't say that, my dear," says a deep voice behind her.

Before she can respond, a large chunk of metal flies over her shoulder and embeds itself in the wall, barely missing Aldtaw's head. Someone tugs on the chain attached to it, and it comes out of the wall and returns to its thrower.

Alithyra whirls around and sees Nakhurd wielding a large executioner's axe. With him is an ogre wielding a meteor hammer, which just missed her, and a pair of war hammers rests back. Nakhurd grins malevolently. "Well, look at this. Now we have two dogs in the cage."

Alithyra raises her bow to fire, but the ogre is quicker. Holding the end of the chain with one hand, he throws the hammer end in a horizontal motion. The meteor hammer hits her bow dead center, snapping it in half. Its momentum keeps it going and the chain wraps around her waist. The ogre smiles wickedly, and grasping the chain in both hands, pulls her off her feet. He turns as he pulls the chain over his shoulder in an overhead swing. The chain unravels, pulling Alithyra to him, and she flies across the dungeon. She hits the wall with a thud and tumbles to the ground.

"Excellent," says Nakhurd. "That should take some of the fight out of her."

Alithyra struggles to her feet. She stands and stares defiantly at her attackers, drawing her tonfas. "I'm much tougher than I look. Trust me, you will not hit me with that weapon again."

"That sounds like a challenge," says the ogre. "Not very wise, canin."

The ogre begins swinging his meteor hammer over his head, lengthening the chain on each pass. After a while, he flings the hammer at her in an underhand throw. The metal piece flies so fast, it makes a whistling sound. At the last second, Alithyra backflips over it, and the hammer end becomes embedded in the wall. She lands on top of the chain, kicking the hammer and using her momentum to drive it farther into the stone. Shocked, the ogre lets out some slack to try to catch her off guard. However, her reflexes are quick, and she lands square on her feet. Before the ogre can react, she takes up the slack and wraps the chain around the key hook.

She rushes forward as the ogre drops the chain and pulls out his war hammers. The ogre takes a few steps forward and swings one of his weapons at her. She drops down mid-run, the hammer passing right over her head, and she slides through his legs. She stands as she comes to a stop and finds herself between her two opponents.

The ogre spins around and swings downward at her, right at the same time as Nakhurd makes the same motion. Reflexively, Alithyra swings her weapons up attempting to block, stopping the axe dead. Her other tonfa shatters, but manages to deflect the war hammers enough to miss her and hit the ground with a thud.

"This is unexpected," says Nakhurd.

"It would seem that you boys have underestimated me," says Alithyra.

Without warning, Nakhurd catches her remaining tonfa in the crook between the handle and the end of the blade. He whirls and wrenches the weapon from her hand. Nakhurd and the ogre swing their weapons simultaneously in a horizontal sweep, one high and one low. Just as they are about to hit her, Alithyra leaps above both weapons, and using her opponents as a base, backflips to the side. She draws two arrows from her quiver as she lands and throws an arrow at each one. An arrow hits the ogre in the knee, causing him to drop his war hammer and slump as he clutches his wound. The other hits Nakhurd in the shoulder. Nakhurd stumbles back a few steps, nearly dropping his axe.

As the ogre struggles to his feet, Alithyra draws what appears to be a simple piece of wood from her quiver, which transforms into the Seeker Bow. She reaches into her quiver and draws ten arrows, nocks them all at once, and looses them in a spread. Each opponent takes five wounds. One hits Nakhurd square in the forehead, snapping his head back. He stumbles and falls into a cell, lying motionless on the floor. The force of five arrows hitting him at once also knocks the ogre back;

however, none of the hits are fatal and he stands there panting and bleeding. After a moment, he takes a step forward before collapsing with a pained grunt. He lies on the floor, conscious and breathing heavily, but also clearly out of the fight.

Alithyra nocks another arrow and approaches him. "Do you surrender?"

The ogre feebly attempts to stand, but immediately crumples back to the floor. "Never."

"Please surrender. I do not wish to kill you."

"Anything you could do is nothing compared to what the master will do if I fail. Kill me or I will rise and kill you."

Although horribly injured, the ogre begins to push himself up. He groans in agony and collapses back to the ground. He reaches and grabs Alithyra's ankle. "If you do not kill me, I will rip off this foot."

Alithyra sighs. "I will take pity on you."

She raises her bow and releases the arrow, which hits the ogre on the top of the head. The force at such a close range drives it all the way through his skull. His grip loosens and he collapses lifelessly to the ground. She enters the cell where Nakhurd fell, and noticing that despite his wounds he is still breathing, nocks another arrow and shoots it directly into his heart. She then replaces her bow and retrieves her remaining tonfa and the keys before returning to Aldtaw's cell. Alithyra pants heavily as she tries to catch her breath and cool down. She winces and grabs her shoulder and she scans the adjoining corridors for any other attackers.

Aldtaw grins weakly as she enters. "That was quite impressive."

"Thank you."

She unlocks Aldtaw's shackles and catches him as he slumps over. She helps him out of his cell and lays him on the stone floor. "I'm going to get you out of here. Are there any others?"

"There are five others in the torture chamber beyond that door," replies Aldtaw.

"I'll get them too," says Alithyra.

"Don't bother," says Aldtaw. "Can't you hear that the screaming has stopped?"

Alithyra listens by the door and realizes that he is right. "What does it mean?"

"It means that they are dead," says Aldtaw. "If Nakhurd's victims stop screaming and he doesn't bring them back to their cells, it means that he has tortured them to death. In this case, he may have executed them before he came out to deal with you."

"I have to check," says Alithyra. "I can't just leave them."

"Trust me," says Aldtaw. "I've witnessed it myself many times. There is nothing you can do for them."

Alithyra sighs sadly. "I suppose I better get you out then."

She helps Aldtaw to his feet, and swinging his arm over her shoulders, supports him with her weight.

"How?" asks Aldtaw.

Alithyra pulls the ball that Shukrat gave her out of her pocket. Then, she tosses it a few feet away and it shatters. A shimmering blue portal appears.

"We're going through there," says Alithyra. "I'll get you some help."

Alithyra helps Aldtaw hobble through the portal, which closes after they enter.

CHAPTER 71

Shukrat is deep in meditation. Suddenly, the air begins to shift, and a whirring sound fills the room. The old goblin opens his eyes and rises to investigate. After several seconds, a portal opens.

"It would appear that I shall soon have company," says Shukrat to himself.

Moments later, Alithyra comes through, holding up a barely conscious Aldtaw. The portal closes after she steps out.

"What happened?" asks Shukrat.

"No time to explain," says Alithyra. "Help me with him."

Shukrat quickly approaches and drapes Aldtaw's other arm over his shoulder. "We'll take him into the guest quarters. He can rest there, and I will tend to his wounds."

They take the injured canin down the hall and through a large doorway. Inside is a second living area, magnificent in size and stature and much larger than should be able to fit inside Shukrat's small house. Several doors line the walls.

"How is it possible for this place to exist within these walls?" asks Alithyra.

"You forget, I am a master of space manipulation," says Shukrat. "I simply magically created a guest house between the realms. A pocket realm, if you like. In it, I can house up to a thousand guests or more if need be."

Shukrat leads them through the first door on the right and into a bedroom. Once inside, he and Alithyra gently lay Aldtaw on an incredibly comfortable bed. Shukrat pulls the covers over Aldtaw and places his hand on the injured canin's head. "Rest now, friend. You are safe here."

He turns to Alithyra. "We need bandages and a cold compress."

"Couldn't we just get the town priest to heal him?" asks Alithyra.

"No," says Shukrat. "We have no large temples here. Only shrines, each one tended by a single priest. Most of them are on a pilgrimage to Rodaria to seek an audience with the Archpriest. The only one who has remained behind is the priest of Rasthor. The death god's priests aren't known for healing, so unless we want to give him last rites, that is not the one to go to. We will have to tend to him ourselves."

Alithyra glances worriedly at Aldtaw. "I don't know if he can make it without magical healing."

"He'll be fine," says Shukrat. "I may not have divine healing powers, but I am fairly skilled with mundane medicine. I have saved people who were in much worse shape. Keep an eye on him for a moment while I go get the supplies I need."

Alithyra turns to watch Aldtaw as Shukrat disappears through the door.

CHAPTER 72

Kevnan trips and crashes noisily into a pile of broken armor as he steps through his door. Rising and dusting himself off, he finds himself in a plain stone room filled with bunk beds. Various articles of clothing, weapons, and armor, among other things, litter the floor and the beds.

"I must be in the barracks," says Kevnan. "Who just leaves heaps of broken armor lying around?"

He begins to explore the area, searching for a way out. After a while, he finds a simple wooden door. He opens it and suddenly finds himself face-to-face with one of Babu's men. He looks human except for his bright green skin, obviously marking him as a daemon. He wears no armor, just simple clothing. His only weapon appears to be a katana on his belt. Kevnan steps back in alarm as the daemon moves through the door, closing it behind him.

"Greetings, intruder," says the daemon. "My name is Julbthu, and by Master Babu's orders, I am your opponent today."

"You're very polite for an enemy," says Kevnan.

"We share no personal enmity," says Julbthu. "There is no need to be rude. Now let's make this quick. Commander Charndergh wants me to report back to the wall as soon as my task is complete."

Kevnan backs up a few feet and draws his sword. Julbthu watches with interest. "A fellow katana wielder, I see. However, your stance is sloppy. I can tell that although you may be skilled with other swords, you are new at this one. I, on the other hand, am a master with the katana."

"I may be new to the fighting style, but I know how to use a sword," says Kevnan. "That said, I hope you won't hold it against me when I win."

Julbthu grins. "I like your spirit. I'll be sure to take it easy on you. I don't wish to end this too quickly."

Julbthu draws his sword and advances toward Kevnan. Kevnan lunges forward and slashes at Julbthu, who parries his blow with ease. "Not bad. A tad predictable though. You can do better, I'm sure. Show me what you've got."

Julbthu attacks. He swings his sword through the air but Kevnan parries the blow. They continue fighting, swords clashing. Although the two fighters seem to be at a stalemate, it is obvious that Julbthu is not trying nearly as hard as Kevnan.

"You have potential, my friend," says Julbthu. "I must say that despite your sloppiness, your amateur skills have me somewhat impressed."

"You're an arrogant one, aren't you?" says Kevnan.

"It's not arrogance if you can back it up," says Julbthu, deflecting another blow. "I am simply confident in my abilities. On the other hand, you seem to think that you can beat me despite your lack of advanced training in this art. That, my friend, is arrogance."

The battle continues with occasional wild swings slicing through supports, causing beds to crash to the floor. Kevnan raises his sword and swings downward, but Julbthu effortlessly blocks his attack.

"You seem to have reached your limit," says Julbthu. "Such a pity. I was just beginning to enjoy our little sparring session. But, as they say, all good things must come to an end, and I'm afraid our fight is over."

Without warning, Julbthu slides his blade down to Kevnan's hilt, and with a rapid motion, twirls it around and yanks the blade from Kevnan's hands. His sword flies through the air and slices through another bed. Julbthu frowns as the bed collapses. "Pity. That was my bed."

Julbthu points his blade at Kevnan's throat. "Do you surrender?"

"Never," says Kevnan.

"Very well," says Julbthu.

Before Kevnan can react, Julbthu spins around and slashes at him diagonally, starting on the stomach just above the thigh and cutting across his chest and over his shoulder. Faster than Kevnan can imagine, Julbthu remains in motion and continues his attack. He brings the blade down in a circular motion, and changing course, cuts horizontally across Kevnan's stomach. He then twirls around and stabs backward, driving his sword into Kevnan's belly. Kevnan grunts in pain when the attack ends. Julbthu quickly withdraws his sword and turns to face Kevnan as the elf drops to his knees. He eyes Kevnan's injuries and sheaths his sword just before Kevnan falls forward and collapses in a heap on the floor. He turns and retrieves Kevnan's sword.

"I claim this blade in my victory," says Julbthu. "Normally, I would kill you now, but I am feeling generous today. I shall not finish you off, but I also will not help you. I must admit that I was somewhat impressed with your skills. Though you are but a beginner in the art, I sense great potential from you. If you should survive and escape this place, continue your katana training. I hope to face you again someday on more equal ground. Farewell for now."

Kevnan tries to push himself up, his arms shaking violently, before collapsing back to the floor. "Why give me a chance at all? Why not just finish me off?"

Julbthu shrugs. "The chance I am giving you is slim. Even if you do manage to get to your feet, you will likely bleed out before you reach the courtyard. My task is complete. If you do survive, good for you. Farewell."

Julbthu leaves through the door as Kevnan fights for life. He struggles to reach Shukrat's portal orb, knowing that his time is running out.

CHAPTER 73

Thakszut appears in the center of a massive circular chamber consisting of black stone, and torches line the walls. A single enormous metal door is on one side of the wall.

Thakszut approaches the door. *I don't like the looks of this. I have never been to this part of the fortress and it gives me a bad feeling. It's probably a trap, but this door seems to be the only way out.*

Thakszut scans the door for a means of opening it and finds a rusty metal lever on the wall beside it. He pulls on it with all his strength, but it won't budge. He climbs up on top of it and starts jumping up and down, but to no avail. Suddenly, the lever gives way, dropping Thakszut to the floor as it moves down. Thakszut covers his ears to drown out the screeching of metal gears and the rattle of large chains. The door slowly begins to rise, creaking noisily. Finally, the door reaches the top and stops. However, to Thakszut's horror, a massive demon steps through.

The creature is over twenty-five feet in height. It has reddish-black skin with streaks of bright orange, as well as large, sharp teeth, massive claws, and large curved horns, obviously marking it as a morag. This monster, known as Basmorg, grins malevolently at Thakszut. Then, it places its massive hand on top of the door and forces it down effortlessly. The door hits the ground with a loud metallic clang and the lever pops back up.

Basmorg glares at Thakszut as the frightened fiendling scurries to the other side of the room. "Seriously? This is the challenge that Master Babu has for me?"

"Don't underestimate me," says Thakszut. "I'll be more of a challenge than you think."

"Because you're smaller and faster?" asks Basmorg. "That will be of little concern. There is nowhere to run in here. After a while, you will tire, and it will be easy to end it. I just have to crush you."

Thakszut thinks for a moment, then steps forward and begins to concentrate. He transforms into a morag himself, surprising Basmorg.

"Impressive," says Basmorg. "Let's see if you can duplicate my abilities as well. Take your best shot."

Thakszut charges forward, head down in a goring charge. He rams Basmorg directly in the chest and comes to a sudden stop. The shooting pain in his head is overwhelming and he nearly stumbles away.

Basmorg sighs. "Is that really the best you've got? Let me show you how it's done."

Basmorg shoves Thakszut back. Then, without warning, he lunges forward and drives his head into Thakszut's chest. The horns dig deep and nearly puncture Thakszut's flesh before Basmorg rapidly pushes his head forward and sends him flying across the room. Thakszut hits the wall with a thud and is barely back on his feet before Basmorg is on him. Basmorg viciously claws him across the face, sending him tumbling to the ground.

Basmorg grabs him by the throat, and lifting him up, glares at him. "Pathetic."

Basmorg pushes Thakszut to the center of the room. A familiar orange glow builds inside Basmorg's mouth. He opens his maw and a beam of fire shoots out. It hits Thakszut in the chest and sends him flying into the back wall. As Thakszut hits the ground, the beam explodes, filling the entire room. When the smoke clears, Thakszut, back in his original form, slumps against the wall, breathing heavily. Basmorg approaches as Thakszut struggles to rise to his feet.

"Still alive, are you?" says Basmorg. "I'm intrigued, but you won't survive another blast."

Thakszut's hair turns white and his size increases dramatically as he plays his trump card and unleashes his Demonic Potential. With an amazing burst of speed, he charges at Basmorg and punches him in the stomach. The force of the blow doubles over the mighty morag, causing him to groan in pain. Before Basmorg can recover, Thakszut clenches his hands together and slams them down on the back of Basmorg's head, driving him face first into the stone floor. He grabs

Basmorg's tail, and after swinging him in a full circle, throws him across the room. Basmorg hits the door with a bang. Basmorg rises to his feet as Thakszut approaches, and the morag laughs.

"Is something funny?" asks Thakszut.

"Not at all," says Basmorg. "I'm just impressed that you're providing such a challenge now. However, if this is all your Demonic Potential, then I'm afraid you still have no chance. Let's see how you fare against me with my Potential unleashed."

The orange streaks on Basmorg's body glow and turn red. Bursts of fire begin to erupt from them as his flesh appears to burn away. Suddenly, a huge burst of flame comes from all the streaks at once, blasting away his skin and revealing a black, fiery skeleton.

Basmorg laughs malevolently as he reveals his new form. "Behold my true Potential. It has been a long time since I had to use it. I just hope you live long enough for me to enjoy it."

Not wanting to waste time, Thakszut charges forward again. However, a searing blast of flame sends him tumbling back; when he recovers, he finds Basmorg standing over him. Basmorg claws at him, cutting into his flesh and cauterizing the wound at the same time. The pain caused by such an attack is nearly unbearable, and Thakszut cries out. Basmorg grabs him by his head and lifts him off the ground. As he stares at Thakszut, the flames build up inside his mouth, spilling out through the gaps between the bones. Thakszut desperately grabs the morag's arm and strikes it. Suddenly, Thakszut turns dark gray; he hits Basmorg's arm one more time, shattering the bone. Basmorg roars in pain and drops Thakszut, wildly unleashing his flame blast to explode harmlessly on the ceiling.

Thakszut lunges forward and punches Basmorg in the ribs, shattering his ribcage. Then, he grabs Basmorg by the neck at the base of the skull with one hand and the top of his head with the other. With one swift motion, he rips the skull right off the spine. A blast of flame consumes Basmorg's headless body, reducing him to ash. Thakszut tosses the skull aside and it clatters on the floor, the flames in its eye sockets snuffing out as it comes to a stop. He approaches the door and forces it open just before returning to his normal form. His previous injuries now catching up, he limps down the hallway to wherever it leads.

CHAPTER 74

Iriemorel steps through a doorway and finds himself in the middle of a jousting arena. The area is quite large, although longer than it is wide. Dirt covers the floor, and wooden beams divide the field in half. Weapons of all sorts hang on both the outer walls and the portable ones set up throughout the arena.

As he gathers himself up, Iriemorel hears galloping hooves coming from one side of the arena. Before he can turn, something hard smashes against the side of his head and knocks off his helmet, which lands a few feet from him as he hits the ground. Iriemorel rises and looks for his attacker. Turning at the far side of the field is an onocentaur wielding a mace. Iriemorel retrieves his helmet but tosses it aside when he notices the massive dent that makes it impossible to wear.

The onocentaur pauses and observes his opponent. "It was quite fortunate that you were wearing that helmet," says the onocentaur. "Without it, that blow would have crushed your skull."

"Perhaps," says Iriemorel, "but you won't get in another cheap shot. I'm ready for you now."

"We shall see. Prepare yourself, dwarf. For I, Yaum, shall defeat you with ease."

Yaum charges down the field. Positioning himself so that the mace can't reach him, Iriemorel stands his ground, ready to swing his maul and strike down his opponent. However, at the last second, Yaum grabs a lance off the wall and quickly aims it in Iriemorel's direction. Unable to react in time, Iriemorel takes the lance directly in the chest. The blow puts a large dent in his armor, knocking him to the ground and shattering the wooden lance.

Yaum turns and charges again as Iriemorel struggles to his feet. He looks up in time to find the onocentaur already on top of him. Yaum swings his mace in a downward sweep, striking the exact spot that his lance hit. The armor covering Iriemorel's chest gives way with a sickening metallic crunch and cracks, once again knocking him to the ground. Yaum grabs another lance, this one with an infernal steel-covered tip, and comes back around. He aims the lance as Iriemorel rises and looks up, hitting him in the same spot once again, punching a hole in the already damaged armor and striking Iriemorel's unprotected chest. The blow knocks him to the ground and he drops his weapon.

As Iriemorel falls to the ground, the lance snags on his armor and pulls the weapon from Yaum's hand. The dwarf tosses the lance aside and rolls on the ground, clutching his chest as he struggles to breathe. Yaum waits at the end of the arena, proudly admiring his handiwork. Somehow, Iriemorel gets to his feet.

"I'm impressed," says Yaum. "Most of my opponents are dead after an attack like that. You've lasted longer than I thought."

Iriemorel stands firm, panting heavily as he tries to catch his breath. "It's not over yet. You should have finished me off while I was helpless on the ground."

"There's no sport in attacking a helpless opponent. If I'm going to kill you, I want to do it while you think you can still fight."

Iriemorel steps forward and retrieves his maul. "How generous of you. Give me your best shot. I'm ready this time."

Yaum grins and charges forward. Iriemorel stands his ground, ready to finally take the offensive. He tries to run forward, but the pain in his chest slows him. Yaum is on him in an instant, swinging his mace at the hole in Iriemorel's armor. Iriemorel swings his maul upward in an attempt to parry the attack. He successfully deflects the blow away from his body, but the mace hits the handle, snapping it. The maul's head hits Iriemorel in the face and knocks him to the ground.

Yaum reaches the other end of the arena and turns around. "I broke your weapon. What a shame."

"I can still fight," says Iriemorel, winded. "I'll rip that mace right out of your hand."

Yaum laughs. "Your overconfidence will be your downfall."

Yaum charges forward, ready to deal the final blow. Iriemorel once again stands his ground, poised to catch the mace and disarm his opponent. Then, when Yaum is merely a few yards from him, he uses his foot to toss the lance into the air, catches it, and lunges forward. Unable to stop, Yaum runs right into the sharp tip. His momentum impales him on the lance and it carries him halfway down the weapon's shaft. He grunts and drops his mace as he comes to a stop with the tip of the lance sticking out his back.

He looks at Iriemorel and manages a weak smile. "Congratulations. You win the games."

Yaum's head drops to his chest and his body goes limp. Iriemorel releases his grip on the lance and Yaum falls lifelessly to the ground.

Iriemorel looks at his damaged armor and scowls. "This was brand-new, you stupid donkey." He releases the clasps, and the section covering his torso hits the ground with a clang. With nothing but the padding underneath, he decides to continue. He picks up the mace and retrieves a large double-bladed axe from the wall. "Typical. All these weapons and the only thing other than the mace that would do me any good in a close proximity fight is an axe. I suppose it will have to do."

Using the mace as a makeshift cane, he finds a door out of the arena and begins to search for Babu's throne room.

CHAPTER 75

Aldtaw is sound asleep in the guest bed, his wounds completely cleaned and bandaged. Shukrat dabs a wet washcloth on Aldtaw's forehead as Alithyra enters the room. She is clutching her left shoulder.

"How is he?" asks Alithyra.

"He'll live," says Shukrat. "If you hadn't saved him when you did, he would probably be dead by now. Assuming, of course, that they weren't keeping him alive."

Shukrat looks at her. "Are you all right?"

"It's only a minor injury," says Alithyra. "I got slammed into a wall during my fight, but I didn't take any other hits."

Shukrat looks concerned. "Let me see. Even a seemingly minor injury should not go untreated."

Alithyra sits and Shukrat examines the back of her shoulder. "Minor, my foot. You've got some nasty bruising and a cracked shoulder blade."

Shukrat grabs some bandages and tends to her wounded shoulder.

"Is it serious?" asks Alithyra.

"It will heal," says Shukrat. "No amputation required. I highly recommend taking it easy for a while. Of course, you may not get the chance. I sense that you want to rejoin your friends."

Alithyra nods. "I don't suppose you could reopen the portal?"

"Once closed, a temporary door cannot be reopened," says Shukrat. "If you want to go back, you'll have to wait until one of the others opens another one. Then, you'll have to go through before they can. Be warned that you may not like what you find."

"I know," says Alithyra. "But I swore to Pelagius that I was in this to the end, and I want to be there for the final confrontation."

Suddenly, a portal opens, but nobody comes through. Alithyra cautiously approaches the magical gateway and pokes her head through. She rapidly pulls back out. "Shukrat, come quick! It's Kevnan!"

Shukrat rushes to her and they both enter the portal. They find themselves in the battle-torn barracks and Kevnan unconscious on the floor.

Shukrat kneels and examines him. "He's alive, but only barely. If I can get him back, I think I can save him."

"Do you need my help?" asks Alithyra.

"No," says Shukrat. "Continue on. I can handle him."

Shukrat concentrates for a moment and begins to glow. Then, his size increases, and he becomes more muscular. He gently picks up Kevnan and hoists him onto his shoulder. "This is only a temporary transformation, but it should last long enough to get him to one of my guest beds. Go now. I promise I will not let him die."

Shukrat takes Kevnan through the portal, which closes behind him. Alithyra opens the door and leaves the barracks, hoping that she is not too late.

CHAPTER 76

Ralkgek finds himself in a vast circular chamber devoid of light. Examining his surroundings, he can vaguely make out five massive pillars circling the room and several dark alcoves. The pillars appear to be covered with vines. The floor is also overgrown, except for the spot where he stands. As he steps forward, he hears a hissing noise and notices that the vines appear to be moving.

"Great shining star, break this darkness," chants Ralkgek.

A shining ball of light appears at the top center of the chamber, illuminating the room except for a few of the larger alcoves at the back. Ralkgek steps back in shock when he discovers that the vines are actually snakes of many sizes and species. Some are venomous and others are not, but all slither over each other as they writhe on the floor and up and down the pillars.

"Welcome to my pit, little mouse," says a voice from the darkness of the largest alcove.

Ralkgek turns to face the alcove in time to see the voice's owner emerge. A muscular cecropsan, human from the waist up and snake below the belt, comes through the opening, parting the sea of snakes as he arrives.

"To whom do I owe this pleasure?" asks Ralkgek.

"I am Tymraal and you shall not leave my pit alive."

Ralkgek scoffs. "Do you really think that I'm worried about your pets? Unless you have magical powers, this will not be a challenge."

Tymraal grins wickedly. "I happen to be a great sorcerer. From the stories I hear about you, I'm at least your equal, if not your superior."

"Let's get started then," says Ralkgek. "I want to see if you can back up your boasts."

Tymraal lifts one finger and waves it back and forth. "Patience, my friend. There's no need to start flinging spells now. First, I want to test your abilities."

"How do you plan to do that?" asks Ralkgek, confused.

"I believe that the Great Serpent will be more of a match for you," replies Tymraal.

"The Great Serpent?"

"Observe."

Tymraal whistles loudly. After a moment of silence, a loud hiss emanates from another large corridor, followed by a shuffling sound. From this alcove emerges a thirty-foot anaconda, which coils up behind Tymraal.

"That's the Great Serpent?" asks Ralkgek, skeptically.

"Not quite," replies Tymraal.

Tymraal hisses loudly and every snake in the room slithers in his direction. To Ralkgek's amazement, they climb up the anaconda, completely covering it at least three times over. Tymraal chants under his breath and the mass of snakes curls into a ball and begins to glow. The orb of shining serpents increases in size. Finally, it uncoils and stops glowing, revealing a single, massive, sixty-foot snake. It opens its mouth and hisses, displaying a pair of foot-long fangs six inches in diameter. Ralkgek looks upon this creature in horror.

Tymraal grins. "This is the Great Serpent. If you can defeat it and survive, you can face me."

Tymraal practically vanishes as the Great Serpent slithers around him, approaching Ralkgek. The Great Serpent lunges forward and strikes with incredible speed. Ralkgek barely jumps aside as its massive jaws snap shut inches from him. The Great Serpent rears back, hisses, and lunges for another strike. Its fangs scrape against the floor as Ralkgek spreads his wings, and flapping furiously, uses them to rapidly jump back and fly across the room.

"Impressive," says Tymraal.

Ralkgek grins and extends one hand, palm up and fingers curled. "Try this on for size. Engulf!"

Ralkgek clenches his fist and flames engulf the Great Serpent. It shrieks as the fire sears its flesh. However, it does not collapse; when the fire clears it still seems completely healthy despite its burns.

"Oh dear," says Tymraal, tauntingly. "I'm afraid you've gotten him angry now."

The Great Serpent whips its tail, striking Ralkgek in the side, sending him flying across the room and to the floor with a thud. The Great Serpent looms over him in an instant. Ralkgek desperately chants, and a ball of flame appears in his hand. The Great Serpent lunges to strike, but Ralkgek continues to chant.

Just before its fangs reach him, the orb turns blue and he flings it into the Great Serpent's open mouth. The massive snake stops mid-strike and freezes solid as a layer of ice covers it from head to tail. Ralkgek slips from underneath the frozen snake and turns to face Tymraal. "Now it's time to take care of you."

A cracking sound comes from the Great Serpent, and Tymraal points to the frozen snake. "It's not over yet."

Ralkgek turns in time to see the Great Serpent rear up, broken ice falling from its flesh. For a moment, they glare at each other. Then, the Great Serpent opens its mouth to hiss and sprays a disgusting green goo in Ralkgek's direction. The spray hits the area around him in a five-foot radius, covering Ralkgek as well. A large blob of the stuff strikes him right in the eyes, obscuring his vision. Ralkgek screams in agony as a burning sensation overcomes him. The Great Serpent once again lunges to strike, but Ralkgek flings a bolt of lightning in its direction. The electric blast hits the snake in the eye, causing it to rear back shrieking in pain. Ralkgek scurries around a pillar to buy himself some time. He wipes the goo from his eyes, but to his horror, his vision does not return.

"Potent stuff, the Great Serpent's venom," says Tymraal. "You'll be completely blind within five minutes and dead within a minute if you get bitten. And the best part is, this venom is magically enhanced. There is no antidote and the damage it does can only be safely reversed by a grand priest or higher."

Ralkgek listens to his words with intent. He begins to concentrate. "Darkness bleak, vision without light. Empower my senses with greater might."

His senses of hearing and smell enhanced, Ralkgek emerges from behind the pillar to face his adversary. Having recovered from the lightning to the eye, the Great Serpent eyes him angrily. Then it rears back to strike once more.

"Fire burns, ice bites," chants Ralkgek. "Lightning dances on earthen might. Electric rock and burning ice, combine to form elemental light."

As he chants, a swirling mixture of fire, blue cold energy, crackling lightning, and crumbling rock forms in his hands and slowly increases in size. The Great Serpent lunges forward, its mouth agape to deliver a fatal bite. When it has nearly reached him, Ralkgek unleashes his spell, throwing the swirling ball of elements into the snake's mouth.

The Great Serpent rears back and emits an unearthly shriek. Electricity flows in and around its body as it both burns and freezes at the same time. Rocky spikes violently erupt from several places on its body, eventually splitting it in half. The frozen parts of its body shatter on the floor and the rest burns to ash.

Tymraal claps slowly. "Well done. I must admit, I'm impressed. I have never seen anyone combine the elements in such a way. Bravo."

"I suppose I face you now," says Ralkgek, breathing heavily.

"I'm afraid so. It's a shame that you won't be at full health for this. I was hoping for a challenge after you defeated the Great Serpent."

"I can still do magic, and I'm still healthy enough to take you on."

Tymraal chuckles. "Your sensory enhancement won't last forever and when it wears off, I won't give you a chance to cast it again. Face it, Ralkgek. It's over for you."

Realizing that he is right, Ralkgek considers his options. His sensory enhancement already starting to fade, he decides that it is time to retreat and pulls out the portal orb. He tries to throw it to the side, but his grip slips and the orb flies right toward Tymraal. The magical item hits the cecropsan on the forehead and explodes. Tymraal briefly screams as the magical energy envelops him. Then, after a brief flash, both the portal and Tymraal are gone. Ralkgek is alone.

"Great," says Ralkgek. "What now?"

He thinks for a moment. "I should probably check on Shukrat."

The blinded daemon begins to concentrate and within minutes an image of Shukrat appears. "Yes? Can I help you, Ralkgek?"

"Did a cecropsan just appear in your house?" asks Ralkgek.

"No," replies Shukrat, slightly confused.

"I have another question then," says Ralkgek. "What happens when one of your portal orbs shatters against a living being?"

"Simple," says Shukrat. "The transport energy unleashed is too unstable to take them to the desired location. Instead, they end up in the Interrealm."

"The Interrealm?" inquires Ralkgek.

"The place between the realms," says Shukrat. "The victim will forever be trapped outside space and time, never on any one of the known or unknown realms, but between them all."

"So, there is no way to get back?" asks Ralkgek.

"It is possible to find a way back, but not likely," says Shukrat.

"Thank you," says Ralkgek.

Shukrat's image fades. Ralkgek makes a quick search of the room and finds a long piece of cloth, which he wraps around his eyes and ties at the back of his head. He then magically fuses together several chunks of wood and stone into a makeshift walking stick. Reactivating his sensory enhancement, he begins his search for the throne room.

CHAPTER 77

Adotiln finds herself standing on a large table roughly twenty-five feet in length. Looking around, she deduces that she must be in the great hall. The room is massive, possibly one hundred and fifty feet wide, four times that in length, and at least twice its width high. Several more tables form a few lines throughout the room, with a few tables towering over the others clearly meant for the larger denizens. A large ornate throne-like chair sits at the end of one of the larger tables, behind which a massive fireplace big enough for a giant to comfortably stand in covers the back wall. A fire burns in the fireplace and an iron pot of bubbling liquid sits in front. Each side wall holds a pair of double doors.

So which way do I go?

Before she can decide, the doors on the right side swing open and an orange-skinned oni enters carrying a dripping sack and a box of various vegetables. He eyes Adotiln suspiciously before proceeding to the cauldron and dumping the contents of both containers in. He stirs the mysterious, foul-smelling soup, watching her the entire time. "Greetings. I am Zygarn, head chef of Devil's Den. I'm afraid dinner is not ready yet. The main course has yet to arrive."

"Thank you," says Adotiln. "I've already eaten anyway. I don't suppose you could direct me to the throne room?"

"Why yes," says Zygarn. "Go out the left door and down the hall on the right. You can't miss it."

A look of realization crosses Zygarn's face. "Excuse me. The main course has just arrived. It seems to be smaller than anticipated, but I'm sure I can work with it. Wait here a moment, please."

Zygarn darts into the kitchen. Adotiln begins to climb down from the table, and Zygarn returns brandishing a kanabo in one hand and a massive cleaver in the other. He kicks a table out of the way, sending it flying across the room and slamming into the exit door. He then strides over to Adotiln's table and glares down at her.

"Now hold still, if you please," says Zygarn. "It'll make this quicker and damage the meat less if you don't move."

Adotiln leaps from the side of the table, barely avoiding the kanabo as it crashes through the wood and slams into the stone floor. She quickly rolls sideways, landing underneath another table, narrowly evading the cleaver. She draws a pair of daggers and begins to pray. However, Zygarn interrupts her by tossing the table to the side.

"I know you're a priestess," says Zygarn. "Don't expect me to give you time to pray in order to use your magic."

He once again brings the kanabo down and Adotiln nimbly sidesteps it. She mutters a very brief prayer and her daggers double in size. Ducking under a sweep from the cleaver, she jumps onto the kanabo and stabs deep into Zygarn's wrist. The oni emits a shrill yelp of pain, releasing his grip on the massive club.

"Don't underestimate me because of my size," says Adotiln. "Even without magic, I can hold my own in a fight."

She leaps off the kanabo just before Zygarn's cleaver slices it in two. She ducks under another table and rolls across the floor to another. Zygarn simply smashes the first table and tosses the second one away. As he throws it aside, Adotiln lunges forward and slashes him across the ankle, causing Zygarn to shout in pain and stumble briefly. He brings his cleaver down, barely missing as Adotiln leaps to safety and rolls under Babu's head table. Blinded by rage, Zygarn begins chopping into the head table. Adotiln nimbly dodges every strike and retreats to the back of the room.

Seeing her standing by the fireplace, Zygarn grins. "There's nowhere left to run now."

He grips the cleaver in both hands and raises it over his head before using the weight of his entire upper body to bring it crashing down. Adotiln leaps forward at the last second, rolling through the oni's legs, stabbing his left foot on the way through. As Zygarn tries to regain his balance, she then stabs both daggers deep into the back of his right heel before spreading her arms and ripping the blades out of opposite sides. Already off balance, the loss of strength in his heel sends him tumbling forward. He comes crashing down, landing headfirst in the boiling pot. He quickly flips over and sits up, screaming in agony as the scalding liquid streams down his body. He wrenches the pot off his head and throws it across the room, revealing his horribly burned and blistered face. He maneuvers himself onto his knees, and using his good leg, struggles to rise to his feet. As he pushes himself up, Adotiln steps behind him and uses the exact same double stab and rip tactic on the back of his left heel. Zygarn shrieks in pain as his foot buckles and tumbles backward into the fire. His screams echo through the chamber as he thrashes before desperately launching himself from the fireplace. His scorched and smoking form slams into the stone floor. Despite his injuries he forces himself up into a kneeling position. Looking around, he spots Adotiln nearby.

"You meaningless little runt!" shouts Zygarn angrily. "I'll serve you up on a platter yet!"

He shuffles toward her, swinging his cleaver wildly. Adotiln rapidly sidesteps a few swipes before one is too fast to dodge. She desperately moves her oversized daggers to block the attack. The force of the blow shatters her blades and sends her tumbling to the floor. Drawing a second pair of daggers from within her robes, she leaps to her feet in time to avoid a downward chop. She sidesteps another chopping attempt before jumping up onto the cleaver and using the momentum from Zygarn pulling it back to leap onto his shoulder.

"Try to get me now," says Adotiln.

She mutters a very quick prayer, increasing the size of her blades, and drives them into the side of Zygarn's neck. Blinded by rage, Zygarn turns the cleaver around in his hand and swings it backward toward Adotiln. Shocked, the nimble little halfling ducks around Zygarn's neck and he imbeds the cleaver deep into his own shoulder. Shrieking in pain, but still enraged beyond reason, he withdraws the cleaver, switches hands, and tries again on the other side of his body with the same results.

"I'm sorry, but I have to end this," says Adotiln.

Before Zygarn can do anything else, Adotiln sinks her daggers into the back of his head right at the base of the skull. Zygarn emits a weak grunt and his eyes roll back in his head. His body goes limp, falls forward like a sack of potatoes, and hits the floor with a thud. Adotiln slides off his body, clears the rubble away from the door, and exits the great hall.

CHAPTER 78

Pelagius barely raises his shield in time to halt Gulvgrum's attack. The morningstar crashes against the shield with a loud clang. The force of the blow reverberates through the shield, rattling Pelagius's arm. Pelagius winces in pain and fearfully takes a step back. Babu watches intently while distractedly crushing a red-eyed raven that lands on his armrest.

"Infuriating as this invasion is, I must say I am disappointed," says Babu. "I have heard tales of the great Pelagius. You do not seem to be the brave warrior that I have heard of."

Gulvgrum advances and brings his sword down, clashing with White Fire as Pelagius parries the blow. Gulvgrum continues his assault, alternating with his sword and morningstar.

Pelagius is on the defensive, blocking blow after blow. The force from the morningstar puts large dents in his shield, which soon weakens and cracks. Suddenly, Gulvgrum lunges forward, attempting to stab Pelagius rather than slash him. Pelagius quickly counters with his shield and the two items clash. Gulvgrum's sword pierces the shield with a terrible metallic crack. Fortunately, it does not go far enough through to stab Pelagius's hand, but the blade is definitely stuck.

Before Pelagius can counter, Gulvgrum twists his sword around, causing Pelagius to briefly lose his grip on the strap. He rapidly moves the shield to the underside of Pelagius's forearm and twists it around so that the strap tightens. Then, he wrenches Pelagius's arm into an excruciating position with the shield facing up and brings his morningstar crashing down on the damaged shield. It shatters, freeing Gulvgrum's sword and impaling Pelagius's hand with the spikes.

Gulvgrum lunges forward with his sword and cuts through a strap holding together the left side of Pelagius's armor, loosening it. In a rapid motion, he brings the blade around and slashes across Pelagius's right thigh. The old hero drops to one knee, using his sword for support. He breathes heavily as he waits for Gulvgrum's final blow. However, Gulvgrum just stares down at him. "Pathetic. I was hoping for a challenge."

Gulvgrum lurches forward and kicks Pelagius in the chest, sending him tumbling backward and sprawling on the floor. Gulvgrum looks over at Babu. "This fight is rather disappointing, master. I expected more from this old man."

Babu glares at Pelagius. "If you can't beat Gulvgrum, what makes you think you can defeat me? Face it, old man. This venture was doomed from the start. Your friends will die elsewhere in the fortress and you will meet your end here. You cannot defeat Gulvgrum and you could never hope to defeat me."

Using White Fire for support, Pelagius rises to his feet, fighting through the pain. "I admit, I've had my moments of doubt. Only moments ago, I would have agreed with you. However, I will not go down like this. If I am to die by your hand, then so be it, but I will not lose to your bodyguard."

Pelagius stands straight and points at Babu. "Your time is at an end, Babu. I will defeat Gulvgrum and I will defeat you."

Babu glares at Pelagius and fails to fight back a small grin. "There's the fire I've heard about. Now we'll be in for a show. Finish him when you're ready, Gulvgrum."

Gulvgrum turns back to Pelagius and advances. He lunges forward and brings his morningstar down toward him. At the right moment, Pelagius sidesteps the morningstar, ignites White Fire, slashes downward, and severs the spiked ball from the handle. Stunned, Gulvgrum barely blocks his next attack, raising his sword just in time to parry a strike. However, Pelagius abruptly changes course and brings his blade around to cut deeply into Gulvgrum's thigh. The mighty demonkin briefly drops to one knee. When Gulvgrum touches the ground, he quickly lunges forward, catching Pelagius momentarily off guard. His strike is not accurate enough to deal further damage to his opponent, but he does cut through the strap on the right side of Pelagius's armor. With nothing to hold it on, the breastplate slips off and crashes to the ground. The only protection his torso now has is the padding underneath.

Both warriors lunge forward simultaneously and stab at each other. Their blades collide and slide down each other, emitting an unearthly screech. Pelagius briefly reignites White Fire, which repels Gulvgrum's sword, sending him off course. The two warriors drive their blades into one another.

Babu leans forward to get a better look. From his vantage point he sees that his bodyguard's sword is piercing Pelagius's already injured thigh, and Pelagius's blade is embedded in Gulvgrum's chest. Fighting through the pain, Pelagius pulls Gulvgrum's blade out of his flesh and he withdraws his own blade. He drops to his knees and Gulvgrum slumps forward slightly, his breathing heavy and labored. Not waiting for his opponent to recover, Pelagius ignites White Fire and makes a vicious slash. He hits Gulvgrum on the side of the neck and cuts clean through, severing the demon's head. Gulvgrum's lifeless body plops to the ground. As Babu watches, Pelagius uses his sword as cane and struggles to his feet. White Fire, still ignited, allows Pelagius to use the magical blade to cauterize his wounds.

Babu scowls and tightly grips the armrests on his throne. "Impressive."

"Now it's your turn," says Pelagius. "Face me, Babu."

Babu's grasp on the armrests tightens, causing a cracking sound to echo through the chamber. "In your condition you can't possibly defeat me. Despite all you have done, I will allow you and any of your surviving friends to make a tactical retreat. Get out now and do not come back."

"No. Whether with my death or yours, this ends today. I will not allow your evil to continue."

"My evil? What about the evil you have done?"

Pelagius stares at Babu. "Exactly what have I done that is evil, Babu?"

Babu's grip tightens to the point that the tips of his armrests shatter. "I am the victim here, Pelagius. Yes, I devour souls, but they provide me sustenance, just as food does for you. I do what I do for survival. Meanwhile, you have broken into my home and killed many of its denizens. This is an assassination attempt, pure and simple."

Pelagius's stance falters and he slightly lowers his blade as Babu's words sink in. After a moment, he raises his sword and points it at his opponent. "I am not the villain here, Babu. It is well known that your kind only needs one soul every three months to survive."

"That is the bare minimum. That would be like your kind going for a month between meals."

"Regardless of that, overindulging doesn't even begin to describe your eating habits, and you illegally hunt outside your designated territory. Your reign of terror must come to an end."

Babu grunts. "As you wish."

Babu rises from his throne and grabs a large longsword made of infernal steel. He glares at Pelagius and steps down to face him.

CHAPTER 79

Alithyra emerges from the barracks into a courtyard. Glancing around to ensure that nobody notices her, she realizes the area is empty. She climbs a nearby ladder onto the battlements and looks around to get her bearings. She immediately ducks down behind the wall and peeks over. Armed troops, mostly comprised of umbra warriors, but including hundreds of individuals of varying species, mill around the grounds, filling the outer courtyard. The main gate and outer wall are also heavily guarded by umbra warriors and a massive oni. Moving slowly around the inner battlement, she sees a second inner wall surrounding a massive keep. The grounds of the fortress stretch back behind the keep for miles with various buildings and courtyards as far as she can see.

She climbs to the first inner courtyard and walks to the gate at the far end. She slowly cracks it open and peeks through. Seeing nobody in immediate view, she slips through the door, closing it quietly. As she turns to enter the courtyard, a door opens on a nearby building. She leaps behind a nearby cart as two dwarves emerge. Between them, his arms firmly grasped in their hands, is a daemon with a cloth tied around his eyes. The two dwarves lead him into the inner bailey while he struggles to break free. One dwarf punches him in the stomach before they continue to drag him toward the keep, but he continues resisting. "Unhand me, you fools. I am here on business with your master."

"You're not fooling us," says the first dwarf. "If that were true, you wouldn't have been in the pit. You are an intruder."

Realizing who the daemon is, Alithyra nocks an arrow and slowly rises. She takes aim and looses an arrow, rapidly drawing and shooting another, striking the guards in the backs of their heads. The dwarves slump to the ground, pulling the daemon down with them. Alithyra approaches as he rises to his feet. "Are you all right, Ralkgek?"

Ralkgek turns to her. "Other than being blind, yes."

"What happened? How did they capture you?"

"In short, magic snake venom to the eyes and pure bad luck. Let's go before more guards arrive."

"We should hide their bodies first so nobody suspects anything."

Alithyra and Ralkgek hoist the dwarves up and, with Alithyra leading, take them to a hay cart. Alithyra places her corpse in the cart and assists Ralkgek in placing his before rearranging the straw to cover them. They then slowly make their way to the keep's entrance. Alithyra cracks open the door and sees an empty hallway. The two heroes enter and quietly walk down the hall, checking doors along the way. When she opens one door, a shadowy figure emerges. Alithyra jumps back and draws her bow, waiting for the guard to come through. As she waits, Thakszut stumbles through the doorway. Alithyra places her arrow back into her quiver. "Thakszut, what happened?"

"Long story," says Thakszut.

"We should keep moving," says Ralkgek. "One of the others could be engaging Babu right now."

Thakszut climbs onto Ralkgek's shoulder. "Agreed. Let's go."

The three heroes resume their trek down the hallway. They reach a round chamber with several doors along the wall. As they reach the center, Alithyra suddenly pauses and looks at the door on the far right, and her ears perk up. "Quiet. Listen."

Coming to a stop and quietly advancing to the door, they hear footsteps approaching, getting steadily closer. Alithyra draws her bow and aims it at the opening as the unknown creature slowly gets closer and closer until the door opens. Alithyra draws back her bow, ready to fire; Iriemorel emerges. He quickly ducks back behind the door. "Don't shoot! It's just me."

Alithyra lowers her bow. "Sorry."

Iriemorel comes through the doorway. "Well, aren't you a sight for sore eyes."

"Sore eyes, yes," says Ralkgek, "but I can't say the same thing for sight."

Iriemorel looks at him. "What happened to you?"

"Magic snake venom," says Ralkgek. "I'll elaborate later."

"I guess we better continue searching for the throne room," says Iriemorel. "By the way, where is Kevnan?"

"He's back at Shukrat's," says Alithyra. "Badly injured, but he should survive."

"Which way to the throne room?" asks Ralkgek.

The others look at Thakszut. "Don't look at me. That business with the door room has got me completely turned around. I've been in parts of the fortress today that I didn't know existed."

The others sigh.

"I guess we'll have to ask for directions," says Alithyra.

Iriemorel scoffs. "We're in enemy territory. Nobody is going to willingly give us directions."

"Willingly, no," says Ralkgek, "but maybe under coercion."

They pick a door on the left and enter a hallway leading to another circular chamber. Sitting in a chair behind a desk is a snoring goblin. Alithyra quietly sneaks up to him and ties him to the chair before waking him up.

The goblin looks around groggily as he slowly realizes what is happening. He helplessly struggles against the ropes. "What? What's going on? Let me go!"

Alithyra approaches him slowly. "In a moment; if you cooperate. Now, can you tell us the way to the throne room?"

The goblin spits in her face. "I know the way, but I'll never tell you."

Alithyra wipes her face and snarls menacingly. Ralkgek sniffs the air and approaches. "I think you'll tell me."

"What makes you think that?" asks the goblin.

Ralkgek pulls the goblin's chair away from the desk and kicks him in the chest, sending the chair falling over backward. It hits the ground with a clunk, as does the goblin's head.

Ralkgek picks the chair back up. "Now, unless you want to repeat that trip, you'll tell me how to get to the throne room."

"Never," says the goblin defiantly.

Ralkgek kicks him over again and turns to Iriemorel. "I need to borrow your axe."

Iriemorel hands him the axe and Ralkgek places it on the ground next to the goblin's neck. He then picks up the chair again and scoots it over slightly.

"Now?" asks Ralkgek.

"No," says the goblin.

He moves to knock the goblin over again, but Alithyra steps between them. "That's too far."

Ralkgek scoffs. "We don't have time for this. Pelagius could be fighting Babu alone. We have to get the information we need."

Alithyra glares at him. "There must be another way."

Iriemorel and Thakszut nod. Ralkgek sighs. "Fine. I have one other trick I can try."

Ralkgek approaches the goblin and grabs him by the chin. He pulls off his blindfold, revealing his bloodshot, clouded-over eyes. He positions his face inches from the goblin's and stares into his eyes. "Enemies once, but no more. Friends from now until the day of four."

Ralkgek's eyes glow bright yellow and he places his free hand on top of the goblin's head and holds his eyes open with his fingers. The goblin struggles, attempting to break the gaze as his eyes slowly turn golden. "No! I will not give in!"

Ralkgek tightens his grip and intensifies his gaze as he repeats the chant. The goblin's struggling grows weaker, the glow in his eyes growing brighter. "No. I cannot betray my master."

Ralkgek repeats the chant several more times until the goblin's eyes are bright yellow and his resistance ends. The glow fades from both their eyes and Ralkgek releases his grip before untying the goblin, who slumps forward in his seat. Ralkgek puts his blindfold back over his eyes and turns to the others, grinning. "Now he'll tell us anything we want to know."

Chapter 80

Babu rushes forward with remarkable speed for his size. He swings his sword in a horizontal arc and the two blades clash. Despite his injuries and the force behind the blow, Pelagius stands his ground and glares at his evil opponent. The blades part and come around again. This time, Pelagius is the aggressor, slashing at Babu with all his might. However, Babu easily parries the blade.

The battle continues as the ringing and clanging of metal on metal goes on. Neither has yet to land a blow on the other. However, after a while Pelagius's injuries catch up with him. His attacks slow and his defenses get sloppy as his breathing becomes heavy.

Babu looks upon him and frowns. "You appear to be tiring, Pelagius. How do you expect to defeat me? I have not yet begun to fight and yet you already appear to be finished."

"I'm not through yet," says Pelagius. "I've still got some tricks up my sleeve."

Pelagius lunges forward and slashes at Babu. However, Babu parries the blow and forces the sword aside. Then, using his free hand, he punches Pelagius, sending him tumbling to the floor. Pelagius lies motionless.

"Is that it?" asks Babu.

Babu approaches the fallen man and pokes at him with the side of his sword. Suddenly, White Fire ignites, and the white flame is quickly joined by swirling green fire. Pelagius whips around and slashes Babu across the chest, the green fire exploding as the blade cuts into him. Babu yells in pain and stumbles back a few steps.

Pelagius struggles to his feet, clearly dazed from the punch. Despite the wound, Babu quickly recovers and glares angrily at Pelagius. "Clever trick, but I will not fall for that again. Next time you try to play possum, I'll just skewer you."

"If swordplay and brawling tactics are all you've got, then I will have no problem defeating you," says Pelagius. "As long as I avoid your strikes, I should be fine."

Babu scowls and furrows his brow as he glares at Pelagius. "You haven't seen anything yet."

Babu grasps his sword with both hands and a blackish-red flame suddenly surrounds it. He steps forward and stands poised to strike, his sword at the ready. He begins to swing, turning completely around and bringing his sword across in a downward arc, striking the ground. He cuts a massive gouge in the floor and continues until his blade comes off the ground and points in Pelagius's direction. When this happens, a massive line of fire shoots off the sword and travels along the ground toward the hero at incredible speed.

Pelagius spins White Fire around until the white flame forms a cone. He drives the blade into the ground in front of him just before the blackish-red fire reaches him. The two flames collide, and White Fire is able to hold it off for a moment. Suddenly, the fire engulfs the white flames and encircles Pelagius, who screams as the hellish fire envelops him.

When the smoke clears, Pelagius is still standing despite the horrific burns. He takes a step forward and falters. He attempts to use White Fire as a cane as he drops to his knees, but the blade slips, and he slumps to the ground. Babu imbeds his own sword in the ground and approaches the injured man. Using his foot, he flips Pelagius over onto his back, causing him to emit a weak groan. The door opens and Adotiln steps in.

"Back away from him!" shouts Adotiln. "Face me, Babu!"

Babu turns to her and gnashes his teeth. "I see you defeated my chef. Very impressive, little one. I may not be as large, but I think you'll find I'm far more of a challenge."

Babu retrieves his sword and advances on Adotiln. He swings the blade around in a downward strike, which Adotiln easily sidesteps. She jumps onto the hilt and rushes up the blade, stabbing Babu in the hand. Babu yelps and drops the sword as Adotiln leaps to the floor.

"Perhaps lighter weaponry is called for here," says Babu. "Daggers versus claws sounds fair."

Babu lunges forward, clawing at Adotiln with remarkable speed. She jumps backward, barely avoiding his strike. She then leaps forward, landing within his grasping range, and starts slashing at his legs. He reaches to stop this onslaught and she jumps onto his hand and runs up his arm to his shoulder. She then drives her daggers into the side of his neck. Babu again shouts in pain and she withdraws the blades.

"I hereby bring justice to my family and all that you have slaughtered," says Adotiln. "Judgment is upon you, Babu."

Adotiln sidesteps an attempt by Babu to swat her off his shoulder. She balances on the back of his neck. She then drives both daggers into his neck at the base of the skull. Babu grunts and slumps to the ground, lying motionless. She hops off the fallen norodrian and goes to heal Pelagius.

Chapter 81

As Adotiln approaches the injured Pelagius, a shadow looms and she turns to see an angry Babu back on his feet.

"Good try," says Babu, "but your puny blades won't pierce my skull that easily."

Babu swings his hand and backhands Adotiln, sending her flying across the room. She slams into the wall, her head bouncing off with a sickening thud, and drops to the floor. As Babu approaches the unconscious halfling, Pelagius struggles to his feet and angrily stumbles toward Babu. Seeing this feeble attempt at an attack, Babu sighs wearily and brings his hand around, backhanding Pelagius across the face and sending him sprawling to the floor.

Babu reaches and grasps the charred remnants of Pelagius's armor padding. He pulls him up and holds him up in the air. "It would appear that I have won. You should have known that you could never defeat me. I want you to know that I take no pleasure in this. We had no quarrel until you took it upon yourself to invade my home and assassinate me."

Babu pulls his free hand back and points his claws in the direction of Pelagius's chest as he prepares to rip the hero's soul from his body. However, only seconds before his claws reach Pelagius's chest, the door flies open with a crash, distracting Babu enough to halt his attack. He turns to the source of the distraction and sees the other four heroes enter the throne room, along with the goblin.

Babu sighs wearily. "So, the battle continues."

Before Babu can make another move, Ralkgek flings a fireball directly behind him, catching him in the ensuing explosion. Babu shrieks as the flames engulf him, and accidentally flings Pelagius away. The wounded hero lands on Gulvgrum's corpse and slides to the floor

As the smoke clears, Babu slowly rises to his feet, glaring at the heroes. Her bow drawn on Babu, Alithyra leads the others to Pelagius.

Iriemorel checks on Pelagius. "He's alive."

"Will he live?" asks Alithyra.

"He's hurt, but not fatally," says Iriemorel. "If we can buy him some time, he may be able to recover enough to rejoin the fight."

"I'll protect him while he recovers," says Ralkgek. "My sensory enhancement isn't accurate enough for me to be much good in this fight, but if Babu tries to approach, it will serve its purpose for defense."

Ralkgek drags Pelagius back toward the door and the other three face off against Babu, their faces intense with fury.

Babu retrieves his sword and surveys the area. "Three against one. This should make things interesting."

Glancing at Ralkgek, he notices the goblin standing passively nearby. "Is that one of mine? Nobody in their right mind would betray me."

Ralkgek grins. "He didn't have much choice in the matter. His mind belongs to me for the next four days."

Babu scowls. "Mental domination. You are a devious one. You should have sent him away. Now he will suffer the same fate as the rest of you."

Babu grasps the end of his hilt and twists it. The lower half of the hilt comes off the sword with a loud pop. However, it is still attached by a large chain of impressive length. Alithyra nocks ten arrows and fires them simultaneously at Babu.

Babu quickly grasps the chain instead of the hilt and rapidly swings the sword around in a circle, blocking every arrow. He then swings the sword in rapid circles above his head before flinging it in an underhand motion and sending the blade flying in the direction of his three opponents, who scatter to get away. The blade impales Gulvgrum's headless body, which comes back with the sword when Babu pulls on the chain to retrieve it.

Alithyra looses more arrows, but Babu uses Gulvgrum as a shield and the dead demon quickly becomes a pincushion. The other two make several attempts to close in, but each time, Babu whirls the sword in a circle, thwarting them. They barely jump back or duck in time and are unable to get closer. Alithyra continues loosing arrows, which either become embedded in Gulvgrum's corpse or knocked aside by the spinning blade. Noticing that all the arrows are hitting the same part of the corpse, Babu pulls his blade back and once again impales Gulvgrum's body. He glares at Alithyra. "So, you have the Seeker Bow. What a nuisance. This should put an end to your game."

Using the blade, he flings Gulvgrum's corpse in her direction. Alithyra jumps to the side, narrowly avoiding the massive body, and readies the bow to fire again. However, Babu's sword rapidly flies in and cuts the bow in half, resulting in a magical explosion that scorches the flesh on Alithyra's left side, nearly disintegrating her hand and forearm, and sends her flying into the wall a few feet from Pelagius.

"Such a pity," says Babu. "It is unfortunate that I had to destroy a legendary artifact, but it was necessary. Farewell, young canin."

Babu flings his blade at her again, and although stunned, she sidesteps it. The sword buzzes her ribs and when the blade is right next to her side, Babu yanks upward on the chain. The sword connects just under her armpit, severing her left arm at the shoulder. Alithyra shrieks in pain and grabs the stump as Babu pulls back to retrieve his weapon. Dragging Pelagius along, Ralkgek quickly moves toward her, summoning a small ball of fire and cauterizing the wound as she passes out from the pain.

When the blade returns to Babu, Iriemorel attempts to interrupt its course. He charges forward with the mace in one hand and the axe in another. He attacks the chain, bringing the mace up into it and chopping down with the axe. However, neither weapon seems to affect it much and the back end of the hilt strikes him. The blow knocks him to the ground and sends the mace flying out of his reach.

"Nice try," says Babu, "but this chain is made of enhanced infernal steel."

Iriemorel rises to his feet and raises his axe just in time to block another attack by the blade. Iriemorel advances on Babu, knocking each attack aside by swinging his axe at just the right moment. When Iriemorel is too close for the distance attack to be useful, Babu grasps the hilt instead of the chain. The two warriors clash, each one alternating between the offense and the defense. Thakszut attempts to close in a few times, but Babu uses the chain to fend him off.

Finally, Iriemorel knocks the sword aside and goes in for the kill. Babu flings the chain in his direction, entangling him as Babu reestablishes his grip on the sword. Babu yanks on the chain, pulling the surprised dwarf into the air.

Babu swings him around, knocking Thakszut back a few feet, and slams him into the ground. He yanks the chain straight back and Iriemorel flies toward the waiting demon. As the dwarf approaches, Babu rapidly pulls back his arm and lunges forward, striking his victim in the center of the back. A loud crack echoes through the chamber as Babu's fist connects with Iriemorel's spine and the dwarf shrieks in agony. He hits the ground with a loud thud. Babu looks upon his handiwork and frowns. He rapidly swings the blade around in a circle, once again repelling Thakszut.

Suddenly, he looks at Iriemorel and mercilessly stomps on his injured back, putting all his strength and weight into the blow. Iriemorel screams and a horrific crack echoes through the room. The evil norodrian pulls up on the chain, launching Iriemorel into the air. Then, he suddenly yanks downward, grabs the dwarf by the chest and legs, forces him plunging faster than he would fall, raises his knee, and jams it into his back, nearly bending him in half with a disturbing crunch filling the air. Iriemorel bounces off the demon's knee and hits the floor with a thud. Babu stomps on his back one more time before pulling on the chain and sending him crashing to the floor on the other side of the room.

Babu yanks on the chain again and sends him flying into a wall. Babu then pulls up on the chain, swings him around, and slams him back first into the walls and floor a few times, dealing more damage to his injured spine. "You appear to have had enough. I'll be merciful and finish you now."

Babu pulls on the chain to retrieve the injured dwarf. As Iriemorel comes toward him, he loosens the chain, allowing it to slide off. Iriemorel continues to soar toward Babu, who is preparing to slash a sword at the incapacitated dwarf. When Iriemorel is in range, Babu begins his attack. Just before his blade connects with Iriemorel's flesh, the severed spiked ball from Gulvgrum's morningstar slams into Babu's head. The spikes pierce his flesh and cause him to stumble to the side, missing Iriemorel, who flies right by and knocks over Thakszut as he descends. The dwarf crashes to the ground and slides to a stop by a wall, lying motionless in a crumpled heap, right next to Adotiln, who is beginning to stir. Pulling the morningstar out of his face, Babu looks in its direction to see that Alithyra has regained consciousness and rejoined the fight. "So, you still have some fight in you after all. Impressive, especially with one arm."

Alithyra pants heavily as she stares him down. "I'll fight to the end."

Babu does not respond. Instead, he angrily grips the chain and sends his sword flying at her. She jumps aside to avoid the blade. However, he anticipated this action and threw the broken morningstar at the same time. The spiked ball hits her in the stomach and she falls backward, hitting the ground with a thud. She groans and screams as she pulls the spikes out of herself. Babu advances on her, sword in hand, but fails to notice Thakszut sneaking up behind him. The powerful little fiendling activates his Demonic Potential and rams into Babu from behind. Caught off guard, Babu drops his sword and stumbles forward. He turns around to face his opponent. "So, this is your Demonic Potential, but not your full potential. I am curious. Show me what you've got."

Thakszut rushes forward and punches Babu in the face. The blow appears ineffective, as Babu's head doesn't even move. Thakszut continues punching and clawing, but to no avail. Thakszut's hair darkens into a light gray and he slugs Babu across the jaw. Unfortunately, Babu doesn't even flinch.

"How disappointing," says Babu.

Babu simply backhands Thakszut, sending him stumbling several feet away. Babu approaches, and grabbing him, proceeds to beat Thakszut to a pulp. After several well-placed punches, he kicks him in the chest. Thakszut tumbles back and sprawls across the floor. His hair takes on the dark gray that allowed him to defeat Basmorg. He lunges forward and drives his fist into Babu's stomach. Babu flinches but seems otherwise unaffected.

"I hope that this isn't the best you've got," says Babu. "Your full Demonic Potential should put you at almost a match for me. If this truly is your full power, then it would seem my expectations were too high."

Thakszut continues his assault but is unable to seriously hurt Babu. The evil norodrian pulls his arm back and brings it forward, smashing his fist into Thakszut's face. Thakszut falls back and hits the ground with a thud.

As Babu approaches, desperation takes over and Thakszut's hair turns jet black. He lunges forward and slugs Babu across the face, sending him crashing to the floor a few feet away. Before he can recover, Thakszut is on top of him. The powerful little demonfolk proceeds to pummel the mighty norodrian, pounding his face mercilessly.

Alithyra crawls toward Pelagius, who is beginning to stir.

"Are you all right?" asks Pelagius.

"I'll live," says Alithyra. "What about you?"

"I'll be fine," says Pelagius. "I have to keep going. Babu must be defeated."

Alithyra looks in the direction of the fight. "It looks like Thakszut will finish him off."

Just as she says this, Babu finally manages to block a punch. He kicks Thakszut off himself and sends the demonfolk halfway across the room. Babu gets to his feet and scrambles to his sword, but Thakszut closes in quickly.

Thakszut leaps through the air, but Babu catches him by the throat and slams him into the ground. He then lifts Thakszut up, releases his grip, and punches him in the face, sending him crashing to the floor. Then, Babu simply stands there and allows the wounded Thakszut to rise to his feet. Still in his final form, Thakszut throws another punch, but Babu catches his fist.

"That's more like it," says Babu. "It seems I actually slightly underestimated your true power. You are almost a match for me. Almost, but not quite."

With his free hand, Babu punches Thakszut across the face, sending him crashing to the floor. He slugs him in the face several more times, not allowing him to stand; then he kicks Thakszut in the stomach, knocking him a few feet away. As Thakszut struggles to get to his feet, Babu approaches him from behind and grabs him by the head, one hand on top and to the right and the other grasping his chin. Babu jerks Thakszut's head to the left before violently twisting it in the other direction beyond its normal range of motion with a sickening snap.

"No!" shouts Pelagius.

Flopping to the ground, Thakszut returns to his normal form and lies motionless. Babu turns to Pelagius, who looks on in horror as the evil norodrian turns in his direction.

"What will we do now?" asks Alithyra.

"We should throw one of the orbs at him," says Ralkgek. "It turns out that if used as a weapon, the orb will send the victim to the Interrealm."

"I was hoping to end his reign forever," says Pelagius, "but that does sound like a good option. We'll use mine."

Pelagius gets out his portal orb and flings it at Babu. However, Babu tosses his sword out and intercepts the orb. The item explodes on impact with the blade and when the light clears, only the chain hits the ground. Puzzled, Babu retrieves what's left of his weapon.

"Nice try," says Babu, "but you'll have to do better than that."

Ralkgek sighs. "I can hear and smell him very well, so maybe I can be of some use after all."

Flapping his wings, Ralkgek flies into the air. The daemon flings another fireball but Babu sidesteps it and avoids the explosion. Ralkgek begins flying around the room, throwing more and more fireballs at the evil norodrian, who nimbly dodges most of them. Then, Babu catches two of the fireballs. He tosses one at the goblin, striking the unfortunate minion directly and incinerating him in the resulting blast. Babu returns his attention to Ralkgek and flings the other one in his direction. The daemon is unable to detect the approaching flame until he feels the heat only feet from his body. He desperately weaves to the side, barely avoiding a direct hit. The fireball explodes on a wall directly behind him, scorching his back and sending him tumbling to the ground. Recovering quickly, Ralkgek stands and plants his feet, waves his arms in a circle, and positions his hands in front of his stomach with palms up and fingers touching. "Freezing fire and burning cold. Frozen flames from times of old."

A blue flame forms between Ralkgek's palms. As Babu approaches, Ralkgek stands firm. He concentrates, and the flame increases in size and intensity until it surrounds his body and forms a dome. As it expands, the temperature of the room plummets and the heroes press themselves as far against the wall as possible. Babu ceases his approach and looks upon the growing fire. When it comes nearer, he reaches out and taps it with his finger, which partially freezes as burns appear. Babu quickly backs away and Ralkgek continues to concentrate on its expansion. Babu curls his fingers and positions his hands in the shape of a ball before he weaves them in a circle. His hands glow orange as flames form around them. He continues gathering power until the expanding blue dome reaches him. Then, he pushes his burning hands onto the dome and begins pushing back. The freezing fire ceases its expansion and shrinks while Babu walks forward. Ralkgek furrows his brow and concentrates harder, increasing the intensity of his coldflame and pushing Babu back. The fire around Babu's hands grows and he resumes his forward push. The two continue to increase their power output, pushing each other back repeatedly. As Ralkgek continues to concentrate, icy burns appear on his hands and arms. The stalemate goes on while the burns reach Ralkgek's face until Babu forces one last push, extinguishing his flames and bursting the dome. A mixture of fire and cold engulfs Ralkgek, covering him with burns as it spins around and knocks him to the ground.

Ralkgek rises to his feet, and Babu approaches from behind, grabs him by the wings, and plants his foot in his back. With one swift motion, he yanks on Ralkgek's wings and kicks him in the spine, ripping the wings from his back and sending him tumbling across the room. Ralkgek shrieks in agony, landing a few feet from Alithyra and Pelagius.

Babu surveys the area and sighs. "What a pitiful sight. The battle may as well be over. Let's finish this. I have important business to attend to."

Ralkgek drags himself over to Alithyra and Pelagius and the three heroes confer with each other. Babu tears Ralkgek's wings in half and begins to approach them, but Adotiln leaps onto his back and stabs him in the shoulders, distracting him from the others.

"What now?" asks Alithyra.

"I have an idea," says Pelagius. "Do you think you and Adotiln can distract him?"

Alithyra sighs wearily, her energy nearly drained. "I'll do what I can. What did you have in mind?"

"First, I'll combine the Flames of Courage with White Fire's flames," says Pelagius. "Then, if I can channel the Righteous Fury into the sword instead of my body, I might be able to destroy him. With any luck, White Fire won't be damaged."

"Why not just call on the Righteous Fury?" asks Ralkgek. "That would make you an even match."

"Babu is too powerful for that," says Pelagius. "Matching him would almost instantly tear my body apart, so I need to channel it into the sword. However, I'll only get one shot. If that's not powerful enough to do the trick, then we're doomed."

"I think I can contribute to the power," says Ralkgek. "I created a spell earlier to destroy a giant magical snake. If I can channel it into the mix, it should increase the power drastically."

The others think for a second.

"Agreed," says Pelagius.

Alithyra nods. Pelagius ignites White Fire, and after muttering a short prayer, adds the green Flames of Courage to it. He then begins to pray and Ralkgek begins to conjure his orb of elements while grasping the sword. Adotiln continues stabbing Babu, and she continues to evade his grasp. Then, he rushes backward, slamming her into the wall and crushing her with his body. As he steps away from the wall, she drops to the ground, stunned.

When Babu turns to grab her, Alithyra fights her way to her feet. Retrieving Iriemorel's mace, she approaches Babu and stares at him defiantly. "I'm ready for another round, Babu. You will not attack my friends while I still stand."

Babu chuckles. "Despite this unprovoked home invasion, you amuse me, my dear. I've already disarmed you once. Perhaps I'll have to do it again."

Babu swings the chain in her direction, and she easily ducks under it. She rushes forward, sidestepping several attempts at a chain whip. She brings the mace down and smashes Babu's foot. He shrieks in pain and backhands her, sending her tumbling to the ground. He places his foot on her head and begins to slowly apply pressure, causing her to shriek in agony. Then, Adotiln leaps onto his chest, driving her daggers into his shoulder. Babu cries out and takes a step back. She withdraws one dagger and stabs him in the throat, stunning him long enough to take a quick survey of the situation. Adotiln glances at Pelagius, who still needs a little more time to put his plan into motion. She quickly looks over at Alithyra, who also needs a moment to regain her senses. She turns back to Babu and locks eyes with the recovered angry norodrian. Desperate to buy the others more time, she remains in her current position, despite the tactical disadvantage, and renews her assault, repeatedly driving her daggers into Babu's chest. As Alithyra begins to show signs of recovery, Babu grabs Adotiln by the head and squeezes, causing her to scream and drop her weapons. Taking advantage of the distraction, he yanks her off his chest and violently slams her into the wall. Then, he draws her in and glares into her eyes. "You've been a nuisance, but I must admit that you've come closer to killing me than any of the others. You've impressed me, little one. I shall grant you a merciful death."

He raises up his free hand and points his claws at her, clenching them together so that all fingers are touching. Then, he shoots his arm forward, plunging his claws into her chest, impaling her. Adotiln grunts as the tips of his claws emerge from her back. Her vision blurs, and she struggles for air as she desperately fights to hang on to life. With great difficulty, Alithyra rises to her feet and steps forward to rescue her friend. However, Babu rapidly spreads his fingers out, his claws carving through Adotiln's body and splattering her remains across the room.

"No!" shouts Alithyra.

Alithyra emits a primal shriek. Enraged, she rushes forward with a burst of energy, smashes the mace onto Babu's foot, and bites him on the leg, her teeth sinking in. Babu emits a surprised yelp of pain, and she repeatedly bashes the mace against his legs and torso. He swings his chain in a whip-like manner and knocks the weapon from her hand. Regaining her composure, Alithyra desperately jumps back to avoid the next strike.

"How was that merciful?" asks Alithyra, trying to buy more time.

"I didn't devour her soul," says Babu. "Considering that all of you attacked me, allowing her to pass into the afterlife is merciful. I may grant you the same courtesy, but your friends won't be so fortunate."

Pelagius finally finishes his prayer and a familiar yellow glow surrounds him. He grasps the sword tightly and concentrates, transferring the energy to White Fire, added to the swirling white and green fire. Then, a brief flash comes from Ralkgek's hands as he adds a swirling mixture of orange fire, blue cold energy, lightning, and crumbling rocks to the vortex. As Pelagius slowly rises to his feet, Babu's chain wraps around Alithyra's waist. He pulls on the chain and catches her in the air. Babu positions his hand so that his claws face her chest. "You put up a valiant fight, but it was all for nothing."

"You're wrong, Babu," says Alithyra.

Alithyra rapidly draws a dagger from her belt and lunges forward, stabbing Babu directly in the eye. The evil norodrian shrieks in agony, drops Alithyra, and puts his hand over the wound.

"I'll destroy you for that!" shouts Babu, glaring at Alithyra.

Alithyra grins and points to Pelagius. "I'm no longer your main concern."

Babu turns in time to see Pelagius's blade in mid-swing and moves to parry the strike, only to remember that his sword has vanished. He watches helplessly as the blade strikes him in the side and cuts diagonally up his stomach and chest, ending at his shoulder. Bringing the blade back around, Pelagius stabs him in the center of the torso, and the energy stored in White Fire explodes, engulfing Babu in a tempest of various magical powers. The sound of the explosion drowns Babu's screams. When the smoke clears, Babu is still standing despite the gaping wounds and horrific burns covering his entire body. He groans and twitches slightly before falling over onto his back.

Exhausted, Pelagius drops to his knees. "Finally."

Suddenly, Babu lurches and raises his head. "Well played, Pelagius. Enjoy your victory while it lasts."

Babu's head flops to the ground with a loud thud. Lying motionless, he breathes his last, exhaling a cloud of dark blue smoke, which quickly dissipates as his body turns ashy gray and crumbles into dust.

Alithyra checks on Thakszut, and Ralkgek feels his way over to Iriemorel, who lies unconscious against a nearby wall.

Alithyra looks at the others. "Amazingly, he's still alive, but he's not doing well. If we can get him back to Shukrat's he may live, but without help he will die very soon."

"We still have one or two portal spheres," says Pelagius.

Ralkgek places his hand on Iriemorel's chest. He mutters something and soft orange light surrounds their wounded companion. After dragging the dwarf to the center of the room, he then finds his way to Thakszut and repeats the procedure.

"What did you do?" asks Alithyra.

"I placed them in stasis," says Ralkgek. "That should keep them in suspended animation until we can set them on a bed at Shukrat's. Without freezing them in time, we could not move them safely."

"How long will it last?" asks Pelagius.

"Five minutes at most," says Ralkgek.

"Then we had better hurry," says Pelagius.

Pelagius reaches into Iriemorel's satchel and removes the sphere. He tosses it across the room, and it bursts right next to the throne, opening a portal. With all their strength, Pelagius and Ralkgek hoist up Iriemorel and drag him toward the portal. Alithyra picks up Thakszut and glances solemnly around the room.

"We should go before any of Babu's underlings arrive," says Pelagius. "None of us will survive another fight."

Alithyra glances over at him with tears in her eyes. "We should gather some of Adotiln's remains so that we may give her a proper burial."

Before they can begin to gather her up, the door behind Babu's throne opens and Hazgor steps out, blocking their way. The heroes freeze in their tracks, slowly and gently set down Iriemorel and Thakszut, and draw their weapons.

"Nobody make any sudden movements," whispers Pelagius. "Rhinorans have terrible eyesight, so he may not see us."

Hazgor's ears perk up and he inhales deeply as he sniffs the air. He squints and scans the room. He then walks toward the heroes, leaning his head forward as he attempts to get a good view. "I may not be able to get a good look from here, but I can still hear and smell you. All of you reek of sweat and blood."

As Hazgor approaches, the door opens and Alasdar emerges into the room. He walks past the heroes and steps in front of the advancing rhinoran. "No. Let them go. They've earned it."

Hazgor stumbles to a stop, waving his arms wildly to prevent himself from toppling over. He clenches his fists and glares down at Alasdar. "What? They killed Lord Babu. Why should we spare them?"

"And where were you during the battle?" asks Alasdar. "You were supposed to come to Babu's aid. You failed, Hazgor."

"He never called for me," says Hazgor. "I wasn't supposed to come out until I was summoned."

"And yet you are here now."

"I decided to investigate when the chamber fell silent. They are still alive and Lord Babu is nowhere to be found. I must avenge him."

Alasdar's skin bulges for a brief second before returning to its natural state. "You should have come out sooner. Avenging Babu is not your task. You let your master down, Hazgor. Live with that shame."

Hazgor loosens his fists and lowers his head. "The master is dead. What do we do now?"

Alasdar grins malevolently. "I am lord of Devil's Den now. Everyone here will answer to me."

Hazgor glares down at him. "Why should we obey you, Alasdar?"

Alasdar's skin roils as though something were moving around underneath it. "You've seen what I can do, Hazgor. Do you wish to suffer that fate?"

Hazgor's eyes grow wide and he steps back in fear. Alasdar grins as his flesh returns to its normal state. "That's what I thought. Now off with you. Your new task is to send out messengers to our forces in the field. Inform them of what has happened and call them back. I have pressing business to attend to."

Hazgor grunts and exits the room. Taking advantage of the argument, the heroes slowly move toward the portal. As they near their goal, Alasdar turns to them. "Not so fast."

They freeze in place, panting heavily, as they begin to expect the worst. Then, Alasdar circles to the other side of the room away from the portal.

"You may go on your way," says Alasdar. "I will let you live for now."

The heroes glance at each other in confusion.

"Why are you sparing us?" asks Pelagius. "Didn't we just kill your master?"

Alasdar grins. "You did me a favor. Had I disposed of Babu myself, the others wouldn't follow me. Not willingly, anyway. This way, I can claim his position legitimately."

"You're not concerned that we may return to finish the job?" asks Ralkgek.

Alasdar laughs as he stops by Adotiln's head. "None of you are a threat to me, and you have no reason to come back."

Alasdar picks up Adotiln's head and gives it a quick but thorough examination. "What a waste. It was such a nice face. Now it's too damaged to be of any use."

He shoves Adotiln's head into a sack, which he tosses to Pelagius. "Something to bury. Leave now before I change my mind."

Pelagius nods solemnly. Alithyra scoops up Thakszut while Pelagius and Ralkgek hoist up Iriemorel and step through the portal.

CHAPTER 82

At their mountain encampment, Eeshlith and Shudgluv emerge from their tents, upon which perch several red-eyed ravens. Glakchog is already up, having taken the first shift on watch.

"Hello, Glakchog," says Eeshlith.

Glakchog simply grunts as he nervously eyes the birds.

"I guess it's safe to say that Pelagius and the others haven't come by yet," says Shudgluv.

"Correct," says Glakchog.

"Maybe they're all dead," says Eeshlith, "Perhaps one of us should go to Devil's Den and check."

Glakchog glares at her. "No. Our orders were to stay here until they come by or we hear from the Green-Eyed Man. That is what we are going to do."

"You can follow those orders," says Shudgluv. "I'm tired of waiting and I want to see what is going on."

"You will do no such thing," says Glakchog.

Glakchog pulls out his hookswords and Shudgluv grabs his weapons as well. They slowly circle the remains of the campfire. They close to attack. Before a fight can start, the Green-Eyed Man appears on the edge of the cliff. "Stop this pointless fighting!"

Shudgluv and Glakchog stow their weapons and back away. Glakchog stands at attention. "Sorry, sir. They wanted to abandon their posts here to see what was going on. I was simply trying to stop them."

The Green-Eyed Man grabs him by the armor. "Well, attacking them is not part of that job. After what happened with the defense force, I will not tolerate any infighting or insubordination. You are all to follow my orders. Is that clear?"

"Yes," reply all three.

"Who was the first to question me?" asks the Green-Eyed Man.

"Eeshlith," replies Glakchog.

The Green-Eyed Man approaches her. "You saw what happened back there. You know that I have had a rough time. I am in no mood for disobedience."

"I'm sorry, sir," says Eeshlith, "I just wasn't sure if the situation was still the same. It won't happen again."

The Green-Eyed Man thinks for a moment. Then, without warning, his hand shoots through the air and he grabs Eeshlith by the throat. Shocked by the sudden outburst, Glakchog takes a step back. Shudgluv, on the other hand, takes a step forward, stretching out his arm in concern. He is quickly rebuked by a vicious glare from the Green-Eyed Man, who then turns his attention back to Eeshlith. He tightens his grasp on her throat as she chokes and desperately claws at his hand for air. "I've been lenient with you before, Eeshlith, but I've reached my limit. I will no longer tolerate your back talk or insubordination. Do I make myself clear?"

Eeshlith's eyes glaze over.

"Boss, that's enough!" exclaims Shudgluv, "She gets the message. Please let her go."

The Green-Eyed Man glares angrily at Shudgluv. "You do not command me!"

Glakchog nervously steps forward. "Sir, if I may. I actually agree with Shudgluv on this. Unless you're planning to kill her now, you should probably release your grip."

"You make a fair point," says the Green-Eyed Man.

The Green-Eyed Man releases his grasp and Eeshlith crumples to the ground, coughing and gasping for air. Shudgluv moves to help her, but the Green-Eyed Man steps in front of him. Eeshlith looks up at him. "You're losing yourself. Please don't give in to your inner darkness. Remember who you used to be and try to return to that."

The Green-Eyed Man's expression softens. "You speak of redemption. What exactly are you trying to say?"

"I'm trying to get you to remain you," says Eeshlith. "Even as a soul hunter, you don't have to lose yourself entirely. I know that some of the old you is still in there."

A look of regret briefly crosses the Green-Eyed Man's face. "Even after all I've done, you really think that I'm still not a complete monster?"

"I know it," says Eeshlith, "I know that my old friend is still in there among the darkness. You just need to help him find his way out."

"I'm sorry," says the Green-Eyed Man. "You're wrong, Eeshlith. It's too late for me."

Suddenly, the Green-Eyed Man lifts his foot and lunges forward. He lands a hard stomp-like kick against Eeshlith's face, knocking her unconscious as her head slams into the ground. Enraged, Shudgluv rushes forward and grabs the Green-Eyed Man by his armor, lifting him into the air. "Why? Why did you do that?"

The Green-Eyed Man glares at him. "Put me down!"

A look of horror crosses Shudgluv's face as he realizes what he is doing. He gently lowers the Green-Eyed Man down and backs away. Before anything else can happen, a portal suddenly opens and someone steps through. The new arrival is an average size human male wielding a massive sword roughly twelve feet in length from the end of the hilt to the tip of the blade and about three feet wide at its widest point. The Green-Eyed Man turns to him. "This is a surprise. To what do we owe the pleasure of your visit?"

"On Alasdar's orders, you are to return to Devil's Den at once," says the man.

"Alasdar's orders?" inquires the Green-Eyed Man.

"Yes," says the man, "Master Babu has been defeated."

A look of horror crosses the Green-Eyed Man's face. He turns to Glakchog and Shudgluv. "Be prepared for an unpleasant homecoming. Shudgluv, come with me. I'll deal with you later. Glakchog, bring Eeshlith and lock her in the dungeon when we get back."

The new arrival turns around and walks back through the portal, followed quickly by the Green-Eyed Man and Shudgluv. Glakchog lifts Eeshlith up onto his shoulders and immediately follows.

CHAPTER 83

Pelagius and the others tumble through the portal into Shukrat's home. Injured and exhausted, they collapse on the floor.

Shukrat rushes out of Kevnan's room. "Good gods! We need to get all of you bandaged up."

Pelagius points to Iriemorel and Thakszut. "Take them first. They need it far worse than we do."

Shukrat examines them. "I should say so."

Shukrat picks up Thakszut and rushes into the Hall of Infinite Guest Rooms. Pelagius uses the last of his strength to hoist Iriemorel up and half carries, half drags him after him. Alithyra follows, leading Ralkgek. Upon entering, Shukrat directs them to various guest rooms. Alithyra and Pelagius place Ralkgek and Iriemorel in one room each. They then each claim a separate room. Shukrat places Thakszut on a bed and looks around at the placement of his patients. "This won't do. I'll have to shift a few things."

Shukrat enters the hall and softly chants. Suddenly, the occupied bedrooms fuse into one large room. Kevnan and Aldtaw sleep in beds at the far end. Without a word, Shukrat goes to Thakszut, bandages him tightly, and sets his neck with a makeshift brace just before the stasis wears off. He walks over to a lab-like area on the far side of the room, tosses some oil and herbs in a bowl, and begins grinding and mashing them up. Taking the mysterious sack from Pelagius and absentmindedly setting it on a table, he applies the salve for everyone else's open wounds and Pelagius's and Ralkgek's burns. Additionally, he splints and slings Pelagius's broken arm and straps a long, thick board to Iriemorel's back before wrapping him from head to toe in bandages. He approaches Ralkgek, wipes off some remaining dried venom with a cloth, and stitches up the wounds on his back.

"I can't cure your blindness," says Shukrat, "but I can help you to master your other senses."

Shukrat looks around, realizing that somebody is missing. "Where's Adotiln?"

Alithyra solemnly points to the sack sitting on a nearby table. Shukrat peeks inside and immediately recoils. As he ties the sack shut, Pelagius tries to sit up.

"Don't do that," says Shukrat. "You need to rest."

"Will Thakszut be all right?" asks Pelagius.

Shukrat casts the same stasis spell that Ralkgek used earlier on the sack containing Adotiln's remains. "I don't know. I cannot do any more than I have with mundane medicine nor fetch any healers at the moment. I can depart to acquire the services of a priest at dawn. The best thing for you and your companions now would be to get some rest. Once you have recovered, you can begin your journey home."

Pelagius sighs. "Rest would be fantastic. After everything that happened, we could all use it."

Shukrat glances at Pelagius. "Tell me what occurred. I would like to know."

Pelagius and the other conscious heroes relate the events of their assault. When they finish, Shukrat sits in silent thought. "A grueling battle if there ever was one."

"What are your thoughts on Alasdar claiming lordship of Devil's Den?" asks Pelagius. "Is it that simple?"

Shukrat shakes his head. "No. Alasdar is not Babu's offspring. Therefore, he is not his heir and has no claim."

Alithyra glances over. "We're not going to have to go back and depose him, are we?"

Shukrat chuckles. "No. That is not your concern. In the event a marquis dies with no heir, the successor is determined by the king. This is a matter for the royal court once they learn of it."

Pelagius's eyes grow wide. "Marquis? Was Babu a member of the court?"

Shukrat nods. "Low-ranking, but yes. You didn't know?"

Alithyra glares at Ralkgek. "Nobody told us."

"I thought they already knew," says Ralkgek. "It wasn't exactly a secret."

"So, that's why Babu accused me of assassination," says Pelagius.

Alithyra looks nervously at Shukrat. "Are we going to have any trouble with the law?"

Shukrat shakes his head. "Not likely. Unless someone reports you to the king, they have no way of knowing who killed Babu."

A red-eyed raven appears at the window and observes the conversation. Shukrat rises, shoos the bird away, and closes the shutters. "It would seem the carcinomancer who has been watching still has an interest in you."

"Until he makes himself known, he is of no immediate concern," says Pelagius.

Shukrat nods. "Agreed. Right now, your main focus should be healing up and preparing for the return trip. Everyone, get some sleep."

Pelagius lies down on his bed and shuts his eyes, ready to rest up for the coming journey home.

About the Author

Eric Balch was born and raised in Texas and attained a Bachelor's degree from Texas Christian University. He went on to co-own a successful business making and selling dog treats and dog food, but that business was sold years ago.

He has been writing for many years now, but it was only recently that he completed his first book. He hopes that the success of it will inspire him to greater efforts and more exciting titles in the future.

In his free time, he likes to read, watch movies and play video games. One of his passions is for cooking and he loves spending time creating great food in the kitchen. Halloween is one of his favorite times of the year and he enjoy nothing more than preparing his house for Trick or Treaters. His yard haunt, Deadman Manor, is popular with both the kids and parents alike and many of his neighbors look forward to the annual home horror

He still lives in Texas today, with his fiancé Jenn and their 3 dogs: a Havanese named Merlin and two Jack Russel Terriers, Kerry and Smidgeon. He is looking forward to continuing to write stories that will appeal to as many as possible. He primarily writes fantasy novels.

You can follow Eric Balch on

Facebook - https://www.facebook.com/eric.balch.1

or you can read more about his book and world setting on his author page at - https://www.facebook.com/ericbalchauthor/ or his website ericbalch.com

www.ingramcontent.com/pod-product-compliance
Lightning Source LLC
Chambersburg PA
CBHW020912060726
47591CB00004B/1211